THE MADWOMAN OF BETHLEHEM

THE MADWOMAN OF BETHLEHEM

a novel

Rosine Nimeh-Mailloux

Second Story Press

Library and Archives Canada Cataloguing in Publication

Nimeh-Mailloux, Rosine, 1937-

The Madwoman of Bethlehem / by Rosine Nimeh-Mailloux.

ISBN 978-1-897187-48-7

I. Title.

PS8577.I56M34 2008 C813'.6 C2008-904626-9

Edited by Anne Millyard
Designed by Melissa Kaita

Printed and bound in Canada

Second Story Press gratefully acknowledges the support of the Ontario Arts Council and the Canada Council for the Arts for our publishing program. We acknowledge the financial support of the Government of Canada through the Book Publishing Industry Development Program.

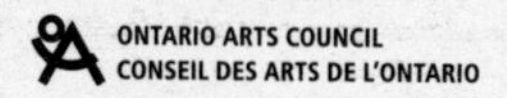

Published by
Second Story Press
20 Maud Street, Suite 401
Toronto, ON M5V 2M5
www.secondstorypress.ca

This, my first novel, I dedicate to all those good Americans who, in 1957, lifted me from a life of poverty to the comfortable present.

Much gratitude I owe to Rose Azoyan, who planted the seed for a wonderful future for me and for my family. I owe so much to Rev. Dr. William C. H. Nelson and Rev. Everette B. Luther, the two ministers of the North Congregational Church of Phoenix, sponsors and supporters for six years. I cannot forget the love and support I received from Muriel and Ivan Speer who took me into their family.

Equally important are Arizona State University for the tuition scholarship over four years and the Phoenix Chapter of Pilot International under the leadership of Mary Selby Lighthall and Norma Synder, the two wonderful women who were instrumental in my receiving the Ruby Newhall scholarship for four years.

To all my supporters and friends, especially Janice Tootell Gittner, I say this: Your magnanimity has made all the difference in the lives of the Nimeh family.

The Madwoman of Bethlehem is a work of fiction. However, the novel was inspired by the lives of two unfortunate family members who suffered from their terrible marriages. One of them lived most of her life in a mental institution and finally suffered a fatal blow. Her life and death have stayed with me since childhood. This novel, in some way, is my song to her.

—Rosine Nimeh-Mailloux

CHAPTER 1

Oasis for Troubled Women
Bethlehem, 1957

SOON, THE ORDERLIES will come knocking on the door of our ward. May Allah* knock them all the way to *Gehannem*, those urchins of the devil!

These sons of Beelzebub think it's time for us inmates to be up, do our penance, and earn our daily bread. This block is for the good ones, though. We're fit only to be put away, but sane enough to earn our shelter and food, such as it is. I've learned to do my keepers' bidding rather than face their shoving and jabbing.

But here, in this home for the mad, this everlasting hell, is where I deserve to be. Until Allah decides I've prayed enough and paid enough for my sin. Maybe then He'll take me and put me next to my kind up there. Must be a big crowd of us in

*Allah, the Arabic word for God, is used by Christians and Muslims alike.

heaven. Why not? This world drives some of us to the very edge. Blessed be His name.

I had better start my morning prayers before they come. Or maybe I should stop praying altogether. Nothing ever changes for me. A million times I've heard the sane say Allah piles suffering and pain on His good subjects to test their faith. That is nothing more than fairy tales! If that's what He does, I don't think the whole business of life is worth a fart.

Now I've gone and done it again! I keep lashing out at life and at Allah. Just pray, you stupid woman! Ask for forgiveness. Every day, I try to say my Lord's Prayer and the psalm The Lord is My Shepherd, and then I ruin it all by swearing and blaspheming. Maybe that's why Allah's gone deaf on me. Blind, too.

Perhaps this drab room of gray-plastered walls, with an iron-barred chink that teases me with tiny morsels of sky, is not a good place to pray. Church is where Allah is more likely to hear me. But church is as far from me as heaven is. So I keep mumbling or grumbling my prayers, before floundering away to the cesspool of my past. There, I wallow in the *kharra*, the shit, I had to eat—this vulgarity does nothing to soothe the pain and the rage. My prayers always end with curses that should fling me to the deepest hole in Gehannem.

I know I should stop dredging up all the dirt and muck of my life. But I can't help trying to find a way to explain it all. I keep asking why—why all that and all this?

Nothing I can say or do now will fix the bloody mess I've made. I can hear my grandmother's voice. "You'll never mend the window pane that you so foolishly cracked." But I also hear my mother say, "Allah is all love. He forgives our sins. We just have to walk in the path of righteousness and pray."

I'd like to tell her it doesn't work. It's never worked for me. And as far as I know, it's never worked for her either. But in case she might be right, I'll go on praying. Can't think of what else to do.

I must start now, before they come. This morning I'll say the Lord's Prayer in Aramaic. Maybe He will hear me if I pray in His son's language.

Bshaim abo, wabro, roho quadeesho, hadhalo shareero, ameen.
Aboon dbash-mayo, nethqa-dash shmokh,
Tethai malkoo-thokh, nehwai sebyonokh, aykano dbashmayo.
Oaf bar'o hablan, lahmo dsunqonan . . .

Knock, knock, knock! They're banging the doors hard enough to wake the dead. They've unlocked the door.

"Up, you women! Get ready for work if you want to eat. You have five minutes to get up and change into your uniforms, then to the bathrooms. Or else!" barks Unwar, bashing the door with the stick he always carries.

I wish I could tell those hairless morons what should happen to them. Because we're insane, they think we're not human—that we don't think or feel. They can never know the suffering that broke our hearts and minds. They only see the rotten bits of what we used to be. To them we are lepers, shattered shells filled with maggots. Damned fools! They know nothing. They swagger with their sticks, jab, scowl, and treat us as if we were slum urchins.

Now that all nine of us are dressed in our ugly, faded blue uniforms, we join the women from the other wards to meet our cursed wardens in the courtyard. I hurry to be first out—first in line, first to the bathrooms. We rush to relieve ourselves and to wash our hands and faces with cool water from the well. Water feels good after a warm night. And then, the wardens are waiting for us with brooms and mops. These days, I'm on sweeping duty.

I'd rather work in the kitchen. There I feel some sanity from being with ordinary people, doing the normal things I used to do—scrubbing potatoes, washing dishes and huge cauldrons. The kitchen chief, Im Issa, is a hard one, but I don't mind. Why should I? I've been ordered around all my life. And while washing dishes, I can sometimes splash on more water to cool my face and neck. When Im Issa catches me doing that, she yells, "Hey you, stop that right now, or I'll call the orderlies."

Once she yelled, "Hey you, empty head, this is not the Baths of Our Lady Marriam!" I laughed so hard that my chest ached, and she raised her eyes and hands toward the ceiling and said, "*Ya Allah*, cure them and spare me their folly!" The stupid woman thought I was laughing at her. What did she know about what's in my head! I was laughing at the sight that her mention of the baths had conjured up.

My mother, grandmother, and I were sitting naked inside the large bathhouse, where women of all ages, completely naked, crowded. Sometimes I couldn't see through the heavy steam rolling in from the small openings in the walls. We sat at our station, scrubbing our skin raw with soapy *loupha* and steaming water.

I had never seen my mother or grandmother naked, and I stared long at their breasts, my mother's large and firm, and my grandmother's sagging bags that fell to her waist. I wanted to ask what those were, but thought it better to keep quiet than to get a tongue lashing. I couldn't help but look down, though, to where I shouldn't.

My mother pretended she didn't notice, but my grandmother—count on her to see all—snapped, "What're you staring at? Keep your eyes to yourself." I knew I'd better not let her catch me looking down there again, but whenever she closed her eyes for a few seconds, there I was staring at the few gray straggling hairs. I couldn't understand it. My mother's was completely hairless. Then I figured out that nice people didn't grow hair there, but bad people grew hair like the *Shaytaan*, the Devil. I was only seven then.

"Here's a broom for you, mother of all heads! I want this whole wing spotless in an hour, you hear? Or there's no breakfast."

I know their idle threats. They want to intimidate us into obedience. "Hahahahaha. Breakfast! *Ya habeeby*, my treasure! Thy will be done. For breakfast this morning I'll have fried eggs with *jambon*, if you please, and white bread with honey and cheese. *Merci beaucoup, Monsieur Diable*."

"Shut up and get to work, unless you . . . " warns Unwar, the one we've secretly named Hell's Ambassador.

"Your orders rest on my head, ya Sheikh il-Arab. Thy will be done, oh master, just like this," I say, snapping my fingers.

"Get to work, now," he says, swinging the arm that's holding the stick in the air.

You ugly bastard! Your mother must have gazed at a mule when she conceived you!

I sweep and shuffle from the grooved stones of the colonnade onto the cobbled courtyard. I try to catch glimpses of who's where in the large square. Some of my wardmates are sweeping inside the colonnades. Others are bending over the stubby handles of their brooms, sweeping the dirt from between the cobblestones. I try to stay clear of the rest as much as I can, just in case a couple of them erupt into a shouting and cursing match. Then the Ambassador from Gehannem is apt to lash the quarreling women into silence.

We sweep three colonnades only. The eastern colonnade is forbidden to us. That's where the gatekeeper keeps watch over everything and every movement around the courtyard. Occasionally, he unlocks the gate to visitors and then locks it behind them. On that side are also the visitors' room, the doctor's office, and the infirmary.

I miss working next to Khadeejeh, who's on kitchen duty this week. Lucky Khadeejeh! I like her mumbling and chattering about her mountain. In the course of the day, she keeps me entertained with fairy tales from her deranged world.

She's from the little village of Beit Safafa, on the southern outskirts of Jerusalem. Sometimes I think she's as sane as those outside these walls. And sometimes she babbles about voices in her head that tell her to go to the mountain. There, a prince in silk robes will come on horseback to bring her the Koran, written and bound in gold. And when she's read it, he will come back to take her to heaven. She laughs and looks so happy.

I remember one of those conversations.

"See those little pines on that mountain west of us, that's where my prince will come for me," Khadeejeh said. She was so excited.

"Those aren't little pines, Kahdeejeh. They're tall and hide the convent of Jabal il-Markal. No one is allowed there."

Suddenly, she turned her furious eyes on me. "You're wrong! That's exactly where my prince will wait for me."

I explained to her that cloistered nuns lived there. They never go out, nor allow anyone in. They spend all their time in prayers.

"Poor Amal! Now I know why they brought you here!" she said, distress in her voice. But soon confusion and sadness transformed her face and she whined, "But I can't go to the mountain. First I must learn to read. Then I must let my hair grow long again. I had such beautiful, long braids that came down to my hips, right here. May Allah break their hands for cutting off my beautiful braids!"

When I tried to console her by pointing out how unimportant the length of her hair is, she stared at me as though I had insulted her. "You should know better. Your hair is your family honor and respect. You Christians have forgotten your traditions. Take Our Lady Marriam—peace on her—she had long hair and always kept it under the white head covering. Her dress came down to her ankles, the way I used to dress before I came here. You Christians imitate those from Orobba. You cut your hair short like them and wear dresses with short sleeves and low necks. It's shameful!"

I wanted to laugh at the way she said "Orobba" instead of Europe, but not knowing how she would react, I kept a straight face. She went on ranting about the foreigners she used to see at the market in Jerusalem who wore shorts, held hands, and kissed each other. "Those people know no shame. But us, we respect the words of the Koran and our honor."

Do I dare tell her I chose to have my hair cut years ago, and that I knew some Muslims who wore their hair short and dressed like Christians, and still were good people? Instead, I decided to have some fun with her.

"Khadeejeh, what's wrong if a man and a woman in love kiss each other?" I knew full well that only a slut would let a man kiss her. Such a woman, if caught in the act, would be locked up at home. Some fathers or brothers might even do away with such daughters who dared to taint their family honor this way.

Khadeejeh, horrified, covered her face and cried, "The shame! Such girls will go straight to Gehannem. I'm going to the mountain, then to heaven." She looked upward toward the clear skies and smiled, as though she'd seen the face of Allah. Suddenly she blurted out, "You should come with me to the mountain, Amal, and I'll ask my prince to take you to heaven to be my maid. I'll be good to you, and we'll be happy there."

"Thank you, habeebty. I've had enough of being a maid. I'd rather be a princess, the beloved wife of a prince. What do you think, Khadeejeh?"

"I'd say it's easier to get you into heaven as a maid than to get you married to a prince."

"Why, Khadeejeh? I'm beautiful. Just as beautiful as my sister Shamiran, the Beauty Queen of Bethlehem. Many princes would die for me!"

"Well, habeebty, we're both beautiful, but no prince is coming here, unless he's insane. And in that case, they'd take him to the Asylum for Men. And you'd be stuck here forever. Poor Amal, tsk, tsk, tsk," she said, shaking her head, feeling sorry for me.

She put her arm around my shoulder to comfort me. "Khadeejeh will take care of you, habeebty! We'll go together to the mountain, and my prince will be good to you. The two of us will help each other, always."

Suddenly I felt sorry for her and thought how like me she was—alone and afraid. "Yes, we'll go to the mountain together," I assured her.

She grabbed me by my shoulders and squeezed me to her chest. I tried to get out of her grip before she squished my breasts into my ribs. When she finally released me, she smiled. "You and I, Amal, will be like two beautiful flowers in paradise."

I know I am no flower and she—Allah forgive me—is not so good-looking. She has yellowed dark skin, a pockmarked face, and bushy, dark eyebrows above brown eyes that are like two squirrel eyes in an elephant's head. But she is tall and very strong. Better as a friend than an enemy. I asked her how she knew she was beautiful.

"Are you blind, woman? The voices tell me. They come from up there."

Suddenly she grew sad and said, "But there's a problem. They won't teach me to read, and they won't let my hair grow in. I'll never be able to go to the mountain. These sons of dogs—curse their religion—tell me short hair keeps the lice away. May Allah fill every hair on their bodies with lice the size of giant wasps! I'd like to see those bastards yelp while they twitch and spin, scratching their heads with one arm, their crotches with the other, driving them insane, until they drop dead."

Suddenly, she began to argue angrily with some invisible tormentor. "Let me go! I want to go with him. You can't stop me. You can't . . . " Her arms flailed and fell on some phantom that only she could see.

"Khadeejeh, habeebty." I tugged at her elbow gently, afraid her arguments might awaken a host of other phantoms hiding in some of the other women around us and trigger an uproar.

"Khadeejeh, your prince is coming to take you. Come, let's go meet him."

She stopped suddenly, her eyes staring at me as though she were seeing me for the first time. I panicked, not knowing what she might do next. I spoke softly and said, "Khadeejeh, I'll teach you to read."

"By Allah's life? But we need a book. Maybe you can ask your husband to get us one."

"My husband is gone for good."

"He's got another woman, ha? Just like my father. He left my mother and me and took another wife. My mother cried and took me with her to live with my grandparents. We worked the fields from sunrise to sunset, just to earn our food. My uncles treated us like beggars. My grandmother felt sorry for us, but could do nothing to help us."

"Such a hard life, Khadeejeh."

"No, not so hard. I loved being in the fields. There, the voices cheered me up, telling me a handsome prince, dressed in white silk with jeweled silver sword at his hip was going to come on horseback to take me to his palace in heaven to be his wife."

"Yes, and then they brought you here!"

"My jealous uncles did. They hated me."

"Well, ask your mother for a book when she visits you next month."

"My poor mother! When she comes here, she keeps wringing her hands and weeps. I tell her about the mountain and my prince, and she weeps even more. You know, maybe she's not quite right up there," she said, her finger touching her head.

"Well, Khadeejeh, we'll find a book somehow and I'll teach you to read."

"And I'll take you with me to the mountain."

Suddenly, I hear the voice of Unwar's partner, the one who looks as ugly as a rat. He barks across the courtyard, and I jump and begin to sweep furiously. The last thing I need is a whack across my back with the stick he carries. That's what my grandmother used to do to me when I didn't obey. "This stick will make you jump," she would growl. "Work never kills anyone. Disobedience will."

And she meant it. Oh, she meant it, all right. I can hear her now . . .

CHAPTER 2

VOICES, SHRILL AND ANGRY, trapped in the dark caverns of Amal's memory crowded in on her. Little things in her present invariably dredged up the detritus of her childhood. As she swept the floor of the asylum on that ordinary July morning, the sun streamed through her bleak world, its harsh light blanching the gray granite walls that girded the huge, square structure. This was another day the sun promised to assault the earth with its scorching heat. Amal recalled how she had to sweep her three-room house and her family's share of the enclave courtyard when she was just six. Her grandmother's ghost loomed less awesome now than the real Sitty seemed to Amal as a child. But this moment, as she swept, the miserable memories rose up before her eyes like the dust from her broom.

Amal was playing hide-and-seek with her friends one day, behind the outhouse. Leaning against the wall, her head resting against her arms and her eyes shut as she counted, she felt a pair of arms suddenly clutch her. Sitty dragged her by one arm across the courtyard, Amal's unwilling legs stumbling behind her grandmother's hurried strides.

Once inside the house, she listened to another harangue about a girl's proper upbringing. Then she received a few whacks to her little behind, to ensure that she learned the golden rule of obedience. "Start with the courtyard, and when that's finished, go inside and sweep all the floors of the house," Sitty commanded.

Sweeping the courtyard was not an unpleasant task for Amal. She liked the vista that lay before her. The enclave, built of granite, squatted on one of the small hills in the southern part of Bethelehem, with a full view of the valley and swelling hills, dotted with fruit trees of all kinds—almonds, figs, apples, plums, peaches, and pomegranates. In the far hills, she could see caves and tents, where Bedouins lived with their goats and sheep. The terraced groves gave the children of the enclave a glimpse of paradise.

For Amal and her friends, it was a forbidden paradise that doled out its own punishment for disobedience. It was imperative that the parents keep their children away from the groves to avoid the risk of eviction. The owners of the groves also owned the enclave. But the children dared each other occasionally to raid a grove and steal whatever fruit was available—ripe or unripe, as much as their pockets and small hands could hold—before the owners spotted them from the windows and verandas of their three-story houses. The little thieves had discovered from experience that pain from a spanking was ephemeral, but the exhilaration in daring to taste of forbidden fruit was forever. Filling their pockets with green almonds and, later, dipping each in salt and munching on the tantalizing salty-sour fruit was worth the risk.

After sweeping the courtyard, Amal went inside to fulfil the rest of Sitty's orders. Her little hands were red, smarting from the stubby handle of the broom that came up to her ribcage. She struggled to hold the broom, as her grandmother walked in and growled, "Here, tilt it like this, and sweep the dirt toward the door. Learn to work now. You'll spare your mother shame when you grow up. No place for lazy women in this world."

"But, Sitty, this is hard."

"Hard! You should have been born in Turkeyya in my time. Then you'd know what hard is. Start sweeping these floors clean. Spotless. Now, get to it, or this," she said, wagging her stick, "will make you."

Little Amal knew her grandmother meant it. She would not hesitate to use her infamous stick to make this "cursed daughter of Eve" toil, despite her age. Amal had tried a few times to beg her mother for help, but never found the support she craved. Her mother was always sick in bed during incessant pregnancies, miscarriages, or deliveries. From these there was little relief. Amal rarely saw her mother up and around like other mothers.

As soon as her grandmother marched back to the outdoor kitchen, some ten feet away from the three-room house, Amal quietly approached her mother's bed and tried to get her to intercede on her behalf.

"Immie," she whispered in a quivering voice. Her mother slowly stretched out her arm, searching for her daughter's head. Gently she stroked Amal's curly chestnut-brown hair, trying to calm her sobbing daughter.

"Immie, tell Sitty to stop being mean to me. I want to play

with my friends, but she won't let me. And this broom is hurting my hands." She uncovered her mother's head and saw her mother's face wet with tears. "Why are you crying, Immie?"

Unable to answer, her mother simply bit her quivering lip and caressed her daughter's face. "Is something hurting you, Immie?" All her mother did was nod.

Amal prayed that her mother would get well enough to take care of her and her siblings, instead of leaving things to Sitty. Then she could play with her friends when she wanted, her grandmother would go away, and she and her mother would be in charge of their own house.

It was only during sleep that Amal attained what she could not during her waking hours. Nightly, she went to sleep wishing for another dream in the lands of magic and joy.

Her most cherished dream was the one in which she stole her grandmother's stick and, with it, glided downhill, toward the neighboring alleys where some school friends lived. Her grandmother was in hot pursuit, but never caught up.

Looking back, she saw the old woman stumble and fall. She retraced her steps to where her grandmother had fallen. "See this stick, Sitty? It's mine, and I'll make it dance on your legs if you don't obey. Now, get up and walk back to the house and be good, or this." She waved a warning with her stick. Amal felt some strange power, as her grandmother got up immediately and marched silently in front of her, head bowed. Arriving at the house, Amal ordered, "Now go clean the kitchen and get dinner ready."

Without a word, her grandmother marched to the kitchen. Then Amal turned to her bedridden mother, "Now, Immie, this stick is mine. It has magic. It made me fly. I bet it can make you feel better. Here, hold it and see." No sooner had her mother held the stick than she got out of bed. She took a few steps, unsure of herself at first, and then she beamed, feeling strong and confident. "From now on, Immie, you're the chief. Send Sitty back to her house." Amal remembered her mother's happy face and laugh, and her own light heart.

But her joy was as fleeting as the dream. Two-month-old Mikhail shattered the visions with his crying, and Amal was jarred back into her grim world, where no magic wand could be found. Covering her head with the blanket, she tried to go back to her dream, perchance to recover her wand, to have her mother healthy again, her grandmother nicer or gone, and above all, to feel the thrill of power.

She never knew the ghosts that imprisoned her grandmother in her dark cell, taunting and torturing her mind and soul with guilt and regret. Many years later, Amal learned of her grandmother's woeful tale, and finally confirmed a philosophy she had by then come to understand: there is no pain so searing as that from guilt, nor grief so piercing as that from regret.

Throughout her childhood, however, little Amal continued to seek fulfillment of her wishes as she slept, and the stick often obliged.

In one of her dreams, she found a stick that glowed lime-green when she held it.

She decided it had magic powers and wanted to test it. She held it up high, made the sign of the cross, imitating the priest during mass when he blessed the congregation, and asked for her favorite chocolate. She loved chocolate, which she rarely had, and even then never more than one or two little squares. Whenever her father decided to show his magnanimity, he would stop at a store on his way back from the quarry and buy a bar for the family. Amal felt like it was Christmas or Easter, when they had special sweets like *baklawa* and *ma'mool.*

"Here, sweeten your mouth," her father would say, proud of his generosity. He would cradle each share lovingly, like the bit of communion bread the priest doled out at the front of the church. Then he would place it, so gingerly, in the children's eager hands, careful not to drop one tiny sliver. Each child kissed his calloused hand. Amal had heard from her mother and grandmother about the delicious manna they'd had in their native Turkey, but she thought chocolate must be sweeter and more uplifting than any manna. The taste lingered in her memory, like her bitter past.

But in this dream, her magic stick gave her all the chocolate she wanted. She gobbled down the first bar, afraid she'd have to share. Now the stick gave her a second bar, a third, and a fourth, until she could no longer savor the food of heaven. Then she asked for Chiclets. How she loved their sweet minty taste! She stuffed the whole thing—twelve squares—into her mouth.

Then she asked the stick for the doll, the one she used to gaze at every day, as she passed the shop on her way to and from school. The doll always stood serene, ruby lips slightly parted in a soft smile, large blue eyes shaded with long, honey-colored lashes, cheeks like pink marble. And her dress! Gorgeous layers of pink chiffon fell in pleats and folds down to the knees and it had bouffant sleeves, and pearls around the collar and hem. This, she thought, must be how they dressed in heaven. She came to think the doll was hers. She even yearned to look like her. She thought her own mother looked a little like this doll. But every day her doll stood there—confident, healthy, happy—ready to take on the world. Amal's mother was always in bed, diffident and silent, sad and sickly, bowing to the will of her husband and mother.

Now the stick had delivered the doll to her arms. But as with the chocolate, the joy lasted only moments, then vanished. Only the memories remained.

Her dark moments always beckoned her to her dreams in which, like the *jinn* of Aladdin's lamp, the stick answered its master's call. She wished for her grandmother to disappear, and just like that, the dream grandmother was gone from her life. But always her happiness ended with the dream. Always she returned to the real world, to the shadow that was her mother, and to the devil that was her grandmother.

CHAPTER 3

WHILE SWEEPING, I look toward the southern colonnade where the violent patients are kept. I spot Pharha some distance away. She's someone from my lost world of childhood and has come here very recently.

Head bent, she's rooted to the ground like a barrelful of sardines, sweeping the same spot, her arms moving slowly, as though she's in a dream.

She looks as repulsive as I remember her—face as big as a *tableh,* our Arabic drum, bulging eyes that stare into space, nose that squats in the middle of her face with two hairy doorways to dark tunnels. Black, bushy, knit eyebrows arch like two gables accenting the permanent anger she wears on that homely face. Her lips—Allah forgive me—are like mulberry wedges, fringed with a thin moustache of dark, bristly hairs. Her thin, burnt coffee-colored hair used to hang down in one oily braid. Now it is mouse-gray, cropped to reveal her large ears. Her dirty, ankle-length gunnysack and men's worn ankle-boots, caked with filth, were replaced by the the same uniform we all wear—blue sack-like dresses that reach a little above our ankles. Pharha makes me feel like a beauty queen.

Back then she went around the streets and neighborhoods begging for food and cigarettes. When we shut the door in her face, she'd rant and rage, invoking Allah's worst curses—to keep our mothers without sons, and to fill our *teeze* with piles.

I often wondered how Allah could make some so ugly and others so angelically beautiful, like Immie and my sister, Shamiran. Of course, you can't question His wisdom, as Immie used to say. So I must stop questioning Him.

I feel guilty about taunting Pharha when we were children. Maybe that's why I feel a spot of pity and have a notion I should talk to her, but I'm afraid of what she might be like now, though a long time ago she was harmless. Leave well enough alone, I say. I have troubles of my own.

Now I'm stuck to this cursed broom. Me and my broom! I must sweep these stone floors clean of dirt and dust if I want to eat. Not that I like the garbage they feed us—some sweetened tea, a little crumb of dark brown bread, dark like their hearts. Now and then, they give us some horrible slop called porridge. We hate it, but eat it just the same. It's better than the pain that squeezes and twists inside our stomachs if we eat nothing.

And so, I sweep and sweep. I like to keep things clean. It does my soul good to scrub until everything turns white and shiny. If only they'd give me some water, I'd get on these knees every day and scrub. With a hard-bristled hand-brush I'd attack every stone and groove with vengeance, until they yielded every last speck of grime. Here, the mad have taught the sane to call me "Killer of Dirt." But water is scarce. I sweep the stones every day but wash them only once a month, or sometimes after a battle, when the bad ones have their evil hour and attack us.

The bastards never show up to break up the fights until the bad ones have drawn blood. I know why, though. They and everyone else here hope someone will die. Then there'll be one less madwoman in this world. When they enter the battleground, they come armed with sticks and whips. They beat and whip the frenzied warriors until they collapse. It always ends with broken bones and open wounds. They break us when we're outside these walls. They finish us when we're within.

Thinking about the bloody battles pumps me into a sudden frenzy. It's as though energy explodes in my arteries and I'm suddenly possessed with a raging desire to scour the bloodied floors. I'd scrub away every last trace of the evil hour. On my knees, I'd scrub and scrub until the stones sparkled. Then I'd feel so clean, my hands white, though all wrinkled and puckered—ugly but clean.

I'm still here after nine years.

It's early morning but I can tell it'll be another burning hot day. It makes the blood boil and the battered brain go berserk. On these sizzling days, some of us get madder than we already are. Some become restless, ready to blow up. One stupid smile or meaningless gaze at another's face, and poof!—a bloody battle.

These torrid days sap all energy from me, and I don't feel like doing much except sitting and brooding over the dreaded memories that nibble away at the tattered edges of my sanity. I hate the hot days that yank me back to those other days, days that simmer with a sun that must have risen from Gehannem. Every ray is a burning shaft that stabs my mind. I want to scream as

I'm flung back and forth from one hell to the other. It feels like a million scorpions are stinging my brain, shooting their poison. So much pain and grief. So much rage and regret. Allah must have mixed in some dried donkey dung when he made me.

Donkey dung. That's what the bastard called me. I haven't heard his voice these nine years, but his words keep popping up. There's no getting away from the past.

I'm hungry. I wish the cursed bell would ring. Suddenly I hear Hala sing. She often bellows her favorite song, which the beautiful Asmahan made famous. That's another pathetic tale. For all her beauty and her voice, her prestige as the mistress of that philanderer King Farouk, she ended up dead—murdered, they say. Well, at least she didn't suffer like me. Or did she? I'll join Hala for fun and to kill time until the breakfast bell rings.

O barge, tell me you're going where?
O barge, tell me you're traveling where?
O barge, tell me,
O barge, tell me,
You're going where,
You're going where?
O barge, tell me you're leaving, why?
O barge, tell me you're traveling, why?
O barge, tell me,
O barge, tell me,
You're leaving, why?
You're traveling, why?

Before we could start the third verse, Lila, who is forever either laughing hysterically or weeping and whimpering, raises her mocking voice and sings:

O barge, tell me if your captain's old?
O barge, tell me if he's rich and bald?
For sure I'll wed him,
And soon bury him,
And take his loot,
And take his loot.

We all start laughing, and a few belt out our favorite warble, *zaghrootah:*

Aayee, Allah strengthen the voice of Hala,
Aayee, and bring the rich old groom to Lila,
Aayee, we'll all give you zaghrootah,
Aayee, we'll dance the *dabkeh* when you're a widow!
Lulululululululululululu

Now everyone is in a good mood, and we raise the brooms above our heads, swaying them, like the men do with their canes. Some of us are clapping hard, while others dance to the rhythm of the clappers. This is hilarious. I'm dancing and singing, forgetting all.

Suddenly, we hear a frightening shriek. Most of us old-timers know what it means. We know we must run.

I drop the broom and start my run toward the gate, to Abu Salem's office. He'll let me in, as he's done in the past. Suddenly, I look back and see Pharha standing, helpless, broom in hand, looking for someone to tell her what to do. I don't know what possesses me, but I run back to get her before she is caught by one of the bad ones. I see wild Soraiya running from her quarters and toward Pharha, screaming, "You daughters of whores. Give me back my baby. I'll kill you, you daughters of bastards!"

I should be running to the gate, but find myself headed toward Pharha. I shout, "Get away from there. Run to me." She begins to waddle in my direction, but cursed Soraiya, shouting obscenities, is closing in on her.

I make a final dash to grab Pharha, but feel an iron hand grab my arm and flip me around. I try to free myself from Soraiya's grip, but she throws me onto the cobblestones, her whole body on top of me. I feel like my forehead is split open, and a million mini-stars explode in my head. She keeps pounding my head into the ground.

I scream from the pain, my arms flapping around my head. I shout for help, but no one comes. Then a shroud of darkness . . .

I wake up and try to open my eyes, but I can't get them open more than a slit, and it hurts. I stop trying and ask, "Where am I?" I can hear myself and wonder why the words are so garbled. Then a gentle voice says, "Amal, wake up. You've been sleeping for nearly five hours."

I try again to ask where I am, this time by turning the palm of my right hand up.

"In the Sick Ward. We're going to take care of you. You've been hurt. Do you remember what happened?"

I try to nod and my head explodes from the pain. "Aaaaay!"

"We've telephoned *il doctore*. He'll be here next week. I've cleaned up the wound in your forehead and all the cuts and bruises. That's all I can do for now."

I tell her how much pain I'm in—my head pounds hard and my whole body throbs. I can't understand my own speech, but she must've understood.

"I know. Do you remember what happened?"

I'm in such pain it hurts to remember. I try to say, "Soraiya," but all I manage is "Raiya."

I lift my right hand to touch my face and lips. My cheeks, nose, and lips all feel bigger. I hear the nurse telling me not to touch my face, but I put my hand on my forehead and feel a huge bump, smack in the middle. I must look more ugly than Pharha, and I start to cry, but that intensifies the pain.

"Don't cry, Amal. You're going to be all right. The pain and swelling will go away in a short time. Now, just rest."

How can I rest when I'm in such pain? There's no rest for the wicked, only trouble and luck black as tar.

I try to tell her I'm hungry. I feel her hand on mine. "I'll go to the kitchen and see what I can find for you." This nurse must be a genius to understand the strange sounds I make.

I hear her open the door, shut and lock it. This place is full of keys, locked doors, and barred windows. Too bad they don't have double locks for Soraiya to keep her in.

How did I let this happen? For nine years I've outsmarted damned Soraiya and the other twisted minds. And now, I'm broken into pieces. My head throbs and my ears pound like twenty drums.

Every inch of me feels like it's being hammered by a giant mallet, like the one my grandmother used to pound lamb meat for her famous raw *kibbeh*. Now I'm the meat.

Stupid Amal! You wanted to have fun. This is what you get. You forgot your golden rule: a little weeping, a little whimpering. Now giggling, then moaning. Laugh a little. Cry a little. Sing your heart out. Dance. Especially when the orderlies or nurses are around. But never let go completely. Always stay alert, on your guard. Don't overdo any of your antics. You've managed to survive these many years by putting on a front, keeping your head clear. Clever like a fox! Now it looks like the fox has turned into a donkey. Once a donkey, always a donkey! Just like my grandmother used to say whenever I did something wrong. "A dog's tail will never be straight."

But now I remember it wasn't just the fun that caught me off guard. It's my stupidity that got me into this when I ran back. I should've left well enough alone. Even when I had been here just a few months, I had my wits about me enough to run to safety the first time I saw Soraiya on a rampage.

I was sitting on a bench inside the colonnade of the west wing, mulling over the bitter events that had brought me here, when I heard screams that froze my blood. Suddenly, the inmates of the north and west wing, who were either sitting on benches or walking inside the courtyard, began to run wildly, some clinging to each other. I began to run behind a woman who was headed toward the gate. Right inside the gate stood the burly, white-haired gatekeeper who let the woman and me into his office and quickly shut the door. I was shaking as I stood at the window of the office and watched the battle that was raging outside.

Soraiya had pinned a poor woman under her and was pummeling her everywhere. That could've been me, I thought. It looked like she meant to kill her victim. She was shouting, "Give me back my baby. Give him back or I'll kill you, you daughter of a *sharmootah.*"

Then, the woman with me said to the gatekeeper, "Ammi Abu Salem, why don't you kill Soraiya and save us all? She's going to finish us one by one."

"Labeebeh, daughter of my brother, what can I say? One

day her maker will take her, when her turn comes." He sighed. "There, the orderlies are dragging her away. Poor Soraiya will be chained for a very long time. You'll be all right."

"We'll be all right, see!" She patted my shoulder and then her chest. "This is my uncle. He takes care of me. He'll take care of you, too. See? You're lucky. We're lucky."

Something in me snapped when I heard the word lucky. I began to whimper, wringing my hands and calling, "Poor little Lucky, where are you now? Did you suffer before you died?"

Lucky was the name I gave the poor cat that used to jump over verandas and rooftops to land on my porch. I used to save little scraps for her. She was all skin and bones, and always hungry. Her meowing was so pitiful—like some starving child begging for a crumb.

The gatekeeper looked worried and asked, "What's wrong?"

"It's Lucky! She flew in the air and then fell down and died," I whimpered.

I remember the poor man raising his hands toward the ceiling, saying, "In the name of Allah the merciful! Allah heal you both!" Then Labeebeh said, "Ya Uncle, you're talking to the ceiling. You have to go out and talk to the sky!"

"Makes no difference," I said. "Allah's plugged His ears and gone to sleep."

And now this! I've had more than my share of beatings, even as a child, but this one could be the end of me. Damn you, stupid Pharha! Damn you, mad Soraiya! I never should've looked back. Should've just gone to Abu Salem's office. Look what I got for doing good.

Ah, if I could just think of something pleasant. It's hard to find something pleasant when you're in such hell. All my life I've paid heavily for every hour of joy I stole.

My mother once said to me, "You came into the world in 1916, in the middle of the First World War. We were so poor then that all we had for you were worn-out clothes and tattered diapers, which poor relations offered."

Now, broken and hurting, I keep thinking I must be the most wicked to deserve all the misery in my life. Sitty was right. When I was young, she often said, "When you're bad, Allah closes His ears and shuts the gates of heaven. He'll never hear you or help you unless you learn to be good and obey your elders."

No, I didn't always listen, but neither did Allah. Instead, He flopped me here. Or perhaps I brought myself here, so far away from all I've known. Far away from the Church of the Nativity, where Immie took me when I was young and still had hopes and dreams to pray for; farther yet from the Church of the Holy Sepulchre in Jerusalem, where I used to pray to Yessou and his mother Marriam to stop my suffering. No good came from all that. No one listened and no one heard my pleas.

I hear the key turn in the door and the soft padding of the nurse's shoes.

"Here we are, finally. Sorry it took so long," she says as she places the tray on the night table beside me.

I tell her she's been gone forever, and she says, "I can't understand what you're saying, but I've brought you something good." Then I hear her say as if to herself, "And you'll never know what lies I had to tell to bring you this. May Allah forgive me."

"Come, let me help you sit up," she says as she circles her arm around my back and gently tries to move me away from the pillow. I cry from the pain as she slides several pillows behind me, one at a time, until I am slightly raised. Please, Allah, stop this pain! I can't bear it. I moan out loud, like an old woman. She comforts me. "Amal, I know you're suffering, dear, but after a few days you'll be fine, back to your old self again."

And what do you know about my old self, you silly head! If you knew, you wouldn't say stupid things like that. I decide it's useless to tell her anything. She wouldn't understand and won't be able to figure out my garbled sounds anyway.

"All right, Amal, let's try some of this wonderful food. Open your mouth and I'll feed you. Then tell me what you think it is."

I want her to stop talking to me like I was a child or deranged. But I have to keep reminding myself I am in a place for the deranged. Shut up, Amal.

I feel something soft soaked in warm liquid, easy to swallow.

"I knew you'd like it! Can you guess what it is?"

My hand speaks for me, and she knows I can't tell what it is. My tongue is swollen and has lost its taste buds. All I know is that it goes down easily.

"Well, it's melba in sweetened warm milk. Delicious!"

I can't believe my ears. Melba in sweetened warm milk is what I prepared for my father when he had all his teeth pulled out. I wish he had lost his tongue too! I still remember how every time I prepared it, I stole a few spoonfuls before I took it to him. My grandmother gave this same heavenly food to my mother after childbirth to help her produce milk to nurse each new baby.

"Here, open your mouth wide. We don't want any of it to dribble down your chin. Open again, bigger. Good girl! This food will help you heal. You must feel better after this." She keeps feeding me. Although I can't taste its loveliness, I can at least savor it in my memory. Sweet milk and velvety melba! I had to be beaten and broken like this to be given the sweetness of heaven.

Whenever we refused to eat the food Sitty prepared for us, she used to say, "It doesn't matter what you eat as long as it's edible." Sometimes we couldn't force it down and preferred to eat the piece of bread we were given with each meal. "Choosy beggars! The hungry will eat stones," she would yell. I used to think, show us how you eat stones, you heart of stone!

Once I told her that when I grew up I wanted to be the best cook, and her answer stunned me. "Then hurry and grow up, because I'm tired of doing everything. Besides, you might be able to catch a husband if you're good at something, since Allah, in His wisdom, denied you your mother's looks."

If I weren't in such pain, I'd think I'm in heaven—a kind nurse feeding me this soothing food. But I know I'm on earth, the darkest side of earth, where I got my worst beating ever. It's the curse Sitty spoke of. How I hated Sitty and her curses! She was so unfair to me, yet she treated my brothers like they were princes of Arabia.

The good nurse is talking again. "Here, Amal, a cup of water with crushed aspirin in it. I'm stirring it, and when I put it to your lips, drink it as fast as you can, so that you can get all the aspirin that's at the bottom."

I know the horrible taste of crushed aspirin and I grimace. I drink it as fast as I can and nearly choke as the cursed remains stick in my throat. The nurse gives me a little water and, with her hand, gently taps between my shoulders. It hurts and I grimace.

I must look like my grandmother when she scowled and accused me of being a curse.

CHAPTER 4

SHE COULD NOT RECALL in all her childhood days when her grandmother ever smiled or looked pleasant when she talked to her or, rather, ordered her around. Mostly, Sitty saved her smiles for Amal's brothers, who invoked her good humor with their swagger and conscious attempts at adult behavior and speech. Meanwhile, for Amal she had only harsh orders: "Sweep this, scrub that." But when she spoke to the boys—Antone and the twins, Youssef and Jiryis—she beamed and her voice turned smooth, like molasses.

Amal was eight then, and Antone a year younger, though he was bigger and stronger than she was. The boys spent their days scouring the neighborhood for twigs or broken branches to whittle into swords and daggers for their world of fun and games. They rode the scooter their father had found abandoned in an alley while on his way home from work. They thought he was a god, but Amal thought he was a thief. She imagined him walking along a street where the rose-granite houses of the rich reached toward the sky. She figured he had seen the scooter abandoned by children of the rich outside the ornate iron fences meant to keep thieves out. He had taken it and brought it to his boys, she was certain, for this wasn't the first time.

Once before, he'd brought home a "find"—a leather soccer ball—and when his wife asked him where he got it, he said, "Some rich children must have left it in the fields. They have plenty of money to buy more."

When Antone was nine, he and the younger twins were free to roam the surrounding hills, looking for anything that caught their fancy. They made slingshots to kill birds. Sometimes they were lucky enough to bring home a couple of small birds, usually sparrows or robins, sometimes a pigeon, or if really lucky, a quail. They tore the feathers off the little things, anxious to slit their stomachs and spill their guts. Their grandmother was proud of the boys' gumption and skill. She taught them how to burn off any fluff that they couldn't pluck by hand, and helped them fry the birds in a pan. Amal watched them thrill at killing such tiny creatures and crunching the fragile bones. As they jumped around and bragged about their hunting skills, they reminded her of primitive men, or jungle animals, seized by blood lust.

They never offered their sister a taste, not that she wanted any of the poor boney birds. They were a selfish clan, and her grandmother helped them feel like the sons of emirs. They played all day and came home to eat, then left in search of another miserable quarry. Amal resented having to clean up after them, though she preferred that to the stick.

According to her grandmother, a girl from the age of five or six should be trained for her future role as a housewife and mother. Amal was not allowed to go beyond the courtyard of their enclave, but she was old enough to do a lot of the housework and relieve her grandmother who had to do the major chores. Amal saw herself as a maid or slave. She worked more than any other girl her age in the enclave and other enclaves nearby.

But she was not willing to surrender all freedom without an occasional attempt at rebellion. Once in a while, she slipped out with the other girls and climbed over the stone fences of the terraced groves that sloped down to a small valley and then up another bigger hill. The girls were careful not to make noise, but crouched as they stepped in the shade of large fruit trees, plucking any fig or almond within their little arms' reach.

Once, they terrorized a crotchety old woman by knocking hard on her gate. Then they ran and hid behind the fence to watch. At the first round of knocking the old woman turned her head left and right, trying to spot a visitor who had perhaps given up after waiting a few minutes. Her room was some way from the gate, and it would take her a few minutes to hobble to the front door. The little tormentors knew how long it would take her to get back to her room, and a couple of them dashed from their hideout and knocked again, a little louder, then ran giggling to their hiding place, proud of their ingenuity. This time the old woman knew it was no visitor, but those miserable neighborhood children.

She opened the door and began hurling oaths and insults. "Allah bring you the trouble you deserve, you cursed children of cursed parents! Can't you find another game and leave an old woman alone!"

The children knew they were in control. She couldn't run.

She could only rave and yell, and who was going to listen to that?

"May Allah send snakes and scorpions to bite you for torturing an old woman, and I'll be rid of you forever!"

Sobered, the children remembered their parents' fear of threats from the angry lips of the old. The mention of snakes and scorpions, common denizens of the groves, was more than enough to spoil their fun. They feared them more than curses or whippings. Those who remained hidden behind the fence scurried back to their enclave.

But the old woman was not yet through. Difficult as it was, she limped along on gravel stones, squawking in her shrill voice, railing against the residents of the whole enclave. The children ran and hid behind the outhouses.

Amal could hear the old woman hitting the gate with her cane, yelling in her native Bethlehem dialect, "Open the gate, breeders of monkeys and imps of Gehannem! Her left arm rested on the cane, her right arm flailed as she spewed her anger. "Can't you teach your children better manners? What kind of people are you? We shouldn't have let you into our country. We give you a place to call home, and you send your imps to spoil our peace. That's gratitude for you. Go back to where you came from, you Syrian gypsies! Go back to your Turkeyya and let the Turks slaughter you!"

That did it.

Amal heard her grandmother's voice, as harsh and strident as the old woman's. "You should be ashamed of yourself, Im Sleiman, to belch out such un-Christian insults. What's your problem?"

"Ask your imps. Let them tell you what they're doing to

me. They keep banging on my gate and throwing stones at my windows."

Liar. We didn't throw stones this time. That was last time.

"Im Sleiman, we don't want our children to misbehave. We'll beat them until they can see stars in daylight. We promise you that. But there's no reason for you to insult us the way you did. If we could've stayed in Turkeyya, we wouldn't have come here for you to throw insults at us. Shame on you, Im Sleiman, at your age to have a poisoned tongue and wicked spirit!"

"Shame on *you* people! You keep breeding children like rabbits. If they don't stop badgering me, I'll get the police after you."

"Go home, Im Sleiman, and stop your belching and bleating. We know how to discipline our children. But you, you should discipline your tongue!"

Amal then heard the gate slam shut and knew that, sooner or later, she would pay. Right away, her grandmother's angry voice rang out, "Where are those fledgelings of the Shaytaan? Where are they?"

"We haven't seen them for a little while now." Amal heard one neighbor's voice and knew it was only a matter of minutes before she was found. Several voices shouted the names of their daughters. Amal panicked more than the rest, for her grandmother's punishment would be more severe than any mother's.

Moments later, someone was pulling on the door of the outhouse where Amal was hiding. She knew the voice to be Im Sammy's.

"Open the door, you in there, right now!" Then she yelled to the others, "There's one in here. I can see her through the crack but don't know which imp it is."

Amal thought if she did not respond, Im Sammy would give up. But then the threat thundered out, "If you don't open now, you'll get a double beating. Open now!"

Amal's shouted from within, "I'm going kaka."

"If you don't get out right now, I'm going to make you shit your apricots, you gypsy!"

Shaken, Amal opened the squeaky door, and Im Sammy grabbed her arm and yanked her out. Where are the rest? Najwa, Lila, Nadia, Janette?"

"I don't know." Amal's voice quivered.

A troup of angry mothers homed in on the others and pulled the little criminals from the outhouses.

Her grandmother grabbed Amal's arm and marched her to their house. "This stick," she shouted furiously, "will do a dance on your legs to teach you to behave." If it hadn't been for the interference of Amal's mother, the grandmother would have given her more whacking on her legs and behind.

"Just wait until your father comes!"

Amal cried harder, knowing there was another whipping yet to come. But her mother interceded. "Immie, she's only a child. She didn't commit a crime. Children think such things are fun, and we have to teach them to distinguish between fun and harassment."

"You're too soft, Marta. Talking is not a good way to teach them anything."

"Immie, I beg you. Stop this and drop the subject. Her father doesn't need to hear anything."

Amal was grateful to her mother and surprised that her intercession worked. But the older woman was not about to leave matters there. "If you don't teach her now, she will be a curse to you when she grows up!" Not knowing how to combat her mother's obsession with Amal and the curse, Marta only shook her head.

Punishment did not discourage Amal from other sorties and mischief. She weighed the risks and felt the thrill was worth it. Whenever she saw her grandmother march toward her with the stick, she would take off, screaming. She had become a great runner. Sometimes she would make the grandmother chase her a couple of times around the huge courtyard of the enclave. Her hand on her heart, the old woman would stop, take short heavy breaths, and sputter threats of what she would do to Amal when she got hold of her. But before she could catch her breath, Amal would run to the house to seek refuge in one of her few hiding places—under her mother's bed, or in the narrow space behind the armoire. There she was temporarily safe and could not be dragged by the hair or arm to wash dishes, sweep and scrub floors, or carry big tubs of laundry to hang on the lines.

Once Amal gathered up enough nerve to ask her grandmother why she couldn't play.

"Because nothing good comes out of playing. A girl should learn how to behave and keep house. Otherwise, she'll bring nothing but trouble to her family when she grows up. The curse will follow her wherever she goes, like her shadow."

"The curse will never catch me. I'm a fast runner," Amal said.

"That's what you think now. Just try to run away," the grandmother challenged.

Amal had no idea then what her grandmother meant. In time, however, she would learn the power of the curse that stuck to her like flesh to her bones.

Shortly after the episode with the old neighbor lady, Amal sneaked away again to play with her friends. By this time, the others knew that Amal was likely to be yanked away and gave her the least important role in their game. Demeaned in the acutely felt way of childhood, Amal decided to reclaim her dignity. She chose her moment with care.

"I have something important to tell you." The little players drew immediately closer to her. "Did you know each one of us is a curse to our parents?"

"No, we're not," one argued.

"Oh yes, you all are. You know why?"

"Why?" a couple chimed together.

"Because you're girls." She said it with the slow deliberation of a seasoned orator.

It took mere seconds for the pronouncement to rouse fear in their hearts. The "curse" was familiar to their ears. They had heard their parents talk in serious tones about the curse that killed babies and children, or mysteriously caused deaths in several generations of a family. They were also believers in the blue-glass eye charms their mothers pinned to the undershirts of their baby brothers to ward off the curse of the Evil Eye.

The leader of the gang, Najwa, questioned, "And who told you that?"

"Uh, I can't say. If I did, I'd die tomorrow. It's a secret." She thought for a second then blurted, "I know something much, much worse than that, but it's a huge secret. I can't mention it to anyone." She assumed a tone of authority.

They were hooked. They gathered around her, the eldest, eager to know, assured her, "We can keep a secret."

"If I tell you, you have to swear in Yessou's name not to

repeat it to anyone, and especially not to your parents. If you don't swear, I won't tell you."

Each in turn, starting with Najwa, swore, repeating after Amal, "Yessou my witness, I promise to love Amal, Lila, Nadia, and Janette, and never tell our big secret."

When they had all sworn, she made them seal the oath by spitting into their hands, which they rubbed against each other's outreached palms.

"Now, tell us," Najwa ordered.

"Come close, closer, closer. Here it is. When a baby girl is born, the curse visits her that first night and kisses her on her forehead."

"So the curse is a person?" one of them asked.

"No, no, it's . . . it's . . . a huge snake!"

They stared at her for a few seconds, unable to speak—until little Janette ran crying to her mother.

Within seconds, Amal heard a furious voice. She turned and saw the tall, bulky figure of Janette's mother. Im Farah was holding her daughter's hand. Her free hand was raised as if ready to deliver a powerful ear cuffing, shoulder shaking, or possibly a slap on the face.

With the speed of a gazelle, Amal ran toward her house, just three doors away, headed for the safety of her hiding place. Im Farah waddled after her as briskly as her heavy behind would permit.

"Where is the imp? Look, Marta, Amal needs some straightening out. It's not normal for a girl her age to say the things she does to our little girl."

"What's she done now?" Amal's mother whined from her bed.

"Go on, Janette, tell Auntie what Amal said."

"She said a snake kissed me on the head when I was born," Janette mumbled.

"Look, Marta, I know you're sick and can't control her, but I don't want Amal poisoning my daughter's mind. Where is she getting these ideas from anyway?"

Marta knew the source full well, but only said, "I don't know, Im Farah. I'm very sorry, and she will never say that again, I guarantee you!"

Though she pretended to be in control of her children and household, the neighbors knew of Marta's timidity and her mother's domineering character. Amal, too, understood that Marta was powerless. Nevertheless, she saved Amal that day. Before leaving in a huff, Im Farah stood in the doorway and issued her final warning. "If you can't take care of her, I promise you, I will!"

You have to catch me first, you barrel of sardines.

After the neighbor left, Marta called Amal out from her hiding place behind the armoire. "Well, you heard what Auntie said. You keep your mouth shut or someone is going to shut it for you."

"But I only told them what Sitty is always saying!"

"With some spicing up. What your grandmother says is for you only, not to be repeated outside these walls. You hear me?"

Amal was inclined to argue. She thought it very unfair that big people could say whatever they wanted, but children couldn't. She was kept indoors for the rest of that day. The real punishment came later, when her grandmother came back with a load of laundry to fold.

Meanwhile, Marta pleaded gently, "Immie, it's not a good

idea to keep harping about the curse. Amal is only a child. She doesn't understand your meaning but will repeat whatever she hears. That could bring her and us a lot of trouble."

The grandmother grabbed Amal by the ear. "You don't go blabbing about anything that goes on within these walls. You understand? Keep your mouth shut or the stick will shut it for you." Amal squirmed and, winced, letting out a long "a-aay." Her grandmother released her red ear and pushed her down on the divan. "Here, start folding the laundry with me. You need to keep busy and learn to work around the house."

Amal obeyed in angry silence. She promised herself she would never call Im Farah "Auntie" again. That was the polite way children addressed their elders, whether they were their real aunties or not. "Kharra on all of them," she muttered to herself. She wished her grandmother would get a home of her own.

If she had been able to express her thoughts at that moment, she would have railed against her grandmother: *You have made my home a prison, and my mother and me prisoners. I can escape from your prison now and then, but my mother cannot. You have turned my beautiful mother into a spineless mouse!*

CHAPTER 5

"AMAL, WAKE UP, habeebty!"

The nurse's voice calls me back from the maelstrom of the past and into the present Gehannem. If only I could go back to start all over again. I would change everything. If only I could have another chance to hold onto the happiness and peace I knew at the Sisters of the Rosary. But now it's useless even to think of "if onlys."

"Amal," I hear the nurse again and feel her hand on my forehead. "You're warm and all sweaty. Perhaps it's only from today's fiery sun. It's so hot—outside and inside—but I'll take your temperature, just in case."

I continue to pretend to sleep. Perhaps I can catch her talking to herself. I might learn the truth about my condition. I can't open my eyes. They're throbbing with pain and feel like they're ready to explode from my head.

"Amal, habeebty, open your mouth for the thermometer." I

feel her hand around my lower jaw trying to open it.

"Uh, uh, uh . . . " My moaning suggests I'm half-awake. And I feel the cold tube go under my tongue. "It'll just be a minute."

I continue to moan, this time for real. My teeth hurt when the thermometer touches them. She removes the thermometer and says, "A little fever, but nothing to worry about. Just a couple of degrees above normal." Then she continues more cheerfully, "You'll be all right. Sleep is the best thing for you. Your body will heal while you sleep."

That's how much you know! You see me sleep and think I'm resting in peace and my body is healing. Well, you know nothing. Nothing! Just like Immie's nonsense, "Pray and He will help you. Things will get better." Fools!

"How's your headache?"

I respond by tapping my head to the rhythm of its throbbing, then I point to my ribs and stomach, and try to say, "Starving!" I hear how garbled my sounds are, but she understands me.

"I don't know what I can get this time. It's four o'clock, and Im Issa is getting supper ready. Then she mutters, "I need Allah and a dozen angels to help me wangle something out of her now, but I'll try."

She leaves. I pass my hand over my face. I feel hardening bumps and cuts in my cheekbones and my lips feel thick. My hand traces the contours of my nose, and it feels sore and huge. Then I go gently over my eyebrows, and find more cuts and swelling. My eyelids worry me the most. Like giant marbles, they are swollen and hard to the touch. I must look uglier than Pharha. I stick my index finger inside my mouth to feel my bottom teeth, and instantly my body shudders with pain that shoots through my head.

I withdraw my fingers. I don't want to know anything more. Ignorance is bliss, some say. Liars! There's no bliss in ignorance or in knowledge.

The thought of losing my teeth torments me. I don't want to look like my grandmother. She was toothless and when she removed her false teeth, her lips disappeared inside her mouth. She lisped and made clucking sounds when she talked. I used to mimic her to make my friends laugh. I'm sorry about it now. Please, Allah, save my teeth!

But I worry even more about my eyes. I can't open them, and I'm afraid to force them open and find out I've gone blind. That would complete my horrible tale. The thought inspires me to complete a poem that I've often begun but have always left unfinished. Now I think I could finish it:

And at my birth, a star blinked once.
Then all went dark and turned to dust.

Why me, ya Allah? I can't bear the thought of being sightless and toothless, and have others laugh at me and play tricks on me the way I used to do to Sitty.

Amal was nine years old, unaware of the ravages that time inflicts on us all. She was consumed by thoughts of revenge against her grandmother, her arch enemy. She would get even with the tyrant who had tattled to her father about her fighting with other children, pulling their hair, and swearing like an adult. She had suffered whippings at the hands of her father, and swore vengeance against her grandmother who was to blame. Amal would inflict a punishment just as severe.

Her grandmother always kept her false teeth in a cup of water on a table in the kitchen. She wore them only when she ate or when company came. They were uncomfortable but too costly to replace.

One afternoon, when guests were coming for a visit, Amal crept into the kitchen, took the cup, and hid it under the bed where her mother was sleeping. A short time before the guests arrived, the grandmother brushed and braided her hair, wrapped her *mandileh* tightly over it, and then walked into the kitchen to get her teeth. She was shocked to find them missing. Worried, she asked the children if they had seen the cup. No one had.

Amal pretended innocence. "No, Sitty, I didn't see it. I didn't touch the cup. Maybe Shamiran did."

"Shamiran can't reach the top of this table. Look for it everywhere. I must have my teeth before the guests arrive."

Amal put on an act of concern and looked everywhere, except where she had hidden the teeth. The guests came, and her grandmother sat on a thick pad on the floor. Company was received in the room that was designated for Amal's parents and the three youngest children. A door separated it from the other room, where Amal, Antone, Jiryis, Youssef, and her grandmother slept. Marta had eventually insisted that her mother live with them for safety reasons. Walking back to her own home alone at night was not wise. Amal missed the relief she used to feel when her grandmother left at the end of each day.

The sleeping room also housed sacks of flour, burghul, jars of rendered butter, goat cheese, jam, and pickles. The jars were placed on a shelf too high for the children to reach, for the food had to last the whole winter.

Her grandmother told Amal to place small dishes of roasted chickpeas, melon, and squash seeds on the condiment tables in front of the guests. Amal also carried glasses of lemonade to each of the guests. She was careful not to spill any of the precious drink and was pleased to hear a couple of the ladies say, "What a nice girl, helping your grandmother!" Another added, "Yes, isn't she well trained. She'll make a good wife one day."

Amal's pleasure vanished when the guests cradled four-year-old Shamiran's face with their hands and, in turn, said, "Oh, how beautiful!" and "She's going to bring many suitors when she grows up." Or "She'll make a good match someday."

The grandmother added, "What a girl needs is luck. Beauty is good, but luck is better." And everyone agreed, especially as they could see Amal's beautiful mother sitting up in bed, unable to care for her family.

Then her grandmother told Amal to go outside but not too far away, as she might be needed. Amal sat behind the door of the adjacent room where she could see through the crack between the hinges and hear everything in the next room. She listened to her grandmother's toothless speech—the lisping, swooshing, and sucking sounds—as she pronounced her "s's" and the "sh's." Struggling valiantly to control the convulsion of giggles that threatened to erupt, Amal clamped her right hand over her mouth and, with the other, held her stomach. If she allowed one squeak to escape her lips, she would surely cause the wrath of Allah to fall upon her.

She especially liked her grandmother's explanation for being toothless. "My gums are all inflamed and I can't wear my teeth."

The women sympathized and then the conversation switched to other subjects. Amal listened to hushed voices exchanging snippets of gossip. Although she did not understand it all, she strained to hear more.

Suddenly she heard her grandmother struggling to rise from the floor. “Ya Allah, stand by me!” Quickly, Amal sprang from her place and rushed outside to the kitchen. Her grandmother told Amal to set the coffee cups on the brass tray, while she made the coffee.

After the guests left, Amal obediently gathered up empty coffee cups. Pretending to pick up a few seed shells the guests had dropped, she bent down and suddenly exclaimed, “Oh! Look where Sitty’s teeth are! They’re under your bed, Immie.”

Her mother looked at her suspiciously, “How did they get there, Amal?”

“I don’t know. I just saw them. By Allah’s life, I’m telling the truth. It must be Shamiran. She must have climbed up on a chair and brought them here to play with later.”

“Amal, Shamiran couldn’t have done that. And it’s a sin to swear by Allah’s life, especially when you lie.”

“But I’m not lying, I swear . . . ”

“Don’t swear. Give me the teeth. Now go and wash the coffee cups.” Amal left the room, put the cups in the kitchen and went back to eavesdrop behind the door. There, she overheard the conversation between her mother and grandmother.

“Look here, Immie, Amal found your teeth. They were under my bed.”

“How did they get there, I bet—”

“Earlier in the day I saw Shamiran squirm to get under my bed, but I didn’t think anything of it. Now I think she must’ve climbed up and got them from the table and hid them under my bed.”

"A likely tale! I know who the culprit is. Here, give them to me. I hope they're not broken. If they are, I'll be a mouth without teeth."

And a mouth without tongue, I hope, Amal thought. On those rare occasions that her mother sheltered her from the grandmother's wrath, Amal was indeed grateful and felt that her mother loved her. She wanted to embrace and kiss her mother, but always her grandmother stood in the way.

If only her mother could stand firm, like a giant guardian, and deflect the tyranny of her grandmother. Amal resented Marta's inability to do the chores, so that Amal could play like all other children. In her mother's face, however, she saw pain. Marta's sad eyes hinted at her longing for good health. Her face revealed both frustration at being an invalid and guilt for burdening her mother with so much. And helplessly from her bed, she endured the more poignant pain of watching her eldest daughter tormented by a grandmother's demons, demons that should have remained in the dungeons of the past.

CHAPTER 6

IF I LOSE MY TEETH, it's Allah punishing me for the sins of childhood. If I lose my eyesight, He's punishing me for the bigger sins of adulthood. I'm full of regrets, but what good does that do?

I know now that circumstances drive us to the edge, and from there, we either retreat or plunge into Gehannem. And plunge I did—into Gehannem's darkest hole. As Immie occasionally would say, "Each of us has a bitter cup to drink and a heavy cross to bear." Poor Immie has had more than her share. I had no idea, then, how grief could turn into bitter myrrh. Now I understand, for I've been belching my myrrh and toting my own cross for most of my life.

I wait and wait, but the nurse hasn't come back. Maybe she couldn't get any food for me. I know Khadeejeh is in the kitchen. She could tell me what goes on there.

That Khadeejeh! When her mind plays tricks and she

hallucinates, she disturbs me. Otherwise, she's the funniest and the most innocent around here.

The door opens and I hear the nurse come in. "Sorry I've taken so long. We live in a world of rub-my-back-and-I'll-rub-yours." She thinks I'm mad and won't understand what she says. I understand perfectly what kind of a world we live in. It's full mostly of thieves, liars, cheaters, and sinners of all kinds. This place is no different. The sane and the insane are alike in their cruelty. But the sane act with full awareness and intent to do harm; the insane are driven by the turmoil in their heads and hearts.

I hope she has something to quiet my stomach.

"Amal, I've got something for you that should keep you until supper time." I hear her set the tray on the table. "I've brought you some broth with little pieces of bread soaked in it. Let me prop you up first."

"You're an angel," I say, but she can't understand me. I can't get my swollen lips to touch each other to make the right sounds. I put my hand on hers and pat it a few times to let her know she's a good soul.

She must've known how I felt. She says, "You need good food and good care," and continues to feed me, spoonful by spoonful. I need a mother like her to nurse my wounds and to feed me. I remember how my mother fussed over me when I fell ill with typhoid fever, a very long time ago when I was a child.

"Now, habeebty, I'll put your head down and you sleep for two hours or so. I'll be back with your supper before I finish my duties for the day. Sleep in peace!"

She leaves, and I try to sleep. *Don't think, Amal. You'll only bring yourself much pain and little rest.*

I hear birds chirping away outside my window, answering each other's call. There must be a tree out there. They put me in mind of a little bird I once heard singing as I sat in the shade of an almond tree, a few terraces down from our enclave, and tried to study. That was such a long time ago, but the memory of it is so very vivid.

She was in her last year of school, studying for a major test in Arabic literature, a subject she loved. The music of a little sparrow was a pleasant distraction. She closed her eyes and imagined herself in heaven, lounging in gardens and groves of fruit, listening to the cheerful songs of birds. No teachers to scream at you or to whack your hands and call you stupid. No house chores to keep you tethered and away from friends. No grandmother to torment you, only beautiful angels to grant you your wishes—beauty and a loving, healthy mother.

Envying the bird, she opened her eyes and addressed it, "You're a lucky one, little bird. You've got nothing to do but fly from tree to tree, pecking at whatever fruit you like. What a wonderful life you have, easy and free, not like mine."

She took the pencil and wrote a few lines of a poem that she never forgot:

Little bird, lovely bird, you're so free,
Chirping and darting from tree to tree.
I wish I were you and you were me,
Just for a day, or two, or three!
You fly in the sky, so carefree,
Not a prisoner, like me.

Suddenly, she heard a pop, followed by a brief rustling among the leaves as the bird tumbled to the dusty ground. "Ha!" She heard her brother jump out of his hiding place, somewhere behind her. Drunk with his triumph and eager to claim his kill, he stepped up and stood near Amal, proudly twirling his slingshot. "I got him with just one little stone. I'm so good, a one-shot hunter."

"And mean! Why kill this little thing that did nothing to you? All he did was perch in the tree and sing."

"Oh, he'll feel a lot better in my stomach. Wait till he's cleaned and fried. A quail would be much better, more filling, but this is better than nothing. This little thing is more useful dead than alive!"

"I hope you choke on one of his bones, you greedy dog!"

"Shut your mouth, animal!"

Shut yours, you big mule! She decided to keep her mouth shut, and her anger contained, lest she risk a punch or a slap. Although he was younger, he had the right, through Father's permission, to discipline his sisters.

Angry with her brother, and sad for the dead bird, Amal could not study. She kept thinking how death comes so suddenly and quickly—at the hand of a ruthless boy. She suddenly realized that even birds that appear happy and free are perhaps not so happy, nor so free. They have their enemies and their killers. Life has a way of teaching us how things really are. It allows the strong to torment the weak, without remorse or accountability, until the weak snap.

I wish I could sleep and escape from the wicked memories. I have to get some rest. But how can the likes of me find rest?

Maybe if I could think of something pleasant and peaceful, of a place that's quieting to the soul—like the convent of the Sisters of the Rosary. Ah, for an hour with those angels, to see their kind faces again, to pray with them. It is such a long time ago, but I still yearn to be with them. If I had one wish, it would be to go back in time and change everything.

CHAPTER 7

SHE WAS THIRTEEN, miserable, and angry at everything and everyone, convinced the whole world had conspired against her.

The premature birth of Gibrail had been costly to Marta's health. Hemorrhaging heavily, she remained bedridden for months. It was the teenaged Amal who took on the role of a mother, before and after school. A bond between the sister and the littlest brother grew, and as a child, Gibrail did not distinguish between his real mother and her surrogate, Amal. She was the one who gave him fresh warm bread right out of the *taboon*, comforted him when he came home crying over his defeat in skirmishes, bandaged his scrapes and scratches, and rebuilt his shattered pride. When he wanted money for candy or ice cream, he knew Amal would give it to him. He never knew what little she was giving him came out of the pennies she had saved for herself.

At school her teacher, Sitt Hannan, often smacked Amal's

palms with a thick ruler to "help" her learn math. At home, her grandmother controlled every minute of her life and kept her slogging away at endless chores. She had little time to study or read her favorite stories of Arab romance, stories steeped in honor, generosity, and revenge. Even so, she exhausted the few available shelves of such literature and then gladly reread them all. Making a pretense of studying, she took whatever opportunity presented itself to steal away and feed her imagination with love stories.

She would leave the house for school very early in the morning and hide behind the outhouses. There, she sat and read until the bell rang, oblivious to both the noise of students in the playground and the putrid air. Very few willingly went near the stench that permeated the vicinity of the outhouses in the spring, or that steamed out into the scorching heat of summer. The outhouses allowed Amal the cherished freedom to adventure into the imagination of writers, who catapulted her into a world graced by romantic love, loyalty, sacrifice, and even death.

She loved to have this privacy, so she lied convincingly about exams she had to study for, and the need to borrow books from her friends. Her father would not hear of money being wasted on mere paper scripted with matters for which girls had no use. "Girls must learn to take care of a house, nothing more," he claimed when approached on the subject. He did not, however, hold the same view when his sons needed to buy books.

She knew it was a sin to lie, and certainly, she would roast in the fires of Gehannem for it, but necessity demanded it, and hell was so far in the future that she would have plenty of time to redeem her soul. She convinced herself that she was too young for death and Allah's judgment. By the time she was old, Allah would have forgotten, unless He had a memory like her grandmother. Amal was willing to take her chances.

The sins she accumulated gave her many a sweet moment—in an orchard, under an almond tree—alone with her book and her imagination. It was like being in heaven; at peace, she lost herself in the pages of a story. Her favorite, which she read and reread, was *Qaiysse and Leila*. Two lovers, cousins, were denied happiness because they had fallen in love, and their open declaration of their feelings brought shame to the house of the young woman. By tribal code, two cousins could rightly marry, but by falling in love, they dishonored their families.

Such kharra of mules, she thought. Qaiysse suffered and went mad, while Leila lived to grieve and mourn. And their families cared only about honor! Honor be damned! First she felt sadness, then rage against the tyrants who manipulated the lives of sons and daughters with the same cold calculation they used to play a game of cribbage.

But as the book explained, the tragedy took place a long time ago, in pre-Islamic times. She was relieved to be living in the twentieth century, when parents would not imprison their children if they fell in love. Though, of course, one could not fall in love with someone from another religion—a Muslim woman with a Christian man, or a Christian woman with a Muslim man.

She had heard of one Christian girl who had eloped with a Muslim, and what a scandal that became! The girl's family was humiliated into self-exile from society. When they were seen in the market, they dropped their heads and slunk away in the silence of their shame.

Amal's cherished escapades into the world of literature and

romance came infrequently. Apart from the tyrannical grandmother who controlled her home life, her math teacher was her worst nightmare. She considered Sitt Hannan to be the daughter of the Shaytaan, the devil, sent to torment students like Amal. The best teacher for stupid girls, Sitt Hannan believed, was a ruler.

After many a smack across the knuckles and countless humiliations, Amal finally could take no more. One day, she ran away from school and swore never to return.

As usual that day, Sitt Hannan had called upon Amal to solve a math problem and, as usual, Amal had failed to give the correct response. Sitt Hannan struck Amal's palms until her hands smarted as though they were on fire. Hate rose in her chest, and her heart pounded. She wanted nothing less than to see her tormentor tumble into the deepest hole in Gehannem and twirl like a dervish in the raging fires.

But, she thought, the teacher was done with her for today. Tearful from the burning in her hands, Amal blew cool breath on her reddened palms and settled down to do something she loved—sketching.

She thought of all the animals she was fond of drawing and settled on one. Angry and vengeful, she sketched a donkey standing on its hind legs. The front legs held a stick, poised and ready to strike. The mouth, opened wide, showed a gap tooth. Two giant breasts were cradled in a brassiere. Decency demanded that she couldn't leave the donkey's private area exposed, so she covered it with a pair of underpants torn in several places. Now and then Amal looked up at the blackboard, faking interest and attention.

Things would have gone on peacefully had the girl next to

her minded her own business and not burst into giggles.

"What's so funny, Sitt Fadwa?" the teacher bellowed.

"Nothing, Sitt Hannan, nothing."

"Well, if you laugh at nothing, then we'd better take you to *beit il-majaneen*."

Several students tittered quietly at the teacher's reference to the Oasis for Troubled Women, the institution for the insane. But Fadwa cringed at the horrid thought. She knew she was going to get the stick and decided to put the blame on the culprit. She pointed at Amal. "It's the funny picture Amal has sketched. It made me laugh. Sorry, Sitt Hannan."

Amal had already crumpled the sketch and hidden it inside the desk, but she knew that Sitt Hannan would settle for nothing less than having the paper and showing it to the class. The teacher always enjoyed such moments of triumph and the victim's subsequent humiliation. Slowly she marched toward her prey and demanded, "Hand over that sketch, you stupid girl!"

Slowly, Amal pulled it out of the desk and gave it to Sitt Hannan, resigned to a terrible consequence.

Eager to demonstrate her own absolute power, Sitt Hannan gave a quick glance to the sketch of a donkey and raised it for the class to see. "Look, girls, what a donkey your classmate is! A nice donkey, isn't she?"

The class erupted with giggles and sniggers. Some girls covered their mouths and looked in Amal's direction, as if to say, "Now you're going to get it!" There was no doubt whose picture it was. How could they mistake Sitt Hannan's gap-tooth and bulging breasts?

Convinced that everyone had enjoyed a good laugh at Amal's expense, the teacher took another look at the sketch. But now her mood flashed from triumph to thundering rage. "You donkey, daughter of donkeys, stand there until I come back with the principal. You're going to wish you were in Gehannem by the time we're through with you!"

Thoughts of the beating she would receive spurred Amal on. As soon as Sitt Hannan had stormed out, Amal ran to the teacher's desk, grabbed the sketch, and bolted out of the classroom. She sprinted over the hilly road to home without stopping. She feared the school would have notified the police to catch her and throw her into prison.

She collapsed just within the gate of the enclave, unable to breathe, her mouth dry, arms crossed around her heaving stomach. She felt safer now. She was ready to put up with her grandmother, rather than suffer strapping and humiliation at the hands of a she-devil. "Sitt Hannan, that piece of kharra, should go to Gehannem herself!" she muttered. "Imagine such a name—Hannan, *compassion*! Whoever named her must have known she would need compassion in her heart. I would have called her Assyeh, the cruel one. That suits her better."

Children playing in the courtyard began to shout, "Amal's back! She's here!"

Before a crowd of neighbors could gather, Amal struggled toward the outhouse on wobbly legs. After urinating, she wiped herself with the beautiful donkey sketch, stuffed it far down in the wastepaper container, and slowly walked into her mother's room. Her grandmother quickly followed. Marta was breastfeeding baby Gibrail.

"What're you doing home at this hour?" her grandmother demanded.

Amal decided to give an abridged version of events. "I quit!

That's it! I'm never going back. I've had enough of being called 'donkey' and getting whacked."

"Best thing," piped in her grandmother.

"What happened?" Amal's mother asked, alarm in her voice.

"Nothing. I got hit hard again today for not giving the right answer to the math problem. Then Sitt Hannan called me donkey, daughter of donkeys. I didn't mind her calling me donkey, but calling you donkeys was more than I could bear. The woman is mad, and she meant to kill me. So I ran out and came home."

"But you have only one more year until you graduate," her mother pleaded.

"If I don't pass math, I will never graduate. I hate Sitt Hannan and she hates me. I can't go back. I won't go back."

If it hadn't been for Sitty, her mother would have marched Amal back to school that afternoon. Instead, she sat down on the divan and wept. "I never had a chance to go to school. If it weren't for my father teaching me to read and write at home, I'd be as dumb as these stones," Marta said, pounding the wall with her fist.

Sitty raised her voice, "Eh, and a lot of good learning would have done you. Amal knows enough to read and write. That's more than any woman in my time ever had. She's better off here with us. She can learn to cook and clean. That's more useful than the silly school learning." She turned to Amal and said, "Stay with me and learn to be a good housekeeper. That's better for you, and for me."

Amal was certain her mother could never win against Sitty, but this time she was wrong. Marta insisted that her daughter should at least learn the arts of sewing, embroidery, and maybe even fashion design. She had seen Amal's sketches of people and animals, and was convinced her daughter had a talent that should be pursued. Then she could support herself if hard times came. Marta prevailed.

"All right, that may be a good idea," Sitty said. "She's going to need a lot to find a husband."

Amal didn't want to know what her grandmother meant by "needing a lot."

The next day her mother surprised her with a sudden show of spunk. She marched to the convent of the Sisters of the Rosary, Amal in tow.

Grumbling and whining about the uselessness of going to another school, Amal occasionally kicked a pebble on the dirt road. At last, they reached the final gentle slope, at the foot of which stood the convent of the Sisters of the Rosary.

Amal remembered talk from girls at school about their Sunday outings to the convent to play on the swings, skip ropes, and play hopscotch. The Sisters of the Rosary kept a boarding school for orphaned girls. On Sundays they opened their playground to girls from the community. But Amal was never allowed to join these girls. Her grandmother thought it indecent to play with other girls who might teach her some horrid and forbidden knowledge.

As the convent loomed before them, Amal pleaded, "I don't want to go to the Sisters of the Rosary. Why can't I just stay home and help Sitty?"

"Stop complaining. You think you're the only one who doesn't get her own way? Just think how unhappy I'm going to be, not being able to read the storybooks you used to sneak home. I love to read when I'm too weak to get up from bed."

That was a revelation—her mother guilty, like her, of reading romances! She had believed Marta was only checking up to make sure the books were from the school library. So, Amal thought, her mother was not as naïve as she often appeared. She, too, used guile to savor moments of forbidden pleasure.

Amal's heart lurched as her mother lifted the heavy knocker on the sturdy metal gate and banged three times. The convent was a fortress surrounded by a high wall that sheltered it from the gawking public. To Amal, it looked like a prison. Her knees began to buckle, and her heart thumped in her chest. She wanted to run, but her mother sensed her agitation and held her hand tight. "You'll love it here."

Soon, a pretty and petite young nun, dressed in a plain, light-blue, ankle-length dress and a white coif, unlocked the gate and smiled at them. "Good day. Can I help you?" she asked in broken Arabic.

My mother smiled back at her. "Yes, I have brought my daughter along to learn to sew and embroider."

The nun welcomed them and ushered them along to a large reception room. "Wait here, and I'll find Mother Superior for you. Make yourselves comfortable."

As soon as she left, Amal whimpered, "I don't want to come here. Why can't I learn to sew at home?"

"Look at it this way, you'll be able to get out of the house for few hours a day, instead of staying home all the time, doing housework and fighting with your grandmother."

Suddenly Amal saw the wisdom of her mother, who was no fool after all. Resigned, she began what became six joyful years with the Sisters of the Rosary.

Her days began at dawn, when she rose to do her cleaning chores, prepare dough, bake it in the taboon, and cook the main meal of the day. Her grandmother valued this help, as it relieved much of the drudgery of keeping house for a family of ten. Even her mother's health seemed to improve with the general brightening of the grandmother's disposition.

Finished with the work that would have taken some women a whole day to do, Amal left the house in the early afternoon and walked to the convent to spend four hours of bliss. At five o'clock, she returned to do her evening duties—washing her younger brothers' faces, hands, and legs, to get them ready for supper before her father's return. Then she served supper and cleaned up afterward. Her mother would ask Shamiran, her eight-year-old sister, to help with the dishes, which sometimes she did, all the while grumbling about how much homework she had to do. Shamiran hated putting her hands in water and faked illness when she was forced to do a few dishes. Her mother seemed always to believe her.

Amal thought that Shamiran must have been born under a lucky star. She was beautiful with golden hair, emerald-green eyes, and skin the color of cream, just like their mother. Allah was unjust in making her sister so beautiful and herself so plain, like her father. The Sisters of the Rosary were the only ones who treated her as though she were the most beautiful girl in the world.

CHAPTER 8

MY HEAD THROBS with regret, while I wait for supper.

God bless the Sisters. How I loved them! They gave me what my own family denied me—love, praise, confidence, and dignity. They cloaked me with kindness, while my family stripped me of all worth. Become a nun . . . one of us . . . Dedicate your life to Jesus . . . use the talent He gave you . . .

The nurse walks in and, I hope, brings some aspirin.

"Hey, Amal, are you awake? I'm sorry to be so late." I answer by turning my hand once, my palm facing up, as if to say, there's nothing I can do about that. I point to my head, and she says, "I've got aspirin here in the cup." I drink the water and the bitter crushed aspirin. I hate the stuff, but it helps a little. Then she says, "I'm going now to see if your supper is ready so I can feed you and get you ready for the night before I have to leave. I have a long walk before I catch the bus to Bethlehem Square, and then another bus to Jerusalem.

Il doctore should be here tomorrow, and will give you good medicine to help you."

I don't like il doctore. I turn my left index finger in my temple, and then flick my right hand toward the door to tell her he's sick in the head and to send him away. The nurse gives a hearty laugh then says, "Is that what you think? Well, we're all a little mad, some more than others. Now, I'll go see what I can wangle out of Im Issa for you."

I think of the kitchen staff—tough Im Issa, Latifeh, Im Nader—and the nonviolent patients who work in the kitchen when it's their turn. Again I wish I could see Khadeejeh. If I live through this beating, I'll have great fun when she next imitates Im Issa. Maybe, in a few days, she could visit me here. I need her mad talk to chase away my ghosts. But the pain is still too much for me to bear Khadeejeh's gabble, although I could use a laugh.

Maybe when il doctore comes, he could give me something strong enough to stop this throbbing. I've never been given any medicine all the years I've been here. My complaints about headaches were always ignored. But this is a new doctor, Doctore Jamayelle. He's better than that old man who didn't even look at me during his annual interviews. He just kept scribbling in his big book and asking his stupid questions—stupid like his face! "Pain anywhere? Any voices in your head? Anything you want to tell me?"

Most of the time I just wanted to get away from the stupid man. I've known others like him, enough for ten lives. But a couple of times, I made up stories that could only have come from a twisted mind. In a way, I enjoyed the sight of him working hard to write down the pile of kharra I gave him.

Doctore Jamayelle is much better. He's young and handsome, and sometimes laughs as he listens to our answers. The first time I met with him, just a year ago, I had such fun. I tried to confuse him.

Nurse Siham, that sour face, escorted me into his office, helped me into the wooden chair facing him, and stood next to me as a guard. Doctore Jamayelle was still writing in his book when I sat down.

"Good morning. I'm Doctore Jamayelle. What's your name?"

"Donkey."

"Donkey? I've never heard anyone with a name like that."

"Well, I'm special, and Donkey's my special name."

"Here in this file, it says your name is Amal Murad!"

"Strange! I've never heard this name before."

"Well, maybe you just forgot."

"I never forget, Doctore. I wish I could."

"What do you wish to forget?"

"Forget what, Doctore?"

"Let's get back to your name."

"I told you, it's Donkey!"

"That's not a good name for a nice woman like you."

"True, but such are the facts, Doctore. But I'm a wonderful donkey."

"Donkeys are ugly and cantankerous."

"You're very wrong! You're a doctore, but you don't see the beauty in donkeys! Some doctore!"

"Explain how a donkey is wonderful."

"The donkey obeys her master all the time. She carries heavy loads of water from the water hole to customers. She carries garbage on garbage day. And when it pleases the master, he even rides on her back. She does everything, except once in a while, when he whips her behind to make her go faster, she will drop a huge dollop on his legs and shoes. Or she might do it right in front of a customer's house. Every dawn she brays on the way to the water hole. Wouldn't you if you were that donkey?"

"I wouldn't know."

"Of course not. A donkey is a beauty—large hazel eyes, nice long face, lovely gray lips, a coat of shiny and velvety fur, strong slender legs, lovely derrière, and a great lock of hair for a tail to shoo the flies away. Do you own a donkey?"

"No. I don't like donkeys."

"But everyone needs a donkey. Even if you don't like donkeys, you should have one to do your work for you. And when you want to take out your anger and frustrations on something, you whip her, and that'll make you feel good again."

"I see. Tell me, then, does the donkey dream?"

"Oh, yes, she dreams all the time."

"But you said you don't dream!"

"I never said that! Doctore, you're confused, or lying. You'll go to Gehannem, if you lie."

"All right. But if a donkey dreams, what would he dream about?"

"He-donkeys don't dream. Only she-donkeys dream. They dream about whippings the cursed owners give them while plodding their way up those slippery cobblestone stairs from the water hole to houses in town. They dream about the insults, the curses heaped on them, the backbreaking labor, the miserable amount of hay they're given . . . "

"What's so terrible about that? Allah made the donkey to serve the human race. It's our beast of burden. Nothing wrong with that."

"Well, in that case Allah must be a man."

"Of course He's a man."

"You're funny and so cute. Isn't he, Sitt Siham? Hahahahahaha . . . "

They look at each other and exchange smiles. I continue to laugh.

He asks, "So, Amal Murad—"

"You keep forgetting my name, Doctore. I'm Sofrenia!"

"I thought you said your name was Donkey."

"Who said anything about a donkey?"

He jerks his head sideways. "You've changed names again."

"No, Doctore. I've been telling you, my name is Sofrenia."

"Who gave you that name?"

"I'll tell you, if you promise not to tell anyone. The old doctore before you, oh, what's his name? Doctore Hmar . . . Hmar . . . Hmarneh! That's it. I heard him say I am Sofrenia. I love that name. Don't you, Doctore? It sounds so Europe-y, a little French, so high class!"

Il doctore and the nurse begin to giggle. The Hamarneh clan is well known in Bethlehem. But I pronounce the name without the first vowel sound and drop the last syllable so that the word means "donkey."

"All right, Sofrenia, do you ever feel pain anywhere?"

"Pain? Don't ask, Doctore. I have pain all over, especially right here and here." I point first to my head, then to my heart.

"You have headaches and pain in your chest?"

"No. No headaches—just hurt. No pain in the chest—just in my heart. Help me, Doctore."

"Tell me, then, how do your head and heart hurt?"

"I'll tell you. My brain churns all the time, like *labann*, the buttermilk in the goatskin flask that the Bedouin women make. I love it. Next time you come, can you bring me some? I'll pay you!"

"You have money?"

"I'm rich. Queen Zenobia can't pay? This world is mad!"

I see him look at the nurse and, smiling, say, "You have so many names. You must be special. Here it says your name is Amal, but you say your name is Donkey, then Sofrenia, and now Queen Zenobia."

"Which one do you like best, Doctore?"

"Well, I think Sofrenia is the most appropriate of the three. What do you think?"

"I think you're a genius, Doctore. A genius!"

He looks at me and says, "You're amusing, to say the least. Now, you have to go back and be good. "You can bring in the next one, please," he tells the nurse.

I turn around and curtsy. "Doctore, Allah be with you." I head toward the door, walking like I was the queen of England or, better still, Queen Zenobia.

In the waiting room, I see Khadeejeh sitting on a bench with another nurse next to her. I wink at Khadeejeh, and both of us break out in a fit of uncontrollable giggling and cackling. I laugh because I think of the pile of donkey dung she'll give il doctore—the palace on the mountain and the prince coming to take her as his bride. She might even tell him about the last offer she made to take me along as her privileged maid.

I hear the door open and the nurse placing a tray on the table. Then, speaking like a mother to her sick child, she says, "Here we are! I've brought you something good—chicken soup, pureed potatoes, white bread, and pudding. That will make you heal fast."

Just give me the pudding and keep your stupid predictions to yourself. But I should be grateful. I raise my arm and with my hand touch my head.

"You like that! Soon you'll be healthy again," she says.

But while the nurse tries to prop me up, I think of what I would really say if I dared express myself and if I could speak clearly. *I don't want to be in good health again. I would much rather remain in this room, in solitude, even with pain as my only companion. Maybe then I would have the time to reweave the frayed tapestry of my life. Here, in this silence, I can hear my thoughts, unbroken by the shrieking and babbling of the mad. If I could stay here, perhaps I could hear Allah's voice. Perhaps He could hear mine. Perhaps . . .*

"Now," the nurse says, excitement in her voice, "Taste this! When you're finished, I'll get you ready for the night, before I have to leave." Perhaps she knows the night nurse would not fuss over a madwoman, even someone as beaten and broken as me.

I begin to feel my spirits gradually lift with the taste of white bread soaked in chicken soup, potatoes mashed with broth. It is food fit for the tables of the rich. I can't believe my good fortune—nourishing high-class food for this madwoman who can't eat by herself, or walk, or talk.

When she gives me the first spoonful of chocolate pudding, I think this is worth dying for. I start to wonder if I'm really eating this food or dreaming again. *Tell me, nurse, am I really alive, here on earth? Or have I died and gone to heaven—or purgatory to cleanse my soul of sins?*

The nuns taught me about hell, purgatory, and heaven.

"Notre Dieu is so merciful that he gives sinners a second chance to repent their sins, do penance, and cleanse themselves before they're allowed into heaven," they'd say. Could it be that I'm in this home for the deranged doing penance? Or is this heavenly food my dying wish before I leave this Gehannem to go to the everlasting one?

Then I hear the nurse's voice, "Hey, Amal, you're not saying anything. Do you like your supper?" Again, I let my hand do the talking for me. I bring my index finger to my thumb to make a circle. I can't quite make the fingers touch, but she gets the idea.

"I'm glad you like it," she says. Then I point toward the ceiling, and she understands, "Ah, yes, it's heavenly. We'll feed you like this until you're well again."

"Angel. Sinner," I say as I point to her and then to me.

I can't believe she understood. "No, Amal. I'm no angel, and you're no sinner. Sinners are those who drive others to this place."

I feel like I've been struck by lightning. *What are you trying to tell me? Are you just blabbing, or are you trying to say something about me?* My heart rumbles with a new terror. Does she know about me? I force myself to snap out of this fear. I must never lose sight of my adopted identity. I try to smile and cry, and I babble unintelligibly about angels and devils, though it hurts to do so. "Allah help you and help us all," she says.

When she finishes feeding me, she says, "I have half an hour before my shift is done. Come. Let's get you ready for the night."

I hate the thought of getting up, but I need to get to the washroom. I moan from the excruciating pain everywhere. I have no strength in my legs. But the nurse supports me by circling me with her arms as I move one step at a time, like a toddler taking his first step. In the tiny bathroom, I yelp, partly from the pain in my ribs and partly from panic at the unfamiliar feel of the porcelain toilet. The only thing I've known is an in-ground cemented hole, with raised footpads. When my ordeal on the toilet is over, the nurse guides me to the sink, puts a bar of soap in my right hand, and opens the tap for few seconds, long enough for me to wet my hands. Water is scarce and sacred.

Supported by the nurse, I limp and shuffle back to bed. Then she says, "Now you are ready for a good sleep. In the morning I'll be back to see how you're doing. We'll take care of you."

You probably can take care of wounds and bruises and broken ribs, but can you take care of the putrid kharra in my head? That's the trick.

"Good night, Amal, I'm leaving now. If I miss the bus, my mother will worry. There's no way for me to let her know if I ever miss the last bus home. Nurse Najlah will be with you tonight if you need anything."

She hesitates and I feel her, still standing by me. "Amal," she says, "would you like to say a prayer before going to sleep?"

Now it's my turn to hesitate. What if she begins the Muslim prayer? I used to hear friends from my school days chant their morning prayer. I actually liked it. I still remember it word for word. But I don't think it'll do anything for me. I'm Christian and Syriac. The only prayer for me is my Syriac one. But it would be cruel to repay her kindness with rudeness. A Muslim prayer is better than no prayer. So I sound my "Aha."

I can't believe my ears when she begins with the Holy Trinity, the introduction to the Syriac prayer,

"*Bshaim abo, wabro, roho quadeesho, hadalo shareero, ameen.*"

"Syriac?" I blurt out.

"Yes, I fooled you, ha?"

"You know me?" I ask her, a little afraid of her answer.

"I know of you."

You know of me! Great news! And what yarns have you heard that have been spun so many times, and in so many ways, by the tongues of gossipmongers?

"Your name?" I struggle to get out.

"Marriam. Marriam Zilpho."

I don't recognize the name. It's not anyone from Bethlehem.

"May you awaken to the goodness of Allah, habeebty," she says as she touches my hand lightly. "I'll see you tomorrow morning." She leaves and closes the door behind her.

I must try to sleep, to get away from the pain and from myself, even for a few hours. All I've done since coming here is to regurgitate the poison that has fermented in my veins. Sometimes I think death is better than this.

Life can be as sweet as sesame brittle, but not for me. I broke Allah's commandments and relinquished grace. Now I know there is no reprieve from the sinful act. None. Nine years later and I'm still in this hell, punished all the more by a beating that might prove the end of me. Now I'm beginning to see the sorry truth. I wish I had killed myself instead, like Nuhad.

My mind burrows back through dark tunnels to that time when my friend decided death was kinder than life. What a terrible way she chose, I thought then. Now I'm not sure which is better, her way or mine.

We were so young, believing in the promise of a fair and happy life.

CHAPTER 9

TOGETHER AMAL AND NUHAD used to walk to and from school. They made a funny pair. Nuhad was a tall and gawky teen, thin as sugar cane. She had a yellow-brown complexion and mouse-brown hair that drooped down her back in two thin braids. Her eyes immediately drew the attention of anyone who saw her. Her eyelids opened but a slit, for they were attached at a low angle to the corner of her eye. She was the only girl in school with eyes so different from almond-shaped Arab eyes.

Beside her stood Amal, short and pudgy. Her hair hung in two thick, shiny braids. Her small jet-black eyes, fringed by short eyelashes, were set deep in a round, honey-brown face. They were indeed an odd couple, not only in their appearance, but also in their character.

Nuhad was a quiet thirteen-year-old who spoke only when spoken to, as though she felt words were too precious to waste. Her consistent demeanor in and out of class, coupled with her academic success, especially in math, earned her respect tainted with envy from her classmates and admiration from her teachers.

Watching Nuhad walk with Amal, schoolmates wondered about the odd pair, so different from each other physically and in personality. Just as Nuhad was stolid, Amal was mercurial. She was quick to reply and easy to draw into a verbal skirmish. Her smile was as ready as her frown. Anyone who wanted to pick a fight with her got more than they wished for. Seasoned in the art of warfare at home—battling her brothers and their grandmother—she was determined to win against aggressors at school.

The bond between Nuhad and Amal was fed and cemented by their silent recognition of their physical unattractiveness and their social ostracism from their classmates' circle. Neither was allowed to visit other students, nor to have others visit them. Nuhad ventured into brief conversations with Amal on their twice-a-day treks, especially on those days when Amal suffered unjustifiably under the tyrant math teacher.

On one of their walks home, while Amal's hands still smarted from that day's punishment, she asked Nuhad, "Do you know an old woman who does black magic?"

"I've heard of such a woman, but I don't know her. Why do you ask?"

"I hear girls talking about a woman who puts a curse of sickness and sudden death on people."

"You're joking, right?"

"No, I'm serious. I want some black magic done to Sitt Hannan."

"You're talking like mad people. Don't say such things in

front of others. They'll take you to beit il-majaneen to live with the mad there!"

"I could kill that piece of dried kharra!"

"And just how do you kill a piece of dried kharra?"

"I'll find a way." Then both looked at each other and began to laugh hysterically. Amal had never seen Nuhad laugh like that.

"But seriously, why don't you think about learning your math. That way she won't have a reason to hit you. Besides, math is fun, a challenge to the brain."

"Now *you're* the one talking like the mad." They laughed again. "Seriously, Nuhad, I just don't have the brain for math. But I love to read and draw all sorts of things. I bet you can't do that."

"No, I can't, but that isn't going to help you finish school."

"If I could only find some magic dust to turn Sitt Hannan into a tiny donkey that would fit into my palm, then I'd show her what terror is."

They giggled then Nuhad said, "That won't help you learn math either. But with a little tutoring, you might become a famous mathematician."

"Since when have you become a comedian?" Amal paused, then added, "If you could help me, maybe I'll learn enough to pass."

"Sure. I can't promise you great results, though. I'm not a real teacher. The biggest problem is my parents. They don't allow girls to visit me. They're very strict."

"Not half as strict as Sitty, I bet. You have no idea what Sitty is like!"

"Anyway, our problem is to find a place to meet where no

one could find us. It has to be near my house. That means you have to find a way to come over."

"Leave that to me. Just tell me where and when, and I'll be there."

And so the stage was set. It was late May, the days long and the sun warm. Amal did everything her grandmother asked and more. She pleaded with her mother to let her get help from a math teacher who lived just at the end of the road to the west. Several students were meeting there, she lied. Her mother prevailed upon her own mother.

That Friday afternoon, Amal bolted from her house, carrying her math textbook, a pencil, and a notebook. Walking briskly, she felt a glimmer of hope. Perhaps Nuhad *could* save her from the humiliation of failure and the ruler.

When she approached the terraces on the last hill at the end of the road, she sneaked over three stone fences and hid under the giant fig tree where Nuhad had told her to wait. Nuhad would work in the garden nearby and surreptitiously cross a couple of stone fences to reach Amal.

While waiting, Amal decided to gorge on the abundant purple figs—the sweetest and most delicious. At first, she devoured as many as she could unpeeled. They were as addictive as baklawa. She recalled the common saying, "Eat unpeeled figs, and when you've had enough, peel and eat some more." Having had more than enough, she squatted down close to the fence near an almond tree. She wished she could reach the high branches, but convinced herself the risk of discovery was not worth it.

Ten minutes later, Nuhad came up quietly from behind. "Stay down. I don't want my brothers to see us."

"All right. Here is my book."

"It seems you've eaten half the figs of this tree," Nuhad remarked, casting a disapproving squint at the ground.

"They're so delicious!"

"And you're so sloppy! You shouldn't leave traces of your crime scattered around."

"The peel is a good fertilizer."

"Well, then, you should've eaten it to fertilize your brain."

"I did, at first. They're addictive. Nevermind the figs, teach me please, Sitt Nuhad!"

"No joking now. I have little time. Let's start with the lesson we had today. Solving problems of fractions. How do we divide fractions? Pay attention."

Nuhad went through two examples, then asked Amal to do one on her own. She was lost. Nuhad explained another one to her. "Do you understand now?"

"I understand when you do them, but I can't do them by myself."

Frustrated, Nuhad lifted her eyes and palms toward heaven, "*Allahu Akbar*!"

Amal cracked up. Nuhad said, "God is great," just as adults do when they're exasperated with children. Nuhad giggled too, then said, "Let's try from the very beginning of the unit on fractions. Maybe we'll have better luck there."

Patiently, she began to explain the basics of fractions. Amal understood the meaning of fractions, but became lost when Nuhad shifted to adding, multiplying, and dividing them. Finding the common denominator was a mystery.

"You know what I think, Amal?"

"What?"

"You should find the woman with magic dust!" Nuhad smiled.

"I told you!"

"I can't believe how clever you are in everything, especially talking, yet you can't understand something as simple as math."

"It's simple for you, because you understand it. You're a genius. I wish I could be like you."

"No, don't wish that on yourself. I sometimes wish I were like you."

"Only the insane would think that!"Amal exclaimed. "Here I wish I could exchange me with you, and *you* wish you were like me! You're so smart."

"I'm so smart I couldn't even teach you simple addition of fractions!"

"It's my brain. It's not made for math. Anyway, you'd make a great teacher."

Nuhad was pleased with the compliment and told Amal that was her dream—to become a teacher. "But my parents won't let me go to Jerusalem to the House of Teachers. They don't think it'll do me any good when I get married. In three years they want to marry me off to my cousin Ali."

"That sounds like Sitty talking. 'What's school for? A girl should train for marriage, housework, and raising children.' Do you love Ali, Nuhad?"

"How do I know? He's five years older. We never speak to each other. We're not allowed. Our fathers are brothers, and they agreed on this plan when I was born."

"Well, I hope he loves you like Qaiysse loved his cousin Leila."

"You're half-mad, you know, Amal. That's just a story from

the imagination of a writer. It's not real life."

"And why shouldn't it be real life? It's so beautiful, so noble, so . . ."

"So mad and so dead! Don't you remember how Qaiysse died in the end?"

"Yes, but a beautiful death, burning with love!"

"And you're burning with insanity. You *do* belong in beit il-majaneen!" Both girls laughed heartily, then parted to begin the walk home.

Several years later, when she learned of Nuhad's fate, Amal was brought to tears. Amal heard talk about a man, Ali Sheriff, who had married his cousin, an unattractive girl of sixteen, who bore him three children—two boys and one girl. But it seemed he had been forced to marry her on pain of losing his inheritance. After four years, he married the cousin he loved, the beautiful Assma, and brought her to live in the same house with his first wife. He cohabited with the new wife and kept the first one as a servant. Two years of taunting from the new wife, and complete estrangement from the husband, drove the first wife to find a way out of her misery. She hanged herself.

Amal was sure this was Nuhad. She remembered the name, Ali, and his last name was the same as Nuhad's. At twenty, Amal wept over the terrible end of her bright and good friend. But suicide, she believed, was a sin against Allah. The good nuns had taught her, "God gives life, and God takes it. Suicide is a deadly sin."

Years later, she would change her mind.

CHAPTER 10

POOR NUHAD! In my younger days, when I believed in the nuns and their teachings, I thought she was so wrong to commit suicide and consign herself to the fires of Gehannem. But let me tell you, all you people who are quick to judge, you have no right to condemn those who take their own lives, not until you've walked in their dark, stormy nights and suffered the same wretchedness.

I sometimes think death is the only way out for me, but then I don't know what's waiting in that other world. If the Sisters of the Rosary are right, much worse awaits those who kill themselves. I believed every word the nuns uttered. Now I question everything and believe in so little.

Ever since deranged Labeebeh killed herself in our ward three years ago, I've thought seriously about ending my life. But I can't suffocate myself by binding my whole head tight with bedsheets. Something else forbids me from acting on my morbid thoughts.

It's probably what the nuns drummed into me about arriving at grace before meeting Allah. Oh, how I need grace. My problem is to find the way to it.

The nuns used to say that hell was for sinners—all those who break God's commandments. As far as I can tell, that's just about everybody. Except for the Sisters of the Rosary. Gehannem must be a crowded place. This place here suits me better, as long as I stay out of some raging madwoman's way. Another encounter would be the end of me. I know death comes to us all, but I don't want to go still filled with the rot that rankles in my soul. But Soeur Micheline's Bon Dieu has shut all the windows of heaven in my face.

I need to go to confession, but how? Even if it's possible, how could I confess everything? I'd be dragged to court and to prison, which would make this place look like paradise. Besides, I don't want to stir up the stinking cesspool again. For the time being, I'll go on as before—hiding, pretending, surviving—until I find my way out of here, or go to the mountain with Khadeejeh.

But a beating like this forces me to think hard about my end. I'm weak, in too much pain to think straight. So I continue to lie in this quagmire, until . . . until . . . I can't think anymore.

I hear you, Soeur Micheline. I hear you and remember every word you uttered. I need you now to help me unload this heavy rock strung around my neck. You were kinder to me than my own family. They dropped me here and vanished. I was left to grief, rage, and regret. But you came to see me so faithfully—every Sunday the first year I was here. After that, you came only occasionally and then you stopped altogether. It's been three years since you've come.

I know I have forever stained my soul. When I could no

longer bear the scorching in my head and the choking of my heart, something in me detonated in a split second, and I lashed out like a lunatic, screaming for revenge. If you judge me, do so with your heart. Had you been forced to walk in the darkness of my past, you might be able to understand how endurance and faith can crack, how hate and rage can explode into vengeance.

Long ago, I found a little book of ancient wisdom in the school library. I've never forgotten the entry about kindness. It said: "Be kind, for everyone you meet is fighting a harder battle." People should remember that!

At fourteen, Amal was still naïve about men and women, and ignorant of where babies came from. Once, when she noticed her mother's belly growing big, she wanted to know why. Her mother explained that soon she was to have another sibling. "But how did the baby get in there, Immie?"

Marta explained. "When a man and woman go to church to be blessed by the priest in a big wedding, Allah later blesses them with babies."

"But how does the baby come out of your belly?"

Marta's explanation was simple and reasonable. "The midwife pulls the baby out of the belly button." That satisfied Amal's curiosity for many years. All she was concerned with was housework and her joyful hours with the Sisters of the Rosary four days a week. Her routine did not leave time for curiosity.

Fridays and Saturdays were the hardest days of the week. On those days, her grandmother woke Amal at the crack of dawn to trot almost a mile to the town's water station—called il 'Aine, though no one knew if the water really did come from a spring. There, Amal would fill a pair of two-gallon containers and carry them back, one in each hand. It was no easy task, but most girls preferred to carry two cans rather than make the trip twice. At first, Amal's arms ached, but in time she became stronger and felt little discomfort.

She preferred the early trek to the water station when there were fewer people fighting and stepping over each other to get to the six faucets, three on each wall. The stronger women were at an advantage. They pushed their way in, yanking the smaller and younger ones out of their way, and pulling them by the hair if they were foolish enough to resist. Amal learned to defer to the strong. She had been clobbered once when she decided to assert her rights.

After filling her containers, she had to struggle, barefoot, against the thick crowd to climb the slippery, steep steps up to the dirt road. Sometimes, a foot would slip and the precious water would rush down the steps to where others stood filling their containers. It happened to Amal and left her wailing inconsolably. She had to take her place at the end of the line again. But even in that place of mayhem, she found some charity. A big, middle-aged woman called her over to stand in front of her, almost in the middle of the line. The others began to complain, but Amal's protector raised her voice and arm, threatening to break the head of anyone who raised a hand against Amal. No one dared, although they continued to rail against the injustices of the world.

One woman yelled, "It's not right, Im Hussein. We've all been waiting in line to get at the water once, and here she gets a second chance. Why?"

"Because she's a little thing, no bigger than your thigh, Im Ali. Wouldn't you do that for your daughter? Shame on you all!

Patting Amal on her shoulder, she said gently, "Stay here and I'll help you fill your gallons and go up the stairs. Don't cry. Be careful next time."

Amal felt her protector was an angel, even though she was a Muslim. Years later, she came to believe angels and devils could be found in any faith.

Once she was back with the water, Amal fed the children their usual hot sweetened tea in bowls filled with small chunks of bread, and sent them to school. Then there were dishes to clean, bed covers to shake outside. She dragged the mattresses out, beat them with a thick stick to drive the dust out, and left them in the sun for few hours. She often wondered how they could get so much dust even after weekly beatings.

Next, she helped her grandmother with dinner to have it ready for noontime when the children returned to devour the labor of her hands. In the early afternoon, she bathed the two-year-old Gibrail, then five-year-old Elias. Later, the rest of the gang came back from school; they would have run away from their bath had not all the food been under lock and key in the kitchen. The noisy rumble in their stomachs convinced them resistance was foolish, and submission to the torture of the loupha necessary. Each received his snack after the bath—a piece of bread with a small piece of cheese or a thin layer of yogurt spread, *labaneh*. Sometimes, Amal spread a little *samneh*, rendered butter, on the bread and sprinkled sugar on top. That had to satisfy them until suppertime.

She poured the bath water on the ground of the courtyard, and with the second bath water, she washed the kitchen floor and the two rooms. Her father took his bath on Saturdays, to be clean for church the next day.

Saturdays were laundry days, even harder and longer than Fridays. Amal and her grandmother would begin at dawn of that day.

After breakfast, the twins—Youssef and Jiryis—accompanied their father and Antone to the building site, where they were trained in the trade. At eleven, her father believed, boys should begin training for their livelihood. Antone was already working full-time alongside his father, who added the boy's wages to the family income. Serious and obedient, Antone was proud to support his family as a man would. Father and son were compatible in temperament.

Mikhail and Elias played in the nearby surrounding hills, hunting birds with their slingshots and stealing fruit off trees. When they were hungry, they came home to fill their bellies. They fought with sticks and daggers they had carved with knives they got from the kitchen. Gibrail stayed to play with other little boys in the neighborhood.

Shamiran was now adept at games and deception. Whenever she was asked to do something, she developed a headache, stomachache, or backache. Her mother believed her and the grandmother, grumbling, ordered Amal to do the dishes and dust the house.

Like Fridays, Saturdays began with trips to and from the water station. A cauldron of water was set on the primos stove for the heavy laundry that would soon begin.

Amal and her grandmother worked hand in hand, scrubbing the laundry in two rounds, then dropping each item into the boiling water for a few minutes. Meanwhile, Amal saved the soapy water in containers to water the flowerpots and wash the floors again.

With a sturdy stick, Amal lifted the steaming clothes and dropped them in the basin of cold indigo-water rinsed them, and hung them in the sun. Each neighbor had an assigned day and time to use the clotheslines.

When the laundry was dry, Amal carried it inside, folded it, and put aside those things in need of mending. Her grandmother set about that job, while Shamiran put everything away. Afterward, Amal still had to help with dinner and supper, and struggle to make Shamiran help with the dishes.

Gradually, Amal shouldered the responsibility of the whole house. And she did so unflinching, uncomplaining, with a measure of pride. She felt important to the family—indispensable.

Perhaps the work she enjoyed most was making a huge batch of dough every other day, and carrying it in its large tub to the taboon, the neighborhood oven. Although this was hard work, she liked it because of the companionship of the few women who sat there,. waiting their turn to bake. It was like a social gathering, each telling of her troubles with children or in-laws, and gossiping about neighbors or relatives—a perfect place for all kinds of chatter—while they waited for each batch of four loaves to bake. They shouted and swore when the mouth of the taboon singed their hands or fingers. That was inevitable, for they had to drop the flattened dough in the right places. Lifting the loaves out was easier as they wrapped their hands with a towel for protection.

Certainly, the children knew about the bliss the manna brought. They gathered at the mouth of the cave that sheltered the taboon like pathetic little beggars, drooling and rubbing their empty bellies. The women tried to shoo them away, but always gave in and lost a couple of loaves to those clever imps, who then scampered away.

When Amal was seventeen, her family became more prosperous. Her father announced his purchase of three acres of land on the western outskirts of Bethlehem, almost across from Rachel's Tomb. It was a moment of pride for everyone in the family, but mostly for her father, who bragged about having saved enough money for the land and a house from his earnings. Although he took pride in Antone, and in the twins who worked full-time with him as masons now, he claimed all the credit for the prosperity of the family.

Every evening, after a long day's labor, the four ate a hefty meal and walked the three-and-a-half miles to the property. They worked on a new house until dark. After a year of hard work, the two-story house stood proudly on the side of a hill, its rose-hued granite drawing more color from the red-brown soil around it. It was a house large enough to begin his dynasty. Soon, his sons would be ready for marriage, and each would have part of the house for his private use. All the women would share in the daily chores of cooking, making bread, and cleaning. He even installed an indoor bathroom to use during the night, and an outhouse to use during the day. The family continued to bathe in the old way, but in a white porcelain bathtub. He even built their very own taboon. Amal could bake bread every day, if need be.

They all felt rich. They owned their own house and land to grow fruit and vegetables. Now they could claim a measure of dignity and equality with the natives of Bethlehem. When her father walked to church, he had a sure foot, a spring in his heel, and pride in his posture. He had finally achieved the respectability he craved. In church, he proudly tossed a handful of coins into the brass tray, to make sure everyone heard the clatter his money made. It mattered little that the coins were mostly pennies.

Once, when Marta asked for a little money to put in the tray, he was quick to silence her. "Allah doesn't need my money. The priest doesn't need much to live. We need much more to get our sons married and settled." Marta, though disappointed, never said anything more. She knew her husband—the moneymaker and master—was always right. She was only the wife and breeder of sons.

Amal continued to labor to keep the large household fed and the house in good order, which were no small things. Babies stopped coming, and her mother's health began to improve. Marta was able to enjoy the daily trip to the market to buy the family's meat, fruit, and vegetables, and she began to help her daughter with the chores. Amal was happy to teach her mother her culinary skills. Since her marriage, Marta had been either pregnant or too sick to do housework.

While mother and daughter spent time together in the kitchen, the grandmother retreated to a corner of her small room, occupying herself with crocheting and the loom. She had long ago abandoned these pastimes to help her daughter raise a large family. Now she could retire and rest from the heavy burdens. Although she did not know her age, she considered herself an old woman. Indeed, she looked old, and her failing sight and chest pain made her feel the end was near.

Most important to Amal was that now her grandmother seemed to like her. Sitty's pleasure at Amal's devotion to the family was obvious in her softened tone of voice. She expressed her contentment one day, while they sat folding the laundry. "Amal, you've turned out so well. I was strict with you when you were young, but that made a good woman out of you. The stick did a good job."

"I don't miss the stick, though, Sitty," Amal replied calmly.

"No," her grandmother said, "but the red-hot stick is from heaven. There's a time and place for everything. It didn't hurt you. Look how you've turned out."

You'll never be able to see the hurt that's buried deep inside. Amal responded only with "uh-huh."

CHAPTER 11

IF I MUST LIE AWAKE remembering, then the only thing I want to recall are those blessed days inside the convent. I wish I could relive those six years but, this time, stay with the nuns and change the course of my life.

If I could return to the age of nineteen, I would do things differently. I wouldn't trade the nuns' world for anything in this one. I would pray with them, sing with them, and learn the arts of sewing, designing patterns, crocheting, embroidery, and drawing—my favorite. I would teach the little orphans and give them the love that every human being needs above all.

I would go back to have the nuns fill the emptiness in me with their praise and love, the poultice for my many wounds. I can't ever remember a frown on their brows, nor a cross word from their lips. They buoyed my spirits, and I sailed through those years, calm and free. Their voices ring in my ear even now. "Le Bon Dieu has given you a great talent . . . stay with us . . .

pray with us . . . become a teacher-nun . . . dedicate your life to Jesus and use the talent to serve Him and the poor who come to us."

I wish I had listened and joined them without anyone's blessing. I should've known better than to ask my father's permission to become a nun. He used to rail against Catholics: "Who are these Catholics who think they're better than us? We Orthodox are the first Christians. Didn't Christ speak Syriac—our language? Now they think they're the chosen ones, and we're heretics. *They're* the only heretics I know!" I would've told him of the nuns' love, compassion, and kindness, things he never had, nor would ever understand, had I not been afraid he would put an end to my daily hours in their paradise. Those few hours with them enabled me to bear all the burdens and bondage of home.

May Allah curse the day I opened my stupid mouth to ask his permission to join the Sisters of the Rosary. "I'll kill you with my own hands before you become a Catholic nun or a Catholic anything," he roared.

Now, after all that's happened to me, I wish he had carried out his threats, right then and there. I would've been spared much grief. From that day on, I was never allowed to leave the house except with my mother, or one of my brothers, as chaperone—even though I had no place to go, nor the desire to go anywhere. I simply wanted to die. For two years, I moved like a ghost through duties that held no meaning for me. My mind and heart paralyzed, I existed without feeling, without hope.

My mother was the only one aware of my mental state. Whenever Sitty approved, she forced me to go with her to the Church of the Nativity and once to Our Lady Marriam, in Jerusalem.

I must've been stupid to think the nuns would've abandoned me, but I heard nothing from them and began to doubt even their love. A few years later, when I expressed disappointment in the nuns, my mother assured me of their love and told me of a visit Soeur Micheline had paid once, while I was away, fetching water. The good nun had wanted to make sure I was all right and to plead for my return. Sitty saw to it that I was kept in the dark about her visit.

I blame myself for much of what happened to me afterward. But more than that, I blame Shamiran and her fair good looks, Sitty's plotting and interference, my mother's timid nature, and my father's tyranny. My own family members are responsible for my being here today. May Allah curse every one of them—especially Shamiran.

Ever since Shamiran had turned fifteen, mothers with sons of marriageable age had been eyeing her. Every mother wanted a beautiful daughter-in-law to produce beautiful granddaughters and handsome grandsons. Black-eyed beauties were on their shopping list, but blue-eyed or green-eyed ones ranked at the top.

With her golden good looks, Shamiran stood out wherever she went. On special occasions, she wore high-heeled shoes to add to her height. And when she walked, she strutted like a peacock, painting a bewitching angelic smile on her oval face. But she never fooled me, that hypocrite. And I avoided her like the plague. I always found excuses for not going to social events with Shamiran—my monthly, headache, toothache, and so on. She made me feel ugly, pudgy, and dark, darker than the bottom of our old cauldron. How could I scrub off my father's dark legacy to me? And how can I believe in a just Allah? He gave my brother

Antone our paternal grandfather's height, his dark hair and eyes, and Father's stodginess. To the twins, he gave our father's stocky build and our mother's golden hair and green eyes. Each of my siblings was blessed with at least one attractive feature. And I, nothing—nothing!

When women visited us under the pretense of a social call, I and everyone else knew they came to get a closer look at our family and to feel out our parents' willingness to marry off my sister or to hold out for the highest bidder. Sitty was always prepared with a rehearsed reply. When she felt an interested family had money, she adopted a friendly tone. "Of course, sooner or later, every girl must marry." But if a family was not the best choice, she would adopt a kind tone. "Shamiran is only fifteen. She doesn't know yet how to boil an egg. She needs a few years to grow up and learn to be a good housekeeper." And if she thought a family completely unfit, she would add, "Of course, you know, she has an older sister who must marry first." That usually brought the visit to an end.

Shamiran and I listened to such conversations from behind the door that separated the visitor's room from the bedroom. Whenever Sitty used me as an obstacle to the proposing family, I felt like she had stripped me of what few rags of dignity I had. The humiliation then turned to anger against Shamiran.

Sitty knew that Shamiran could catch twenty rich men before I could attract the attention of an old widower with one foot in the grave. I was almost twenty-four, approaching the threshold of spinsterhood, I complained to Immie about Sitty's remarks to mothers of eligible men interested in Shamiran. "Sitty means well," she said. "She's worried about you and wants to secure your future. After we're gone, we worry how you'd fare under the authority of six sisters-in-law. Marriage is a woman's fortress, sheltering her from scandalous gossip and shame."

Marriage gives young women respectable status in society, they say. Ha! Let me tell the fools what sheltering fortress and respectability I gained. How I wish Shamiran *had* married at fifteen, and I had remained a maid to my brothers' wives. Instead, Sitty and Father held out for the highest bidder, the rich son of a pompous *shaytaaneh*, a she-devil.

I remember every moment of that sunny Sunday afternoon in June when a group of six women paid us a social visit. Four of the women were acquaintances from our Syriac community who visited us once a year and, as custom demanded, received a return visit from Immie and Sitty. The other two, complete strangers, alerted my mother and grandmother to their purpose. It was as clear as the cloudless summer skies of Bethlehem.

CHAPTER 12

ONE OF THE TWO strangers, Hilaneh Murad, was a Syriac from Jerusalem who had long ago turned Catholic. This wasn't uncommon in the 1915 diaspora of Armenians and Syriacs who had escaped the Turkish massacre. Survival demanded a change of religious affiliation, in order to get cheap housing, employment, and free schooling for their children.

During her first visit, Hilaneh and her friend Miladeh, brazenly studied everything—the furniture and curtains, the quality of glass the lemonade was served in, and even fingered the embroidered doilies on the little serving tables. Crass and impervious to their hosts' feelings, they looked from floor to ceiling, searching for cobwebs that might have been missed, assessing everything with the trained eyes of detectives.

Her grandmother seethed but remained silent, as a proper hostess should, although she revealed her disapproval by squinting her eyes from time to time. Marta sat, her face as imperturbable as a seasoned poker player.

As soon as the demure Shamiran walked in to offer cigarettes to the visitors, Hilaneh sat up and scrutinized every detail of the young girl. By now, everyone knew Hilaneh's purpose. It was not uncommon to receive several lady visitors at one time, but the presence of a stranger among them unveiled any mystery.

Amal brought in napkins, fruit, and the usual snacks—roasted melon and watermelon seeds, roasted chickpeas and pistachios. She went around the room offering the crystal dishes to each guest, "*Tfaddally, Khalty.*" Please, help yourself, Auntie. Every woman your mother's age was an auntie, and every man your father's age an uncle.

What struck Amal was the smug, superior air of this strange visitor. She sat straight, as though ready for a challenge. Her short auburn hair was permed; her large hazel eyes lined with dark kohl and accented by high-arched, diasapproving eyebrows; her lips painted with deep red lipstick that matched the color on her painted cheeks. It all hinted of a woman who had broken with tradition and assumed the role of a high-class lady. Her wrists were covered with wide gold bracelets and several bangles. On her chest lay a gold chain that was more like a rope, and on it hung a huge gold medallion of the Virgin Mary. She wore a short-sleeved, crimson silk dress, its low V-neck, revealing deep cleavage.

Everyone was struck with her brazen display of gold and flesh, so unlike Marta, so intimidating. Amal did not know anyone of her mother's generation who wore short hair and makeup. But Hilaneh Murad was from Jerusalem, the big city, and Amal, with a measure of uncertainty, guessed that some city folks must look like this.

After the visitors left, Amal heard her grandmother say, "She came here to examine us. Who does she think she is? The Queen of Sheba? I don't like her but whoever she is, we'll find out more about her. Farideh El Kiki, that busybody, should know. I'll send for her tomorrow."

The speculations lasted only days, for Farideh El Kiki obliged with pleasure.

Hilaneh Murad's oldest son, Kareem, was a successful thirty-two-year-old businessman in Jerusalem. He had heard from some relatives about the Dannos' beautiful daughter. The fact that he was fourteen years Shamiran's senior, with no distinguishing physical features, was of no concern, for he knew his money would buy him the youngest and most beautiful girl anywhere. Neither was his age of concern to Shamiran or her family. Young girls grew up hearing their mothers say, "A man is not a corsage to wear on your breast, especially if he's rich. But a woman is like a beautiful rosebud in a man's lapel."

Very soon, following Kareem Murad's instructions, Father Barhoom from the Bethlehem Church of Virgin Marriam came to visit and to inform Amal's father, Jabra Danno, that a delegation of elders from the Bethlehem and Jerusalem communities wished to discuss a proposal for Shamiran's hand in marriage. That was what conventional protocol deemed the initial step. Usually, the *tulbeh*, the official request, came a week later, followed by the engagement and the wedding—all within a month's time or less.

The purpose of the first delegation was to check out the family's willingness to receive Kareem Murad's proposal of marriage to Shamiran. As soon as the grandmother heard about the pending visit, she embarked on a scheme.

Amal's father had invited two elders, distant uncles, to be

present at the pre-tulbeh. Antone and the twins were also there to receive the delegation. No woman was allowed to be part of the men's social or business gatherings.

When the delegation of three elders arrived at the Dannos' home one late afternoon, they spoke briefly about insignificant matters and, as protocol dictated, approached the subject of marriage gradually. Jabra Danno waited patiently.

"Abu Antone, Father of Antone," the eldest of the delegation addressed Jabra in the traditional manner as the father of his eldest son, "we've come to know if you would consider a proposal for your daughter Shamiran's hand in marriage, from the very respectable Kareem Murad of Jerusalem."

"We welcome you all. How old is he?'

"Kareem is thirty," the elder lied, " very respectable and very rich!"

Jabra pretended he didn't know who this rich man was. "Who are his parents and grandparents?"

"His father, Murad Murad, died suddenly when Kareem was only fourteen. Kareem has worked in his father's bakery since he was six and took it over with his widowed mother. Now it's a big business, and Kareem also owns a Goodyear tire store, a Shell gas station, a garage, and several taxis serving travelers from Jerusalem to Damascus and Beirut."

Jabra, who had not known the extent of Kareem's wealth, became excited but pretended that it was of little concern to him. He continued the customary investigation of a candidate for son-in-law. "Which village in Turkeyya does his family come from?"

"His parents are from Urfa."

Jabra camouflaged his feelings of disappointment at Murad's

birthplace and carried on with the business at hand. "Money is least important. What's important is character and reputation." He lied with great dignity, and while no one believed his sincerity, everyone understood the propriety of stock expressions on such occasions.

One dignitary declared, "His reputation is as white as the candles on the altar. The best!" And another added, "He's a pillar in our community in Jerusalem. Any girl he marries will find her hands full." Full of gold they meant.

Jabra had heard enough and was anxious to give his approval. He could not believe his luck. His future son-in-law was a millionaire, and some of that would spill over into his family. "We should be very happy to have him come for the tulbeh." The elders were pleased, but not as pleased as Jabra.

The grandmother, mother, and two daughters were sitting in the adjacent family room behind the closed door to the salon. Amal made the coffee and Marta signaled to her eldest son to take in the brass tray on which stood the Arabic coffee pot and cups.

Jabra stood taller, his posture more straight than usual, as he showed the delegation out and then turned to his family to announce smugly, "I've agreed to hold the tulbeh Saturday evening. He's a millionaire. We're the luckiest in Bethlehem."

"Tell us about him," his wife urged, as though they hadn't heard it already.

He repeated the details, embellishing as he went on. "You could say he owns Jerusalem. A prince!"

Shamiran pretended to crochet, while thrilling to the prospect of marrying the richest man in Jerusalem. Amal sat quietly at the sewing machine and acted like this was ordinary news. She lifted her head to listen for a brief minute and then returned to her work, seemingly unconcerned.

Now the grandmother asked the granddaughters to go clean up the sitting room and the kitchen, but as soon as Amal and Shamiran walked out, she made her pitch, "Father of Antone, have you thought of Amal's future?"

"What future? She's not had one proposal. Unless she marries a widower with a houseful of orphans, we have to take care of her. Allah's will."

"She'll be twenty-four when the olive harvest begins. That's three months away. Until then, she's marriageable. Abu Antone, this is your chance to help Amal find a husband to shelter her from shame or need," his mother-in-law spoke gently.

"What are you talking about?"

"Well, I've been thinking. If Kareem really wants to marry Shamiran, you could use her as bait to catch a husband for Amal. You could tell him our tradition doesn't permit us to have the younger girl marry before the older sister. So, yes, we accept their proposal, but they'll have to wait until the older one is married."

"So we risk this great chance to trap a man for Amal?"

His wife stepped in, "What my mother is trying to say is that if Kareem wants Shamiran so badly, then he could talk some friend, or even his brother, into marrying Amal."

"You won't lose him. After all, you're not refusing him but just putting a little challenge his way. Successful men like challenges." Her grandmother was bent on helping Amal.

Jabra was growing interested but did not want the women to have the upper hand. "Let me think about it tonight. In the morning, I'll tell you of my decision."

The day of the tulbeh, the elders from Jerusalem arrived at the Danno home. Kareem's brother, Boulos, who should've been among Kareem's party, had stayed behind to keep an eye on one of Kareem's businesses. Perhaps, Kareem meant to keep his brother away, for he could not count on Boulos' sobriety or good conduct. Kareem brought with him two bottles of arrack and two huge trays of sweets from the famous pastry maker Ja'phar, in Old Jerusalem.

After the general welcome of guests, the eldest of this dignified delegation began, "Our dear brother, Abu Antone, today we've come to ask you, on behalf of our son Kareem, if you would be willing to accept Kareem's proposal to marry Shamiran. We hope to hear your approval."

"*Ahlan wa sahlan* one and all. We give you welcome. You have graced our home with your visit. We would be honored to accept Kareem's proposal."

Then it was the nearest of Kareem's relations, Jalil Munsoor, who spoke. "Abu Antone, on behalf of Kareem, my cousin's son, I thank you from the bottom of my heart for accepting Kareem into your family as your son-in-law. I'm sure this union will be the happiest in all Falastine. Kareem, thank your uncle, Abu Antone, and kiss his generous hand."

Kareem followed every letter of their tradition and kissed the knobby, calloused hand of Jabra, who now swelled with importance. "*Mabrook,* my son. May Allah bless you and bless your marriage to our daughter."

Everyone got up and shook hands with Jabra and then with Kareem, uttering their traditional mabrook—congratulations. After they were all seated, Jabra asked Antone to tell the women to get coffee ready.

While they waited, Kareem's uncle said, "My brother, Kareem wants to make it clear he's ready to pay for everything. The wedding is all on him."

"May Allah bless you, my son, and compensate you a thousand fold. We accept your offer."

"Allah's blessings on you all," the priest added.

Jabra shifted in his chair, his right hand caressing his thick moustache, twisting and curling the wisps at the end of it. Now was the time to test the plan. He said, "My son Kareem, there is one little matter I must tell you about. Our family tradition says the eldest daughter must marry first. I hope you would be willing to wait a short while before marrying Shamiran."

"How long, do you think?"

"It's hard to tell. I hope in a few months, but only Allah knows how long. But as soon as Amal is married, you can marry Shamiran the week after."

"I don't think that should be a problem. I am prepared to wait."

His uncle gave him a look that hinted of disapproval, but Kareem ignored it.

Before the guests had arrived, Amal had watched her grandmother take out a special comb, gently caressing it as though it were a newborn son. She saw the old woman's eyes gazing into empty space, as she hummed a heart-wrenching, plaintive tune from the southern hills of Turkey. Once, while Amal was preparing supper, she had asked her mother, "Why does Sitty do that, rocking herself back and forth, humming such a sorrowful tune?" Marta then told Amal of the grandmother's tragic loss of her husband and about the comb she had treasured since her wedding in 1892.

Amal's grandmother had married her maternal cousin, Samu'eel, a man unlike the men of Azekh—bold, tough men, ready to use their fists, canes, stones, daggers, or guns against an aggressor. They lived in a place where life was a hazardous business, at a time when brawn superseded brain. There were always Kurds who sneaked down from the nearby hills in the darkness of the night, raiding farms and storage bins during harvest time, and stealing livestock. Sometimes, vineyard owners awakened to discover their unfinished harvest had been completed and hauled away during the night. Deprived of their staples, their guarantors against starvation during the harsh winter months, they sought revenge against the marauders. The resultant skirmishes often ended up in the death of defender, marauder, or both. Bloodshed hardened the men on both sides, and hate burrowed deep into their hearts.

Marta's velvety voice thickened and came in staccato bursts as she told of her father, a quiet and reclusive man, who enjoyed serenity among his books. He preferred to read the Bible and histories of his Aramaic nation. Sometimes he left his labor in the fields and rode his horse to the Monastery of Mor Gabriel—a two-hour ride from Azekh, where he would spend a week, buried in the tomes written at the dawn of the Christian Era.

His behavior angered his six elder siblings, who felt their youngest was a deviant or an idiot who never did a solid day's work, and who often returned from shepherding duties with fewer sheep than he had left with. An angry brother would have to scour the hills for the missing sheep.

Marta spoke of her mother's frustration and disappointment with a husband unfit for survival in the harsh environment. Her position in his family was undermined, even though she worked much harder than the rest of the daughters-in-law to make up for her husband's uselessness. And when she privately chided him about his laziness, he never raised his head from his book.

Not only did his family consider him a failure, but they also thought him to be deranged. Even when thieves raided their harvest and livestock, he would say, "If anyone risked his life to steal food, he must need it. Let him take it."

"In spite of what everyone thought of him, I loved him, just as he was," Marta admitted. "I would've preferred to spend time with him and his books, rather than being stuck in the kitchen. When he was found dead at the far edge of their land, with a big gash in his head, and a book of poetry in his lap, my mother forgot her frustrations and mourned his death. Sometimes I'd hear her mumbling, 'A strange husband is better than no husband.'"

While they were waiting for the water to boil for the coffee, Amal's grandmother rose slowly from her mattress and beckoned Amal to her. "This is a precious gift from my father on my wedding day. He bought it in Istanbul. These precious amber stones come from the Baltic Sea, and the opals and turquoise from Turkeyya, home of the best turquoise. Of course, it's known to ward off the Evil Eye. I should've given it to my eldest daughter Salma, before I left Turkeyya. I should've. But that's a wish lying in the dust of another time."

She paused a few seconds then resumed, her voice breaking, "Here, it's yours. Wear it in good health, and may it bring you better luck than it has brought me." She held Amal's shoulders, gently turned her around, and placed the exquisite comb in her braid.

Amal was overwhelmed with this show of kindness and

generosity. She had never known of the comb, nor expected anything from her grandmother. She was unused to feeling special.

She lowered her head and kissed her grandmother's hand. "Allah give you long and healthy life, Sitty. I'll always treasure it." She was deeply touched when she saw her grandmother's tearful eyes and grief-etched face. She had never thought her grandmother was capable of shedding a tear.

"Allah bless you, *ya binty*." Sitty's scratchy voice called Amal "daughter."

Marta was pleased with this precious gift to her eldest, who needed more than a jeweled comb in her life, but Shamiran's reaction poisoned the moment. She stared at her grandmother and Amal, venom suffusing her face, her eyes like green daggers.

"What's my gift, Sitty?" Shamiran demanded.

"You be quiet! You'll be getting more gold and diamonds to deck yourself with than you have arms, hands, and ears to put them on."

"But this is my engagement. This comb should be mine."

The grandmother shot back, barely controlling her anger, "Shut your mouth! You'll have more than most girls ever will. This comb is nothing compared to what you'll soon be getting. You're not only greedy, but too bold. Now, I'll say no more, and neither will you. Go!" She dismissed Shamiran with the back of her hand.

Marta turned to her youngest daughter. "You know, Shamiran, your grandmother gave her special comb to Amal because she's the eldest. That's our tradition. The eldest son inherits the largest share of the father's wealth, and the eldest daughter gets the mother's favorite piece of jewelry. This comb is the only thing of value your grandmother kept. All her jewelry has been sold since fleeing Turkeyya, just to survive. This comb should have gone to my unfortunate sister Salma, who died in her prime. If your grandmother had given it to me, it would still have to go to the eldest, to Amal."

Amal was shocked to see the hostility her grandmother showed toward Shamiran. And although she was overjoyed that her grandmother had conferred on her this emblem of privilege, she did not understand why the old woman had chosen that day, special only to Shamiran. In spite of her muddled feelings, for the first time she felt a measure of self-worth and exhilaration. The nagging question, however, continued to dog her.

The grandmother sat down once again on her soft mattress and issued her orders. "Shamiran, take the cigarettes and pass them around to the guests and, like a well-brought-up girl, don't look anyone straight in the eye, especially your future husband. Keep your head bent and your eyes lowered. You, Amal, will conduct yourself the same, as you serve the coffee. Now, go."

"May Allah bless my plan and make it work." The two conspirators exchanged knowing smiles.

When Shamiran entered the room, the old men, seated on wooden chairs placed against the walls, suddenly sat up to take in her dazzling beauty. She followed her grandmother's instruction and walked with practiced modesty, head slightly bowed, eyes lowered to demonstrate her bashfulness—a quality most desirable in a young girl. She looked ravishing in the green satin dress, tied in the front with a wide waistband. Before entering the salon, she had raised her shoulders in order to lift the skirt a little to reveal her shapely calves. The two long braids that she had wrapped twice around her head, one atop the other, looked like a golden crown. The old men's eyes were riveted to her curvaceous body and breathtaking, youthful face—porcelain complexion, cheeks mantled with a rosy hue, and large almond-shaped emerald-green eyes, fringed with long eyelashes the color of honey.

Kareem had seen her only once before, from a window of a relative's house, as Shamiran walked home from her lessons at the seamstress's shop. Now, seeing her just a foot away, he was struck all the more by her extraordinary beauty.

Although Amal was heavier and had a plain face, today she was rather pleasant looking. Her long braids, wound in two circles, one on each side of her head and crowned with her new comb, made her face attractive. She was dressed in a soft, floral material—rust-brown background sprinkled with small yellow flowers and green leaves. Amal had made herself a skirt that reached past her mid-calf, with the least amount of gathering at the waist, and a buttoned-down tunic that came to five inches above her knees. She was clever in choosing that style. It minimized her large waist and wide hips.

Unaware of her grandmother's plot, she served the coffee without anxiety. Today, she felt special in her own way—thanks to Sitty's gift. She placed the tray on the table in the middle of the room and walked out. Later, Antone would collect the cups.

CHAPTER 13

OH, DEAR LORD, I awake again to the darkness of the blind. I still can't open my eyes, but I know it's morning. I can tell it's not the dark of the night. I hear noises and mumblings in the corridor. Now and then a muffled scream, a cackle, or a shout reaches me from the colonnades and courtyard, even here in this isolated room. It must be another hot day. I'm all sweaty and sticky.

"Good morning, Amal. How did you sleep last night? You must've slept well. You're probably hungry, right? Well, you've made a professional beggar out of me. Back to Im Issa to see what we can wring from her hands this morning. But first, I'll clean your eyes with boric acid and then put some ointment on them."

I recall Sitty's treatment for infected eyes. She used the urine of one of my brothers, usually the youngest. The older ones would run away as soon as they heard her say, "Boys, I need the urine of one of you!"

Once she tried to get urine from the youngest, Gibrail, nicknamed Gabby. He must've been two or three then. She held the wide-lipped Arabic coffee cup over the potty we used in the room at night. She told Gabby to pee in the cup. He was half-asleep when she pulled out his penis and he began to urinate. It came out with all the pressure built up through the night and bounced off the shallow cup, onto Sitty's face and clothes. She shouted for him to stop, but he kept on going. Sitty ordered him to stop, and the poor child began to cry.

"After I've cleaned your eyes, you might be able to open them," the nurse says gently.

Open my eyes! What for? To better see my ugly face turned uglier than the faces of sinners in Gehannem? No, better not see. You're a kind nurse, but you've got no idea what torments plague my body and mind.

"Now we're off to the washroom to get cleaned up for il doctore."

"No! Can't get up. A shower will kill me. Pneumonia . . . die." I pretend to weep though it hurts to do that.

"It's been a steaming week since your last shower. We must wash away the sweat. Stop crying and help me get you out of bed. Now, slowly and gently, take one step at a time to the bathroom. Don't worry. I'm holding you. It's just a few feet away.

"We're there. I'm going to put you on the toilet seat. After that I'll put you under a warm shower."

"Oh, Allah help me. The water will get my bruises and broken bones infected."

"No, Amal, water doesn't cause infection. It will help you heal."

"That's not what Sitty used to say."

"Well, your grandmother lived in a different time. She wouldn't know what we know today."

You think you're so clever! Sitty may have been a wraith from Gehannem, but she knew how to cure burns without leaving behind a scar to tell what had happened. She could cure stomachaches, headaches, colds, and even pneumonia. And what do you know? Just to dole out aspirin. "Sitty knew it was bad to give a bath to the sick."

"You're not sick. Sick means you have a disease."

"I have a disease. A big one," I tell her.

"No, you don't. You were beaten up badly, and you have bad bruises. But you're not sick."

"Yes, I'm very sick. I'm going to die from pneumonia."

"Pneumonia in this sizzling heat? Anyway, it's Saturday, shower day! Now, let's slip this gown off and step into the shower stall."

"No!" I scream.

"Here, let me tie this plastic around your head. I won't wash your hair. You're not going to get lice while you're here. Now, stand here, and stop shaking."

"I'm freezing. Get me out!"

"Not before I scrub you once."

"At least keep the warm water running."

"There's only so much water for each patient. It's measured."

It is torture lifting my legs so she can slip on clean underpants. Putting on the clean blue uniform is even worse. I can't stop groaning. Nothing fake about my pain.

"Now, habeebty, let's get you settled in bed. Then you'll be able to sleep for a few hours before il doctore comes. Oof! What an ordeal you've put me through!"

This young thing is full of donkey kharra! She thinks a two-minute wash is an ordeal! "Ordeal! You don't know what that is."

"You complain too much. Look how nice and clean you are now, and how wet I am. I need to change, but before I go I'll give you the aspirin."

"*Shookrun*, nurse. Allah's mercy on your dead relatives!"

"Allah's mercy on all of us, and on you."

"I'm not dead yet." I argue.

"That's certain, but the living need Allah's mercy more than the dead. All right. I'll leave you to rest. Il doctore should be here by the time you wake up, to find you pretty as a bride. Sleep well!"

In her innocence, she has stabbed my mind with that cursed word "bride." One word—that word—and I'm locked into a black hole, the darkest night of my life.

Ever since the day I was marched to church to be wedded and fettered to a handsome groom, my life has been branded with humiliation, pain, terror, grief, and despair. I feel like I've been caught in the contest between Allah and the Shaytaan. I've suffered tribulations just like Ayyoub, and like Job, I was patient. But unlike him, I failed in the most important thing—my faith in Allah. In a moment, the faith that held me together ripped at the seams, and I detonated with all the anger and hate I had long repressed. *Bride*. Damn the word and everyone who had a hand in making me one, starting with Father Barhoom!

CHAPTER 14

A WEEK AFTER THE blessing of Shamiran's tulbeh, Father Barhoom paid Amal's father another visit.

Her grandmother sent Amal and her sister to the back of the house to prepare hummos and salad, which had not been in the plans for supper that evening. Both knew it was to get them out of earshot of the conversation. Her grandmother and mother sat mending clothes in the corridor, eavesdropping on the conversation in the salon.

Shamiran could not contain her curiosity. The priest was sometimes the ambassador of bad news but, more often, a respectable matchmaker. "Let's go crouch under the salon's window and listen," she said to Amal, who was as curious as her sister. They sneaked out the back door and hunkered down under the salon window.

"Abu Antone, my son, I bring you sweet news," Father Barhoom began cheerfully.

"Good news, *inshallah*!"

"Good news, indeed. Kareem Murad would like to know if you'd be willing to give Amal to his younger brother, Boulos."

"What does he do for a living?"

"I understand he is a manager of one of his brother's stores."

Jabra could not believe his luck. His eldest daughter would be married. He did not need to worry about her future. But he didn't want to sound too eager. "Father, how old is Boulos?"

"Oh, he's about ten years, more or less, younger than Kareem. Father Barhoom knew the age of every young man and woman in his parish and those in other Syriac parishes. He made it his business to know every detail surrounding eligible men and women. That made him almost four years younger than Amal, an unusual match. But the priest was thrilled at the prospect of performing two weddings and receiving two gifts of money from Jabra and from Kareem.

"Is it unwise, Father, for a woman to marry a man younger than herself?" Jabra's tone suggested he did not think it a serious matter.

"What are a few years? What matters is that both brothers come from a good family. And they're rich, my son! Any father would grab a rich son-in-law, no matter if he was sixteen or sixty-four," the priest argued.

"Of course. It's not like he's ten years younger." Jabra agreed. "He's Kareem's brother, and that's good enough."

"Do I tell them to come for the tulbeh?"

"Of course! This Saturday evening would be good. That's three days from now. You can tell them, Father, that I will be pleased to receive them."

"Allah bless you, Abu Antone, and bless your home."

Amal's father walked the priest out of the house and, as he bent to kiss his hand, he slipped ten shillings into it. The priest would have thought himself lucky if he'd gotten one-tenth of the sum from this man, who was not known for his generosity. But the great tiding of a second daughter's pending marriage was worth a lot to him. For the priest, ten shillings was enough to supply his family with food for two weeks or more. "Allah bless you and your family. May you receive multiples of this gift."

Before their father and the priest walked out of the house, Shamiran and Amal ran back to the kitchen. Shamiran was subdued. Amal, however, felt the blood race through her veins, her heart beating against her ribs, and she quivered at this new and strange sensation. The unexpected and unimaginable had happened.

Amal had rarely allowed herself to be entertained by thoughts of marriage to a man who would love her, and when she did, they were brief moments of delicious self-delusion. She had, for the most part, resigned herself to a spinster's life, as a servant to the family. Now, she was intoxicated, dizzied by this sudden promise of love and the revelation that she would marry Kareem's brother. She felt impregnable, shielded from the harsh world by a man's love.

Having indulged in her own glory long enough, she threw a glance at the silent Shamiran. She was busying herself with chopping lettuce and tomatoes for the salad, leaving the onions for Amal, as she had always done. A chill seized Amal's heart as she noticed her sister's surly face.

"I can't believe it. First, Kareem asks for your hand, then his brother asks for mine!"

"It does sound ridiculous," mumbled Shamiran, turning her back to her sister, as though the salad were more important than her sister's happy news.

"Maybe we'll have a double wedding!" Amal said hopefully.

"I don't think so."

"Why not, Shamiran? I've seen it happen once."

"You won't see it this time. I'll have my wedding, and then you'll have yours," she said with a sharp edge to her voice.

Amal felt her sister's hostility slap her face. "It's not for us to decide. Father will say what will happen." Amal's voice was low and spiritless.

Meanwhile, Jabra hurrired to tell his womenfolk of his great act of wisdom and fatherly concern for his daughter. "Allah has smiled on us. I've found a groom for Amal. I've sent word to Kareem Murad that I accept his brother's proposal to marry our eldest daughter. Where are the girls? Marta, go get them."

Marta called her daughters and both hurried from the kitchen to the living room. Smiling, she ushered them in. Their father sat in a chair and waited, weighing the importance of this ponderous matter. The girls stood waiting for the pronouncement.

"Amal, you should know I've just sent word to Kareem Murad that I accept his brother's request for your hand. Boulos, his younger brother, will come with Kareem and their chosen group to receive our formal approval this Saturday. Now my heart and mind will be at peace, knowing I've married off my two daughters to two good men. I'll never have to worry about your welfare or happiness. Let's get ready. Make sure we have enough cigarettes, tobacco for the nargileh, and coffee. Amal, come here, ya binty."

Amal approached her father with an addled brain. She was

visibly nervous. Her eyes lowered, she took her father's extended hand and kissed it, as was expected. "Mabrook, ya binty," he said. "May Allah bless you and bless us all. Two wonderful grooms for our two daughters! What else could we ask for?"

Had her skin been of a lighter shade, the rush of blood to her face might have been noticeable. It came partly from diffidence and partly from a new and pleasant feeling. For the first time she felt herself to be the center of attention and recipient of her father's love. It was a moment to cherish.

Only Marta wanted to know more about Boulos' character, his work, and financial circumstances. It was rather unusual for her to take the lead in any questioning—she usually deferred to her mother and husband. Today, something stirred in her as she recalled how her gentle father was so different from his own brothers.

"What did the priest say about his character? Is he like his brother—serious, steady, successful?"

"Of course. What do you think? He's Kareem's brother."

Amal sensed her mother's concern, but wished she would stop prying and spoiling the glorious moment. *What are you trying to do? This is my chance! You know I don't have your good looks.*

Once, when she was ten, she had confronted her mother. "Why did you give Shamiran golden hair and green eyes and me this dark skin and hair? She's beautiful and I look like a *ghouleh*!"

"Amal, habeebty, you don't look like a ghouleh. Don't say such things. You blaspheme your maker. He chose to make you the way you are. And in my eyes, you're beautiful. If it were up to me, I would've given you the best. You are my firstborn, and I love you dearly. I wish it were up to me." Amal half believed her but always felt someone was not fair to her. Maybe Allah, maybe her mother, maybe both.

"Now," the father went on, "to more important business. I want the engagement to be a week from this Sunday, and the wedding a week later."

"But that won't give us enough time to have the trousseau ready," Marta said, concerned.

The grandmother was quick to interject. "We will be ready, even if we have to hire a seamstress. The Murads are rich. They'll pay for everything. And why give time to the busybodies of the town to do us mischief?" She knew enough of the jealous tongues that could mangle their plans.

Shamiran stood still, expressionless. She had no say in any of this, but it was not what she was hoping for. A deep resentment, bordering on hate toward her sister, rankled in her heart. She wanted to be the first to marry. After all, she was the first to receive a proposal.

Marta looked at her mother in silent admiration of her shrewdness.

That Saturday, in the late afternoon, Kareem brought Boulos and the elders to the Danno home for the tulbeh. That was the first time Amal had a glimpse of her groom, and Boulos of his bride-to-be.

For Amal, it began as an evening in heaven. She felt so light that she could have soared on the wings of her ecstasy. She and Shamiran stood at a window on the second floor, peering through the curtain to watch the delegates and the prospective grooms walk up the path. Shamiran was excited to see her fiance again, and Amal anxious to see what the man who sought her for a bride looked like.

What she saw was beyond her greatest dreams. She could not contain her joy when she spotted the groom-to-be walking beside Kareem. He stood about a foot taller than his brother, and had golden hair, a stunning contrast to his brother's dark head. Without thinking, she blurted, "He's so handsome! I never imagined him to look so beautiful. He'd make girls lose their minds!"

"Don't get excited," Shamiran was quick to interject. "You know what they say. A man's not a corsage to wear on your breast. It's wealth that counts. Kareem is very rich. No one has said anything about Boulos' money, or his businesses. The talk is all about Kareem."

Stunned, Amal turned to look at her sister. She felt as though Shamiran had aimed a poisoned arrow at her heart. Amal's moist eyes, her silence, and her attempt to control her quivering lips may have made Shamiran feel a little sorry for her cruelty. She tried to cover her jealousy by adding, "Of course, he's Kareem's brother, and Father said that was good enough."

Amal gathered up enough courage to say, "I can't believe your heart could let you say things that cut a deep wound in mine. Could you be so jealous and selfish that you'd spray poison in my face, Shamiran?"

"That's a big joke! What would I be jealous of, dear sister? Please, tell me!"

Amal's eyes conveyed how mean-spirited an animal she considered Shamiran. She clenched her fists and said, "You are selfish and ungrateful. Allah has wasted my mother's beauty on a heart made of stone. I have always envied your beauty, but I was pleased for your good fortune. But you, you've always had everything through lies and manipulations, yet you can't feel even a little happy for me."

Amal quickly turned and left the room. She went down the stairs on leaden feet. She wanted to hide and cry, but there was no time for that now.

Shamiran, on the other hand, felt a shadow of remorse. Yet her conceit was shaken at the sight of Boulos, who definitely was more handsome than her betrothed. As always, she felt entitled to the best, for she was the best.

The tulbeh went according to tradition. Amal, dressed in a new dress of burnt orange, trimmed with chocolate-brown crocheted collar and cuffs, served the coffee with a quiet heart. An aura of composure and tranquility settled about her, and the elders must have noted it and approved. Older men preferred a quiet woman, even if she was not the most beautiful. "A mouth without a tongue makes for a happy home," was their favorite proverb.

One week later, on a Sunday, close members of the Murad family gathered at the Dannos' home for a double engagement ceremony. When the Murads approached the house, Jabra, his six sons, and a few elders close to the family stood on the veranda and welcomed the male members of the Murad party into the large salon. The Murad women, led by Hilaneh, the future mother-in-law, followed behind and were greeted by Sitty, Marta, and the few women they had invited.

Her grandmother was vexed when she embraced Hilaneh and kissed her on both cheeks, as Hilaneh merely offered her heavily rouged cheeks but did not kiss her hostess. It was an insult her grandmother would not easily forgive. Later, Amal overheard her complaining to Marta. "She dresses like a lady but smears her face in red like a woman of the streets. Some mother-in-law she's going to be!"

Amal and Shamiran remained in the room prepared for the women. When their future mother-in-law entered, the brides-to-be walked up to embrace and kiss her. Both felt her coldness as she gave them her red cheeks but not her lips. Amal tried to ignore it, though it threw a dark shadow across her heart. Shamiran seemed unperturbed and immediately guided Hilaneh to the best chair in the room, next to her own.

Amal began to think that perhaps this was how city folks behaved—aloof and unemotional. The sisters sat, smiles plastered on their faces. They had been properly coached on how to greet their future mother-in-law, how to sit, to stand, to look, and how to smile. Engagement day was usually a feast for those who loved to find fault and criticize. Every facial expression, every gesture, the way the brides-to-be sat, stood, or turned would be reported. Every fault of both bearing and dress would be elaborated or exaggerated throughout Bethlehem and Jerusalem.

The men sat in one room smoking cigarettes or the nargileh and chatting about a range of topics. The older ones were fond of reminiscing about their native towns and villages in Turkey, while sipping their coffee. The younger men discussed business and politics—the latest anxieties over the influx of Jewish immigrants into Palestine, their acquisition of more Arab land, British colonialism, and World War II. In the next room, the women talked about the best seamstresses for trousseaus, the best hairdresser, and the latest fashions. They repeated rumors of upcoming tulbehs or engagements, as they sipped lemonade and munched on roasted melon seeds and nuts.

Although most women closely eyed the brides to-be, they were also keen to watch Hilaneh. They sized up her black suit and the white blouse that spilled over the jacket to form a collar. Her inappropriate choice of black—the color of mourning—drew silent criticism from everyone.

The Danno guests, though jealous of the good fortune that had befallen the two daughters of their relatives, took offense at Hilaneh's supercilious attitude toward her hostesses. They did not need to dig deep to know of her dissatisfaction with the choices her sons had made. Hilaneh's companions were less obvious.

Hilaneh meant to show her disapproval more convincingly than words could craft. Quietly she sat, flanked by Shamiran on one side, and by the women she had brought along, barely acknowledging anyone else, even her future daughters-in-law. Once in a while she glanced sideways at one or both brides-to-be, then turned her head to a friend next to her to mumble something. The grandmother put on a happy face and ignored her, but Marta was more flustered and struggled to make conversation with Hilaneh.

Amal tried to suppress the commotion in her heart. A nameless trepidation ran through her veins and contaminated the joy that had filled her heart since the tulbeh. Watching Shamiran's composure—her confident strut across the room to ask a friend to pass around the condiments, her perfect smiles that camouflaged the resentment she felt toward Hilaneh—Amal thought that she, too, should ignore Hilaneh's unpleasantness. She sat up straight, shoulders pushed back, her head turning now and then from left to right to dole out measured smiles to everyone and no one in particular.

Suddenly, Amal's eldest brother, Antone, appeared in the

doorway to announce that the engagement ceremony was about to begin. Led by her grandmother, Marta and Hilaneh, Amal and Shamiran—followed by the other women—entered the large salon, at whose center the priest now stood. He directed the Murads to his left, and the Dannos to his right. He took the right hand of Amal and brought her next to him, then motioned to Shamiran to stand next to Amal. Boulos and Kareem stood on his left.

The priest nodded his head to a young man he had brought with him, and immediately his helper—the Shammas—brought out a gold-trimmed scapular and carefully placed it around the priest's shoulders. Father Barhoom cleared his throat and began to chant the Lord's Prayer in Aramaic; his Shammas and the men joined in. He opened a small book and read an invocation of God's blessings on the engagement of Boulos and Amal, and Kareem and Shamiran. Then, he turned to Boulos, nodding his head and opening his hand to offer two gold bands.

After the blessing of the rings, he placed one on the fourth finger of Amal's right hand, and she bent her head to kiss his hand. Boulos did the same after the priest placed the ring on his finger. The priest repeated the ceremony with the rings that Kareem handed him. Several women let out their traditional zaghrootah. Everyone broke into loud cheers and applause.

At that moment, Amal felt a quick stab of fear.

Hilaneh did not clap; she managed a strained smile, however, and was the first to congratulate Amal and Shamiran, "Mabrook, habeebty," she said, kissing each one on both cheeks. Then she turned to Kareem and Boulos, congratulating each with a kiss. The priest said, "Make room for the brides and grooms. Amal and Boulos, you sit here, and you two, sit beside them. Let the party begin."

One man took out the *'ood*, and began to pluck at the strings; another beat the tableh. The older women coaxed the young women into dancing to the spirited music. Then the men were offered liqueur-glasses of arrack, a piece of chocolate, and baklawa. The women ate sweets and drank lemonade.

Throughout the afternoon, the refreshments and pastries kept going around. No one turned down anything. Engagements and weddings were times to enjoy delicious sweets.

Amal was uncomfortable sitting next to a man, a stranger, and her future husband. When his arm touched hers, a jolt, like a powerful electric current, shot through her. She did not understand why a touch of his arm should cause such a stir inside her. Boulos did not say anything to her but sat there, his lips frozen in a perpetual attempt to smile.

Kareem's happiness, though, was evident in his broad smiles and sparkling eyes. After a few minutes he asked Shamiran if the ring fit well, or did it need sizing, all the while gazing into her eyes, as if to tell her how much he loved her.

Boulos took the cue from his brother and asked Amal the same thing. Amal then felt as though she were in heaven. Her Boulos was not only handsome, but he was also kind. He asked her where she wanted to shop for her trousseau and jewelry. No one had ever asked her for an opinion.

"Wherever you think is best," she replied, as tradition demanded. Women shall cede to men, especially before marriage. In return, no doubt, Boulos would care for her, protect her, and give her happiness.

CHAPTER 15

JUST WHEN I'M AT the edge of sleep, I hear the key turn, and the lowered voices of a man and woman. "No, Doctore Jamayelle won't be back for two weeks. He got married yesterday and has gone to England for his honeymoon."

"How wonderful," I hear Nurse Marriam say.

I remember that il doctore was supposed to be here by noon, so it must be lunchtime. I can't hear screams coming from the courtyard.

"This is Amal, Doctore Ansara."

"Is she asleep?" he asks in a dry voice.

I feel Nurse Marriam's hand patting my arm, trying to wake me. I pretend to be asleep.

"The report says she was beaten up by Soraiya."

"Yes, Doctore."

"Is this one violent?"

He's afraid I'll jump from my bed and take a big bite out of his face. Stupid! I wouldn't touch you or any man for that matter. You men of crocodile skin!

"No, Doctore. I've been here three years now, and I've never seen her violent."

"I have her full report here, but I've had no time to read it. Maybe you could fill me in on her condition."

"Amal suffers from delusions and hallucinations. Doctore Hamarneh had diagnosed her with schizophrenia. She's moody. She goes from extreme happiness to morbid silence and depression."

"Now, I think we better wake her up. I don't have much time. I have to get back to my clinic."

"I'm sorry, Amal. This is Doctore Ansara. He wants to examine you."

"She's badly bruised," he says as his hands and fingers touch and press my head first, then my cheeks. That's when I yelp and moan. He ignores me and continues to jab and press down my whole body—face, mouth, neck, and all the way down to my legs.

Finally he stops the torture and I hear scratching of pen and paper, then his voice. "She has an ugly wound in her forehead and other cuts in her scalp. Badly bruised eyelids, contusions on her face, shoulders, and chest. Probably cracked ribs. You have to keep an eye on her for signs of concussion, although it's difficult to assess in cases of mental illness.

"Now I'll check her eyes." That's when I cry out, "No, no, hurts, hurts!" The nurse holds my arms, and I'm too sore and too weak to fight. He raises one eyelid enough to see, then releases me from the terrible throbbing and smarting in my eye.

He says, "Blood vessels have burst in her eyes. I can't tell the extent of the damage until the swelling goes down and the vessels have healed. She may have permanent or temporary damage, but no one can tell now. These eye drops will help. Apply penicillin ointment to all the cuts and bruises. I'll prescribe ointment for her eyes, too. Continue to give her aspirin, and if that doesn't work, you can give her codeine. Is there an X-ray machine here?"

"No, Doctore. We'll have to take her to a lab in Jerusalem for that."

"All right, in the meantime, keep bandaging her chest tightly."

I hear the door shutting behind them as they leave me to my pain.

The thing that frightens me the most is the prospect of blindness. *Oh, my Lord, make me deaf, make me a cripple, but not blind. I wouldn't care if I couldn't hear. But I have to see. I need my eyes to see where I'm going. I promised Khadeejeh to teach her to read. How can I find my way around without sight? I can't live in darkness. Haven't I eaten enough kharra? When is enough enough?* I'm suddenly weeping. I don't know what has gotten into me. I've never found the ointment to soothe my wounds, and no one has offered any.

Suddenly I hear Sitt Marriam's voice. "Amal, what's the matter? Is it the pain?"

My moaning prevented me from hearing her come in. I want her to give me something to stop the banging in my head. "I want deen. My head! I can't bear it. Give me deen."

"Deen?" she asks. "You want religion?"

"Il Doctore said to give me deen when I have too much pain."

"You mean codeine. Hey, not much damage to your memory. That's very good," she says with a little laugh. "Well then, I'll get you some lunch first, and then give you a codeine pill. It's strong stuff. You have to take it with food."

After what seems like forever, the nurse returns, chirping as usual. She puts a spoonful of food between my swollen lips. I try to swallow but it sticks in my throat. I panic and she pats my bruised back, until my throat clears. "I'll take out the little meat and feed you only the mashed potato."

She feeds me and babbles about my luck to have such good food. The more she speaks the more riled up I get. When she finishes, she asks, "Feel better now?"

"Better." *I won't bite the hand that feeds me. Although sometimes you dare the devil in me, you silly girl!*

"That's it. You did well, Amal. Now I'll give you the codeine and some hot tea, take you to the washroom, and then you'll be able to sleep like a baby."

I raise my hand to indicate I want only five spoonfuls, but she misunderstands me.

"You don't want the tea?"

Again I try, this time by pointing my forefinger down and then raising four fingers.

"Oh, you changed your mind? You want only four spoonfuls?"

Yes, I'm a madwoman who can't make up her mind, and you're so stupid!

"The sweet tea is good for you. Warms up your insides so you don't feel the heat of the afternoon. And the sugar lifts your spirits!"

She puts her hand on mine ever so lightly and, with the

other, caresses my hair, as though I were her child. It puts me in mind of my mother smoothing my hair when Sitty was not around.

She straightens the bed covers and gently adjusts my head on the pillow. "Look at you now!" she chirps. "In a short time, everything will heal and all this will be over, and you'll look pretty as a bride."

And you're a dumb donkey! Why do you keep jarring my most painful memories? "Sleep in peace, Amal," she says and leaves.

Like the peace in Gehannem! It's strange how my mind works. Just when I think I've buried the bloodied fragments of my life, one word from careless lips reopens all the old wounds. How can I sleep now?

But slowly, I begin to feel my limbs relax. The pounding in my head grows faint and distant—giving way to raucous memories.

CHAPTER 16

AS IF THE WORD "BRIDE" were a magical invocation, the ghosts of Amal's past now rise, twirling like frenzied dervishes, flailing their swords above their heads. Every detail of her wedding—from the final preparations of the evening before to the nightmare of the nuptial night—now dance before her in garish colors.

The last night she spent as the daughter of the Danno family should have been one of enlightenment—the usual explanations and advice from mother to daughter. All Amal received, however, were veiled words that made her fear that some calamity lurked just beyond the merriment of her wedding. This nameless fear nibbled at the edges of her mind and caused tremors in her heart.

That same night, her father and brothers, along with both close and distant male relatives, went to Kareem's villa in Katamon, a rich suburb southwest of Jerusalem, to attend the traditional party they called "the Groom's Night." Kareem hired a bus to convey the guests to Katamon and back to Bethlehem around midnight. Although no woman was allowed to share in the ribald party, Amal had heard about such evenings.

Supposedly, the Groom's Night is a ritual meant to cheer and console the groom, who is about to lose his carefree life and assume the heavy burden of marriage.

Boulos' party was organized and paid for by Kareem, the Best Man. As soon as the bottles of arrack and whiskey were opened, the party turned into a noisy affair as men danced, sang, and drank. Kareem made sure that Boulos did not have more than a couple of drinks, for he knew of his brother's bad habit. A drunken groom sends a strong signal to the bride's family that their new son-in-law will bring them trouble. Undesirable qualities must be kept well camouflaged.

After a time, the bachelors swarmed around the groom, plunked him down in a chair in the middle of the room, and covered him from the neck down with a sheet. Just as tradition in the Middle East requires men to grow their beards the first week of mourning their dead, each groom must grow his beard a week before the wedding, to mourn the loss of his bachelorhood. Then, on the eve of his wedding, the beard is shaved.

The single men around Boulos squabbled over who was to shave his beard. For very good reason, the groom's brother always ensured that only a sober man would be chosen to shave the groom. And like all grooms, Boulos pretended to be sad, grieving for the end of his carefree life, until his beard was shaved and his head washed.

The boisterous party continued until midnight.

As her agitated mind reeled from image to image, Amal saw herself that night, in the house with only her sister, mother, and grandmother. A bride's last night in her family home is usually sad, punctuated with uncertainties, for it signifies an exchange of her family for another, a familiar life for one unfamiliar.

In the kitchen, Marta prepared the *halaweh*, the sticky concoction used for yanking unwanted hair from the root. Women apply it to their legs, arms, underarms, and sometimes faces, to remove dark fuzz on upper lips and sideburns. Married women clear their private areas with it, willing to bear the pain to please their men, for hair on a woman's body, except on the head, is disgusting to many. Hair on men, however, is deemed a sign of heightened sexuality. Women would often comfort each other with the saying, "Beauty demands a high price."

On turning eighteen, Amal and Shamiran had been allowed to use halaweh to remove hair from their legs, arms, and underarms. A mother who allowed her daughter to remove her hair before eighteen brought disapproval. The Dannos' impeccable honor and reputation would not be breached.

That night, the three women went about ridding themselves of body hair as usual. Then, when Shamiran had finished doing her legs, arms, and underarms, Marta asked her to leave the kitchen and go take her bath. Gladly Shamiran left to wash away the sticky residue of the halaweh.

Seconds later, hesitating a little, Marta mumbled, "Now, Amal, take off your underwear and remove the hair between your legs."

Shock registered on Amal's face. "What're you saying? Why?"

"Married women must keep that part clean."

"But that will hurt a hundred times more than in the armpits."

"Amal, I've been doing it ever since my wedding night, and it hasn't killed me," Marta answered gently, without looking her daughter in the eye.

"Why do I have to?" Amal asked, with all the strength she could muster. "Shamiran didn't. Why should I?"

"She will when her time comes. Now I can help you, if you want."

Stricken with the unthinkable thought of her mother seeing the most private part of her, and the pain of yanking coarse hair from the root, she began to sense something sinister imbued in all this ritual. "I don't need help. I'll do it by myself!" she grumbled.

Marta got up to take her bath, and Amal grabbed a small ball of halaweh, angrily pulling on it to soften it to the consistency of masticated chewing gum. The task was agonizing. Even when she had finished, she continued to feel the smarting pain, like hundreds of giant ants forcing their mandibles into the bare patch. Such senseless torture and needless humiliation, she thought.

Strangest of all was the nakedness she felt, though she was now fully clad. Something that had been part of her had been plucked out. Worse than that were the droplets of blood oozing out of torn hair follicles.

The kitchen door opened and Marta stood there drying her hair, "Are you ready for your bath?" she asked gently. Silently, Amal got up from the floor and, without looking at her mother, walked out toward the washroom to take her last bath in her parents' home.

Later, in the bedroom she shared with her sister, she watched her mother arrange the last of her clothes and effects in a suitcase. Amal would need some of these clothes for the one-night honeymoon at the only hotel in Ramallah. All of her other belongings had been hauled away by the groom's family on Friday, after the traditional display of her trousseau.

Amal sat on the edge of her bed drying her hair with a towel; sorrow clogged her throat, and apprehension filled her heart. The life she had known was about to vanish forever, and in its place would spring a strange world, full of uncertainties. Soon she would have to please and serve a husband, who was a stranger in every way. And she would have to defer to and venerate a mother-in-law whose coldness was already evident.

Even more intimidating was the prospect of living in a small two-room dwelling in a strange place, in the bustling, grim atmosphere of Jerusalem's Old City. She wished she had been offered a three-room home in the New Jerusalem, one with an indoor bathroom, something she had become accustomed to in the last few years. New Jerusalem had wide asphalt streets and large, modern buildings. And from there she could have caught a bus near Jaffa Gate to Bethlehem to visit her family.

But a bride-to-be must defer to the decisions of her in-laws.

Hilaneh had insisted that Amal accept the generous offer to live in the two-room house in the Old City. After all, it was the first home of Hilaneh and her husband, the one that the Catholic Church allowed them to live in rent-free, a reward for leaving their Syriac parish and joining the Catholic faith.

Amal had no choice in the matter. "I can't give up the right to my first home," Hilaneh told her. One never knows what troubles will find us. Besides, the rent is very cheap, five shillings a month, and the location is the best. You just walk out the gate and down the alley, and in a few minutes you're in Souk Khan il-Zeit. There you can buy whatever you need. You'll love it."

Amal was no stranger to Hilaneh's philosophy of frugality. To hang on to their cheap dwellings, refugees from Turkey had to lie and cheat—necessary tactics and common survival strategies. Life, at best, had been precarious and often subject to the will of many conquerors, such as the Ottomans and, since World War I, to the English and their Mandate. People learned to survive. In hostile environments and hard times, survival is a natural imperative, permitting—and forgiving—lying, cheating, hoarding, and even killing. In time, such behavior becomes embedded in the common psyche. When better times arrive, people find themselves still trapped in the old fears of losing everything once again. They had come to believe their prosperity ephemeral, and their stability fragile. The only morality they could afford, therefore, was one that allowed them to prepare for the next catastrophe, to survive the next diaspora that, once again, was bound to happen.

Hilaneh was trying to preserve her right to cheap housing. But as Amal later learned, her mother-in-law also much preferred to live in Kareem's spacious new villa in Katamon. There, it was easy to hop on a bus any day of the week to eat in Café Europe and restaurants on Jaffa Street and to shop in Jewish boutiques in Tel Aviv and Jerusalem. She could not have dared, as a widowed Syriac woman, to sit in restaurants without inspiring censure and malicious gossip from neighbors and relatives.

"You don't look like you've heard a word I've said." Marta sounded almost apologetic.

Jarred from her thoughts, Amal looked up at her mother. "I've put your undergarments at the bottom, your clothes for Monday over them, your nightgown and robe on top of everything. And I also put in this piece of flannel for tomorrow night."

"All right," she replied, having heard only the first few words, as her mind wandered again through her unnamed fears.

Marta sat down beside Amal, who kept her head bent low, chin almost touching her chest, face curtained with grief. The mother put her arms around her daughter. "Don't look so sad, habeebty. Marriage is the only end for a decent woman. You should feel happy now that you will sheltered from disrespect and protected from all harm. You're a lucky girl to have finally found not just a husband, but a handsome one at that."

In a quivering voice, Amal spoke. "My heart is heavy with fear. I don't know why I'm afraid. Maybe it's losing my place here. This is the only world I've known, and I feel like a blind person suddenly finding himself in a strange place, not knowing in which direction to move, or where to place his foot." And she began to sob.

Tears came to Marta's eyes. She tightened her arms around the girl. "Amal, don't weep, daughter. We're just fulfilling what Allah, in his wisdom, created us for—to marry, serve our men, and bring forth children—a mother's true pride and joy."

Wiping her own tears, she continued to counsel and console her daughter. "I was only fifteen when I married your father, who was thirty years old then. It happened after my father died.

"After his death, my uncles were fed up with battling thieves—poverty-stricken Kurds or Turks. That was in 1915, during World War I, when Turkey fought with Germany against England and France. My uncles sold their home and land and decided to settle in the plains of El Quamishleh, in northeastern Syria. There, with no one to plague them, they felt certain they would prosper in peace.

"So before my uncles finished the sale of their lands, my mother secretly made a deal with one of her father's distant cousins, who lived in a nearby village. The shrewd relation advised her to accompany him, his two sons, and a small group of people who were planning to go to Falastine. From those who had already left to settle there, he'd heard that the Holy Land was under Turkish control, but refugees from Turkey found support from many churches in Jerusalem. Most important, there were no Kurds to harass them. He proposed to have me marry his childless widowed son, and promised my mother the necessities for the trek to Falastine and security for me for the rest of my life.

"I don't know how your Sitty managed it. She packed only the necessary clothes in one cloth bag, and some bread and goat cheese in a smaller bag. On the appointed night, we stole away to be met by a group of men, among them, your father and his father. In silence, and like ghosts, we hurried to meet the rest of the band that had already begun the march southward toward Syria.

"After a month of walking and sometimes riding trains through northern Syria, then westward toward Lebanon and south toward Falastine, we finally made it to Jerusalem. We were guided to the main Syriac Diocese of Mar Murcoss in the Old City. They housed us for a few days and then brought us here, to Bethlehem, and helped us find shelter. Immediately, the men began their search for jobs. To help feed their families, the women went to work as maids or washerwomen.

"Within three months, your father had earned enough money to rent a house with two rooms, a small kitchen, and an outhouse. And I was married in a simple dress that I sewed from material your father's mother bought. I had a wedding band on my finger to bind me to your father forever. My mother lived with us at first but then decided to rent a room down the street. She worked hard for a rich family, washing their clothes and scrubbing their floors—the price of her independence. But there's deep sadness in her heart for my older sister Salma and her three little children. That's another story for another time."

Listening to her mother's tale, Amal stopped weeping as she journeyed across the years to strange lands. She lifted her head to look at her mother, who began again, "And look at you! A handsome young husband, a wealthy family, and a life of security. What else could a woman want?"

Amal knew what else she wanted, but dared not utter it. She did not have the courage to say that she desired to expel the nagging fear in her heart, and to replace it with something called love—that gentle and noble love she used to read about, the kind that sacrifices all for the beloved. She could not bring herself to answer her mother's question, to express her shameful romantic sentiments. The stories she read told of secret meetings of lovers, promises of another encounter, and love more powerful than parental dominion. Yes, Boulos was handsome, but she had seen him only twice, and always with the whole family present. Her other unspoken fear was of the intimidating mother-in-law.

Marta hugged her daughter and kissed her many times on the cheeks and head. "You know my heart is filled with love for you, my firstborn. You have a special place here. That will always be the same, no matter where you are. We are always here for you, though starting tomorrow you will belong to the Murads first."

Amal was comforted by her mother's assertions of love. There had never been a time like this, when she and her mother sat together, alone. Amal began to think that she had nothing to worry about. Hearing about her mother's life and marriage had helped to convince her that she was a lucky woman, certainly luckier than her mother.

Before Marta left the room, she stood up and gave Amal some final words of wisdom that had resisted the march of time. "Now, Amal, bring us honor. Obey your husband in every way. You must please him, and . . . do whatever he asks of you . . . " She hesitated, her face blushing.

"I've always obeyed you, my father, and Sitty. I know how to do that. You don't need to worry, Immie," Amal replied, her voice low, her tone subdued.

"I know. Tomorrow is a hectic day, and I might not have a chance to say much. That's why I wanted to say these things now. May Allah bless you and give you many children, as he has blessed me. Try to sleep early; tomorrow will be a long and tiring day."

After her mother left the room, Amal fell into gloom again. She laid her head on the pillow and began to pray. "Please, *Elahi,* my Lord," she pleaded, "quiet my mind and still my heart. Give me the courage to face tomorrow and the days that follow, whatever they may bring. Help me, and I'll always be your servant, always."

CHAPTER 17

"AMAL, HABEEBTY, wake up!"

"Are you bringing me roasted lamb?"

"Ooh, aren't we being fancy today. I'll go see what supper Im Issa has for us this evening," Sitt Marriam says cheerfully.

I wonder when they're going to take me for X-rays. It's a good thing I can't open my eyes. I don't want to see the light of Jerusalem when they take me there—that cruel city that condemned me to eternal torment. May Allah's wrath fall on you, Jerusalem, Land of Peace!

Sitt Marriam is back. "Hey, Amal, are you ready for a feast?"

"Roasted donkey balls?"

"Shame on you! Nice women don't talk like that."

You should know I'm not a nice woman. There was a time when I was very nice, but nothing good came out of that. So now, to Gehannem with "nice."

I don't know why I have this uncontrollable urge to be vulgar. I used to cringe when I heard anyone use vile language.

"That's ungrateful, Amal."

I think I've upset Sitt Marriam. I shouldn't do that to my only lifeline.

"You've heard the expression, 'Kiss the dog on his lips, you'll get the bone from his mouth'?"

"Who's staying with me tonight?"

"Sitt Najlah."

"That fat cow!"

"That's a terrible thing to say. She's staying in the next room to help you if you need anything. Be kind now, and don't give her trouble."

I put my right hand to my head to tell her I will obey all her commands. "The codeine," I add.

She laughs, "You're something! Sometimes I wonder who is mad, you or the rest of us. Anyway, here, swallow the codeine, and I wish you sound sleep. It's already six and I have to run to the bus stop. Inshallah you awaken to the goodness of tomorrow. And don't forget to have a sweet dream, like the dreams of brides!" she say as she leaves.

She's forever bringing me trouble as she spouts her sweet words. Bride! How am I going to find her sweet dreams!

When are you going to have pity on me, oh Lord, and fill my head and heart with peace? You've abandoned me these many years, and I've turned away from you. Now help me out of this darkness, and into the light.

Maybe I should try to remember some of the psalms I used to recite when I languished in Jerusalem. I loved the one that began "God is our refuge." Let's see . . .

"God is our refuge and strength, a very true help in trouble. Therefore, we will not fear, though the earth be removed, and the mountains carried into the sea. Though . . . though the waters roar and be troubled . . . and the mountains tremble. There is a river that flows . . . through the City of God and brings it joy."

And I don't believe a word of it. All I know now is my own raging fire—and the bride in white burning in it. I try to sleep but am plagued with the memory of the day that made me a bride.

CHAPTER 18

SHE SAT IN THE SALON of her house, surrounded by a large crowd of the Danno guests, women of all ages. Some of the men sat in another room, but most stood outside chatting and smoking cigarettes, as they waited to greet the groom's party when it arrived.

Amal felt the stares of the older women sitting on chairs that lined three walls, their eyes riveted on her to scrutinize and silently sit in judgment—their hearts ready to condemn or approve. But the younger ones, infected with the fever of this most thrilling day in the life of any woman, envious of the bride of the hour, somehow lifted Amal's spirits. As they danced, they clapped loudly to the beat of the romantic songs, their sensual gyrations and quivering hips spurred by the excited tableh. The gaiety of the moment stirred in Amal a feeling that resembled happiness. She could feel their intoxication and hear the crackle of the fire of their dreams. She knew she was the envy of every eligible woman. She felt a strange sense of being elevated above the single women there, raised to the prestigious position of the married ones.

Suddenly, she heard a shout, "They're here! The groom's people are here! One, two, three, four cars! And one . . . two . . . three buses!"

There followed a sudden rush out of the salon and onto the porch. Only the older women remained. Amal was soon to learn what kept them so sedate amid the fever of the moment—a woman is the center of the world for one short day only, a few brief hours.

Her grandmother and mother walked out to greet their soon-to-be in-laws. The crowd of women divided to make way for them, for they must be the first to welcome the groom's family. Shamiran stood at the window, longing for a glimpse of her fiancé. Amal heard the horns honking in sporadic staccato and the loud excited noise from the crowds that walked up the hill, led by the groom's male guests. The women always followed behind.

When the first warble pierced the air, Amal knew the moment had come:

Aayee, ya honorable beit Abu Antone,
Aayee, ya builder of castles, high and mighty,
Aayee, father of six lions, all handsome and noble,
Aayee, Allah bless your home and table,
And reward you for giving us your precious Amal!

The rest of the women joined in the deafening ululululululu that followed.

Amal's heart began to beat in her chest with all the doubts and fears of the defining moment that must now drive her out of her home and into the unknown. Tears welled in her eyes as she saw her future mother-in-law lead her women guests into the crowded salon. Amal feared the woman, as though she were her judge and jailer, all in one. The salon throbbed with the pounding drum and the excited clatter of chairs being removed to make more room.

Suddenly, there was a hush as, led by her father and his eldest son, Antone, the men came to the open door. The women intuitively parted to make way for them.

The proud father approached his daughter, took her hand to raise her from her seat, preparing to entrust her to her brother who would lead her out of the house and down the hill toward the decorated car waiting to take her to the church.

Amal, warm tears streaming down her face, heard her father's hoarse voice. "Daughter, Allah bless this day and bless your marriage, and bring you happiness. Don't weep, ya binty. You're leaving this home to build another, with Allah's blessings." Looking as sad as the moment demanded of fathers, he gazed up at the twenty-two-year-old Antone, who stood taller by almost a foot. "Son, take your sister's arm and lead her out. Yalla, let's go. It's time!"

Behind him stood her grandmother and mother, waiting to bid farewell to Amal, as though she were embarking on a journey from which there was little chance of return. First her grandmother embraced her, kissed her on both cheeks, and then uttered her final words: "May this day bring you lifelong happiness. Allah be with you."

When Marta approached, there were no words, only tears.

Locked in an embrace, the mother wept for the well-known burdens that her daughter, like all women, must take up—pleasing her husband, bearing his children, slaving silently to help build her husband's fortune. Amal's tears were for the loss of the known, and the dread of the unknown.

Behind stood Amal's brothers—Youssef and Jiryis, Mikhail, and the two youngest boys, Elias and Gibrail, aged fourteen and eleven. None of them realized the depth of her misery on that happy occasion, except Gibrail, who struggled to keep his tears away. He was her favorite.

Now he stood at the end of the line of brothers who were caught up in the excitement of the wedding celebrations. They were the privileged brothers of the bride, showing off their new suits and shoes. Each brother approached Amal to plant light kisses on her cheeks. Shamiran again dabbed her sister's tears, gently whispering, "All right, Amal, enough weeping. This is your happy day. Don't turn it into a funeral in front of all the guests. Look how your face is now smudged with kohl."

When his turn came to bid her farewell, Gibrail made a painful attempt at a smile, but could not trust himself to look into her eyes. Amal knew his pain and, choking back her tears, put her arms around him and held him in a long embrace. When she loosened her embrace, he turned around and dashed out of the room, elbowing his way through the crowd of women, before his tears betrayed him.

Antone took Amal's arm to lead her out of the house. "*Yalla, yakhtie*—come, my sister—put a smile on your face and let's go out of here without any more tears. The people are waiting. Let's go."

"Let me first fix her smudged eyes," Shamiran said, her

own emerald eyes glistening. To Amal she said, "No more tears, yakhtie! Don't ruin the maquillage I worked so hard to fix!" Feeling like a younger sister admonished by her elder sibling, Amal attempted a feeble smile.

Quietly Antone gave her his left arm and Shamiran his right. They marched slowly out of the room, toward the veranda. The crowd had already begun to spill out of the house. The younger guests rushed down to the waiting buses to find good seats, while the older ones waited for the bride to step out of the house to give her the customary warbling.

Aayee, Allah walk with you, Allah be with you;
Aayee, tears will do no good to you;
Aayee, if you spot a nail nailed to your father's house,
Aayee, yank it out and take it with you!
Ululululululu . . . !

When the bride and the immediate families of the bride and groom were comfortably seated in taxis, the procession began, taxis in front of buses, all honking horns.

As soon as the buses came to rest at the foot of a steep hill, they belched out their excited cargo. At the top of the hill, the Church of the Virgin Marriam pierced the jumble of the terraced rooftops of Aramaic-Syriac parishioners, its steeple rising high above all buildings to declare its spiritual and moral authority.

Amid honking cars and buses and the jostling jubilant crowd, Amal was supported by Antone and Shamiran up the two dozen wide steps to the church. Shop owners and residents of homes nearby crowded the doorways and barred windows, eager to see the bride, and to share in the excitement of the traditional ululus. After all, not every Sunday provided such a joyous occasion.

Even Amal became somewhat caught up in the celebration. After all, it was for her. Pride in being the woman of the hour—a bride—accompanied her until she reached the door of the church.

As she stood at the threshold, she caught a glimpse of her groom and his brother, standing near the altar waiting to receive her. At that moment, whatever pride she had felt fled from her, and in its place, fear coursed through her veins. Antone noticed her trembling arm, and whispered something in her ear. Her legs moved as though by some power other than her will. She felt her heart bounce against her chest and the blood drain from her head. When she reached the altar, her trembling was obvious to all those near her, and to those standing in the first few pews. Her brother again whispered in her ear; then he disengaged his arm from hers and moved aside to make way for the groom. The priest approached the groom, took his arm, and led him to Amal's side. Following the priest's prompting, Boulos took Amal's trembling arm and placed it in the crook of his own. Kareem paused a few extra moments to watch his beautiful Shamiran, then moved to stand next to his brother. This was, after all, his moment of triumph. Amal's wedding was the guarantor of his own, soon to come.

Shamiran held Amal's arm firmly and whispered in her ear. Another panic struck Amal when she felt as though she would soon lose control of her bladder. She squeezed her thighs tight and forced her mind to focus on the complete disgrace she would bring to herself and her family. She would forever be remembered as the only bride in history to desecrate the church in such an unspeakably dishonorable way.

Then she felt Boulos pat her hand a few times, as if to tell her it was all right. She reminded herself that she was in the house of the Lord, the one she believed in and prayed to. Fortified by her faith, she was able to hear the beautiful melodies of the ancient Aramaic chants that dated back to early Christianity. Then, she was suddenly wrenched from her silent prayers into the present by the voice of the priest calling her and her groom by name.

He paused, waiting for silence as mothers yanked their children and held them by the collar of their shirts, forcing them to stand still next to them. Some men turned around in their pews to shake their heads and frown at the women on the opposite side of the aisle; a few raised their right hand to command silence. Two white-haired, elderly men, frowning in disgust at the incorrigible chatterers, rose from their seats and marched briskly and menacingly to the women's section. One stood midway and the other at the back, each raising his index finger, as a teacher would in disciplining misbehaving children.

Amal was familiar with men's handling of women in church and how women, young and old, after a reprimand, resumed their chatter. As soon as the men turned to go to their seats, some of the brazen young nudged each other, as they muffled their giggles at the men's familiar display of authority. The older women frowned and turned to scold the young ones, blaming them for the humiliation they had received.

And finally, the priest's voice rang out, calling the attention of Amal, Boulos, and the crowd to the reading from the Bible. He began, "The Lord instructs us in the Gospel as to what he wants us to know, and how he wants us to conduct our lives in marriage. This will now be read for our bride and groom, and should also serve as a reminder to all you married men and women."

In his most reverential voice he resumed, "Glory to the Father and Son and the Holy Spirit, now and forever," to which the cantor chanted, "*Ameen*."

Then Father Barhoom spoke to the whole congregation: "Man is the image and glory of God, but woman is the glory of man. For the man is not of the woman, but the woman of the man. Neither was the man created for the woman, but the woman for the man.

"The Apostle Paul says to us: 'Husbands, love your wives, and wives be subject to your husbands, as Sarah was subject to Abraham and called him Lord.'"

Amal felt comfort in St. Paul's command to love each other. Obeying her husband was something she took for granted. The idea of being loved by her husband was most comforting to hear.

"What therefore God hath joined together, let not man put asunder. Whoever shall put away his wife, and marry another, commits adultery. And if a woman shall put away her husband, and be married to another, she commits adultery."

Then the priest continued to read: "And God said, 'Oh ye men, you are the head of your wife and household, as Christ is the head of the church. Love her as Christ loved His church, and keep her from straying into darkness. In the strength of your love, she will remain pure of heart, far from the paths of evil.'"

Amal wondered what the priest meant by her straying into darkness and into the paths of evil. She had never consciously or subconsciously done evil to anyone. Why would she now?

The priest surveyed the crowd for few seconds, then resumed in a most commanding tone, first addressing the groom: "Our son, Boulos, this our daughter, Amal, has today left her parents and brothers and has entrusted herself to you as your wedded wife. Therefore, take care of her and be mindful of that which is due to her in food, drink, dress, and home; guard her with all that is right and just. Be kind in your treatment of her, and pleasant in your speech to her, always ready to do what pleases her."

Then, softening his voice, he turned to Amal, "Our daughter, Amal, pay attention to the word of God as he laid it down in the Holy Book. And God said, 'Since a woman is the weaker vessel, she must submit unto her husband, as unto the Lord. The husband is the head of the wife, even as Christ is the head of the church and the savior of the body. Therefore, as the church is subject unto Christ, so let the wives be to their own husbands in everything.'

"Amal, obey your husband, serve him with a good heart, and receive him with a pleasant tongue. Be faithful to him. And be like the dove in gentleness, and the turtledove in devotion."

He paused, then addressing both bride and groom, he read from the book: "We charge you both to walk in fear of God, to labor to find harmony, be it in things of pleasure or of displeasure. Bear all hardships that may befall you—sickness, adversity, or catastrophe—with the patience of Job . . . "

After leading the congregation in a chant, he paused, turned to Shamiran, and asked for the white ribbons in her hand. He took them and gently draped them over his left palm and over the heads of the bride and groom. His voice rose in a melodious chant in Syriac, punctuated by the loud rattle of the shakers.

Then he tied one ribbon around Boulos' neck, "This ribbon, Boulos, signifies the holy bond of matrimony to your wife. Let this knot bind you to her for the rest of your days."

He turned to Amal and, tying the ribbon around her neck, repeated the same command, adding, "Allah's blessings on you both, and may He who created you fill your house with children." He then asked Kareem for the rings. Taking the bigger band and holding Boulos' right hand, the priest said, "This is the ring that Allah has blessed today, and that I place on your finger, there to remain for as long as you live." With that, he slid the ring on his finger. Repeating the same ceremonious words, he placed the other ring on Amal's finger.

He addressed the congregation. "Now, our bride and groom will go to the hall and there you can offer them your congratulations."

The crowd hardly needed instructions. They rushed out of the church and toward the church hall. They wanted to get the best spot possible to see the bride and groom enter the hall, and to make sure they received their share of the sweets that the groom's family traditionally provided. The children waited excitedly for the shower of pennies and colorful candied almonds as the bride entered the hall. For the children, that was all there was to a wedding.

Once in the hall, the bride and groom were given the center of the back wall to receive the guests and their gifts. Of course, only immediate family and extended family offered gifts of any significance.

Now that the couple was married, it was the immediate family of the groom who stepped forward first. Hilaneh, accompanied by her brother-in-law, came forward, a big smile on her face, embraced and kissed her son, then raised her arm to put ten dinar bills on his forehead, which she let drop into his hands. Then she took his left hand, slipped a gold ring on his fourth finger, and gave the customary wish: "A thousand mabrook, habeeby. Inshallah you find happiness." Turning to Amal, she embraced and kissed her on both cheeks, and placed a gold necklace around her neck. "Mabrook, habeebty! May you be happy in your marriage!" Amal now felt less uneasy about her mother-in-law, and more secure in her acceptance as a daughter-in-law.

Each in turn, Boulos' uncle and Amal's father came forward to embrace the couple and to offer their own good wishes, as well as gifts of money and jewelry. And following custom and her upbringing, Amal kissed the hand of each to express her respect and gratitude.

Her grandmother, waiting behind her son-in-law, stepped in front of the groom. She was dressed in a new but unadorned gray suit, long-sleeved, the skirt down to the ankles. On her head was a black shawl covering the new mandileh that older women wore at all times. Boulos lowered his head to kiss her hand, as she kissed his forehead and placed three dinars on it. Turning to Amal, she lifted her hands in supplication and, eyes toward the ceiling, began a solemn invocation. "Allah bring you happiness! Allah bless you with good health and fill your hands with gold and your home with sons!" She embraced Amal, kissed her on both cheeks, and placed a gold ring with a large turquoise stone on the ring finger of her left hand. "Wear this ring that your grandfather gave to me when I was married. May it bring you good fortune and ward off the Evil Eye from your new home."

Amal was deeply moved, and her eyes brimmed with tears, but these were tears of joy. Through years of obeisance and toil, she had earned her grandmother's love, and now felt triumphant. Never before had Amal put her lips to her grandmother's hand with so much love and gratitude.

In his turn, Kareem embraced his brother and put a ten-dinar bill on his forehead, and a gold watch on his wrist. He would have given a lot more to his brother, but he did not want to outdo his future father-in-law, who had gone out of his way to give ten dinars. Privately, he would do a lot for his brother. To Amal, he presented six gold bangles, which he slipped on her arm.

As soon as the congratulations were finished, Boulos led Amal through the crowd, out of the hall, through the parish gate, and down the steps to the waiting cars. Only the wedding party and the immediate families were driven to Boulos' uncle's house, which was within walking distance from the church.

Around nine o'clock Jabra Danno and Kareem stepped forward, Jabra standing in front of Amal and Kareem in front of Boulos. Everyone knew this was the moment that the bride and groom would leave the festive evening to go to their destination. Most newlyweds spent their nuptial night at the groom's family home, where they would live for many years. The few fortunate wealthy grooms would go to the famous resort town of Ramallah and spend that first night at the Qubeibeh Hotel.

Jabra was the first to speak, "Yalla ya ibny, ya binty, come my son and my daughter, it's time to go. The car is waiting. Allah bless your marriage and give you many children!"

Bride and groom stood up. Boulos wore a smile on his face, and Amal, though smiling, was obviously nervous. If her mother had asked her at that moment what her one wish was, she would have said without hesitation, "To go home with you!"

Boulos led her to the car, which took them to Ramallah. The tremors in her heart turned into loud rumblings as they arrived at the hotel, and her night of terror began.

CHAPTER 19

NO NO NO, STOP! Take me home! I want my mother! Stop hitting me. Don't do this to me. You're killing me.

The harder I fight him off, the angrier he becomes, and the harder he beats me. He grabs my arms and brings them down to my chest, dropping all his weight on them. With his other hand, he forces himself between my legs. Suddenly, I feel as if my flesh is torn. A million stars explode in my head as I scream from the pain burning down below. I hear his heavy breathing and then he removes himself from me and lies beside me. I can't stop weeping.

I sit up and find blood on the inside of my thighs, and some on the sheet under me. I'm terrified at the sight of blood.

Help, I'm dying! He's killed me. Help me!

"Hey, hey, what's the matter? What's wrong?" I hear the night nurse, Sitt Najlah.

I feel something streaming down my inner thighs. "I'm

bleeding. Take me to the bathroom to clean myself. Help me, help me," I cry out, feeling the burning inside me.

"You've had a bad dream. That's all!" She shakes my arm. She flings the bed covers off me and says, "There's no blood here." Then she lifts my nightgown. "You're all dry and clean. You've had a nightmare, that's all. Go back to sleep."

I close my eyes and say my prayers until I can feel myself drifting off to sleep.

I'm sitting in a tub full of warm water. Standing over me I see Beelzebub, tall, muscular, dressed in red, with horns on his head, a flaming sword in one hand, and a snake in the other. Suddenly, his wicked grin blurs and I see Boulos' face. He laughs as he threatens me with the snake in his hand. I want to scream from my terror of snakes, but my voice is tripped in my throat. I'm screaming.

"Amal, wake up and stop that noise! You're full of nightmares tonight." The nurse's voice is gruff and she's holding my arms tightly. "Can't you sleep without this racket? Everyone needs a rest."

I continue to sob. Does she think I enjoy terrorizing myself? She brings me a glass of water and before she leaves orders me to sleep and give her peace. I close my eyes and say my prayers over and over again until I can't tell where one ends and the other begins.

Alone in the hotel bathroom I scrub myself with the soapy loupha, as if that could cleanse the horror I feel. I'm still burning down there and, weeping again.

I hear Boulos knocking at the door, and when I don't answer, he walks in. "Are you all right?" he asks gently, as though he is not the monster who has inflicted pain and shame on me. He sits on the toilet seat and asks, "Didn't your mother tell you this is what happens when you get married?"

"No! She only told me to obey you in everything."

"Well, it would've been better if she had told you more. The hotel owner won't be happy when he finds you've stained the sheet. You should've brought a little towel or something to put under you for the first time."

Now I realize why my mother packed that little flannelette in my luggage.

"I didn't know!"

"It's not your fault. Anyway, I'll give him bakhsheesh and that will please him enough."

I begin to feel he's not such a monster, after all. But I still don't trust him. Why did he hit me so hard, instead of being patient and explaining things to me? I must admit I wouldn't have listened to explanations anyway.

He helps me out of the tub and wraps me with a towel. "Dry yourself, and come to bed."

I hesitate then mumble, "I need my nightgown."

He smiles and says, "All right, I'll bring it."

I walk out of the bathroom and sit in a chair.

"Come here to bed," he says gently, patting the pillow beside him.

"I want to sleep here."

He gets up from the bed, and I begin to shake again. I'm afraid he's going to hit me again. But he takes me by the arm, rather gently, and walks me to bed.

I lie down and he puts his arms around me and tells me the way of men and women. He assures me the blood was that of my virginity, and my parents would be proud, and his mother satisfied she didn't buy "spoiled goods" for her son.

He tries again to enter me, but I move away. He assures me it's all right and won't hurt this time. But it does. I have no choice now but to submit to his desires.

I wake up and find myself naked next to him. I cringe as though I've done some vile thing. I hear him snoring. I leave the bed, wrap myself with the robe on the chair, and go to the bathroom. I come back and sit on the chair, not knowing what to do. It's late morning, and the sun is streaming through the flimsy curtains.

Suddenly, there is a knock at the door. I panic and try to awaken him. He opens his eyes and asks, "What's the matter?"

"Someone is knocking on the door."

Then we hear his mother's voice, "Open the door, you sleepy heads! Open the door!"

"Why is she here?"

"My mother and yours have come to see proof of your virginity. Your honor!"

What humiliation! I should've been prepared for all this. It might've been easier.

He quickly puts on his pyjamas and robe, and opens the door. I rush to the bathroom and shut the door behind me, embarrassed mostly about the night before, but also afraid to face a loudmouth like Hilenah. Then I hear her loud kisses and teasing. "Oh, my poor son is so sleepy. Where's the bride? Come in, Marta. Sit in this chair." Then she shouts, "Where is she? She didn't run away, did she?"

I want the earth to open up and swallow me. How can I face her and my mother? Then I hear her threaten, "If you don't come out by yourself, I'm coming to get you!"

I hear Boulos say, "Immie, lower your voice. Give her a minute then I'll get her. You stay in your chair."

"Where's her honor? That's why we're here. I want to see her honor!"

"Right here," I hear him say. "She forgot to put something under her."

"Well, it's good to know we didn't get spoiled goods," his mother says. I'm beginning to understand what she meant by that.

Then the doorknob turns and he walks in, all smiles. He puts his arm around me and coaxes me to come out with him. I have no choice but to obey.

I walk out, my head bent low, ashamed to look her or my mother in the eye. Hilaneh spreads her arms. "Come here, habeebty! Mabrook, mabrook! Inshallah, soon we'll hear the good news of a grandson on the way!"

My mother gets up to embrace me, but without Hilaneh's vulgarity. Perhaps being the mother of the groom gives Hilaneh license to say whatever she feels like. My mother is obviously of a different class. I want to cry in my mother's arms, and blame her for not explaining things to me, but it must wait.

I sit down and look at my mother. I notice a hint of disappointment in her face. In her quiet way, she says, "I'm sorry we didn't bring the traditional sweets and breakfast with us. I was sure Hilaneh would've brought everything with her. Had I known, I would've bought a few things myself."

"We people of Jerusalem don't have such customs. Are you hungry, son?"

"Sure I'm hungry. I'll order breakfast from the hotel for all of us."

"That's my wonderful son!"

"After breakfast, we'll go with you to Jerusalem and help you settle in your new home. That's what your mother and I decided on our way here."

I'm suddenly gripped with terror of this woman and want to run away from her, but I can't. She's blocking my way with both arms, while her son laughs. My mother tries to reach me, but Hilaneh blocks her way. I beg for help, but my voice is jammed in my throat. I try to run toward the door, but Beelzebub now blocks the way. My terror multiplies as the devil's face now looks like Hilaneh's, now like Boulos', both laughing like hyenas.

I see my mother standing in her misery, her face contorted with pain, weeping silently. Her lips part, but her voice is muffled. She's trying to get around Hilaneh, who's blocking her way with both arms. Powerless, she lifts her eyes and arms toward the ceiling, her lips pleading for help from above, but all I hear is Boulos cheering his mother on, and Hilaneh taunting, "She's ours now. You can't have her back. She's ours. We'll take care of her from now on. You'll see! Right, son?"

I awaken to my scream, and now I'm afraid the fat night nurse will be furious with me.

But when the door opens, and I am comforted by hearing Sitt Marriam's gentle voice. "Good morning, Amal. How do you feel this morning, habeebty?"

After the horror of last night and the hard-hearted night nurse, I decide to be more grateful to Sitt Marriam. "Better," I tell her.

"Hey, that's good! Did you have any trouble last night?"

"Trouble? No, no, I was in heaven!" I decide to give her an outrageous lie, rather than talk about my nightmare.

"The night nurse said you woke up screaming about blood."

"No, I didn't. I just woke up now. She's a liar!"

"Well, maybe you just don't remember," she says kindly.

"I slept the whole night and didn't even move once."

"All right. Let's get your eyes washed, and maybe you'll be able to open them a little today. Wouldn't that be nice? Then I'll change the dressing on the big cut in your forehead, clean your wounds, and put ointment on them. I notice less swelling in your lips. Things are looking up."

"I need a bath," I tell her flatly.

"A bath? Why, I gave you one yesterday, and you raised your screams all the way to heaven! I'll give you a nice bath again on bath day, Saturday. No one is allowed a bath during the week. We have to be very careful with the little water we have. Now, I'll tend to your wounds, and then I'll get you a good breakfast, and that will lift your spirits."

"I've already had breakfast."

"No! When? Who gave it to you?"

I really must stop frustrating her. But I have to protect myself too. If I don't confuse them now and then, they'll think I'm sane, and then where would I be?

"I'll go see about breakfast. I'll be back soon."

She leaves behind the sharp, sickly odor of alcohol. How I hate that smell! It fills my nostrils and takes me back to where I never again want to be—trapped in a cage called home.

CHAPTER 20

THREE WEEKS AFTER her wedding, Amal's real troubles began.

She had become inured to her mother-in-law's daily visits, which began the first day she entered her marital home. Although she felt the visits were nothing less than intrusions upon her new life, she masked her feelings with the deference and congeniality befitting a new daughter-in-law. Amal's eagerness to please and her obvious fluster were not lost on Hilaneh, who was certain of the impact she had on the daughter-in-law she deemed unworthy of her handsome son. It was her intent to keep Amal in mind of her subordinate position in the marriage triangle. She wanted to ensure that Amal understood her home was really Hilaneh's, and that her husband was Hilaneh's son, first and foremost.

Whenever Amal heard the menacing thumping of her mother-in-law's heels on the stairway, she felt trepidation. Immediately she dropped whatever she was doing and gave Hilaneh the warmest welcome, kissing her on both cheeks and inquiring after her health. Hilaneh rejoiced in Amal's overtures and her own success at keeping her daughter-in-law intimidated.

On each of her visits, Hilenah would scrutinize the four corners of the room, the kitchen, floors, and ceilings. When she could find nothing to criticize in Amal's impeccable housekeeping, she would say, "Well, you could change the furniture around. You could put the bed here, and the *diwan* there . . . or there. The room would look better."

Always deferring to her, Amal would say, "You're right. I have to try different ways." And she would have, had there been more space in that small room.

Now, three weeks after the wedding, when the warm sun of summer crested the cloudless blue skies of Jerusalem, Hilaneh proclaimed her dominance once again. The role of every new wife has always been the breeding of children for the in-laws. But Hilaneh injected her quizzing with the venom of her strong dislike of Amal.

"Well, is there bread in the basket yet?"

Amal was taken aback. She had no idea what Hilaneh meant. She wondered why the woman would ask such a silly question. Of course, she always had bread in the basket! She hesitated before replying, "There's a loaf in the cupboard from yesterday. Boulos will bring home one or two fresh loaves in the evening. Would you like me to fix you something to eat?"

"That's not what I'm talking about." Hilaneh patted Amal's belly with her hand. "I mean anything here yet? Are you pregnant?"

"I don't know."

"What do you mean you don't know?" She straightened her

jacket's lapel and mustered all her sarcasm to drive the insult through Amal's heart. "You must know when your monthly comes! Or maybe you don't know that either!"

Feeling Hilaneh's hostility, Amal replied timidly, "Every four weeks."

"I know that, but when in the month? Which week—first, second, third, fourth?"

"Usually in the fourth week of the month."

"Well, we're entering the fourth week. Has it come?"

"Yesterday," she answered in a low, dispirited voice, as though she had committed a crime.

"Let's hope you won't see it next month! That'd be mid-August. Let's see now. If you become pregnant soon, you would deliver sometime in spring of next year. Perfect! I'll have a grandson around Easter. I'll be able to celebrate the Resurrection of Christ and the birth of a grandson at the same time. That would be the greatest Easter. What do you think?"

"Inshallah from your mouth to the gate of heaven!"

Even Amal's own mother had not been so bold as to question her about her monthly, one of the subjects both mother and daughter considered taboo. But as she had just learned, her mother-in-law had the right to break all taboos, and to encroach on every private detail of her life. She knew, from now on, there would be more questions, more investigations, more needling, and little peace. She turned to Hilaneh. "I'll make a cup of coffee."

"Don't trouble yourself. I've had a whole pot this morning with my Kareem before he went to work. Oh, how I miss having coffee with Boulos every morning, as I used to before you married him," she said with an exaggerated sigh.

Amal felt the sharp prick but pretended not to recognize it. "Why don't you join us some early morning for coffee and breakfast?"

"It's not the same, habeebty. After a son marries, it's never the same." Then, sighing, she got up, "I have to go now. I've got some groceries to pick up and supper to prepare for Kareem and me. In one month, Kareem will be married to your sister. Then Shamiran will take over these chores."

Dream on, mother-in-law! You need Shamiran in your life to break your turned-up nose and lower your head! She'll burn your heart with a hot iron, and you won't know where it came from! Do it, Shamiran. Make a humble maid out of her with your well-known weapons—your charm and your sweet, innocent smile.

"Shamiran will surely be the best thing for you," Amal said, enjoying the irony that went over Hilaneh's head.

Except for Hilaneh's badgering, however, Amal's life in those early days of marriage had taken on a quiet routine. The somber atmosphere within her walls was tempered by the genuine pleasure she found in her new city, its breast basking in the bone-whitening sun of mid-summer.

She became accustomed to getting up early in the morning to make her husband's coffee and to serve it to him in bed. He slurped one demitasse after another, emptying the pot before getting up to wash his face with cold water. He dressed while listening to the radio. Amal busied herself in the kitchen frying eggs and making a fresh pot of coffee.

Before she finished fixing an egg for herself, he began to eat. The only conversation between them was when Amal asked if he wanted more bread, cheese, olives, or coffee. She respected his quiet ways, as her mother had respected her own husband's sullenness.

After breakfast, he rose from the table, full of gratitude, "Thanks to Allah, my stomach is full."

"*Sahtain*—with double good health," she responded.

He pushed his chair back and, as he got up, invoked heavenly help, "Ya Allah!" That was Amal's cue to get his coat and help him into it. And, as usual, he dug into his pocket, jangling the coins before he brought up one shilling and placed it in her hand. "There's the money for today's food."

"May Allah bless your hands!" came the stock expression of gratitude. "Is there anything special you wish to eat today?"

"No, whatever you make will be good," came the indirect compliment. "I must go now."

"Go with peace!" came the automatic traditional response, as she watched him sprint down the stairs.

In those days, she felt a sense of pride and pleasure at being married to such a handsome, hard-working man who never complained nor demanded anything. He always provided for their daily bread and always returned home for supper with his usual placidity. That is as it should be, she thought. His silence she interpreted as a sign of wisdom and contentment.

But deep in her heart, an unquiet feeling nagged at her own presumed contentment. She wondered if those stories of love and romance were just lies—fantasies born in the imagination of men and women who knew the anguish of unfulfilled desire. She yearned for even one of the smiles that he reserved for his mother and brother, or for a tender touch of his arm. When she saw newlyweds walking to church on Sunday morning, the woman's arm in her husband's, she wished she could do the same. Yet his demeanor and aloofness thwarted such dreams. She attempted to console herself with the fact that she had never seen her father touch her mother's hand or arm. Some men are like that, she thought, unemotional, undemonstrative.

And except for the thorns his mother stuck in her side, she was content, filling her days with a routine she enjoyed. Daily she aired the bedding under the hot sun of summer and the gentle breeze of autumn for an hour. Then she made the bed, swept, mopped, and dusted.

When he returned between seven and eight in the evening, he greeted her dispassionately, his face expressionless, voice spiritless—not unlike her own father's—which, she was certain, came from spending long and hard hours at work.

"What's for supper? I'm starving."

In a submissive, almost apologetic tone, she replied, "I made hummos, salata, and burghol with lahem and bandorah." Then, before she had the time to sit down, he made a quick sign of the cross and attacked the food with furious energy. He kept his eyes on the full plate before him, while his hand shovelled spoonfuls of the warm and spicy spread into his gaping mouth.

In the early days of her marriage, she attempted to make conversation by infusing questions into the silence of the meal. "How was business at the store today?"

"All right," he replied quickly and curtly. That squelched further inquiries.

Rejecting her efforts at conversation made her feel uncomfortable and unworthy. If, by his silence and short grunts, he meant to proclaim his authority over her and confirm her in the role of a mute maid, he succeeded.

Although she was confident and proud of her culinary and

homemaking skills, she craved a modicum of praise, or a word that would acknowledge her existence in his world. Even her father, stodgy as he was, always managed a word or two in praise of each meal.

The highlight of her tedious routine was her daily trip to the market. From her house she walked down the Alley of the Melons and into the street of Khan il-Zeit.

At first, she was afraid to venture into the ancient bazaars of the Old City. She was intimidated by the grim and narrow, crowded streets, hemmed in by grimy walls rising three stories high.

Even more daunting were the dingy labyrinthine souks. The walls were pocked with the small openings of shops displaying many goods that spilled over onto the street. The fragrance of spices and baked goods combined with the pungent smells of cheeses, olives, fish, newly tanned leather goods, and the musty odors of fruit and vegetables assaulted the city dweller. It was all so different from the open-air market in Bethlehem, where she could see blue sky, breathe fresh air, and never worry about getting lost. But soon Amal learned to appreciate the smells and sounds of the souk, and gradually became a seasoned haggler, enjoying the game of cunning and bartering between vendor and shopper.

Apart from the regimen of cooking, cleaning, and shopping, Amal's daily ritual included visits to the first-floor outhouse. The small outhouse stood in direct view of her neighbor's door, and invariably, her neighbor either appeared in the courtyard or busied herself just inside or outside the doorway. She was always ready with her cheerful morning, midday, and evening salutations. There was no doubt in Amal's mind that Nahla sought her friendship and company, but she was always mindful of her grandmother's favorite proverb: "Play alone, and you'll go home a contented soul."

Amal was afraid of starting an open friendship with a woman she did not know anything about, and who had four children. What if her husband were to come home and find her visiting with Nahla, or Nahla with her? She did not want to risk her peace and quiet.

All the same, Amal's obliging character was forging a silent friendship. Whenever she found Nahla's children had left smudges here and there in the outhouse, she quietly climbed her stairs and came back down with a basin of dishwater she saved for watering her three pots of flowers and for cleaning the outhouse on her assigned days. She cleaned up the children's mess without a word of complaint or hint of displeasure. Another neighbor might have raised the roof, squawking about the obligation of cleaning up after the children, and the need to teach them how to squat over the hole properly. As she later found out, that was how Hilaneh had handled the situation.

Amal's good nature and kindness registered in Nahla's heart. She often apologized to Amal and asked to be informed if the children made a mess on the footpads or floor. Amal's response was always the same, "It's all right. You must have plenty to do with four children. I don't mind." Amal was grateful for even the most unpleasant distraction from the silence of her home. She could hear her grandmother's warning, "Sow goodness and reap wickedness." But she never believed in her grandmother's cynical dictum and chose to ignore it. Now, more than ever, she felt the need for a kind word, a smile, and friendship.

In spite of Hilaneh's badgerings and Boulos' surliness, Amal came to appreciate her new city. One of the few things that delighted her was the glorious view from the threshold of her home. Beyond the front step of her living room, she watched the Old City, a kaleidoscope of hills and valleys, all cluttered with red-roofed, sun-bathed white houses and the steeples and domes of three faiths, among which rose some century-old olive, pine, and cedar trees.

Directly before her, in the distance, rose the high steeple of the Church of the Mount of Olives that seemed to touch the cerulean skies. Her eyes followed a hill down toward the Church of Mary Magdelena perched in a cluster of domes, and below that rested the Church of Gesthemane. To the far right, she could see the edge of the Church of the Holy Sepulchre, and off-center, to her left, the Dome of the Rock.

She turned to her chores, unwilling to surrender to the darkness and gloom that sometimes seeped into her heart.

CHAPTER 21

"HEY, HEY, look here, Amal! We're in luck today. Now, are you ready for the breakfast of princes? But perhaps you need to go to the washroom first." Nurse Marriam's gentle voice chases away my tormenting ghosts.

"Later," I say groggily.

She feeds me the first bite and I immediately know the taste. It reminds me of something I had years ago. "Jambon," I blurt out.

"Bravo! It is jambon. Im Issa ground it to a paste so you could eat it."

I pat my palm on my sore chest to tell her it's delicious. She understands. "Well," she says laughingly, "we won the lottery this Sunday."

"Sunday?" I ask, confused as to what day I was carried in here, and how long I've been here.

"Yes, it's Sunday. Everyone has a better meal on Sunday."

"Never jambon!" I tell her, wagging my finger. "Never!"

"Well, if you can keep a secret, I'll tell you where it came from."

I let my hand speak for me, instead of a nod that would surely give me sharp pain.

"I brought it with me from home. I told my mother how badly you were beaten, and she said, 'Feed her meat, eggs, and goat milk to get her strength back.' The English colonel's wife for whom my mother works sometimes gives her chocolatta, pudding, or a can of jambon. Now promise not to breathe a word of this to anyone."

"I promise," I say and quickly add, "but what am I promising?"

"You mean you've already forgotten the jambon and the food I've been losing my soul to the Shaytaan to get for you?" she teases.

I'm convinced now that although things change, life remains unchanged. Only fools think otherwise. That's how I see it anyway. And I know there's no way out, only darkness here and raging fires there.

A long, long time ago, Sitt Marriam, when I was a girl, I still held hope that life would change and bring with it what my heart desired—love, freedom, and joy. But now I'm here to tell you, if there's any fortune in this life, it must fall in the lap of the undeserving. That's life's justice, a terrible injustice.

"Well, the jambon is all gone. Come, now, let's have the soft-boiled egg and the melba in warm milk from Im Issa. If you don't get better soon with all this food, then I'll lose faith in my mother's wisdom, 'Feed your body, nourish your soul.'"

"I wish I could see what I'm eating."

"Soon. Doctore Jamayelle will help you see."

"I don't want to see. I wish I had been born blind!"

"First you want to see, then you don't. You know what my mother always says?"

"More pearls have dropped from your mother's mouth?"

"She says, 'Whatever Allah does, He does it for a good reason.' She can't read, but she's wise and lives by the word of Allah."

"So does my mother, but what good has it done me? Allah has taken a holiday on Lake Tabarieah or the Sea of Galilea to bless the undeserving and to punish the deserving."

"Allah forgive you for such blasphemy."

Silly girl. Don't you know He doesn't forgive?

I touch my head gently several times to tell her it hurts. "I'll take the tray back and bring aspirin." She gathers her tray and leaves.

Although I'm grateful to her and moved by the goodness of her heart and her mother's, I envy her. She has an angel for a mother. I bet her mother would die for her daughter, if she can feel pity for a mad stranger like me.

"All right," I hear her say, "there's your aspirin in water."

She puts the cup to my lips, while she supports my back with her other arm.

"Very good, habeebty. Do you want to go to the bathroom now, before I leave?"

"No. I want to save it until there's a huge pile of kharra to drop on her head."

"Whose head?"

"Hers. Wife of the Shaytaan."

"I never knew the Shaytaan had a wife. Who is she?"

"Oh, she goes by many names, but mostly by Hilaneh."

"Hilaneh who?"

I should shut my mouth. My head hurts and I pretend to be asleep.

"Let's go to the washroom, Amal, and then you can sleep until noon." She helps me out of bed and to the washroom and back.

"Sleep in the peace of Allah, *ya roahy,*" she says and leaves. Every time she calls me ya roahy, she reminds me of my mother, when she used to call me that, "my soul." Now I think hers were nothing but empty words.

My mother, that fool, also used to say, "Do good, and Allah will reward you tenfold." I tell you, the truth lies so far away from this naïve view. Do good, and He'll punish you a hundredfold. It's not your good deeds that determine the peace and plenty of your life. It's what others do to you and for you. Your life is determined, controlled, and molded by others—their selfishness and delusions, their demented minds and cruel hearts.

Sitt Marriam, though, is beginning to shake all these convictions. If only I could see her. Maybe then I could find out if she was really good, or pretending to be good. Another stupid thought! Wasn't I once fooled with both eyes open? What difference does seeing make?

I have to be careful what I say to the nurse. I have to remain between the two flimsy worlds of the sane and the insane. It's safer for me, for the time being. But her kindness makes me feel guilty. What she must have told her mother to make her give up a precious food for someone like me, a stranger and insane! I never knew such kindness. Oh, I thought I knew an angel once, a long time ago, but I was wrong, completely. Some people look like angels, but deep down they're cowards. I was blind to so much.

I try to sleep, but I see my mother looking at me from far away. I can't see her face clearly enough to know what she feels or thinks. *"Go away, go away! Stay away and hide in your safe cranny, like the mouse that you are! I can never forget how you shrank away when I needed you most."*

A month after her marriage, during her Sunday visit to her parents, Amal decided to speak privately to her mother about Hilaneh's inquisitions and the doubts they had sown in her heart. She had begun to suspect her own fertility and to feel cursed. The possibility of being unable to bear children now plagued her mind and heart.

That Sunday, while helping her mother in the kitchen, she began by asking, "Immie, is it very serious that I'm not pregnant yet?"

"It's only been a month. Sometimes it happens from the first time, and other times, it takes several months and, in some cases, years. Don't worry about it now. It will happen, inshallah."

"But my mother-in-law, keeps questioning me about it in her daily visits. She makes me nervous, and I'm beginning to think of nothing else but becoming pregnant."

"Ignore her comments, habeebty, and humor her. Everything will happen as Allah wishes."

"Humor her! I do everything but the bellydance, but she never stops. Daily she comes to inspect every inch of the house and, just like the Chief of Police, interrogates me about everything, including when my monthly comes."

"Don't pay attention to her. She's the controlling kind, and she must have had a hard time, a young widow having to raise her sons alone. Now she's lost one son and in a week's time, the other will marry. Some mothers find it difficult to have another woman share their sons' lives. In time, everything will be all right."

"And in the meantime?"

"Be patient and sweet. Someone like Hilaneh is better kept as a friend than as an enemy. You know the saying, 'Make a friend of your enemy, and you'll win the war.'"

Amal heeded her mother's advice and exercised patience, until the Grand Inquisitor came in the last week of September. Amal braced herself to answer the dreaded question.

"Good morning, habeebty! Already scrubbing floors?" Hilaneh chirped with her usual metallic vivacity.

"Good morning! Welcome!" *Snake under the sheep dung*! Amal's tone was over-cordial. Immediately, she dropped her brush on the wet kitchen floor, washed her hands, and walked into the front room, where Hilaneh had already ensconced herself on the divan. Amal decided to follow her mother's advice. She embraced Hilaneh, kissed her on both cheeks, and then asked in a genuine voice, "How are you, wife of my uncle?" in the usual way a daughter-in-law addresses her mother-in-law.

"Everything is good, as long as the health is good. And my health is very good, thanks to Allah."

"We thank Allah. Inshallah you're always in good health," her voice dripped with charm. *May Allah send you a stroke to paralyze your tongue!*

"How's my son?"

"In good health, thanks to Allah."

"What's new?" she inquired as though she hadn't asked the same question only days before.

"Nothing new. Oh, Boulos said he might take me to Cinema Rex on Jaffa Street to see Laila Murad and Muhammad Fowzi in *Al Majnooneh*."

"You want to spend hard-earned money on a film about a madwoman?"

"It's said to be very good. You know, those actors are famous."

"A waste of money."

"Two years ago, my brothers took me and Shamiran to see *Les Miserables*. I cried through the whole film. I've loved the cinema ever since, though that is the only film I've ever seen. That's why I hope he'll take me to the cinema on Sunday."

"It's all lies and fairy tales. You waste your money and fill your head with ridiculous stories."

"But it could be real. Isn't life like that, full of troubles?"

"Ah, it's all nonsense. Is there anything happening in here?" she asked while her hand patted Amal's belly.

"Not yet. When Allah wishes, it will happen."

"This is not a good sign. Not a good sign. My poor handsome young son will have no children to care for him in his old age."

"My mother says not every woman becomes pregnant right away. Sometimes, she says, it takes several months or years before it happens. My mother is not worried."

"Well, I am," she asserted, blatantly ignoring the undeniable fact that it took a year to bear her first child, Kareem, and ten years more to bear Boulos. "Look at your mother! She gave birth to you nine months after her wedding and never stopped dropping a child every one or two years. I thought daughters turned out like their mothers in every way—character and childbearing. That's why we agreed to have *you* for my son." Pursing her lips, she added, "Of course, you're much older than your mother was when she got married.

"Well, habeebty, pray He'll bless you soon. I'll pray for you, too. Now, I've taken you away from your housework. I don't want to make you waste any more time. And I have to buy groceries and help Shamiran with the dinner. I'm teaching her how to cook."

"Very good! Shamiran is a quick learner, and you're a great cook. You'll teach her, and soon she'll be your right arm. You'll never need to tire yourself out with all the housework, cooking, and shopping," Amal struggled to sound sincere.

"Oh, she will, I hope, but I don't think she's as strong and healthy as you. She often has headaches or backaches. She seems to have delicate health."

"Always, very delicate." *Aha! She's fooled you too.*

"Did she tell you her monthly hasn't come? It's been a month since her wedding, and she seems to have grabbed. It should've come two weeks ago. Soon we'll know for sure. In that case, I should have, I hope, a grandson around the end of May. Isn't it great news?"

Amal felt a convulsion deep inside her.

"I really must leave."

"Oh, can't you stay a little longer? You haven't had a cup of coffee or anything to eat. You can't leave without at least a cup of coffee!"

"Thank you, habeebty, but I have to go. Don't worry. I'll see you again very soon."

I wish soon were fifty years away, you big sow. "A hundred *ahlan wa sahlan*, wife of my uncle!"

After kissing Amal, Hilaneh left.

Amal stood watching her go down the stairs. In her frustration and anger, her thoughts rang in her head. *You deserve the tribulations of Job, or at the least you deserve Shamiran to bring your swollen head down to your feet! Don't disappoint me, Shamiran. I'm counting on you!*

Amal stood silent for a few minutes. Although she never wished her sister ill, she felt hurt and betrayed by the news of her possible pregnancy. She turned her tearful eyes toward the heavens and whispered, "I've always believed in You, ya Elahi, my Lord, the one who is all love and justice, but where is your love and justice? I see none. I know jealousy is a sin, but I can't help being jealous. I've been jealous of Shamiran all my life, and now You've given her another gift that gives me a dull ache in my belly. You have to give me a child. Make me pregnant, I beg You."

How foolish I was back then, thinking a desperate vow would help me. But I was still so young—young enough, also, to harbor the faint hope that my weak mother might lend me some support. Perhaps I could have excused her for not standing up for me at first, when my troubles began. But I'll never forgive her for closing her eyes and shutting her ears against my pleas when the bastard and his mother joined arms to beat me into the ground. Never!

CHAPTER 22

BY MID-OCTOBER, the autumn sky had turned a sullen gray, and the air had lost its warmth. Occasional rain clouded Amal's view and dimmed her spirits. Soon the billowing, howling winds of winter and the unyielding pounding of rain would imprison her within her walls. But the autumn also brought a new terror.

In the fourth month of her son's marriage, Hilaneh, with eyes more inimical then ever, came to conduct her usual interrogation.

"So, what're you cooking for my son today?"

"*Fasoolia bzeit*, green beans in olive oil and tomato sauce," she replied half-heartedly.

"Is this how you feed my son? No meat! My poor son! He's used to a lot of grilled kebabs, and *coussa mahshi* and *kibbeh,*" she sneered.

Attempting to find a good reason for the meatless dish,

Amal replied, "Well, it's Friday, a day for meatless meals. That's tradition."

"We don't hold such traditions. That's for old people and the old days. My son deserves to be fed the best."

"I don't have enough money to buy meat every day. I try to manage with the little I have." Amal sounded apologetic.

"Are you accusing my son of being stingy with you? How dare you?"

Amal felt the dagger slice her heart as Hilaneh stormed out and down the stairs.

That evening, when Amal heard Boulos' hurried steps up the stairs, and saw him from the doorway of her kitchen, she immediately sensed something new and ominous in his demeanor. He glared at her with the ferocity of a baited beast. He stomped into the living room and shouted, "Leave everything and come here now, this minute!"

Shocked and frightened by the anger in his voice, she obeyed. She stood facing him, while he approached her in deliberate, slow steps. He stood so close that she could hear his rasping breath. "How dare you tell my mother I'm stingy and don't give you enough money to buy meat!"

"I never said such a thing," she defended herself.

"And now you dare to call my mother a liar!" he shouted, raising his right arm and slapping her face. The blow had come with such force and suddenness that she did not have time to protect herself, but staggered backward. She felt like hundreds of needles had stung her face. More loud accusations accompanied blows to her shoulders. She muffled her cries of pain to avoid being heard by the neighbors.

Amal sat on the divan, sobbing, more wounded in spirit than in body.

Though Boulos was still breathing heavily, his rage had subsided, and from the kitchen he brought a towel rinsed in cold water to wipe her face and arms. That did nothing to soothe her wounded heart.

In a voice that had lost its harsh edge, he said, "Get up, now, and let's have supper. Now you know the punishment for talking behind my back, especially to my mother, and for lying. Let's go to the kitchen!" If she had dared look into his face, she might have spotted vestiges of guilt.

She did not feel like getting up, let alone eating. She did not, however, want to risk another explosion. He stood watching as she slowly propped herself up with both arms and shuffled her way to the kitchen. She scooped rice from one pot and put it on the plate. She ladled the string beans in tomato sauce over the rice and placed the plate in front of him. She took a bowl from the cupboard, put a small helping of beans into it, and sat down to eat.

Amal stared at her food, aware of the clatter of his spoon against his plate. She could not bring herself to dip the spoon in the bowl and bring it to her mouth. She had lost her appetite along with any dignity, however tenuous it had been.

Calmly he asked, "Why aren't you eating? Eat!"

In a quivering voice, and without looking at him, she mumbled, "I can't."

"You have to eat." He spoke in a quiet voice.

She was confused.

I don't understand how you can hit me and then coax me to eat, concerned about my well-being. You've crushed my spirits, but you're worried about my health.

Suddenly, she felt nausea rise from her stomach to her throat. She rushed from the table to the little porch and began to retch. When the retching did not stop, he left the table and went outside. Amal began to heave the bitter bile, as he looked on guiltily. And when she could not bring up any more, she collapsed on the floor and began to weep again, from exhaustion and self-pity.

"All right, come. Let's go inside."

With his arms under hers, he lifted her off the floor and walked her to the divan. He then got a towel and cleaned her face and wiped her tears. He placed a pillow under her head and told her to relax. Then he found an old rag and took the bottle of alcohol and went outside to clean up the vomit. Back inside, he moved her legs to make room for himself on the divan. When she looked up, she saw his anguish and guilt-ridden face.

Good, I hope you feel my pain, you son of a sharmootah!

In a voice of genuine concern, he spoke, "Amal, you have to learn to keep your mouth shut. My mother cannot be contradicted or slighted. I have only her and my brother. Nothing is coming between them and me. You should also know I don't deserve to be criticized, especially to my mother."

"I didn't criticize, and I didn't contradict her. I swear by the Bible!" came her quick self-defense.

"There you go again, accusing my mother of lying. Why would she lie?"

"Because she hates me!"

"I don't believe a word of it. Now, just remember this, I will not have my wife standing up to my mother in any way. Unless you like what you just got."

I bet she doesn't interrogate Shamiran daily about what she is going to cook for her son. I bet Shamiran continues to play her tricks of migraine and whatnot, and uses your mother like a maid. She may be angry at Shamiran but she takes it out on me. Curses on all of you!

"She comes here every day, and badgers me about what I'm doing, criticizing everything I do or say, calling me ugly and barren!"

He hesitated then explained, "She doesn't come to badger you. She comes because she cares about me—er—about us. I don't believe she calls you ugly or . . . anything bad."

"No? You have to hear her!"

"See how rude you are! I tell you this is not going to continue. Either you improve your manners, or this," he said, raising his fist to intimidate her.

You're either blind or stupid! Or under her spell! You simply refuse to see the truth. I have a family and six brothers who'll make you shit apricots, you bastard son of the sharmootah. Forgive me, Allah!

"Now, let's go to the kitchen and eat something." It was a command.

Convinced her brothers would beat some sense into him, she got up and ate in silence. He ate with his usual appetite; she toyed with her food and managed to swallow a few spoonfuls. When he finished his supper, he walked away to recline on the divan and listen to his radio.

After she had done her chores, she entered the living room with a heavy heart. Usually she sat in a wooden chair next to the divan. But that night she could not listen to the music of love and lovers. Leave it to hypocrites or fools who live in a dream world of juvenile romance, she thought. "My head is throbbing. Would you, please, lower the radio?"

"Go to bed. I'll lower the radio and sit up for a while."

That night heralded the beginning of a new era in her life.

Three weeks after her beating, Boulos finally decided that the swelling in her face and bruises on her arms and shoulders were sufficiently healed, and it was safe to take her to visit her family.

Although Amal's visible bruises had disappeared, the invisible ones ran deep. At the first opportunity, she got up from her chair, offering to help her mother set up the table and serve the dinner, "Sitty, you sit there, and I'll help Immie."

In the kitchen, Amal stood next to her mother who was adding the finishing touches of fresh lemon juice to the pot on the primos. It was full of grape leaves that Marta and her mother had spent the previous evening stuffing with lamb and rice and rolling into finger shapes. On the other primos perched a pot of stuffed zuccini. Sunday meals were the best of the week.

Amal began to speak, but couldn't prevent her tears from falling. Marta stopped abruptly. Holding a pinch of salt, her fingers hung still over the pot, "Amal, why are you crying? What's wrong, habeebty?" she asked.

Weeping softly and uncontrollably she murmered, "Nothing, nothing!"

"You're weeping like this for nothing? I want to know what's going on," Marta insisted, concern in her voice and face.

Then, in a rush, Amal blurted out, "He hit me three weeks ago, for no reason. None! I ask for nothing. I do everything. I obey his every wish."

"What brought this on?"

"His mother came that day, like every day, and questioned me about the supper I was preparing for him, a Lenten meal of green beans in tomato sauce. She complained that I don't feed her son well. I told her I manage with the little money I have. She called me a liar and accused me of calling her son stingy. She left my place like a madwoman. When he came home for supper he accused me of lying and smearing his name. And as soon as I defended myself he hit me."

Marta stood almost paralyzed. Then she managed to ask, "Is that all true?"

"Truer than the truth, ya Immie. May Allah paralyze my mouth if I lied to you!"

Marta put both hands on Amal's shoulders and spoke gently but firmly, "Men are sometimes in the grip of their mothers. She must've filled his head with her own poison. We've heard from people how she has no control over Kareem but keeps a strong hold over her younger son. I felt from the beginning she was going to be someone to fear."

She stopped for few seconds then continued, "Listen to me, habeebty, we can't have people talking about us. We have to keep this quiet. Maybe that's the end of it. Your father is ready to ask for the hand of the Nissans' daughter for your brother Antone. He will never hear of anything to spoil the chance. You know how one word of trouble can start a huge fire. Let's keep troubles away. Certainly, at this time. But if he beats you again, we'll deal with him then. Now, wash the tears from your face, and let's have dinner as if nothing happened."

Amal was stunned, though she could understand her mother's reasoning. She knew that Bethlehem, like every little town, loved gossip. Nevertheless, she had expected her mother to do more, to promise to have her brothers teach him a lesson he would never forget.

Betrayed by the one who should have stood by her, how would she now defend herself against the demons that plagued her life?

Amal wondered how Shamiran could be so impervious or so blind to the humiliation that her own sister suffered at the hands of Boulos and his mother. Three Sundays of each month, Amal and Boulos went to Shamiran and Kareem's home for dinner after attending mass. Hilaneh insisted the whole family have Sunday dinner together.

Right after mass, they walked up the wide, cobblestoned street that led to Jaffa Gate, where they boarded a bus to Katamone. Her sister's beautiful villa was a short walk up a hill from where the bus dropped them off. Hilaneh was always busy preparing the dinner, while Shamiran, dressed in her Sunday best, fussed around with setting the table and arranging flowers. Amal could not help but notice the way Shamiran would turn to Kareem, who sat reading the newspaper, to ask what he thought of the table setting or the flower arrangement. He would put aside the paper and approach her, putting his arms around her waist and admiring all that she had done.

Minutes after they arrived, Hilaneh would call Amal to the kitchen to help with the dinner. Amal was always ready to help, but she wondered why she, the guest, must help with the preparation, and not her sister, the lady of the house. She would have gladly offered to help, but was sensitive to being ordered to earn her Sunday meal, while her sister strutted in front of Kareem and Boulos.

As soon as they finished eating dinner, Boulos would show his appreciation for his mother's hard work by saying, "The best food in the world, Immie. Allah bless those hands! Inshallah we eat together in happy times."

"Double good health to you, my love. Inshallah we feast at the birth of grandsons!"

Although Amal always complimented her mother-in-law on the delicious food, she hated every morsel at her sister's table. To her, it was like feeding on poison. If she had the choice, she would never go near the place to watch Shamiran pretend to be the sophisticated fragile flower, saying little, strutting around the house with a permanent, vacuous smile on her lips.

"Now, Amal, let my mother relax and you go do the dishes," Boulos would say to demonstrate his love for his mother and appreciation for a good meal.

Stripped of dignity once more, Amal cleared the dishes and went to the kitchen to clean up.

In early December Boulos told her, "From now on, you're going to Kareem's house three days a week to help your sister out."

"Why?" she asked, surprised.

"Your sister is four months pregnant, and the doctor ordered her off her feet for the next couple of months."

"But your mother is there. She does most of the work as it is."

"My mother helps, but she's not going to be Shamiran's maid. She's too old to work hard seven days a week."

"Why doesn't Kareem hire a maid? He's rich and can afford to get Shamiran a maid."

"It's none of your business what they do with their money."

"But I can't go there three days a week and leave my work here."

"You have so little to do here. It's not like you have a whole farm full of children!"

This hurt. "I can help her once a week, but not three times."

"What kind of woman are you? Shamiran is pregnant and has to stay in bed for fear of miscarriage, and you refuse to help her? You'll do as I say. Mondays, Wednesdays, and Fridays you will go there in the morning. I'll take you there the first time and bring you back at night. After that, you'll be able to get there on your own."

"Boulos, I'm afraid of your mother. She hates me, and she'll find ways to get me in trouble. Besides, three women in the same house will be enough to start a world war."

"You just shut your mouth and nothing will happen. Besides, my mother won't be there. She needs to get out and visit friends."

"Boulos, I'm your wife, not a servant."

Suddenly, he was on his feet bristling with rage. He grabbed her by the shoulder and shoved her down on the divan. "A servant-and-a-half! Who do you think you are, daughter of lords?"

She began to cry, "No, but I don't want to feel I'm my sister's maid."

That was the last straw from a woman who did not know her place. His face grew dark; the air turned electric with his wrath. And the blows came down—on her face, head, back, and arms. Helpless against his fury and the pain he was inflicting, she screamed, begging him to stop—her only defense.

"Doesn't anything get through your donkey head? You're going to learn the hard way to do as you're told and never to answer back. Keep your tongue in your mouth."

When his wrath was spent, he stepped outside in his undershirt and saw Nahla and her husband staring up, listening. He walked back in. "Look what your screaming has done? You've rattled the whole neighborhood. They're all out watching and listening. Are you happy now?"

She covered her face and continued to weep. This time, however, she was seething with anger and bitterness.

My family should stick your head in the cesspool of Wadi M'ali!

The next morning, in the bone-chilling wind of December, and the dampness left by the torrential rain of the night before, she walked behind him, her head wrapped in a wool scarf, and her body in a heavy coat. In silence, they marched quickly through the dingy streets of the Old City, toward Jaffa Gate and to Bus #4.

There was no doubt in anyone's mind that Amal was not at her sister's house with a glad heart. Shamiran was still in bed, but Kareem and Hilaneh were up having their second cup of coffee.

Amal became convinced that Kareem did not expect to see her at his house early Monday morning, when he welcomed her in his congenial way. "Good morning, Amal, Boulos. What brings you both so early today?"

Amal spoke before her husband, "Boulos told me I have to come three days a week to help Shamiran."

"Why, Boulos? Amal has her own place to take care of. We can manage with my mother here, and I can hire someone if we need more help."

Amal kept her eyes focused on Hilaneh and Boulos. She caught the quick glances exchanged between them.

"Isn't your brother thoughtful, Kareem?" Hilaneh was quick to jump in. "He wants to help us. He knows I'm not what I used to be. Thank you, Boulos, my heart! Thank you, Amal, habeebty."

You snake!

"I hope this is not going to be too much for you, Amal," Kareem said kindly. "If you feel after a week it's not possible to continue, all you need to do is speak up."

"Oh, Amal is a great worker and a great cook. You couldn't find better," Hilaneh said. Amal was not fooled by her hypocrisy.

For a second time in the privacy of the kitchen, Marta listened to her daughter's tale. Sighing deeply, she said, "Amal, my heart weeps for you. I wish I knew what to do or say. This is not what I wanted for you. It seems your life was charted with tar. I know how you're suffering. But each woman has a cross to bear. Yours is a heavy one.

I spoke with your father that first time you told me about Boulos beating you, and he would not hear of any meddling between husband and wife. I wish I could do something to help you, habeebty. My hands are tied. But if he does it again, I'll talk to your sister, and she'll get Kareem to take care of his brother."

"That's it? I'm alone, burning in a fire and no water to put it out!" Amal sobbed.

"No, you're not alone. Allah's with you all the way. Follow His word and read the Bible, especially the psalms. Before you leave today, I'll give you my Bible. Put your faith in it and use the gifts Allah gave you to avoid the situations that bring on his bad temper."

That was the last time Amal pleaded to her mother for help. Her pleas fell on hard stone.

Meanwhile, she moved with the mechanical precision of a robot, her face expressionless, her voice lifeless, her prayers nothing more than empty words mumbled between unwilling lips.

> God is our refuge and strength, a very present help in trouble. Therefore will not we fear, though the earth be removed, and though the mountains be carried into the midst of the sea . . .

Now Jerusalem did not appear as a city of beauty; nor the city of peace she had thought it to be. Instead, she saw a city of beauty and brutality, light and gloom, love and betrayal.

CHAPTER 23

I WISH I COULD SLEEP and awaken to find the coils in my brain had been dredged of the charred residue of all the years of my life. I might then begin a new life and take my chances again.

I have no idea what day it is, or how long I've been here. We must be at the end of summer. It feels warm, but not as hot as in midsummer. Soon everything will turn cold and damp. I hope I'm out of here before the cold winds begin their orchestra of bellowing and keening. I'd rather be with my friends in our ward when winter unleashes its fury.

But, here or there, I need my sight back. My head is better, and so are my bruises, but my sight hasn't come back. I only see shadows of light and dark. And when the howling winds of winter lash the little window, and rattle the shutters, as though they mean to crash in to freeze me half to death, I'll feel the pain of loneliness and know the agony of sightlessness.

It's quiet here where I sleep undisturbed, unlike my restless nights in the regular ward, where I used to be jolted awake by the sudden scream of an inmate. There I breathed the same sour air of nine roommates.

Here, from the little barred window near the ceiling, I hear the breeze soughing through the leaves of the silvery olive trees outside, which some of us trusted patients are allowed to harvest every September. I wonder if harvest time has come and gone. I enjoyed being among the "good" inmates who were given the privilege of going outside this prison to pick olives. Outside these walls, we can breathe the fresh air, harvest olives, sing our hearts out, tell jokes, and tease each other. The orderlies stand guard, amused at our behavior. Now and then they shout at us to be quiet and to work faster.

It's definitely getting a little cooler in here and quieter outside. I can still hear the birds chirping and calling to each other. Soon they'll be gone to warmer places, like the valley of Jericho, to bide their time until winter retreats and spring dawns again.

Suddenly, heaviness seizes my heart, and I feel the room closing in on me. What hope do I have of finding my own spring? My head hurts and my chest is so tight that I can hardly breathe. I hear voices in the room, then a familiar voice calling me, "Amal, habeebty, it's your best friend, Khadeejeh. They let me come visit you." I feel her hand caress mine. "Amal, I've missed you so much. It's been so long. I've been asking to see you. Finally, Sitt Marriam let me."

I don't know if this is real or another dream. I manage to open my eyes halfway, but I can only see shadows. "Is it true or a dream?"

"It's true, my soul. Here, feel my hand."

"How long have I been here, Khadeejeh?"

Khadeejeh pauses for few seconds, as though she's trying to find an answer. That's so unlike her. She never had to stop for an answer before. She used to babble away for hours. Then she says, "You've been here a very long time, habeebty. Three years, I think."

I know Khadeejeh gets confused so easily, and you can't believe everything she says. But just the same, the idea frightens me. "Impossible. I've been here three weeks, at the most."

Again, Khadeejeh pauses, then says, "Well, I'm not sure. You know how time is. It comes and goes, and we don't know how. So it could be three years." She pauses before she speaks again, "Oh, I think it's been three months. But I feel you've been away for years."

"Khadeejeh, I've missed you, too." I should be happy my friend is here, but she's pitiful and I feel sad. We're both helpless.

"You don't look happy, habeebty. Khadeejeh will make you laugh. I know things that will make your brain jump out of your head. Do you want Khadeejeh to tell you?"

When I take too long to answer her, she bends down and whispers in my ears, "l have funny stories about Im Issa."

"Tell me."

"I've been working in the kitchen ever since that sow Soraiya beat you up. And I've been making all the food you've been getting. Good food, right? We have to take enough of that kind of food with us when we go to the mountain. We have to make a dress with pockets to the ankle, like Im Issa's, or steal one of hers. Then we could fill them with food we steal from the kitchen. Anyway, when I tell you how Sitt Marriam managed to get you all that good food from Im Issa, you're going to die laughing."

I begin to feel like the old days, when Khadeejeh and I had our insane talks about going to the mountain and then to paradise with her prince.

Khadeejeh clears her throat and begins. "You know the first day they brought you here, Sitt Marriam came into the kitchen and talked to that ghouleh, Im Issa. You should have heard her—so sweet: 'Im Issa, I have a patient who was beaten up badly this morning and missed her breakfast. I know it's past breakfast and too early for lunch, but can you find something to give her now? She's starving, the poor woman!'"

Now Khadeejeh's voice grows harsh to imitate Im Issa's, "'I'm busy preparing dinner. Your patient has to wait until noon.'

"Sitt Marriam says in a pitiful voice, 'Im Issa, if you were to see her, you would weep. Soraiya got her this morning.'

"'I heard the ruckus. Well, something gets us all in time. What's new?'

"'Please, Im Issa, what do you think of a piece of melba and some warm milk?'

"'Is she the daughter of princes, or the descendant of the prophet Muhammad, Sitt Marriam?'"

Khadeejeh stops to take a breath and begins to cackle. "You'll never guess what next, Amal. Sitt Marriam looks right at her and says, 'She's my cousin.'

"'By Allah's life, I didn't know she was your cousin,' Im Issa says. 'Whatever you need, just come and ask me. What happened to her? What brought her here?'

"'What can I tell you, Im Issa? You know how life can be for some women.'

"'Don't remind me! I know. My own sister, childless after three years of marriage, now lives like a maid to her husband's new wife. Life is a toss-up between the black luck and the white.'"

Now I understand how the nurse got me that good food. I laugh as I visualize the scene in the kitchen.

"Oh, I can tell you so much more. You'd really want to laugh when I tell you about the aspi . . . "

"Khadeejeh, I think Amal is tired now. Perhaps tomorrow you can come again and you can talk a little more. A little at a time. Now say good-bye to Amal."

"But I want to tell her about the aspir . . . "

"Later, Khadeejeh. You promised to leave when I say. Remember what I told you about losing my job, if anyone finds out you're here? If you want to come again, you have to listen to me. And remember, this is our little secret."

"Promise you bring me here tomorrow?"

"I promise, but no one is to know. No one."

Khadeejeh kisses me on the cheek and whimpers, "Habeebty, inshallah you get well soon. We have a lot to do, you and I, before we can go to the mountain."

"Of course," I tell her. "Remember Sitt Marriam's secret, Khadeejeh. You don't say a word, and you'll come back tomorrow."

"Khadeejeh never forgets a promise. Like you. You promised to teach me to read, and you will, right?"

"Yes, I promised. Now what did you promise Sitt Marriam?"

"Not to tell anyone I visited you," she says, proud of herself.

"Very good. Go with peace!"

I see the shadow of the nurse taking Khadeejeh toward the

door. I can tell which is which. Khadeejeh is very tall, and the nurse is short. Though I'm alone now, the dark cloud that has shrouded me, is gone. My head feels a little better, my heart a little lighter. It's strange that just a short visit, even with someone as mad as Khadeejeh, takes away some of my gloom.

Khadeejeh's friendship brings me the same comfort as Nahla's once did, though the two women are so very different. Nahla, my former neighbor and friend, is free from the scum that floats in the heads of the likes of Khadeejeh and me. Nahla and I used to have coffee for an hour or two every afternoon and talk about anything and everything. Sometimes, she read my cup and both of us laughed at the strange claims and far-fetched predictions she swore were so clearly visible in the coffee grains. In those days, she was like a salve for my wounds. She came to see me here a few times but then disappeared from my life, like all those who should've stood by me.

Soon the nurse is back and I thank her for letting Khadeejeh visit me.

"It's nothing. I just want you to get better and see you walk out of here the way you were before this happened."

"Khadeejeh said I've been here three months. That can't be true!"

"Well, it's true. For the last month you've been heavily sedated. Dr. Jamayelle's orders."

"Don't sedate me."

"We had to, because you were crying all the time and refusing to eat. We had to do something."

"Crying is good. Tears clean the soot from the heart."

"But you weren't eating or drinking. And that isn't good. You know what they say, 'Feed the body and nourish the mind.'"

"They've got it all wrong. They should say, 'Feed your soul, and your body will nourish itself.'"

"Hmm! You're full of surprises."

I should shut my mouth sometimes. "My head is full of kharra, and it churns and churns."

"You know what my mother used to do to me whenever I said that bad word?"

"She used to wash your mouth with soap, or rub pepper into it."

"How did you know?"

"Mad people know everything. You're not mad. You know nothing."

"To know things I have to become mad! Well, Amal, who'd take care of you if I became mad?"

"I'd take care of you. The mad take care of the mad." I laugh hysterically.

"You must be tired from the visit with Khadeejeh. Why don't you rest for a while?"

I wag my index finger as if to warn her. "Thief! Thieves go to hot Gehannem."

"How am I a thief?"

"You steal food for a cousin with no teeth!"

She laughs. "You don't believe Khadeejeh, do you? You know how she imagines all sorts of stories."

"Khadeejeh never lies. She's going to paradise! I'm taking her there."

"So you and Khadeejeh are going to paradise, and I'm going to Gehannem!"

"I'm just taking Khadeejeh there, and coming back here."

"You want to come back here? Why?"

"To get you out of Gehannem!"

"You seem to know your way around."

"You want to get out of Gehannem or not?"

"Sure. I'm not interested in going there in the first place."

"You're going there. Everyone is going there."

"It must be a popular place."

"Like Jericho in summer."

She laughs out loud, "I hear Jericho's hotter than Gehannem in the summer."

"But I'll help you out of there."

"And I'll help you out of here. A deal? In fact, my mother and I read the Bible every night before going to bed, and we pray for others and for ourselves. We've been praying for you."

"You and your mother have been praying for me? No wonder Allah's gone deaf on me!"

"Why wouldn't He hear our prayers?"

"Because He doesn't listen to thieves and liars."

"Oh, He will hear us."

"Who's *He*?"

"He's the one above who we love and who loves us."

"I never thought nurses could be mad! Careful, habeebty. They might lock you up."

"In the name of the Father, Son, and the Holy Spirit!"

"Ameen!"

"You make me want to laugh and cry at the same time."

"See what I mean! You're showing all the good signs of madness. If you stay in this place long enough, you'll become one of us. I'm afraid you've caught the mad germ."

"You can't catch it. It's not like a normal disease."

"Yes, it is, and worse. You don't even know that you've caught it. That's why Soeur Micheline and Nahla stopped coming to see me. They're afraid they'd catch my disease."

"Who are Soeur Micheline and Nahla?"

"I dreamed of gold, but tin was all I got."

"What? Who's talking about dreams of gold or tin."

"Of course, we were. What do you think we were talking about?"

"You were talking about Soeur Micheline and Nahla."

"How long have you been here, three years? Tsk, tsk, tsk! Such a pity to lose you! I have to tell Doctore Jamayelle to help you, poor girl! He'll give you a new name, like they gave me when I first came here. He'll name you Sitt Sophrenia!"

"Why Sophrenia?"

"I don't know, but it sounds lovely."

"I see," she says, humoring me. "Now I think you're getting tired. I'll leave so you can get some sleep, maybe till suppertime. I'll come then to feed you."

"You sound just like Nahla."

"Who's Nahla?"

"She's not as beautiful as Queen Zenobia, and not as ugly as I am."

"You're not ugly. Why do you think you are?"

"Because I am, you sweet liar, Sitt Sophrenia!"

"Well, Sitt Amal! Say your prayers and sleep in peace." She leaves closing the door behind her.

I like to tease her like Nahla used to do to me. With Nahla, it was more real though. She knew my problems and tried, in her way, to cheer me up. With Khadeejeh, it's a game, and I go along with her strange notions and hallucinations, but she cheers me up, too. Now that I'm feeling better, I'm going to have a bit more fun with the nurse.

CHAPTER 24

SHE TRIED TO SWEEP away Nahla's image and to muffle her voice. Finally, she surrendered to the memories of her neighbor in Jerusalem, whom she had kept at arm's length for two years. Once it began, their friendship—the only one she'd ever had—brought joy into her somber home.

Three days after another beating, Amal shut herself into her room, emerging only for a quick trip to the market to get the daily groceries and for surreptitious visits to the outhouse. She purposely avoided Nahla. She couldn't show her puffed-up face or red eyes. Passing in front of Nahla's door, she lowered her head and kept her eyes on the granite floor of the small courtyard. She was mostly afraid that one kind word from her neighbor might unleash more tears of self-pity.

Besides, she did not want to exacerbate the situation by defying Boulos' wishes. He had told her, from the very beginning, to stay away from Nahla and her family. She was not to be trusted, he said, and he did not want to see her children anywhere near his house. Although Amal knew nothing about Nahla, she thought it best to obey.

Boulos' volcanic eruptions, his unprovoked assaults, and the knowledge that the whole neighborhood was aware of her humiliation added to her pain and shame, and made her avoid everyone. They must feel I've deserved my husband's rage, she thought. Even women, especially old mothers-in-law, agreed with the men's common excuse for wife-beating: She must have deserved it and needed a reminder that her husband is her master, never to be contradicted. A wife only received sympathy from others if the husband was a known gambler, drunkard, or both.

But Nahla, it seemed, could no longer bear to hear Amal's screams pierce the thick night air. She knew enough about Hilaneh and Boulos to believe her neighbor was a victim of their wickedness. Disregarding her mother's advice and her husband's warnings against meddling in other people's affairs, Nahla climbed the stairs, steadying a brass tray on which was a pot of coffee and two demitasse cups.

When she heard the three knocks on her door, Amal quickly sat up, pulled her hair away from her face and, straightening up her dress, limped to the door. She did not expect to see Nahla with her easy smile and cheerful voice.

"I haven't seen you for three days and thought perhaps you're not well. I decided to come and have a cup of coffee with you."

Amal's voice was scratchy and weak, "Please, come in." She was well entrenched in the Arab tradition of hospitality to visitors or neighbors who knock on the door. Bad timing, low spirits, or sickness could not muffle the voice of hospitality.

Both were nervous and awkward during that first visit, though for different reasons.

"I thought after two years of being neighbors, it was time we had a cup of coffee together and a little chat now and then."

"Of course, we should. I . . . I always felt you were so busy with the four children and didn't want to take precious time away from your day," came Amal's polite excuse.

"Oh, no, no. I have enough of the children and their skirmishes. Frankly, I hate housework! I put the twins down for a nap every afternoon, whether they need it or not, because I want to spend an hour by myself, reading my magazines and the newspaper. Children are precious, but they frustrate me so much that I sometimes wish I hadn't got married. Each day is like the other, full of chores—cleaning house, cooking, feeding everyone, doing dishes, and then going to bed. Sunday is the only day that I get a break. We go to church and then to my mother's for dinner. She usually gives me the leftovers to bring home for our supper." Nahla prattled on from one topic to another.

"I thought you were the happiest woman in the world!"

"Well, I'm not miserable, but a married woman's life is dull. I feel that I, too, deserve some time for myself, just to do what I want."

"You must've gotten married very young."

"I was only sixteen when my mother decided I should marry."

"So young!"

"Can't do anything about it now." She stopped for few seconds and then asked, "Why don't you come down for coffee in the afternoons, around two o'clock, when I put the two-year-olds down for a nap?"

At first, Amal hesitated, but quickly realized she needed to get out of her room now and then. Since Shamiran had given birth, Kareem had hired a nanny to care for the child. He did not want to burden Amal any longer. Although Amal had resented helping her sister three days a week for several months, she had enjoyed the chance to get out of her home.

She accepted Nahla's gracious invitation. And during those visits, Amal learned much about Nahla and her life.

"I don't know why your mother pushed you into an early marriage, and to a man fifteen years older," Amal remarked during one of her first visits to Nahla. She already felt enough at ease to speak freely.

"My mother was afraid I'd bring her another *nakbeh*, like my older sister did," Nahla said.

"What calamity did she bring?"

"Aida is two years older than me. My mother was widowed soon after I was born, and worked for rich families to support us. She wanted my sister and me to get an education, become teachers. She believed that way we could at least support ourselves and our children if we ever became widows like her. So she sent us to Saint Joseph school, right at Bab-il-Khalil, Jaffa Gate. We used to be Greek Orthodox, but my mother went to the Catholic Church, and we became Catholics. So my mother didn't have to pay rent or tuition.

"In her secondary years, Aida became friends with some Armenian girls. She started going with them after school to meet some English soldiers at Café Oroppa on Yaffa Street. Armenians came from Oroppa. They're basically Oroppeieen. They think it's all right to talk to men or go out with them. And you know how Arabs are—if a girl only looks at a man, they call her—far from your ears—sharmootah.

"To make a long story short, my mother found out from a relative that Aida was seen with an English soldier, walking arm in arm near the King David Hotel. My mother was furious and threatened to lock her up in the house. But Aida was smart. She promised to come home after school and not go anywhere. And you know what she did? She eloped with the Englishman and married him. And she's the happiest woman I know. Sometimes, I think every girl should marry an English soldier. My mother was scandalized, and forgot about the education and decided that before I could bring her another shame, she'd marry me off to the only son of her widowed second cousin. And here I am."

"But you seem happy, always smiling or laughing with the children."

"Oh, I can't complain. I find ways to bring some fun into my life. Saleem's so much older than I am—but he's quiet and kind. He keeps us fed and clothed, never complains or demands. He works for the Falastine newspaper, repairing machines and doing all sorts of work around the place. He doesn't make a lot of money, but he's lucky to have steady employment."

"You're blessed. A good husband and four children! What else would a woman want?"

"Saleem at least goes to work and has someone to talk with. Me? I'm stuck here day in, day out."

"I never thought of it that way. It does sound boring. Men have it better." Although Amal thought Nahla had nothing to complain about, she did not want to disagree with the only friend she had.

"Look at Aida. Some days she doesn't have to cook. She goes

with Ed to the soldiers' club for lunch or supper. She has enough money to go shopping for clothes in the Jewish stores. They go to parties and dance all night. And she's always cheerful, chattering away about all kinds of people she knows, or things she's bought. And when she brings her husband to visit us, I can't help envying her. It's like there's some sort of magic there, a kind of life that we read about in romantic stories, or see in Egyptian films."

"It does sound exciting."

"But whenever they come, Saleem walks out, disgusted with their behavior. He can't stand to see them always laughing, touching, kissing. He thinks they're immoral and will corrupt our children. Can you imagine how fun, laughter, and love could corrupt anyone?"

"That's how Arabs think, our tradition."

"Throw tradition out! I prefer the English way, don't you? I love my sister, but after each visit, I feel empty and miserable. Of course, the children love their Auntie Aida and their Uncle Ed, who bring them English chocolate, and biscuits filled with sweet cream, and toys. Saleem thinks when the English leave Falastine, Ed will leave Aida behind. But I don't think so. He reads the newspapers and says, 'These English boys are having fun while they're away from home. I tell you, Nahla, the English love the Zionists. They brought them here and give them guns to kill us and take our land. And if the Arabs rebel and kill one Zionist, the English kill all the Arabs involved. That's how much the English love the Arabs! That's how much this funny Ed loves Aida!'"

"How could anyone be sure about anything in this world? One can't tell the good from the bad. Things are not always what they seem," Amal reflected, more as a commentary on her own life than on the English and the Arabs.

"True. Like you said, I'm always cheerful, but my heart isn't, and no one sees what's in it. But Aida and Ed really love each other and they show it." She paused and, with the palm of her right hand, gave a light push to Amal's arm. "What do you think, Amal? Should we dump our husbands and find fun-loving, good-looking, English soldiers who will hug and kiss us all day and all night long?"

Now Amal chuckled at the wild idea, "Too much of a good thing is the same as too much of a bad thing, as Sitty would say."

"Not for me! I think I could take all of that."

"You're funny, Nahla. You do make me laugh."

"And that's what you need, Amal, a little laughter in your life. You're too serious. You should get out now and then and find some fun things to do."

"Fun things might turn to . . . " She checked herself from saying anything that might hint of her troubles.

"Amal, I wish you wouldn't lock yourself in your house after Boulos . . . you know, gets all angry and . . . and takes it out on you. I know, as well as everyone else, you suffer in silence. The neighborhood women feel for you. They know what Boulos is like."

"What are you talking about? What do they know about him?"

"You forget he grew up in this very house, and these neighbors have seen him grow up from a toddler to a man. I could tell you a lot, but I don't want to add to your troubles. Perhaps one day . . . "

Friendship with the lively Nahla was the best medicine Amal could have had. In two hours every afternoon, the young women shared everything that touched their lives. For Amal, they provided enlightenment, amusement, and insight about how to cope with her life.

Their daily chats over coffee and Nahla's readings of Amal's fortune in the coffee grounds provided excitement and laughter. Although both women knew reading fortunes was nothing but an exercise of the imagination and a harmless pastime, deep in their hearts they wanted to believe wonderful things would someday happen to them.

Once, when Amal asked Nahla how she could see all that promise in the cup, she leaned over and said, "Look here, Amal. See this person, a woman, I think, short and dark-skinned, her arms stretched out ready to embrace you? She's like your angel."

"Go on! Angels are beautiful, with golden long hair. I've never heard of a short, dark-skinned angel," Amal teased.

"Well, that's what I see. You can believe it or not. Take a look here. See this? Anyway, if you don't want her for your angel, I'll take her."

"And what is she going to do for you?"

"Oh, I don't know. She might give me what I ask for."

"What's that?"

"Swear by the Gospel you would never tell anyone?"

"I will never tell, and if it makes you feel better, I swear to you by the Gospel."

"If an angel should grant me one wish, it would be for a handsome young man like Ed. I feel so ashamed to tell you that when Saleem comes to me, I close my eyes and think of someone like Ed. Of course, you don't have to imagine anything like that.

Boulos is young and handsome, so . . . so . . . You must feel good all over every time."

Amal could not believe her ears. She had never heard or engaged in conversation about men and women. How could Nahla talk so easily about such private matters? All she wished was for Boulos never to touch her again. She had never felt anything but revulsion. She put up with him for the sake of having children. And that was not happening.

"It's a good thing you don't tell Saleem that."

"Are you mad? There are things a woman should never tell her husband. That's what my mother taught me, anyway. But, tell me, Amal, is Boulos . . . you know what I mean?"

"No, I don't know what you mean, and even if I knew, I wouldn't be able to talk about such things. Not because I don't want to tell you, but I just can't."

"You're so good at getting things from me, but so hard to get anything from. Maybe you don't trust me."

"Oh, I trust you, but I can't talk about such things."

"Some day, when you've had a few children, you'll change."

"May Allah hear you!"

Amal's visits with Nahla provided even more than light conversation and easy friendship. On Nahla's coffee table, there was always a day-old newspaper that Saleem had brought home from work. He usually read it during lunchtime and brought it home for his wife to thumb through, then use as toilet paper.

The first time Amal saw the newspaper, she reached for it, curious about what people read daily. "My father can't read. So we never had a newspaper at home. I've never held one in my hands." She immediately began to read.

"I only read the headlines," Nahla jabbered. "I don't like to read about crimes in the city, or about Jewish bombings and their driving poor Arab farmers from their lands. I hear enough from Saleem to tear anyone's heart. I prefer this: *Majallet Hawwa*, Eve's Magazine. She took a magazine from the bottom shelf of her armoire and held it out for Amal. "Now this is entertainment!"

Amal, deep into an article by Khalil-il-Sakakini, did not hear a word Nahla said. She was moved by the plight of the Palestinians under the English Mandate and the threat of Zionist acquisitions of Palestinian farms.

"Don't waste your time on the miserable stories in there. Read this magazine instead. There, you'll find good jokes, stories of romantic love, advice to women on handling difficult mothers-in-law, reviews of Egyptian films, news about actors and actresses, singers, and all kinds of fun things. That's what you need, Amal. Not more misery than you already have."

"I'll read it, but I can't believe how beautifully this Sakakini writes. There's such power in his words. It's as though each word is wrenched from his heart. This is beautiful writing."

"Amal, you're so dramatic about his writing. I think you love misery. That's why you keep quiet about your troubles."

"This is different. Talking about my troubles is a waste of time—pointless. But here, the story is about injustices against a whole nation."

"Really. Amal. You should know that these are just stories to sell newspapers."

"And the magazines don't exaggerate?"

"They exaggerate to entertain us. Newspapers depress us."

"Well, I'd rather know the truth, even if it depresses me."

"I'd rather not know. There's one truth here and several

others there that makes me wonder. How we can know the whole truth, Amal?"

"You want to live with your head in the sand, like an ostrich?"

"Isn't that better than to live with a head full of problems and miseries?"

"I must be made that way." Amal folded the newspaper.

"Anyway, you can borrow any magazine anytime you want."

"Thank you, Nahla, but I'll just read here."

"I know. You're afraid of Boulos!"

"Why ask for more trouble?"

"I don't know why your family doesn't make him eat his own kharra. If Saleem ever raised a hand against me, my mother, an old widow, would get up an army of relatives to break his arms. And if they didn't, she'd take her old shoe and beat him on his head until he changed his ways. What's wrong with your family, anyway?"

"My father is full of his sense of honor. He doesn't want to have gossip around his family. My mother feels for me, but she's powerless against my father. So she prays for me, and the last time I complained to her, she gave me the Bible to read. And that's what I do—pray and read the Bible."

"You just stick to the Bible, and you'll have the calamities of Ayyoub."

"I just hope I have his faith. Remember Nahla, Job was saved by his unwavering faith in Allah."

"You and the Bible! May Allah pardon me! I have such a fool for a best friend."

CHAPTER 25

"AMAL, WAKE UP, habeebty. I have to give you a quick sponge bath before Doctore Jamayelle comes to see you."

I wake up, but have no idea if this is morning, afternoon, or evening. "Who's coming?" I ask, unsure that I heard right.

"Doctore Jamayelle. He wants to see how you're doing."

"Tell him not to come unless he can help me see."

"I'm sure he's going to help you. Hasn't he helped you so far? You feel better now, and you don't have as much pain."

"I still have pain in my head and heart, and my eyes are still curtained with a white veil."

"Everything will get better now."

"You promised to bring Khadeejeh here. I haven't seen her in a year."

"A year! Well, if you're good, I'll bring her after il doctore leaves."

"Swear by the ashes of your dead!"

"I swear by my father's ashes."

"I wish I could swear by my father's ashes, but he still breathes!"

"That's a sin to wish death on anyone, especially your own father."

"I don't care. I have no father."

"And how did you come into the world?"

"I rose from Wadi M'ali, the cesspool where all the mad come from."

"That's terrible, and a sin against Allah."

"I'm a sin all right and I married a jinn. I could write a stinking poem about that."

"Write a poem?"

"You don't know? I'm a famous poet."

"Really?"

"But I'm bad and condemned to Gehannem."

"How can you can be in Gehannem when I take such good care of you?"

"Where were you when he clobbered me last night?" I stop suddenly, realizing I shouldn't have said that.

"Who did?"

"Who did what? Why do you ask such strange questions?"

"Well, it's time to get your breakfast."

"Absolutely! A good breakfast, a delicious dinner, and a feast for supper, like the feast Shamiran had when she baptized her firstborn. See these hands! They made all the food. Poor unthanked hands! Everybody thanked the sharmootah, like I wasn't even there. Like I was invisible. Before my mother left, though, she hugged me and thanked me for all the work I had done, and Kareem was full of gratitude."

"Who's the bad woman that got all the thanks?"

"What bad woman? Why are you always bothering me with strange questions?"

"May Allah heal all the sick of the world." The nurse let out a sigh.

I decide to say something nice. "Allah has blessed your mother. He gave her the best daughter in the world."

"What a nice thing to say!"

"And when your mother felt she had enough peace and contentment, she sent you to me. You take such good care of me. I'll keep you—I just wish I could see you."

"Soon. Once you've eaten, I'll take you for another short walk in this corridor. You need to work your muscles."

"I can't walk."

"You're getting better and stronger with these daily walks. You'll surely lose your mobility lying in bed for months."

"What month are we in?"

"The end of September. You'll hear your friends harvesting the late olives in the back of this wall today."

"Let me sleep."

She leaves, and I feel drained. Sitt Marriam tends to me like a mother tending her child, but I can't help myself when she spouts off about Allah. I've had it with Him, and I lash out at her. Anger and fear swirl around in my head, and I just want to sleep . . .

From far away, I hear a man's voice, "Does she sleep during the day?"

"Sometimes, especially after she's been riled up about something or other. She becomes furious and screams, and then quiets down exhausted. Then she sleeps for an hour or so."

Now I know I'm awake. I know Sitt Marriam's voice, and the man with her is Doctore Jamayelle. She said he was coming to see me. I might as well keep my eyes shut and pretend to be still asleep.

"What about at night? Any disturbance?"

"It seems everything is fine, according to the notes the night nurse leaves on the chart. She says occasionally Amal cries and screams, begging someone to stop hurting her. She has nightmares."

"Does she ever mention names?"

"To me she's mentioned her sister, Shamiran. Once she mentioned some woman, Queen Hilaneh, and another time she talked about her best friend, Nahla."

"Has she ever said anything about men or her husband?"

"I don't remember anything about a husband."

"From now on, write down names you hear her say, and things you think are important. I have to construct her story and what really happened to her. She's a smart woman. Not much is known about her case other than she witnessed someone kill her husband, which caused her breakdown. She's been here nine years and hasn't recovered from the shock. That's strange."

"Doctore, it's hard to know what's important and what's not. Sometimes I swear she's saying something deep and sane, and the next second she's in a rage and doesn't know what she's said, or recall anything she's mentioned. She says the strangest things."

"Let's try to keep track."

"Amal," she calls, while gently shaking my shoulder, "Doctore Jamayelle is here to see you. Wake up!"

I moan and pretend to be coming back from a deep sleep. She shakes me again, calling my name.

"Akh, ya Immie! Aaay! Let me sleep. Why do you torture me?"

"Nobody would dare torture you! I'm Doctore Jamayelle. I won't let anything happen to you. Open your eyes. Let me see what they're like now."

"No, no, you'll hurt me."

"No, I won't hurt you. Just open them as wide as you can. There, you can open them nice and big. That's good."

I see a small flash of light in one eye, and then in the other, but can't see much else. Suddenly the light disappears, and he covers one eye.

"What do you see now?"

"A shadow."

"Good! Can you tell what it is?"

"Mini donkey."

"Now what do you see?"

"Two knives."

"Now how many?"

"Five!"

"Very good! Now what do you see?"

"Biscotte? . . . Chocolatta? . . . Donkey ears? . . . Donkey balls?"

I hear muffled giggles.

"Now let me examine your head and chest. Everything looks better, much better."

"It hurts all over. I'm in agony," I insist. "I don't want to go back to the ward. Not yet. Ask Sitt Marriam how much pain I feel. Medicine helps very little."

"But you're well enough to have the blue water removed from your eyes. There's a famous doctore Inglizi who'll do it."

I'm dumb with fear. Then he speaks to the nurse, "I'll call Doctore Boone and make an appointment for her. It may take a while, but she's ready for the operation."

"Operation? Never! No one will put a knife to my eyes."

"There's no knife. He'll just lift the blue water, and then you'll wear eyeglasses so you can see."

"I'm a good woman. Don't hurt me. I kiss your hands and feet! No knife!"

"Don't worry. There won't be any pain. Just listen to Sitt Marrriam and don't give her a hard time."

From now on, I'll be careful what I say and the names I drop in front of Sitt Marriam. I never thought she would remember a name I mentioned once, like the shaytaaneh, Hilaneh, or my best friend, Nahla.

Nahla. What a friend! What loyalty, what courage, and what a big heart. Whenever I suffered another thrashing, she comforted me, pumping into me courage and hope. She railed against Boulos and his mother, always invoking Allah to send them their due punishment. "Allah will one day smite them. Sooner than later, I hope!" she often said.

Oh Nahla, you'll never know how you sustained me in those years. You dared to entangle yourself in my life. You shredded the curtain that hid the wickedness of my tormentors. If only I had been wiser.

CHAPTER 26

FOR ALL THE FRIENDSHIP Nahla brought, Amal's world continued to grow darker.

In the first four years of marriage, she had not considered Boulos' occasional drinking to be a serious matter. Once in a while, he came home with a faint smell of arrack lingering on his breath. But, she thought, a man had a right to a drink, especially with friends, if he so desired. Who was she to stop him? During those evenings, she just tried to be invisible, lest he explode into a barrage of insults, smacking, and shoving.

In the four years that followed, he came home drunk at least once a week. She would keep her eyes lowered and head bent, afraid that one glance at him might ignite the rage within. He would eat nothing, throw his plate on the kitchen floor, and shout obscenities against her and the food she'd so carefully prepared. Quietly and silently she'd clean the floor and put everything away.

She would remain in the kitchen, out of his way, lest her mere presence provoked his demons and stoked his fury into another round of violence. Those times always left her too ashamed to see anyone, including Nahla.

But six years of friendship had forged loyalty and love for Amal in Nahla's heart, alongside hatred for Boulos and his mother. Every time Nahla heard Boulos' voice yelling insults and violent threats, she became more enraged. Amal's cries for mercy struck her like blows to her own body.

One such night, in the summer of 1947, residents of Jerusalem sweltered under the searing heat of the day and the smothering heaviness of the still night air. In the middle of that week, Amal's usual two-hour afternoon visit at Nahla's had been extended to five. Amal, realizing her house was as hot as the taboon, had given in to Nahla's insistence, but not without trepidation. Nahla's place on the first floor was a little more bearable.

"Oof!" sighed Nahla. "This weather makes me wish for a snow storm."

Amal glanced at her watch, then stood up. "I should go up and leave you take care of the children."

"Stay a while, at least until sundown. Besides, you can't cook in this heat."

"My supper is all ready. It only needs a little warming up when Boulos comes home."

"You're so efficient. Me, I refuse to cook when it's hot. I told Saleem to bring a watermelon and goat cheese and bread on his way home. The children love it, and Saleem is easy to please."

"I told you, he's one in a million."

"I guess so, but . . . well, life is never perfect."

"Still, I'd take a thousand like him before someone we both know."

In spite of Nahla's insistence, Amal could not risk staying past six o'clock. She never forgot the lessons in good manners her grandmother had taught her: "Visiting for more than two hours is not only a waste of time, but in bad taste. Your host won't kick you out, but you make her wish she could." Once, when Shamiran came home after sundown, her grandmother preached, "There's no thicker skin than that of the guest who doesn't know when to leave." Now Amal's training and, most of all, fear of Boulos fortified her resistence to Nahla's pleadings to stay longer.

For several hours, Amal sat on the threshold of her house, fanning herself with a piece of cardboard and drinking lukewarm water from one of the clay pitchers on her porch. She would wait for Boulos, whenever he chose to come home.

She could hear neighbors on all sides hauling mattresses, pillows, and sheets up to their rooftops or to their porches, where they spent the nights entertaining themselves until exhaustion claimed them, sometimes in the small hours of the morning. From one rooftop wafted idle chatter and gossip. From another came the rise and fall of voices full of sleep, droning in the warm air.

Weary and irritable, the men of the Old City argued heatedly about the outcome of the skirmishes with the Zionists, who were gaining more land. Some blamed the English for the problem; others blamed the Zionists or themselves for not being more effective in fighting back. Older heads cooled the heated arguments with their faith in Allah's wisdom and even-handed justice, "Allah knows best. He wouldn't allow such injustice to come to us. He would help us."

The younger men disagreed but politely deferred to their elders. The conversations shifted from significant to insignificant subjects. Late into the night and through such discussions, the women slept the sleep of the weary, and the children the sleep of the innocent.

Amal, however, sat listening to the men—their whisperings, murmurings, and sudden outbursts of laughter. Several times she jarred herself awake when her head suddenly nodded into her lap. She forced herself to remain awake until he came home; his supper was still in the pan, ready for warming up. Occasionally she went to the kitchen sink, and splashed a little water over her face and neck.

Around eleven o'clock, she heard the latch of the gate click open and footsteps shuffling against the stone floor. Instantly, she got up and stepped into the steaming kitchen to start the primos. She could hear Boulos mutter curses as he stumbled over the mattresses that Nahla had spread outside her threshold for her family's sleep-out. He managed to make it to the staircase. He gripped the railing as he struggled to haul his legs over the dozen stairs and into the steaming house.

From the kitchen, Amal could smell his arrack breath and, for a time, stayed put. Finally, she stepped into the doorway between the kitchen and the front room and, with trepidation, whispered, "Good evening."

As soon as she finished her salutation, he spun around to face her. His glowering visage told her trouble was coming.

Allah, be my succor in the hour of your wickedness. She quietly stepped down into the kitchen again. She thought it best to stay out of his way, and to keep busy warming up his supper. She did not dare ask him if he wanted to eat.

Then she heard him shout, "Come here, you donkey head! Come here," he shouted, his speech slurred.

She obeyed. Very quietly she stepped into the middle of the room. Fear invaded every fiber of her body. She saw him sitting on the divan, holding his head with both hands as if to steady it. His red eyes stared menacingly, and she was certain of having to pay again for another of his mother's vile fabrications.

"I said come here!" he roared.

She stood trembling. *What a night for a beating, and what a scandal with the whole neighborhood awake on their rooftops!*

Then, his voice falsely gentle, he patted the divan beside him. "Come and sit here."

No way out of this, whether I listen to him or not. She took small nervous steps and sat down, not knowing when or where the first blow would fall.

Slowly, he brought his left arm up and grabbed her long braid. He gave a sudden jerk to her head.

She gasped from the sudden pain. "Don't hurt me, I beg you, for Allah's sake. I've done nothing wrong, as Allah's my witness."

"You want to know what you've done, you head of stone? I'll tell you, after I've taught you how to listen," he shouted, tugging at her braid. His speech was slurred, his mouth frothing with anger.

"I always listen to you. I keep my mouth shut." She squealed at his painful tugging on her hair, and from panic at what was to follow.

"Shut your big ugly . . . mouth, you liar!" he snarled.

"I've never lied to you, I swear it!"

"Well, let's see," he said smiling maliciously, while pulling again on her braid. He asked as a mother would a child, "And how did you spend the day today?"

Weeping, she answered, her voice breaking with each tug of her hair, "I went to the market, cleaned, and made your supper. Please, stop hurting me!"

"That's all, ha?" his voice was full of malice.

"That's all," she sobbed.

"You need to be taught a lesson so you'll never lie to me again!"

His voice exploded, spewing ugly curses and insults as he yanked her braid with his left hand and, with his right, slapped hard at her face and head. "I'm going to make sure you've learned your lesson once and for all."

He got up pulling Amal's braid with him, while she twisted and screamed from the pain. Then he pummelled her wherever his fist fell.

Suddenly, he ceased his attack and pulled her braid away from him so that his face was only inches away from hers. His arrack breath added to the cloying atmosphere in the sweltering room.

"I . . . told you . . . a long time ago . . . a long time ago . . . not to visit with the neighbors downstairs. You didn't listen. You didn't know my mother has friends in the neighborhood!" He let out a loud cackle and shook his head as he released her braid. He tottered a few steps back and prepared to give Amal a final fist. At that moment Amal dropped down on the couch and his fist fell on the hard wood of the divan's hand rest.

He swore at the couch, at her, and at the whole world.

Exhausted, he flopped on the bed and soon passed out—fully dressed and with his shoes still on.

Amal remained curled up on the divan until she heard him snore. She struggled to stand up and dragged herself down the steps to the kitchen to wash her face and arms. She did not want to dry her face. She sat on the floor of her porch and leaned against the wall, facing the Old City that perched, unperturbed, on the terraced ridge of the Mount of Olives. The star-studded sky hung above the city like a jewelled canopy. The brilliant sky and tranquil city seemed to mock her sordid life and gloomy heart.

Amal gazed at the silhouettes of trees and steeples that seemed to kiss the stars, and she began to weep, her throat constricted with the pain and misery of her life. She felt completely abandoned, unworthy of motherhood, unblessed by love and dignity. Silently, she wept for her helplessness against this demon and his mother, and for all the black days yet to come.

So many thoughts whirled around in her head.

When will it end, O Lord? When? I'm afraid of what I might do if this continues. I can't take it anymore. Death is kinder than this life. Perhaps I should go to the Sisters of the Rosary. If I had the courage, I would take the bus to the city by the sea, to Yaffa. There I could work as a maid for some rich family and hope no one would ever find me. But I'm afraid of the world. Dreaming is easy. Acting on your dreams is another matter.

Sitty always said, "When Allah shuts a door, He opens a window." Well, You've shut both window and door against me. What do I have to do to earn Your blessing? How much longer, my Lord? How much longer do I have to wait?

Finally, overcome by exhaustion, she drifted slowly into sleep.

She awakened to the stillness of early dawn and could just

make out the dark outline of the church on the Mount of Olives as it rested against the deep blue-gray horizon. To the east, a band of deep purple grew and spread upward forming a fusion of small bands of pale hues—peach, pink, and orange.

She did not need another hot day to make her aching head and bruised body feel worse. Her head felt as if it were bound by bands of steel. The skin of her head felt sore against the lightest touch. Heart and mind numb, she wanted only to retreat into an eternal slumber.

She forced her weak legs to rise and to carry her aching body down the stairs to the outhouse, slowly and quietly, afraid of awakening Nahla and her family. She leaned against the railing for support. Then she struggled up the stairs again and, by force of habit, began to make coffee for her husband.

Suddenly, she grabbed a cup and filled it with coffee, as she had always done. She paused a few seconds, then sat down on the threshold and took a sip. She had never done that. The first cup was always for her husband, but as he slept, she finished it and refilled it four times.

When she saw that she had actually drunk the whole pot by herself, she felt shocked at first, then guilty, and finally exhilarated. The shock came from the realization that she had drunk coffee made for her husband. The guilt arose from her recognition of having committed an act of transgression. On the other hand, a new identity, a new sense of self-worth and courage rose to defend her against the guilt dragon. She felt as though someone who had been imprisoned within her had just been liberated, to stand by her, to fortify her against aggressors.

She tipped her cup over as Nahla had taught her and waited a minute before she picked it up, cradling it between her thumb and her fingers. She turned it slowly around, peering in to see what Nahla often saw in her cups.

There's a mountain I have to climb, but the road there is full of stones, small and large. I see someone else walking beside me. I can't tell if it's a friend or an enemy. With my luck, it's an enemy, but I'll get to the mountain, if it kills me.

With that silent reading of her cup, she sat for a full minute, smiling as she slowly turned the cup to find something else to boost her spirits.

Suddenly, she heard Boulos make his usual sound of awakening. "Is coffee ready?" he asked, his voice rough and scratchy. He tried to clear it with a series of coughs.

"Yes, but it got cold. I'll make you a fresh pot in a minute," she lied without a hint of guilt.

In the few minutes it took to make it, she felt something strange come upon her. She did not know what it was, but of one thing she was certain. She now had a sense—however vague—that she was a deserving person. The tide of fear had begun to ebb, and her heart felt a little lighter, her mind clearer. For the first time, she began to see herself as a worthy person, entitled to make a pot of coffee and drink it while her husband slept.

Then, when the coffee was ready, she poured the first cup for him and the second for herself. She sipped it in silence, feeling some kind of victory in her game of lies and hypocrisy.

Sitting in bed, he was shaking his head and rubbing his right palm. "I must have hit it against something hard, or slept on it," he said, as if to himself. Silence. "I don't know how I slept with my clothes and shoes on," he said, again as if to himself.

She remained silent.

When Boulos finished the pot of coffee he tried to get up. "Ya Allah!" He struggled to bring his legs from the bed and down to the floor. "I'm so tired and stiff. Help me take my shoes and socks off."

Warily, she approached the bed, unsure if his request was another trick to pounce on her again, or a sincere call for help. She untied his shoes and slipped them off. Immediately, a whiff of his sour, sweaty socks assaulted her. She bent her head down lest he should notice her contorted face and pursed lips as she tried not to breathe in the rancid odor. Quickly she removed his socks, scurried with them toward the doorway, and flung them to the farthest side of the porch.

"Ya Allah," he said again, as he limped to the kitchen.

May Allah blind your eyes and paralyze your arms!

While he splashed cool water on his face, neck, and arms, she quietly made another pot of coffee, and began to make his breakfast. He devoured it, as was his habit, then got up from the table and asked her for a change of clothes. "I have to leave very early today. Too much work."

She knew he would shower, as he often did in those sweltering days of summer, at his brother's house in Katamon. Leaving early, he would avoid the crowded bus and be able to return with Kareem in his new car.

"I'm going," he announced under his breath and left with his clean clothes in a paper bag tucked under his arm.

May you leave and never come back!

"Oh, I almost forgot. Your sister wants you to visit her on Monday to help her with a dress."

After he left for work, she was relieved to be alone again. She felt soreness in her head and arms. While she vacillated between the desire to sleep or do her daily chores, she slumped on the divan and drifted into sleep.

For the next two days, Amal remained in her home, and Nahla stayed away.

Early Monday morning, Amal got ready as soon as Boulos left for work.

On a few occasions, Shamiran would ask Boulos to bring Amal for a little help whenever the maid was sick. Although Amal could never refuse to help her sister, she was adamant against accepting her offer of money. Amid all the indignities in her life, she was determined to salvage one little sliver of her shattered pride.

Amal did not relish the thought of spending a whole day with her sister, which only stoked the smouldering coals of jealousy in her heart, but she dared not object. She would do anything to avoid Boulos' rage and blows.

Amal was content, even glad, to go alone. She had the same uplifting feeling she experienced in her daily outings to the market, where she haggled with the merchants. How proud she was whenever she thought she had struck a bargain and saved a few piastres. Those were precious piastres she kept, along with the Christmas and Easter gifts of money she received from her father and the secret gifts her mother on few occasions sent with Amal's youngest brother.

Whenever she saved enough coins, she took them to the market to exchange for a bill of half or one English pound, known as lira. These she tied it in a little handkerchief that she tucked inside the burlap lining covering the springs of the divan. She removed one of the tacks holding the backside and carefully slipped her small treasure inside. No one would ever turn her furniture upside down. Her little bundle was safe. And whenever Boulos sat on the divan, her trove safely under him, she felt pleasure and pride in deceiving him, and in having a secret all her own.

At seven o'clock that morning, before Nahla was up, Amal climbed down the stairs and tiptoed across the yard in front of Nahla's door. Gingerly she opened the front gate and closed it behind her.

The fear that had gripped her in her early days in Jerusalem was now replaced with the confidence of seasoned dwellers in the Old City's crowded labyrinth. Roaming its many souks and bazaars, she frequented the fabric shops, fingering the silk, muslin, or cashmere materials, dreaming of Sunday strolls with a loving husband.

Most of all, she cherished her secret visits to the Church of the Holy Sepulchre. In her first year of marriage, when Boulos took her a few times to Jerusalem's most holy church, she memorized the right and left turns into the intimidating and sooty arched, cobblestone alleys and souks that led to the Christian Quarter, where the church stood.

As soon as she came out of Jaffa Gate, she headed quickly toward the buses lined up along the city wall. She could see bus #4 to Katamon and hear the revving of engines. Half running, she worried that the bus would depart without her, leaving her to wait another twenty minutes for the next one.

She sat in the back of the half-empty bus. A short while later, the driver started the engine, and the bus whined and heaved out of its position, making a sharp turn to the left to go toward Katamon. She had begun to delight in the journey of twenty minutes all by herself.

Along the way, she watched the countryside with the keen interest of one seeing it for the first time. She gazed dreamily at the Sultan's Pool to her right, at the red-brown fields newly harvested, and the various patches of olive groves, some in the process of being harvested. Her mind wandered far away to those times when she picked olives from the trees in the back of their new house on the outskirts of Bethlehem. She remembered the pride she took in pickling huge jarfuls of olives to last the family a whole year.

She was so deep in reliving those days that she missed the stop nearest her sister's house. The bus driver's voice jarred her back to reality. "Sister, are you staying on the bus and going back to Jerusalem, or are you getting off here?"

She was shocked and embarrassed. She got up and walked to the front of the bus, and confessed, "I don't know how I missed my stop. I'm at least twenty-minutes' walk from where I should be."

"That's all right, sister. If you want to wait here a few minutes, I can drop you off wherever you want on my way back to Jerusalem." Then, as he got up to stretch his arms and legs, he uttered the common invocation to prayer: "In the name of Allah, the Beneficent, the Merciful!"

She realized the driver was Muslim. *Oh, my Lord! I've been sitting here all alone with a Muslim driver! What would people say if they were to see me?* She was filled with anxiety, although the chance that someone should see her was remote. A woman seen alone with a man, Christian or Muslim, is subject to gossip of the unsavory sort.

As soon as she recognized her sister's street, she got up. The driver stopped the bus, "With peace, sister."

Shamiran greeted Amal with the usual hug and kisses. She led her to the kitchen, where two children—Murad, six, and Elaine, four—sat at the table finishing their breakfast. Two-year-old Saleeba, born on September 27, the day Orthodox Christians celebrated *'Eed il-Saleeb*, the Feast of the Cross, was banging on his dish with his spoon and screaming excitedly at the sound he was making. Six-month-old George was propped up in his pram, cooing away.

Amal embraced the children and gave the oldest two a small chocolate bar and packet of chewing gum. The children screamed with delight, even though they had become accustomed to receiving such gifts.

"Is your maid here today?"

"No, I gave her the day off. She hasn't looked well of late."

"Where's our mother-in-law?"

"I talked a friend of mine into taking her as a companion for her mother, to spend the day in Yaffa. They own orange groves there. So Hilaneh couldn't say no to them. You know how she loves to associate with the higher class."

"Good. So what kind of material did you buy?"

"Oh, nothing so great. Just some woollen material. I thought it would be nice to have a new suit for the winter."

"Do you know what style you want?"

"I like some suits I've seen in *vetrinas*, in Jewish stores on Yaffa Street. But I haven't really decided on anything definite yet. We don't have to start on it right away. Let's have breakfast first, just the two of us. We never get to do that. That ghouleh Hilaneh is always here when you come with Boulos, and we never have time alone."

"How could we? My days are full of chores—going to the

market, cooking, cleaning, laundry, and the rest of it. I don't go anywhere except when Boulos brings me here. Even visits to our parents are few and far between."

"He doesn't take you out?" Shamiran sounded surprised.

"No. In the first year of our marriage, he took me to Yaffa Street twice, and to Cinema Rex once. That's all."

"That son of dogs! Kareem asked him several times to come with us and bring you along, when we went to Tel Aviv, or Tabariah, or Jericho. Each time Boulos said he was taking you someplace else."

"Oh, he went someplace else, for sure, but not with me."

"The bastard! He's no better than his mother. Both are dirty liars!"

"I never knew that's how you felt about them, especially Hilaneh."

"We've never had a chance to have a private minute to ourselves."

That's an excuse. You could've found time, if you'd really wanted to. Instead, she said, "You don't come down to the bazaars of the Old City to do your daily shopping. That would've given us a chance to visit once in a while."

"Grocery shopping isn't for me, and Hilaneh loves to do that. So she can shop, cook, and clean all she wants. I have enough to do with four children."

Amal asked, "I gather you're not fond of her?"

"Only an idiot would like a sow like her! Let's forget about her now and make some eggs with jambon. You look like you need to put some meat on your bones."

"I don't have much appetite these days. I'd like to get started on your new suit, because I have to be home before dark."

"Didn't Boulos tell you he's coming here and we're having supper together?"

"No, he didn't."

Amal became quiet, and noticing her anxiety, Shamiran asked, "Amal, why do you look so worried? You're not afraid of him?"

"Let's drop the subject."

"Well, then, let's have breakfast, then we can sit and enjoy a pot of coffee together. I'm even going to make your breakfast."

While Shamiran prepared breakfast, Amal played with her nephews and niece. She felt somewhat uneasy about the visit. The maid and Hilaneh were both gone and Shamiran was not all that interested in the new suit—the reason Amal was asked to come. Amal decided something was up.

"Now, let's have our coffee," Shamiran said as she carried the pot to the salon, followed by Amal with the cups.

"What are you making for supper?" Amal asked.

"I don't know. I have all kinds of vegetables and meat. We'll think of something."

They sipped coffee and Shamiran began to speak. "You know Amal, as your sister, I'm worried about how much weight you've lost in recent years. Our mother has mentioned many times how thin you look, and how quiet you are. She's worried about you."

"I was too fat. I feel lighter now."

"I've also noticed how you don't say much when you come for supper some Sundays."

"You remember how Sitty always preached about what goes on within the walls of your house must remain there. Well, I think it's better to keep quiet than to open the gate of troubles."

Shamiran continued to press her. "But are you happy? You

look so sad whenever Boulos decides to bring you here for supper."

"I don't know why he doesn't want to come every Sunday like before."

"He doesn't like to come as often ever since Kareem kicked him out of the Goodyear Store. You must know the story."

Suddenly, Amal's eyes opened wide, staring at her sister. "No, I never knew that! When did this happen?"

"About . . . oh, three months ago. Didn't he tell you?"

"He never talks about anything with me. Why did Kareem dismiss him?"

"It's a long story, and I don't know if I should tell you about it."

"Why is it nobody tells me anything? Why am I treated like an idiot!" Amal's voice revealed her anger.

"Don't say such things, Amal. I'll tell you what I know. The store was losing money, although sales were good. Someone was taking money from the till, and at first Kareem was sure it was the hired man. After grilling the employee, he found out Boulos was taking money from the till and leaving the store for several hours a few times a week. Of course, Boulos went into a rage and denied the accusations. Imagine the big liar! Of course, you know what he does now for a living."

"No, I don't," Amal responded, almost in a whisper, her face revealing her dismay.

"You don't? He never told you?"

"No. All I know is that a lot of things have changed in the last three months. He's been giving me less grocery money. About the same time, he stopped bringing me over for Sunday dinners, claiming he had a lot of work to do. I didn't believe him, but

I didn't argue. Even going to Bethlehem has stopped. It's been three months since we visited our parents."

"He now sells shirts, ties, socks, perfume, and wine."

"That explains the different fragrances on his shirt, and the alcohol on his breath. I didn't think too much of it at first, but lately, he comes home late at night, drunk."

"You should hear Hilaneh cry and plead with Kareem every night to give him back his job. But Kareem is so furious, he refuses to give him a red penny. He knows, though, that his mother gives the thieving bastard whatever he wants. Lately she's been asking for more money every week. Kareem knows she doesn't spend it all on herself."

"I haven't seen his stock of wine or perfume. Where does he keep his merchandise?"

"Oh, he keeps his stock at Kareem's office."

"I'm surprised he goes to Kareem's office."

"He has no choice. The dirty dog knows he's guilty and wants to stay close to his brother. Kareem knows Boulos is using him, but hopes someday Boulos will turn away from his bad ways. He goes there in the morning for breakfast and then takes his supplies and leaves. Before Kareem closes his office in the evening, he comes back to store them for the night."

"I think you know more than you're telling me. He comes home very late. He must go someplace else after work. I need to know the whole truth." Anxiety constricted her face and voice.

"I don't know, Amal. Kareem has never said more." She paused a moment then blurted out, "All I wanted was to ask you if he abused you physically."

Amal kept silent.

"Amal, does he beat you?"

"Why? Have you heard anything? You never asked before. Why now?" she asked accusingly.

"I know I should've asked before, but I've always been so busy or not well, with pregnancies and children and . . . "

"I know all about that. The time to intervene is gone. It's too late."

"No, Amal, it's not too late. He has to stop beating you."

"I never told you he beat me. How did you know?"

"I . . . I've heard."

"From whom?"

"From someone who cares."

"Mother?"

"No. She wasn't the first to tell me. After I heard from someone in your neighborhood, I went to Bethlehem and asked our mother if she knew anything."

"And?"

"She said she knew he occasionally hit you, and that she couldn't do anything because father said not to meddle."

"Did she tell you I told her about the first two beatings in the first six months of marriage, eight years ago?"

"What! Has he been beating you since your wedding?" Shamiran's shock was visible.

"Did our mother tell you she gave me the Bible to read her favorite psalms, and told me to avoid anything that might trigger his temper?" Amal asked bitterly.

"No."

Amal looked directly into her sister's eyes. "You must've at times guessed something was wrong. You could've asked why I looked so miserable."

Shamiran hesitated then tried to explain, "I noticed sometimes you were too quiet, and thought maybe you're not happy because . . . because you couldn't get pregnant. But now, I'm sorry, my sister. You know I was pregnant from my wedding night and was always sick during my pregnancies. Then, you know, four children in eight years have sapped all my energies and attention, and . . . but we have to put a stop to him. That bastard and his sharmootah of a mother! How can two brothers be so different?"

"Just one of life's mysteries."

"Maybe it's a good thing you can't have . . . " She stopped abruptly, not wanting to add to her sister's grief.

"Children? Well, maybe if I was able to have children, he might have become a responsible family man. Or his mother might have left me alone."

"Hilaneh will carry her anger to the grave. And I hope sooner rather than later. She never wanted either one of us for her sons, and that's killing her. She resents me because Kareem worships the ground I walk on. She doesn't dare say one word to me, because she knows Kareem will put her out the door."

"What I want to know is when did you find out he beats me."

"Oh, a little while ago."

"Then I know who told you. There's one person only who cares enough to tell you. Let's stop talking about my problem. I'm convinced misery follows some people from the cradle to the grave, and I'm one of those. So I beg you not to breathe a word to Kareem."

She paused, then garnering enough willpower to sound high-spirited, asked, "Anyway, why don't we start making supper early?"

"Why don't you sit and play with the children, and I'll do the cooking?"

Amal looked at her sister with mischief in her eyes. "You're cooking? I hope you have enough Alka Seltzer in the house!"

"Oh, I do. But we won't need it." Seconds after, she added, "With you coaching me, I might surprise Kareem."

Amal smiled. She could not remember a time when she felt such warm kinship with her sister. Shamiran's genuine caring endowed Amal with the will to endure her miserable life and withstand the news of Boulos' dishonesty. After the sisterly talk with Shamiran, Amal's heart felt a little lighter, her head clearer, and her spirits a little uplifted.

CHAPTER 27

"WAKE UP, AMAL. It's dinner time." Sitt Marriam stands at my bedside and shakes my shoulders. "You need to get up and walk a little, go to the washroom, and then you'll be ready for dinner."

"Yes, I need to get strong to fight my enemies."

"You have no enemies here. You're among friends."

"Nahla told me I have to be strong to fight my enemies."

"Who's Nahla? I don't know any Nahla here."

You think I'm going to tell you about Nahla so you can tell il doctore, and then dig into my past! "Nahla lives here," I tell her, pointing to my head. "She talks to me sometimes and makes me laugh."

"What does she tell you to make you laugh?" she asks while helping me walk from my bed to the corridor.

Snooping again. You think you're smart. Ha!

"She tells me there are snakes and scorpions crawling around me. Oh, there's one snake there! Look over there! It's all curled up in the corner."

"I don't see a snake anywhere. And you can't see a snake either, not with the blue water over your eyes!"

"I can see just the same."

"How would you like to sit for a while? You're well enough to sit in a chair now, and that will make it easier to take a few walks each day."

"I want to sleep."

"If you sleep now, you'll miss your dinner."

"I want to see Khadeejeh."

"You be a good girl and I'll bring Khadeejeh after you eat."

"I'm a good girl. Always good. Never bad."

She leaves, the sweet soul, and I sit and feel like always, triumph and guilt for the way I treat her. I have to do what I have to do. Protecting myself is first and foremost. Nahla was right. I should've done things to help myself earlier, instead of living with my misery. Now, I'm sure, I would have found the courage to get out of my hell. But what good is it to know this now?

The good nurse is back with *mujaddarah*, some olives, and salad. She helps me eat.

"Enjoy it. Sahtaine!" Double good health.

"Ya habeeby, how delicious!"

"Im Issa makes the best food for you."

Keep humoring me. "My stomach is so full. Thanks to you and to Im Issa. Now, you'll bring Khadeejeh?"

"But she can't stay long. She has to help finish the olive harvest today. When they get to this side, you'll be able to hear them."

"I love picking olives and pickling them. Do you know how to pickle olives?"

"My mother used to do it when I was little, but she's too old now, and I have no time to learn to cook."

"Khadeejeh will teach you to pickle olives."

"That's nice. Now sit here and wait for me."

After a while, the door suddenly opens, and two shadows slowly glide in, wanting to surprise me, I know. "Ghosts!" I scream. "Help! Help!"

"Amal, don't scream. It's only Khadeejeh and me. If you scream, the orderlies will come and take Khadeejeh away."

"Kadeejeh, habeebty, come here, let me touch you."

She comes rushing and, in her village dialect, says, "You don't know how long I've been waiting to see you. I miss you."

She bends down to kiss me. "You must get better and come back to me, to all of us," she says, and I try not to breathe in that sweaty odor.

"Allah kareem, Khadeejeh."

"Sitt Marriam brings you good food. Soon you'll come out."

I don't want to tell her I don't want to come out until I've figured out how to deal with the ghosts that haunt me.

"Habeebty, you must get better soon," Khadeejeh insists. "I'm waiting for you to start teaching me to read. You promised."

"I know."

"Immie is bringing me paper and pencil next time she comes."

"Did you tell her why?"

"Of course! I think she was a little happy and a little sad about it. First she smiled a big smile and asked, 'Who told you that?' and when I told her the voices in my head did, she slapped her leg and said, '*Ya harram alaiky!*' and she went on slapping her leg while she rocked back and forth. My poor mother! She smiles one minute and weeps the next. I think she's not right in her head."

"When is she coming to see you again?"

"I don't know. Soon. Very soon."

"Is Sitt Marriam still here?" I whisper to her, knowing well she's around. She wouldn't leave Khadeejeh here alone.

"Yes, she's writing in her book," she whispers back.

She must be writing down what we say so she can tell il doctore. I'll give her something to write about!

"So, Khadeejeh, what do you see and hear in the kitchen?"

"I see and hear Im Issa, the big vixen."

"Tell me what she's been doing and saying lately."

"Open your ears big and hear this. This is the truth or may Allah paralyze my tongue."

She clears her throat a few times to get ready for her famous imitation of Im Issa. She's funniest when she tries the dialect of Jerusalem. I'd howl if I could when she squeaks, forcing her throat to sound the softer and longer vowel sounds.

"I'll speak in Sitt Marriam's dialect and Im Issa's and you'll know who's saying what. I was on kitchen duty. I sat near the door picking little stones and straw from the rice, when Sitt Marriam came back with the tray Im Issa prepared for your dinner.

"'Allah reward your hands and your good heart, Im Issa.'

"'And reward you, too, Sitt Marriam, and heal your cousin. Is she better?'

"'Better, but she has a long way yet to be able to function on her own and return to the ward. She still has bad headaches and blue water on both eyes.'

"'What a pity! Oh, the troubles of this life!' Then she let out a long sigh, and leaned her head closer to whisper to Sit Marriam, and I leaned my head closer to catch everything.

"'Sitt Marriam, my daughter has been suffering from very bad headaches for a year now. I don't know what to do for her.'

"'Aspirin is what we give for headaches. Has she taken any?'

"'Sometimes, when there's extra money after feeding her seven children. You know how it is.'

"'Does the aspirin help?'

"'A little, the poor thing. She sometimes holds her head and screams from the pain and says her head is ready to explode.'

"'Has she seen a doctore?'

"'What doctore, Sitt Marriam! She doesn't have the heart to spend her children's food money, and I don't make enough here to help her.'

"I started to mumble to myself, as I always do, and then glanced at Sitt Marriam and caught her giving Im Issa a wink. A little later, I was mopping the floor, when Sitt Marriam came back. I turned around so I could see their faces. And do you know what I saw?"

"What?"

"Im Issa was standing with her back to the kitchen workers, and Sitt Marriam stood facing her. I saw her put her closed right hand right into Im Issa's hand. She said, 'Im Issa, you must buy her the stronger kind of aspirin and tell her to take one or two at a time. Maybe that will help her.' Then she left.

"No one else saw that. She's clever, that Sitt Marriam. Maybe they fooled everyone there, but they can never fool me. I'm Khadeejeh, soon-to-be-bride of a prince. I see like a hawk, and I hear like a cat, and like a snake I crawl, sure of my way. I don't bite, you know. But I'm sure of what I hear, when I hear something."

"I know you do. You're very good."

"But you didn't laugh at the story as you always do."

"Oh, it's a very funny story. I'd laugh if I could. I have a big headache today, Khadeejeh. You were very funny, like always. Come again, Khadeejeh, when I don't have a headache. Now I want to sleep."

"All right, habeebty. Sleep, sleep now."

"Yalla, Khadeejeh, we have to go now and let her rest. You'll see her again," Sitt Marriam tells her gently.

Soon the nurse returns. "You must've liked the story she told. She has the best imagination of anyone I know."

"You mean anyone in beit il-majaneen?"

"That's what people call it, but it's a hospital for the mentally ill."

"It's a hospital that drives people mad and blind."

"And on that subject, I have good news for you. Doctore Jamayelle called to tell us he spoke with Doctore Boone, who's going to try to schedule you within the next month or so. Late October or early November, you're going to the Hospital for Ocular Diseases in Jerusalem. You'll be able to see again."

Suddenly, I'm in the claws of that monster of fear. I never thought I would ever have to face that dreadful city again. I'm in such a panic that my whole body is shaking, and I begin to cry out loud, "I don't want to go there. I beg you, don't let them take me there. I'll die there. I'll die." I don't know where all the tears and the sobbing are coming from. Never did I expect I would go hysterical at the thought of going back to Jerusalem.

Sitt Marriam tries to comfort me. "You don't have to go if

you don't want to. If you want to stay blind, though, it will not be an easy life. Soon you're going to be well enough to return to the ward and live like the rest. Who's going to take care of you there?"

"I don't want to go to Jerusalem, city of thieves, torturers, murderers . . . "

"Why? It's not any worse than any other city."

"You know nothing."

"Well, you're only going to the hospital for a few days, then you're coming back here."

"Why can't il doctore come here?"

"They don't have the equipment they need here. There, they have the best hospital and the best doctore."

"The best hospital in the worst city."

"It's not all bad. It's got a bit of everything, the good and the bad. Who knows but you'll meet some good people there."

"I don't want to meet anybody there. I like it here. It's where I want to be. It's my *baladdie*." My town. And the only one I would want to see is Nahla, but who knows where she is now!

CHAPTER 28

AMAL'S LATEST ORDEAL had strengthened Nahla's will to tread the dangerous waters to help her poor friend. She had gathered enough courage to abandon her promise to her mother and to defy her husband's wishes. She wanted to help her best friend, to arm her with terrible secrets that could defend her against the abuses of her husband and mother-in-law.

The morning after Amal had visited her sister, and after Saleem left for work, Nahla hurried upstairs carrying a pot of coffee.

"Good morning, Amal. How are you?"

"Thank Allah, still alive," Amal answered in a subdued voice.

"Look, Amal, there has to be an end to this abuse. Stop pretending everything is fine. I haven't slept well since he beat you a few days ago. I wanted to see you after, as I usually do, but I was worried when I didn't see you all day Monday. You have no idea of the horrible thoughts that crossed my mind. Where were you?"

"Shamiran asked for my help with a dress."

"I'm curious why he beat you this last time."

"Oh, he came home so very late and drunk."

"Amal, don't hide things from me. I overheard him shouting about visiting neighbors."

"Well, then, you know why. I never wanted to hurt your feelings. I was warned from the very beginning not to visit you or any neighbor. How he found out baffles me."

"Yesterday I discovered how. It seems Hilaneh recently visited old Im Hanny and questioned her about what she thought of you. The poor woman spoke well of you and told her you only went to the market, and visited with me every afternoon. She told me so herself."

"But why they don't want me to visit with you is beyond me."

"I know why. Boulos and his mother want you kept in the dark about their past."

"What past?"

"A past that will help you defend yourself against mother and son."

"What 'past'?"

"A powerful weapon! What you'll hear now will be sweeter than Ja'phar's pastries. First thing, Hilaneh is a *real* sharmootah."

"What do you mean?"

"Exactly what the word means."

"You don't mean she goes with . . . ?"

"Yes, with men or with one man, what's the difference? She's a bad sort."

"I can't believe it! She must be in her fifties, too old for such things."

"You make me laugh. You should read my magazines instead of the newspapers. You'd learn a few things. You're so smart in so many ways, but when it comes to men and women, you're really naïve!"

"And how do you know about her past?"

"Don't ask how. I don't want others dragged into this."

"Tell me what you know."

"I'll start by saying that Hilaneh couldn't have had enough when her husband was alive. Don't forget my mother raised us here when Hilaneh lived upstairs. Figure it out.

"There must be at least ten years between Kareem and Boulos. Just think. The father worked hard from four in the morning to eight at night. He limped home every night, my mother said. And he was fifteen years older than Hilaneh. She wanted more than she was getting."

"How's this going to help me?"

"Just be patient and listen! My mother told me how Hilaneh always tried to pass herself off as superior to most. When her husband was still alive, she used to go to the bakery to help him from ten in the morning until four in the afternoon. She was very attractive then, always dressed up in bright colors and tight-fitting clothes. Her cheeks were always smeared with pink, and her eyes lined with kohl. My mother and all the other women in the neighborhood thought she looked cheap.

"Ten years later, when Boulos was born, she hated staying home with him. Three days a week she would wrap him up and take him with her to the bakery. What a good woman, my mother thought, until one day when she left the house right after

Hilaneh, to do laundry for a wealthy family in the Old City. My mother was surprised to see Hilaneh some little distance in front of her, walking briskly in the opposite direction from the bakery. At first, she thought that perhaps Hilaneh had some errands to run before going to the bakery. But soon she found out something that disturbed her. At the end of Khan il- Zeit, Hilaneh turned left and soon entered a textile shop.

"When my mother walked in front of the shop, she saw a tall, handsome young man with blond hair and green eyes, standing at the counter and talking to a younger man of about sixteen. But there was no sign of Hilaneh. My mother thought she had imagined seeing her enter the shop. She continued on her way to work and returned in the early afternoon. As usual, she saw Hilaneh return at four o'clock, the baby in her arms, and in one hand a cloth bag full of groceries and fresh bread from the bakery. Now and then she gave my mother a day-old loaf of bread. My mother appreciated any gift of food, since she had to raise us with the little money she made from being a washerwoman.

"Anyway, the following week, my mother decided to leave right after Hilaneh, not so much to spy on her, you know, but to ease the nagging suspicions about her neighbor's character. Again, she saw Hilaneh enter the same shop and disappear from sight. From that moment, my mother's opinion of the good mother and wife quickly vanished. In its place grew a suspicion of the most wicked and unspeakable kind—Hilaneh was a fallen woman, a sharmootah!

"After that day, my mother had nothing to do with her. She needed no further proof of Hilaneh's infidelity as Boulos grew up. He resembled neither parent. Perhaps my mother was the only one who knew whose seed Boulos came from. Whenever

Boulos ran down the stairs to play with my brother, she made the sign of the cross and mumbled, 'in the name of the cross.' She preferred not to have him play with my brother but didn't have the heart to stop him.

"When Boulos was four, my mother noticed a change in Hilaneh's character. She became ill humored, always screaming at little Boulos, with or without reason. Sometimes, she called out to him, 'Come here, you seed of the Shaytaan!' She looked unhappy and angry, and didn't take care of herself as before. My mother suspected the source of her unhappiness was in that textile shop, and her curiosity got the better of her.

"One day, on her way to work, she stopped at the textile shop under the pretence of buying material. She found some excuse to refuse every kind of material the old man brought down for her. 'The young man that was here gave me a better price for the same material. I'll come back when the young man is here,' she told the old man.

"'That's my nephew,' the man told my mother. 'He's in Istanbul taking care of business there. He's going to be there for a long time.'

"My mother was then sure of the reason for Hilaneh's unhappiness but felt sorry for her husband, who had no idea his wife was a tramp and his beautiful son, the seed of a Turk. I'm so sorry, Amal, but Boulos has no Christian blood in him, although he was baptized, and he's a bastard, on top of that.

"Boulos grew up to give her plenty of trouble, at school and on the streets. He went around with a gang of wild boys. They swore, stole, and fought often. And when he turned thirteen, she dragged him to a special school for troubled boys in Ramallah and left him there.

"Four years later, the teachers had had enough of his wild behavior and language and expelled him. He never learned a trade and became a street swaggerer, strutting the streets of this city like a peacock, proud of his good looks, unwilling to work for a living. And why should he? His mother now kept his pocket full, against the will of Kareem, who argued often with her about the way she was ruining him."

Nahla stopped and looked at Amal, who had kept silent throughout. Nor had her face shown either satisfaction or displeasure.

"Amal, now you have the weapon to make him and his mother your slaves."

Amal remained quiet and expressionless, as though she'd heard nothing.

"Say something, Amal. Aren't you at least surprised to hear their story?"

"I'm shocked, but I don't know how this story is going to help me."

"You don't? Well, maybe this next bit of information will make it plain. You can make Hilaneh grovel to you with what you know. Blackmail, my dear Amal."

"With my luck, it will backfire on me, Nahla."

"This is your chance to do something, instead of sitting and taking it, Amal. Allah said, 'Walk and I'll walk with you. Knock and you shall find.'"

"All right. Let me hear it."

"First, I must explain to you how this wonderful surprise has come about. And you must swear by the Gospel not to repeat a word of what you've heard and what you'll hear."

"Of course I would never repeat a letter of it, and I do swear by the Gospel."

"Here it is. Aida had mentioned a little while back that on one of her trips to Yaffa with Ed, she saw Hilaneh in a café sitting next to a man of distinguished appearance, dressed in a dark suit and a fez. They appeared to be at ease with each other as they engaged in conversation, smiles, and laughter.

"When Aida told me that, I jumped. I asked her to take pictures if she spotted Hilaneh and the man again. I explained the reason and she agreed to help. Now I'm waiting for the proof and your victory. Aida promised she would go again to the same café. So very soon you'll be lifted from the abyss to the top of Mount of Olives."

"It sounds all too good to be true, but I'm not sure I'm up to such battles."

"Oh, you will be and you have to be. You can't wait until he finishes you."

"Let's see what happens when the pictures get here."

CHAPTER 29

I HEAR THE BELL RING and there's quite a commotion out there. They must be lining up for supper.

This has been one of the longest days. I wanted to sleep, but it wouldn't come. If only I could enjoy the sleep of babies—dreamless, colorless, and soundless. If only I could go back in time and rewrite my dark story. But "if only" are the sorriest words I've come to know. My whole life has been dreaming, wishing, and praying, and look where that's got me! Nothing good has come to me. Why should it now?

I hear the door open, and I shut my eyes quickly. I hear Sitt Marriam's gentle voice, "Amal, wake up. I brought you supper."

I pretend to be groggy, waking from a deep sleep. "You brought me Salome's head on a platter?"

"Now what have you been dreaming about?"

"A sow's head cooked in sauce."

"Ugh!"

She must have decided against continuing a stupid conversation with a cantankerous mad woman. She says, "I brought you soup and rice."

"What? Is that the food you feed to the daughter of princes?"

"Soup is good for the daughter of princes and the daughter of beggars. It's made with marrow bones, full of nourishment. Let's hurry up. I'm running late. I still have to go back to Jerusalem. My mother will worry when it's dark and I'm not home."

After I eat, she walks me to the bathroom, then helps me into bed, gives me aspirin and water, and tucks me in. She hurriedly recites the Lord's Prayer in Syriac. I am content to hear her say the prayer, but can't bring myself to say it, not silently or aloud. She bids me good night and I start to sing the way people in Bethlehem do, "*We're going to Jerusalem to learn the dialect of city folks, but then return to Bethlehem where people would laugh at your new dialect.*"

She laughs, "Be good now, or I won't bring you a special dessert."

"Kenapheh!"

"If you're good!"

"Go to sleep now, and I'll see you in the morning." She shuts the door behind her.

Alone in bed, my mind wanders back to Jerusalem and Nahla. I wonder where she is now, and what she looks like. Does she think about me? Does she still love me? She visited me twice in the first six months after I was brought here. Nothing ever stays the same. I thought she might visit me, even once a year. But then, why should she, when my own mother hasn't come once? I feel a lump in my throat and I weep.

Oh, Nahla, we were better than sisters. You put your neck on the line for me. You brought shafts of sunshine into the dark pit I was in.

For three weeks after Boulos had beaten her and her visit with Shamiran, Amal lived in relative peace. Boulos left early in the morning and returned late at night, around eleven o'clock or midnight. Without even a glance at her or a word, he would undress, throw his clothes on the divan, and go to bed. He filled the room with the pungent smell of arrack. Occasionally, he would order her in his slurred speech to serve him supper. She hoped the food would choke him. To herself she thought, even the Shaytaan doesn't want him!

Now that the weather had turned cooler, she saved the suppers he did not eat for the next day. "Waste is a sin," her grandmother had drilled into her. She was raised to believe in the sanctity of bread and food. She often recalled her grandmother's wrath if she saw a crumb of bread on the floor. "This," she used to rage, "is like the bread of communion, the body of Christ!" Fortunately, Amal liked leftovers—she thought food tasted better the second day. Often, she would offer some to Nahla, who could never resist Amal's cooking.

In spite of the relative calm, Amal felt uneasy. Tremors of anxiety were part of her life, but those three weeks were darkened by anxiety over Shamiran's possible meddling. She hoped she wouldn't rue the day she had told her sister about Boulos' violence. Nahla's footsteps on the porch interrupted her dark thoughts.

Nahla appeared in the doorway, hardly able to contain her excitement. "Look at this fortune!" she whispered, waving an envelope in front of Amal's face.

"What is it?"

"The pictures, silly!"

"Let me see them," she said as she grabbed the envelope from her hand. She ripped it open and took out the five pictures. She stared at them, her body rigid.

Finally, Nahla asked, "What do you suppose we do with these?"

"These are my passport to freedom land." Amal raised them above her head and praised Allah for finally giving her something to deliver her from the present.

"What are you going to do now?"

"I must think of a plan, a strategy, before Hilaneh decides to come."

"Why wait? Call your sister now and ask her to send Hilaneh over."

"I don't want to involve Shamiran."

"Just tell her you have something here for Hilaneh."

"That might work."

"It will work. Go down right now to the grocer, give him a piaster, and call your sister."

"Oh, I'm shaking. I'm afraid. I'll wait until I've had time to think this through."

"Amal, you should be more afraid of the next time Boulos bashes your head against the wall. Don't be a coward. Be a tiger, Amal. When we were young, my mother taught us to break the arm that's raised against us. Sometimes it's the only way to survive. Go, Amal. Allah's with you!"

Amal grabbed her purse and headed for the shop. She asked the grocer to dial the number for her. Flustered and trembling, she lost her thought and tongue when he handed her the phone.

Her heart nearly stopped when she heard Hilaneh's imperial voice. "Allo, who's speaking?"

Amal froze. When she heard Hilaneh repeat the question, Amal tried to control her agitation before speaking. "Wife of my uncle, can you come over tomorrow?"

"Why? I'm too busy tomorrow," Hilaneh replied sharply.

Amal felt her courage trickle back. "I have something important to show you."

"What's so important that can't wait until next week?"

"It's something you'd want to see now." Amal began to feel the power surge in her veins.

There came a pause before Hilaneh answered. "Listen here. I have no time to waste. But maybe I can stop for a minute this afternoon, before I visit an old friend. It better be important."

"Oh, it is. Good-bye, wife of my uncle."

When she hung up the phone, she felt blood rush to her face. The triumph she felt was tainted with fear.

She rushed back to Nahla. Her friend would be proud of her, but how would she handle the termagant Hilaneh! "Nahla, she's coming this afternoon, but I haven't planned how to approach the subject. I should have thought of all the details before I called."

"Stop panicking! Remember, you bear the sword, and she's your hostage. Tell her exactly how you feel—the beatings, the insults, and the misery you live under. If she doesn't cooperate, then hold the pictures for her to see. That'll give her a heart attack."

"I'd better plan what I have to say. She could be here in an hour."

"Remember," Nahla said, "you hold the sword."

Sitting on the divan, Amal felt her courage ebb and the tide of fear advance. She regretted agreeing to the plan. What was I thinking, she wondered, to throw myself into the slimy green waters of the pools of King Suleiman, when I don't know how to swim!

While standing in front of the mirror, she tried several approaches to explain her position. An hour later, she heard Hilaneh's footsteps on the stairs. Her heart beating hard, Amal walked to the threshold. "Ahlan wa sahlan, wife of my uncle," she greeted her, kissing her on both cheeks. *The kiss of Yehuda I give you, Shaytaaneh.*

Hilaneh narrowed her eyes and pursed her lips before she spoke, "What's so important that you had to disturb me at home?"

"Why don't you sit down before we talk?"

"I don't have time to visit. Just tell me what you want and I'll be on my way to visit a friend."

Although Amal was stung with Hilaneh's imperial manner, she reminded herself that she held the sword. "I'll start by telling you that your son has made a mop out me, beating me for no reason, bruising me, and threatening to kill me. Here, touch this spot."

"What do you want me to do about it? It's between you and him."

"No, it's between you and me. You have to tell him to treat me like a human being, as a wife should be treated."

"Is this the very important thing you brought me here for?" Hilaneh started toward the door. "I have better things to do."

Amal held out the pictures. "And what about these? Are these important enough for you?"

Hilaneh froze as she stared at the photos. Slowly she walked back, snatched one of them from Amal's hand, and sat in a chair. "What's this? Whose pictures are they?"

"Look closer. Don't you recognize the man and the woman?"

"Is this a joke?"

"No, don't you recognize yourself and your man-friend?"

"Shut up, ya kalbeh! How dare you talk to me like that?"

"Because I've had enough. Maybe you'd like me to show them to Kareem. He has good eyesight."

"Give me the pictures, or I'll tell Boulos to finish you."

"Here, you can have them. I have the negatives and many more pictures. And before you have the chance to talk to Boulos, I'll have them in a few hands."

Hilaneh's eyes blazed, but her shoulders slumped and her hands shook. "Alright. I'll talk to him about his behavior, but you have to give me all the pictures and negatives."

"I can't, but I promise you this: no one will ever see them, as long as you make him stop beating me, and give me the respect a wife should have, and enough money to live on."

"What does he give you now?" she asked, her voice subdued.

"Four shillings a week. He thinks I can live on air and water. I'm finished with the old life. I want something better. I want to be treated better. And if he raises his hand against me again, I swear to you, Gehannem will fling its gates open, and the raging flames will burn whoever is responsible, you included."

"All of a sudden you have the mouth to threaten me. You have no manners, no respect for your elders. Shame on your upbringing!"

Hilaneh held her tongue for a few seconds, then said, "I'll do all I can. I'll talk to Boulos. If he doesn't give you enough money, let me know, and I'll give you what you need. I'll come here once a month and take care of things. But whatever you do, don't call me at home. No one is to know of this."

"As long as you keep your word, no one will ever know."

"Tell me one thing. How did you get hold of these pictures?"

"I can't tell you." Feeling her newfound power, Amal looked Hilaneh in the eye. Hilaneh flushed, then turned on her heels and stormed out.

Amal wiped the perspiration from her face. She stood before the mirror and scrutinized herself. She saw the reflection of a stranger—someone taller, a sparkle in her eyes, a triumphant smile on her lips, and confidence in her demeanor. Yet, apprehension fluttered in her heart. She was in unfamiliar territory now.

She turned away and sat down, feeling as though she had been transported to a strange place with no compass to guide her. Fear and agitation mingled with quiet satisfaction. Suddenly, she got up and went downstairs to Nahla's. She needed her friend's approval and applause. "Nahla, I can't believe I did it!"

"I told you, you could do it. All you needed was a weapon." They embraced and kissed each other.

CHAPTER 30

I'M SLUMPED IN THE CHAIR next to my bed. Life isn't worth the effort it takes to breathe, I figure. From outside these walls, I hear the occasional swearing and screaming of the inmates. Now and then, I hear the orderlies yelling at the poor women, as if yelling or shoving could fix mangled minds or broken hearts.

I sit up at the sound of the doorknob turning. Sitt Marriam walks in and fills the room with her cheerful voice.

"Well, look at her, sitting in the chair, strong and straight, like she's ready to tackle the world."

"You're hallucinating again!" I tell her.

"I brought your lunch and a surprise."

"I'm thrilled."

"You should be."

"Go away," I tell her, flicking my hand toward the wall.

She humors me like a mother soothing her sick child, "I

brought you *mujaddara bi ruz*, and green olives on the side. I know you like lentils with rice."

"I'd like it with salad—lots of tomatoes, cucumber and onions, lemon juice and olive oil. That helps to swallow the dry mujaddara."

"Next time. Now this is what we have."

"And the surprise?"

"After lunch."

Afterward, she asks me to open my mouth for the last bite, and I taste the sweet kenapheh.

I can't help thinking how sweetness is so short-lived, be it food or good fortune. That's how my life has been.

Alone the day after Hilaneh's visit, Amal wondered if her mother-in-law had prevailed in reining in her son.

As she stood in the kitchen making the midday meal, she heard Boulos' footsteps on the stairs. He walked into the room, tossed his suit coat on the bed and asked in a voice that had lost its gruffness, "Where are you?"

"Here," she replied in a monotone.

That was the first time in eight years of marriage that his wife did not rush to greet him. He sensed the change in her behavior but decided to ignore it. "What's for lunch?" he asked, as if nothing had happened.

"Fried zucchini and baba ghannouj," she answered.

"You know I don't like that."

"I'm making it for me. I didn't know you were coming back."

"This is my house, I will come and go as I please."

"That's fine, but I can't cook and throw food away. You

are often not here and I have little enough money as it is for groceries."

Boulos paused. He was not used to her answering in that steady, unapologetic voice. "You don't need money when I stay away."

"I need to eat," she answered calmly.

He took a few steps and stood in the kitchen doorway, "Since when have you learned to talk this way?"

She ignored his question and continued cooking.

"Look at me when I talk to you. Answer me! Don't stand there like a wall."

She turned her head to look at him and, in a steady voice, said, "Since the last time you laid hands on me. The *last* time."

"Looks to me like your tongue has grown a foot since then. It needs trimming," he threatened, though his voice had lost its pugnacity and razor-edge tone.

"I'm answering your questions."

"Stop what you're doing and come here. I have something to settle with you."

She had made her point and believing that his mother must have talked to him, she rinsed her hands and stepped into the room. In the past she'd stood waiting for the storm, her body trembling inside and out. Now, without a tremor, she sat in the chair facing him.

"From now on, I am away from Sunday until Friday night. Then I leave again Sunday morning. I will do as I please. I'm the master of my house. I'm the one who feeds you and houses you. I and no one else."

She continued to watch him, her face expressionless, her eyes fixed on him, as though she had not heard a word. Inside, she felt the reverberations of confidence.

"You should bow, kneel, and kiss my feet every day of your life, and do you know why? Because I married you and saved you from becoming a spinster. I had, and still have, hundreds of beautiful young women running after me. Beauty queens—Arab, Armenian, Jewish—I could have my pick. But your father knew what he was doing, that fox! Kareem couldn't marry Shamiran until her older sister married. Nice trick, don't you think! He knew the sky and the earth would part before he found a husband for you. So Kareem bribed me to marry—with money and a business of my own.

"Now you see how grateful you should be to me for making a respectable woman out of you! And besides, you can't even bear a child! What do you say to that?"

She could not believe her ears. Although she remained speechless, her heart was pounding and her head swimming with this revelation of her humiliating marriage. She seethed with anger, but remained seated, stolid, and silent. She feared getting up, lest her legs fail her.

"What do you have to say to all this? Nothing?" He waited a few seconds then added, "At least, you're smart enough not to say anything. Here are two shillings for the week. I'm going out."

As soon as he left, her walls crumbled around her. Every fiber in her shook, and the tears came. How could her family have done that to her, thrown her in a loveless marriage built on deceit! Just as I've tasted the sweetness of victory, I must drink a cup of myrrh, she thought. Now she felt like a worthless rag that her father had tossed away. With the tears came the bitterness against everyone who had anything to do with her marriage.

CHAPTER 31

"GOOD MORNING, Amal. Wake up. It's breakfast time," Sitt Marriam chirps.

I've been feeling better for the past week. But I'm not going to tell her that. Why should I? Things get better and then get worse. When she finishes feeding me, she says, "I've got very good news for you."

"What bad news do you have now?"

"In three weeks you're going to Jerusalem to have the blue water removed from both eyes. Then you'll be able to see. You'll join your friends. They miss you."

"I'm not going to that wicked city," I tell her firmly. I hate that city and everyone in it.

"You're not going to live there. Just a few days. I'll be there to take care of you and bring you back. You'll feel like a changed woman, with a new pair of eyes."

She thinks if I could see again, I'd be a different person. Only the stupid think seeing changes things.

"Now, if you're good, you might see Khadeejeh today."

"Give her a bath before you bring her here. Her perfume nearly killed me last time she came."

"But that was because of the olive harvest."

"Where's Khadeejeh? You haven't brought her to see me for a year now," I deliberately exaggerate.

"She's in the next room."

"You've hidden her in the next room?"

"Something like that. Maybe you can raise her spirits."

"Raise her spirits? I'm not a spell brewer."

"Just cheer her up. She refuses to eat and keeps arguing with herself. Maybe you can talk her into eating. She's very weak."

"What have you done to her?"

"No one has done anything to her. She's just not feeling good."

I can't believe my ears. I feel bad that I made those nasty comments about her. She's the only one who really loves me. She did lift my spirits when she visited me. I have to do the same for her. So I tell the nurse, "Khadeejeh will listen to me. I'm her cousin. Take me to her now."

"You have to promise me one thing: you must try to keep her calm, and to encourage her anyway you can. She might listen to you better than to any of us."

We go in and the nurse guides me to Khadeejeh's bed. She takes my hand and places it on Khadeejeh's arm very gently. Khadeejeh sighs, *"Ya yamma!"* That's how they call a mother in towns and villages. Very softly I call her name. She's quiet, and I try again, "Khadeejeh, this is your cousin, Amal."

I can tell white from dark shapes, and I know she's turning her head to face me. In a hoarse and weak voice, she asks, "Amal! My sister, is it you?"

"It's me, habeebty. I've come to see you. I've missed you so much. Why haven't you come to see your cousin Amal?"

"You're not my cousin. You're my sister. Amal, I'm going to die." Her voice is so weak, so unlike her.

"No, who ever told you that?"

"Allah told me. He took Immie, Amal."

"Oh, habeebty, you shouldn't say things like that!"

"Amal, I haven't seen Immie in a long, long time. She promised to come and bring me pencils and paper, but she never came back. Then a voice told me she's dead and gone to heaven."

"Khadeejeh, she may be sick, that's all. She'll come when she's better."

"Voices don't lie, Amal. They're my friends. My only friends, since you went to live in the Sick Ward, and Immie stopped coming. She's dead, dead, dead!" She begins to weep.

"Listen to me, Khadeejeh. My voices told me your mother is sick like me, but she's getting better and she's coming to see you soon. See, I'm going to be better soon, too. Il doctore is going to make me see again. Then we'll be together again, like before. Everything will be the same as before." I'm trying hard to give her some hope. Her mother could be dead, for all I know. Poor Khadeejeh!

"Promise!"

"I promise, but you have to eat and get well. Otherwise, how am I going to live without you, Khadeejeh?" And suddenly I remember the thing she wants more than anything else. "Khadeejeh, remember you have to learn to read before you go to the mountain to meet your prince!"

"I need paper and pencil."

"From Sitt Marriam. She promised."

I could picture Sitt Marriam's surprise. "She promised to let us come here for an hour each day to learn to read. Ask her!"

"Is it true, Sitt Marriam?"

"We'll see. It depends on you. If you eat and get better, maybe it'll happen."

"Swear by the Koran!"

"I swear by the Koran and the Holy Book and all the saints."

"No good. You must swear by the life of the Prophet Muhammad, peace on Him, then I know it will happen."

"Alright. By the life of the Prophet Muhammad, peace on Him, I'll do my best."

"Amal, what do I do if the voices tell me not to eat?"

"You tell them you're going to listen to your sister who loves you. Who do you love more, those voices that you can't see or me?"

She pauses for a few seconds and says, "You."

"That's my good sister. Now start eating and get well soon. Look at you. You're all skin and bones. How do you expect to learn? Your brain needs food."

"My brain needs to eat, too?

"Of course!"

"Will you come again to see me?"

"Every day, to see if you're keeping your promise." I don't tell her that in three weeks I'll be gone for the operation. I'll tell her when the time comes. By then, she'll be stronger and better able to handle it.

I hold her in both my arms, hug her tight, and kiss her on

the head. She latches onto me, and I slowly tell her I have to leave but will come again. Sitt Marriam reassures her and we leave.

Back in my room, the nurse helps me into the chair and says, "You were a great help, Amal. Sometimes, you're more sane than those on the outside."

For a few seconds I'm at a loss, and so I say nothing. Then I decide I'd best play silly. "Listen, here, you don't talk to Princess Lila, Daughter of King Ni'mann like that!" I don't know how I thought of that just now. Once I played the part of the maid of Princess Lila in a school play, such a long time ago.

"Who's that?"

"You don't know? You mean you've known me for many, many years, and you don't know who I am!"

"Oh, I should know, but sometimes my memory isn't so good."

"A nurse without a good memory! Allah help us!"

"Allah help us all! Oh, I just remembered something. My mother gave me this spearmint gum and this small chocolatta to give to you. She said the gum would strengthen your jaws and the chocolatta your spirits. Here," she says and places them in my hand. Do you want some now or later?"

"One square of chocolatta and one stick of gum now, and hide the rest under my mattress, so Sitt Najlah doesn't steal them."

"She doesn't steal."

"She steals everything. She's jealous of me."

"Jealous! I see." She picks up the tray and leaves.

I could never tell what thoughts pop into my head. Like now. How did I think of the night nurse being jealous! And such thoughts always bring back those bits of my life that I'd rather forget, like being jealous of Shamiran, even unkind to her, like the time she came to visit me.

It was on one of those days a few weeks after Boulos had set down his new routine. Amal sat in her room contemplating the malaise in her life and how she would like to change it. Her reveries were interrupted by the clicking of high heels on the stairs. She wondered if it was Hilaneh.

Then Shamiran appeared in the doorway, and Amal's sulfurous anger began to rise. She remained seated, an insult to the incoming visitor.

Shamiran was dressed in a pale green suit, her neck decked with pearls, and her hands sparkling with a large emerald ring on one finger and a diamond on the other. Her right arm displayed half a dozen gold bangles and a wider filigreed bracelet. Her golden hair was raised in the front with the rest pulled back behind her ears. In one hand she held a small box, like the ones Nahla brought sweets in.

What catastrophic event brought you here in mid-morning!

Shamiran entered the room and stood almost paralyzed, unable to think of what to say or do. It was so unlike Amal to sit staring, arms crossed, and not invite her own sister to sit down. No one treated a visitor that way. Finally, Shamiran gathered enough courage, "I . . . I had an appointment with the dentist this morning and had enough time to stop and share some kenapheh with you. I wondered how you were doing."

"How kind of you! I'm doing fine, as you can see, sweet sister!" she said, her tongue laced with malice.

"What do you mean?" Shamiran faltered.

"You know what I mean." Amal's anger was all too obvious. "You knew all along of the dirty trick your Kareem played on his brother, and it ruined my life."

"What trick are you talking about, Amal?" she asked, surprised at Amal's tone and her meaning.

"Don't pretend you're innocent!"

"I have no idea what you're talking about, Amal. Why don't you explain?"

"You and everyone else in the family knew of the way Kareem plotted to have Boulos marry me so that he could marry you much sooner."

Shamiran's face turned pale. She sat down in a chair facing her sister. "Amal, you have to believe me. I had no knowledge of it until a month ago when Kareem told me how guilty he feels about the part he played in your marriage. At the time, he had no idea how incorrigible his brother was. He thought marriage to a mature woman would settle him down, would be the best thing for him."

"As you can see, I'm not the best thing for him. Imagine my humiliation! But I can't believe you just heard of it only recently."

"I swear on the Gospel, Amal, it is the truth. How would I have known about that? In fact, I was quite angry when you got married before me. You must remember how badly I behaved with you at the time. I was jealous."

"Well, you should have at least told me as soon as you learned of it."

"And what would that have accomplished? There's nothing that can be done to change the past. But I want to help you in anyway I can. I'm not going to let Boulos abuse you as he has done."

"I hear guilt speaking! You needn't worry about it. Boulos, through some miracle, doesn't beat me now, and I exist in relative peace, frail as it is."

"I'm glad to hear that. What made him change, I wonder?"

"Who knows! But now I know too much meddling has made my life Gehannem. Allah will punish those who played a part in dirty games behind my back. He doesn't have stones to throw at the wicked, but His terrible punishment will come in due time."

Shamiran's fear showed in her eyes. Allah's punishment was something no one wanted to hear of or endure.

"Look, I've heard enough. Why don't you go home and live your charmed life. And our parents can stay in the safety of their home, too."

Suddenly, Amal got up from the couch, limped toward the little commode beside the bed, and picked up the Bible Marta had given her. She turned toward Shamiran, "Here," she said, her voice full of bitterness, "give this back to *your* mother. Tell her a head of cabbage has more use."

Looking at her sister in disbelief, Shamiran pleaded, "Amal, you can't be serious. You can't return our mother's most cherished gift. You know she's helpless. Father's word is from Allah. You must know how much she loves you—more than she loves any of us. The times she's visited you—very few times, I know—she did so by sneaking away with Gibrail, pretending she's going to see a doctore. You can't hurt her this way."

"Keep your sentiments to yourself! From now on, I'll do what I want and the rest can go to Gehannem. I don't want you or Kareem interfering anymore."

"Amal, come stay with me for a while. I'll take care of you."

Her voice broke and her eyes filled with tears.

"Too late, too late. I must do things my way now."

"We can help you, Amal."

"Don't waste your breath! I'll find my own way."

Tears spilling down her rouged cheeks, Shamiran got up, embraced her sister and pleaded, "Forgive me, yakhtie, and forgive Kareem. He meant to help you, but it backfired. We should've paid attention long ago. We're guilty. Can you find it in your heart to forgive us?"

Amal wondered when her sister had acquired so much humility and compassion. Not that it mattered at this point. She was determined now to live her life the way she saw fit. Seeing her sister weep, though, she softened her voice and said, "Shamiran, go home to your children. I'll take care of myself."

"Would you let me give you a small gift, ten liras, to help you in the next little while?"

"Thank you, Shamiran. I don't need money. What I need no one can give." Only a fool would have turned down that much money.

Shamiran embracd her sister and, kissing her on both cheeks, surreptitiously slipped the money behind the cushion supporting Amal's back.

"*Ma' il salameh*," Go in peace, Amal said dispassionately. She stood on the stoop and, as she watched her sister go down the stairs, began to feel a little guilty about the way she'd treated her. "Shamiran, thanks for coming."

Shamiran looked up at her and, with trembling lips and broken voice, replied, "You're welcome. Allah be with you!"

Amal stood there, wondering what had gotten into her. Although she felt a little sorry for the way she had treated her sister, mostly she felt stronger than ever before, capable of doing whatever needed to be done.

She went into her house, got dressed, combed her hair, and wrapped her thick braid twice around her head. She reached into the armoir, pulled out a small box, took out the comb her grandmother had given her, and stuck it through the two layers of braids on the right side of her head. Then she reached for the box that cradled her black hat and gingerly settled the hat, slightly tilted sideways, atop her head. This is insane, she told herself, but I like it!

CHAPTER 32

I WAKE UP to another dreary, idle day. Now that Khadeejeh is well again and back in the ward, I miss her. I had gotten used to visiting with her daily and chatting about all sorts of mad stuff. I enjoyed the feeling of doing something useful with my time.

"*Sabah il-khaire*, Amal!" Sitt Marriam wishes me good morning amid the clatter of the breakfast tray. "Hurry and eat. We have important things to do to this morning."

"What important things, Your Majesty?"

"You'll know after you eat."

After breakfast, she leads me to the washroom, and then to the shower room. "I'm going to give you a quick shower and get you dressed in a clean gown."

"This is not bath day."

"No, it's Thursday, but it's a special day."

"I don't need special days. They always turn out ugly."

"Not this one. We're going to the Hospital for Ocular Diseases in Jerusalem."

"I don't want to go to any hospital, especially in Jerusalem. I'm not having anyone take the knife to my eyes." I whimper.

"This is a special hospital, and a very famous doctore will remove the blue water without any cutting. It's done quickly and without pain."

"All these lies about special this and famous that. Special kharra!"

"Now, be nice. You can't talk like that there, or they won't help you."

"Damn them all!"

"Everything will turn out for the best, you'll see."

"But I can't see. I can only hear the philosopher of Baghdad."

"Who's that?"

"Ask Sitty. She called us that when we pretended to know everything."

Now I'm really frightened. I am miserable with her as she takes my clothes off. When she's fed up, she threatens to call an orderly, and that shuts me up quick. Meanwhile I'm shaking, afraid of what they'll do to me in that city. I swore a long time ago to burn in red Gehannem before I went back. You can never swear to anything in this world.

She finishes combing my hair, all the while complimenting me with lies about how thick and silky it is. If only she could've seen the braids I had! That was ages and ages ago.

"Take your time," I tell her, as she departs for a few minutes. "I'm not going anywhere." But I wish I could run away to the Sisters of the Rosary, and shut myself up in the convent of the nuns.

Suddenly, I remember the little square of chocolate and stick of spearmint gum hidden under my mattress. They won't be here when I get back. Sitt Najlah would find them. The ghouleh is fat enough! Luckily, the chair is near my bed. I pass my hand under the mattress and find my treasures. I suddenly think I'd like to give them to Khadeejeh.

"I want to see Khadeejeh," I tell Sitt Marriam on her return.

"We don't have time. The car is ready. Look, Amal, enough of this. We have a schedule to meet."

Now I start crying in earnest. She softens up and asks, "Why do you want to see her now? You'll see her in few days."

"I have something for her."

"What?"

I open my hand for her to see.

"Oh, I tell you what. I'll give them to her. I promise," she says in a gentle voice.

"But I want to say good-bye to her."

"It would be worse for you and her. You know how upset she gets. Why don't we surprise her when we return?"

I mumble all kinds of stupid things to quell the fear that has gripped me while she wraps me in a winter coat, covers my head with a scarf, and ties it under my chin. "You need to dress warm. This is one of the coldest Novembers I've seen."

I keep up my stupid rhyming as I'm led from the room and into the courtyard of beit il-majaneen, which has sheltered me all these years. I can tell you she's right about the coldest November.

When I step outside the metal gate, my head spins, and I feel like I'm going to faint. Sitt Marriam holds my arm tight. An orderly's hand grips my other arm. I'm lifted and settled inside a taxi between the nurse and the orderly.

"Let's go!" the orderly tells the chauffeur.

The car grumbles, shudders, then moves. The orderly and the chauffeur chat and Sitt Marriam and I listen quietly. Women couldn't understand the important and serious issues that men—*fatheads!*—talk about. I have nothing to distract me from listening to their every word.

My memory of the way to beit il-majaneen is as flimsy as old cobwebs. Nine years ago they brought me there. It was in May of 1948, when the war between the Palestinians and the Zionists broke out. That miserable day that pitched me into a deep pit, swarming with snakes and scorpions.

I concentrate on the discussion between the two morons. They probably can't read or write. The dumbhead next to me asks, "What's new, Abu Waleed?"

"*Wallah*, as you see, Sayyed Ghassan." They always invoke Allah to witness their stupidity.

"How's business these days?"

"Like tar. Some days I don't make enough to buy bread for the children."

I used to hear this line a long time ago. Nothing has changed.

"It will change, inshallah!" the idiot next to me says.

"From your lips to the gates of heaven, I hope."

They carry on with their stupid conversation for too long. I don't remember that it took this long from Bethlehem to Jerusalem. The car seems to be descending and swerving around sharp curves, sometimes to the left, then to the right. That's not how I remember it. After a while the car appears to be climbing up a mountainside, until suddenly it comes to a stop. I grab Sitt Marriam's arm.

She holds me gently and pats my arm to quiet my nerves. "Everything is alright, Amal. I'm with you."

Sitt Marriam tells Ghassan to come over to her side of the car. He lets go of my arm and gets out. She whispers to me, "Keep quiet and say nothing."

She opens the door and takes my arm and helps me out. Then Ghassan holds my other arm and they walk me up some stairs. I'm shaking, especially my legs, and for a minute I think I might empty my bladder. *"Here's a madwoman who urinated on the floor," someone would shout laughing, and others would follow me, taunting like children used to do to Pharha.*

I start saying the Lord's Prayer and I don't know how many times I've said it before Ghassan says, "We're bringing this patient in for Doctore Boone."

A woman's voice asks, "The name?"

"Amal Murad," he replies.

My heart stops. I know that woman's voice. I keep saying to myself, I know that voice, but it can't be. Impossible! Perhaps fear is making my mind play tricks. Now she says more gently, "Take her down this corridor on the left, through that door, and to Room 5. Someone will be there to take care of you."

"Shookrun," Sitt Marriam says.

She and Ghassan lead me to the assigned room and ease me into a chair. Minutes later, I hear a woman's voice, "Name?"

Ghassan answers, "Amal Murad."

"We need to take off her clothes and put this gown on. Ghassan says, "I'll wait outside."

After they finish changing me, the woman says, "Follow me."

I refuse to stand up. Ghassan comes in and grabs my arm so hard that he could've pulled my shoulder from its socket. It hurt and I let out a cry for help. Sitt Marriam says, "Wait, Ghassan. I'll handle her." She brings her lips to my ears and whispers, "Amal, no one will hurt you, because I'll be holding your hand all the time. Trust in Allah. Yalla, habeebty."

That gives me little comfort, and I weep quietly. It might go worse for me if I raise a stink. They lead me down a long corridor, and suddenly a door opens, and I can tell the room is well lit. I hear male voices speaking Inglizi. I still remember some of il Inglizi I learned in school, a very long time ago, but I can only understand simple words and sentences. I have no idea what they're saying. Maybe it's better not to know. Let the knife fall and finish me off.

Then four arms suddenly lift me off the floor and I scream. "Put me down," I keep crying. Sitt Marriam holds my hand and says, "It's alright, Amal. You're going to be placed on a high bed so il doctore can help you."

I'm trembling and mumbling. Formless faces, menacing ghosts, loom over me. Hands push me down onto a flat surface. It doesn't feel like a bed. They begin to tie my hands and legs down. I resist. "Don't kill me. I'm innocent, innocent!"

"Amal, they have to tie you down so you don't hurt yourself. I'm right here beside you," Sitt Marriam says while holding my hand. "I'd never let anyone hurt you."

Suddenly, someone presses a handkerchief against my face, and as I breathe in, I sink into darkness . . .

"Amal, you're waking up. Just stay quiet." It's comforting to hear Sitt Marriam's voice. But soon it fades away.

I hear her again from far away and try to open my eyes. But they feel like they're bandaged. I can't move—they've wedged my head between two bricks. I can't even lift my arms. They're still tied down and my legs too. "Where am I?" my voice sounds weak and hoarse.

"In a special room. You're doing very well. See? You didn't feel a th . . ."

Then I hear her voice again. "You're doing fine, Amal. Soon, you'll be awake, and your eyes will be as good as new."

"I'm still blind," I mutter, half asleep.

"You're not blind. Your eyes are kept covered to give them time to heal."

"Take the bandage off!"

"Il doctore will do that soon."

I feel half asleep and half awake. I didn't quite hear or understand what she said, and I ask, "When can I go back to Bethlehem?"

"You miss it that much?"

"I don't want to stay here. Take me back now!"

"I can't do that. The doctore will have to examine your eyes first and give us instructions how to care for them; then he'll release you."

"I'm afraid! This is an evil place. I don't want to stay."

"No more evil than Bethlehem."

She has no idea what I'm talking about. I try to say a prayer or two to quell the demon of fear. Maybe Allah will hear me now that I'm in the city that crucified His Son. Suddenly there's a knock at the door, and I wonder what's going to happen to me now. I'm all ears.

Sitt Marriam goes to the door and I hear her whispering, " . . . doing fine . . . related . . . ?"

The stranger at the door whispers back, " . . . friends . . . long ago . . . alright?"

" . . . like this . . . like that . . . "

"Poor . . . see her . . . ?"

" . . . later . . . maybe . . . good . . . "

Then I hear the door close and the nurse at my side again.

"Who was that?"

"Oh, just . . . a nurse, asking how you're doing."

Such a liar! She thinks I couldn't hear. She doesn't know my ears picked up enough words to know it wasn't a nurse. Let her think I don't know anything.

The words I heard keep turning around and around in my head. " . . . friends . . . see . . . later . . . " *Nahla.* Was that voice really hers? Or am I hallucinating like poor Khadeejeh? I must be. I have no friends in this city. The only friend I had wouldn't be working at a front desk. How could she? From what I remember, she didn't finish more than her Grade 7, and she wasn't a very good student. But that voice tantalizes me.

My heart trembles. What does Nahla think of me now? Does she still love me? She couldn't love someone like me. Just a couple of visits in all these years! If by some miracle it's her, how do I behave with her? Why do I face one problem after another?

If it's Nahla, I wish she would just go away and leave me be! She, of all people, knows the whole truth. I can't face her. Facing her brings everything back, smack in my face. I'll tell Sitt Marriam I don't want to see anyone. It's easier that way. Why stir the cesspool and choke on the stench of the old kharra! No, I don't want to remember.

"Where am I going to sleep tonight?"

"Right in this special room, in this comfortable bed."

"You're sleeping here with me. Don't leave me. I'm afraid!"

"There's nothing to be afraid of. They take good care of patients here. Soon, it'll be suppertime and I'll feed you, just like always." She squeezes my hand.

"There are many ghosts lurking here," I protest.

"Don't worry. I'll be here every minute of the night and day, and if I see one, I'll beat him with this chair until he's dead."

I choke on the laugh bubbling in my throat. I say to her, "Shookrun. Allah strengthen your arms."

I feel better, knowing she's sleeping in the same room with me. A knock at the door and a woman's voice breaks the silence. "Supper for Room 5!" Her voice is firm, her tone matter-of-fact.

"Here's your supper," Sitt Marriam says. "I'll crank up the bed to raise your head a little. You have to keep calm while I feed you. You shouldn't shout or move your head. If you do, you'll hurt your eyes."

She puts the spoon in my mouth and I feel the soaked bread and taste the salty broth with its hint of tomatoes and some rice.

"You like it?"

"What kind of supper is this?"

"A light supper after your operation."

Frankly, I don't want to eat anything. But I know I have to, and I can't cause trouble here and draw attention to myself. I want things to go well so I can go back to the safety of my home—beit il-majaneen, my only refuge now.

She finishes feeding me, then gives me sweet tea.

I thank her softly.

"Now, I'll give you a needle so you'll have a good sleep through the night."

"You're not putting the needle in my eyes, by Allah's life!" I meant to sound dumb.

"Of course not! I'll give it to you where you have some meat."

And she sticks the needle in my hip.

"Akh! You're killing me!"

"Oh, stop your bellyaching!"

I begin to feel my body relax. I close my eyes and begin to say the Lord's Prayer . . . and I hear Nahla's voice.

CHAPTER 33

NOW THAT BOULOS was living up to his promise, Amal did not worry about spending time with Nahla. She could do whatever she wanted during the week—visit with Nahla, buy whatever she needed. Hilaneh became her generous banker. Boulos gave her the weekly allowance for food, while Hilaneh secretly gave her a few liras. Amal had more money than ever before and was able to do more for herself, including making monthly payments on a sewing machine.

One day, during one of their chats over coffee, Nahla suggested that Amal become more modern. "Why don't you get rid of all that hair, Amal? For one thing it's easier to take care of, and you'll come out of the old century."

Amal smiled. "I might just do that and more!"

"Yes! Some lipstick and maquillage! Wouldn't you look wonderful!"

"I don't know how wonderful, but I'd like to try new things."

"I'll help you. Aida knows a great hairdresser, Sarkis. You know Armenians are the best hairdressers around."

"I didn't know that. But I'd rather go to a woman. I'd feel more comfortable."

"Don't be silly. He won't bite you!"

Amal asked if she could read one of Nahla's magazines. After a few minutes, she raised her head, "What a horrible story!"

"What story?" inquired Nahla.

"Here is a story of a fifteen-year-old girl who stabbed a man to death for assaulting her."

"Good for her. I'd do the same thing," snapped Nahla.

"You wouldn't! It takes a certain kind of person to kill another," Amal insisted.

"Not really. A girl has to defend herself if anyone threatens her honor."

"What about 'Thou shall not kill!'"

"You don't kill for just any reason, but for honor, I'd stab the bastard fifty times."

"And go to hell for it?" Amal asked.

"I'd rather take my chances with Allah than with a threat to my honor. It's hell whichever way you look at it. What kind of a life would a raped woman have? No man would ever marry her, and she'd live the rest of her days in guilt and shame. I'd rather send the bastard to hell, too."

Amal looked serious. "Let's change the subject."

"What have you got out of yesterday's paper?"

"Another depressing tale—more bombings, killings, and bloodshed."

"It doesn't look good. I wonder if the world has always been like this—fighting and killing one another!"

"From what I remember of my history classes, there were always wars and killings, victories and defeats—the rise and downfall of every nation. In the Middle East alone, empires came and went—Persians, Macedonians, Aramaens, Assyrians, Chaldeans, Romans, and Greeks. I don't remember the order of these empires. Then, the Arabs conquered almost the whole world, bringing Islam to the region. Did you know, we Syriacs descended from the great Aramaic nation that ruled the lands from Egypt to the Eastern borders of Iraq, to the northern borders of Turkey? And look at us now, enclaves scattered all over the world. Every nation has its glorious days before crumbling into dust."

"Don't tell me anymore, Amal!"

"I won't. I'm beginning to think you have the right idea not to take life seriously, but to eat, drink, laugh, and do whatever makes your life bearable."

"And that's exactly what you're going to do. I'll call Aida tomorrow and have her take you to the hair salon."

"Sounds like a threat," Amal teased.

As Nahla wished, Aida took her to a famous coiffeur to have her hair cut and styled. When they arrived at the hair salon, Amal was mortified to see a man, all smiles and friendliness, ready to chop her hair up. She looked at Aida, panic in her face.

"For your first cut you need the best. He's the best. Just relax! He's only going to touch your hair."

"*La howla wala!*" She whispered the common expression of exasperation and sat in the swivel chair. She was flustered when the coiffeur asked, "How short do you want it, and how do you like it styled?"

She stammered and turned to look at Aida, who immediately came to her rescue. "You want your hair just below the shoulder. Right, Amal?"

"Yes," she replied in a low voice.

"And you want it styled in today's fashion—raised on both sides in the front, and curled inside at the end, right?"

"Yes," she managed to say, regretting the moment she'd listened to Nahla and Aida.

"Sarkis, cut it to about here," Aida said, touching Amal's back just below the shoulders. "That's good, Amal?" she asked.

Amal gave a tacit approval.

She watched as Sarkis undid her braids and caressed the thick cascade between his fingers. She cringed when she saw the smile on his face. *He's mocking me.* She wished she had never come.

Sarkis turned to Aida. "About here?"

Aida agreed. He then took a sharp knife and held it still in his right hand, while his left hand lifted half of her hair, raising and lowering his grip, trying to decide the exact place where the knife should fall.

Seeing the knife in his hand, Amal quivered with fear. She wanted to cry to him to stop but was worried Aida might be upset with her. She closed her eyes and said a prayer instead.

Sarkis sensed her anxiety. "You have such beautiful, thick hair that a knife will do a better job than scissors. Don't worry. It won't hurt."

Even Aida's comforting hand on her shoulder did not quell her panic. Closing her eyes, she felt the horror of an animal about to be slaughtered. Her stomach twisted tightly when the knife hacked off the first handful. And when she opened her eyes and saw her hair cut, and a long thick bundle in Sarkis' hand, the tears came. But neither tears nor regret could return her to her former self, she realized.

She got off the chair and looked at Aida and Sarkis with a suggestion of a smile on her lips. *What's done is done*, she told herself. She opened her purse and paid Sarkis. Half a lira! A whole week's grocery money for a haircut. She reminded herself that the money came from Hilaneh and was meant to make life better, easier, and more pleasurable.

It did not take her long to realize that she did indeed look better, more modern. Now she needed more time to keep her hair groomed and styled. After the first few days, she learned how to shape it and put the pins in the right places. What pleased her the most was the reaction of the shopkeepers who had known her for years. These permanent residents of the markets and bazaars were skilled in the study of women. When the neighborhood shopkeepers from whom she bought most of her groceries saw the new Amal, they gave their tacit approval with a smile and showed their pleasure by their keen desire to haggle longer for the best price they could get.

When Boulos came home Friday night and saw his wife with her new hairstyle and makeup, there was mockery in his voice, "Huh, what's this? You've gone mad!"

She didn't answer, and he went on, "Maybe you think you'll look like your sister? What a waste of money! Maybe I'm giving you too much money, if you can throw it away on stupidities."

"Your mother gave me the money for it," Amal finally said. "Everyone, including your mother, thought it was a good idea."

"My mother, huh! Just listen to everyone and see where that's going to lead you!" He made it sound like a threat, but it was a toothless one, both knew.

After that initial step, with encouragement from Nahla and Aida, Amal became more daring and decided she should indulge in the latest styles in materials and shoes. On Sundays, once Boulos was gone for next five days, she accepted invitations from Nahla and her husband to accompany them to visit Nahla's old mother or, occasionally, to see a film. During the week, Aida took her shopping in the fancy stores in Jewish West Jerusalem.

At first, Amal was intimidated by venturing into new territories, but she found the experience so uplifting that she came to enjoy her outings with Aida. They went to cafés in Jaffa, where Amal had café-au-lait. This she preferred to eating dinner. Every time she went with Aida, she suggested going for café-au-lait and insisted on paying. Hilaneh would give her more if she needed extra money. But when Aida suggested that they go to Tel Aviv, Amal panicked. She was afraid she might see, or be seen, by someone who might recognize her. On the other hand, she wanted to go and see other places. Besides, she could not insult friendly Aida, who had taken Amal under her wing and was opening her eyes to a brand new world. Allah knew she needed friends.

So when Aida insisted on taking her one Thursday, Amal had no choice but to go, if only out of gratitude. It was Aida who'd taken the initiative to blackmail Hilaneh. Helping Amal became Aida's mission in life. Her husband was on duty every day, and she was free to enjoy life.

That first trip to Tel Aviv kept Amal's heart in a constant double beat. She sat in the back of the military jeep with Aida and Ed, while one of the two other British soldiers in the front seat drove. If ever she had felt like a cheap woman, it was then. Deep in her soul, she thought Aida was outrageously bold. She avoided glancing at her as she nestled in her husband's arms, laughing and kissing. *What kind of a girl is this?* Amal regretted having accepted the invitation to go with her. When one of the soldiers looked at her and asked if she spoke English, she turned red, her heart beating hard in her chest.

Aida came to her rescue, "She's very shy, and I don't think she speaks English."

"I could teach her, love!"

"I don't think so, Blaine. She's married."

"That's too bad, Aida. Couldn't you have brought along a younger woman, and single?"

"Hey, Blaine, I'm not in that line of business. This is a good friend who's never been outside the Old City, and I just wanted to show her another part of the world."

"No problem, darling. I'm a good friend too, and you could be good to me by bringing a single friend along next time, okay?"

Everyone laughed except for Amal. She was not used to English being spoken so rapidly and missed the drift of the conversation. The few words she caught here and there were enough to make her feel they were making fun of her. If she'd had the courage, she would have jumped out of the jeep.

Aida sensed her friend's embarrassment and, in Arabic, gave her an abridged version of the conversation. But this did little to ease Amal's discomfort.

When the jeep stopped at the side of a wide road, flanked by shops and cafés, the soldier sitting in the passenger seat quickly got out to open the door for Amal. She was too embarrassed to take the hand he offered to assist her, "Come, darling. I'm just helping you down the step. Come on now."

He took her hand and helped her down. She was still shaking and unable to look at him. She wanted to thank him but could not bring herself to say the words.

Aida joined Amal, whose face spoke of distress and mortification. "Amal, you're too shy. I've never seen anyone so shy. My goodness! Stop shaking."

"Aida. I've never been in a car with strange men before."

"Well, you never have to worry about being near English soldiers. They're very polite and nice. They treat a woman like a precious piece of jewelry."

"They were laughing at me."

"No, no, they weren't laughing at you. They were just having fun. Being so far away from their families, they try to make life easier by joking around. Relax!"

"I don't know how. I'm not used to this."

"Remember, you're as good as anyone else. Never think someone is trying to make fun of you.

It was the first time Amal had eaten in a fancy restaurant. The specialness of the moment somewhat diminished her fear of being recognized. And after that first experience, Amal felt more comfortable when she went anywhere with Aida, although silent fears of exposure still nibbled away at her pleasure.

Bit by bit, and in spite of Boulos' weekly intrusions, Amal's days were infused with the joy of freedom, more peace, and much less pain. What added to her happiness was an addition to her family in December of that year.

One day, she came home from the market to find a kitten on the ledge of the house adjacent to hers. The little creature was meowing pitifully and looked as though it wanted to jump down, but was afraid. Amal put the bag down, held her arms high, and called to it, "Come down, kitten. I'll catch you. Don't be afraid!" After a minute of hesitation, and Amal's constant encouragement, the kitten jumped, screeching from fear. It landed just beyond where Amal stood, and for seconds did not know whether to run or remain. Amal's kind voice reassured it to take a few slow steps toward the open kitchen door.

From that day on, Amal could not have gotten rid of the kitten if she'd wanted to. It became her constant companion, sometimes following her and risking some rough-and-tumble play from Nahla's twin boys. It sat beside her on the threshold of her room or in the kitchen, sometimes jumping into her lap and purring as Amal stroked her soft black-and-white fur. When Amal got into bed, the kitten meowed, begging to be lifted up to sleep in her arms. Lovingly she made a bed from a cardboard box, put an old towel inside it, and placed it in the kitchen, where the kitten slept during the cold, wet winter months.

The first Friday that Boulos saw the kitten on the stoop, he looked at it for a second and, suddenly, kicked it in the abdomen. Amal's hand went immediately to her heart. She felt the pain of the screeching little thing as it scrambled and tumbled down the stairs. She contained her anger against the devil who only knew how to torment the helpless. For the first time since her marriage, the thought of doing him harm entered her head. She wanted to go down to hold her little friend and comfort her, but she knew better.

Staring at Amal, who stood rigid and speechless, he scowled. "So, I see you've given birth to a cat!" Then, making the sign of the cross in the air, he slowly pronounced, "Allah's name on you and your firstborn!"

She remained silent, though her heart brimmed with anger at the meanspirited remark and the insult he had flung in her face.

"Throw it out! My house is not for stray animals!" he shouted.

A stray animal is better fit to live in this house than you, you kaffir! "It's cruel in this cold and windy night to put the little creature out," she objected.

"And since when do you have the right to bring anyone or anything into my house? Throw it out, or the next time I see it around, I'll kill it!"

And I pray for someone to kill you soon. She decided silence was her best strategy for the time being. She hoped Nahla had heard the kitten's screeching and had given her refuge for the night.

That was the only unpleasantness in her life then, and she managed to circumvent Boulos' despicable acts by leaving the kitten in its box in Nahla's kitchen from Friday to Sunday. The rest of the time, she was free to sew at Nahla's, have coffee, go to the market, or gallivant with Aida. It was a good life, perhaps the best she had ever enjoyed, with the possible exception of her time with the nuns.

CHAPTER 34

AFTER BREAKFAST, Sitt Marriam gives me an injection to help me sleep, she says. The next thing I know I'm awakened for dinner. I eat and fall asleep again until suppertime. She feeds me supper—good food. I wanted her to take me to the bathroom, but she put a pot under me instead. After she cleaned me up, she gave me another injection and I must've slept until morning.

Doctore Boone arrives. I'm quiet as he takes off the bandages and gently examines my eyes. Light floods them and he asks, "How many fingers do you see?" I tell him I see one, then five, then two. "Good," he says, "everything is good. Day after tomorrow, you go back to Bethlehem, inshallah!"

He pats my shoulder and leaves.

Soon, someone knocks and opens the door.

I hear two voices whispering. That always makes me nervous. I want to know everything that goes on, when I can't see.

Then I hear Sitt Marriam near me. "Amal, do you feel like having a visitor now?"

"A visitor? Who in this Gehannem has come to visit me?"

"Someone. She says you were best of friends at one time."

"I don't know any best friend."

"She's brought fresh kenapheh with her. She says you two used to have that often."

Now I'm sure it's Nahla, but I pretend not to know her, "I don't know her."

"Amal, it wouldn't hurt to just say *marhaba*. That's all."

"Marhaba, Amal!"

I hear that and my heart sinks to my belly. My head screams for her to leave me alone. I knew it was her. I wish she would go away. I'm suffering enough paying my dues. Isn't that enough? I refuse to answer. Maybe she'll go away.

"Amal, this is Nahla. I wanted to visit you. I brought us some kenapheh for old time's sake."

"I don't like kenapheh."

"Well, I'll keep it on the table. Maybe later on you'll feel like eating it. How are you, Amal?"

"Who knows? I can't see how I am. I'm blind."

"I'm very sorry. I know you had the operation two days ago. The best doctore did your operation, and you're going to see in a few days."

"How do you know all that? You're a fortune-teller?"

"No, I don't read coffee grains anymore. I haven't ever since you . . . left."

"Left? I never left. I'm where I've always been, in beit il-shayateen."

After a pause, Nahla went on. "You remember my two

daughters, Therese and Georgette? They're now young women. Therese is twenty-four. She went to England on a scholarship to study nursing. While there, she met a doctore Inglizi, and he followed her here and married her. She works with him in the operating room. His name is Doctore Boone. Georgette is in England, in her last year of studying nursing. And do you remember the two imps—the twins—Tony and George? They're nineteen now. Both are going to England to become male nurses. Allah has been good to His little orphans."

I'm shocked to hear Doctore Boone is Nahla's son-in-law. "Orphans! Poor orphans, like me!"

"You're not an orphan, Amal. You have parents."

"No, I don't. They died a long time ago. Everyone in my family is dead."

Nahla was silent for few seconds, not knowing how to respond, then said, "Allah have mercy on their souls, and on my mother's and my husband's."

"Where are they?"

"In heaven, I'm sure."

"Your husband?"

"In heaven, too."

"What does he do there? Does he still bring home the newspaper?" I ask. I have to make sure she knows I'm not all there.

"No, but I buy it now."

"You shouldn't have to buy it when he can get it for free!"

Silence again, and then she says, "I've missed you so much."

"Sing to me '*Zurooni kille sinay marra* . . . '"

"I'm out of practice," she says, laughing.

"Sing," I say in a hoarse voice. I know I'm going to start crying. There's a hard lump in my throat. She starts to sing, and to my surprise, her voice breaks and she weeps as she sings. Now I can't control myself and I cry too. Then she breaks off, holds my hand, and sobs.

Soon, I feel Sitt Marriam's hand gently stroking my hair and patting my shoulder. She tells both of us, "Come, come! This is a happy meeting of old friends. No tears now. Amal, don't cry, habeebty. It's not good for your eyes. Enough, Nahla! Let's not turn this happy day into mourning," she says in a voice soft and gentle. "Think of some nice things to tell each other."

I have so much I want to ask Nahla, but I can't say anything in front of Sitt Marriam. I've got to get rid of her and then I could have a real conversation.

"You know, Amal, I moved from the Old City, and now I live in Sheikh Jarrah, a new suburb in West Jerusalem, not far from this hospital. I walk here to work every day. Amal, how about having a piece of kenapheh with me and Sitt Marriam? I brought three forks from home."

"Sitt Marriam doesn't like kenapheh."

"I don't?" Sitt Marriam sounds surprised. "Let's raise your bed so you can eat."

"How can I eat? I can't see."

"I'll guide your hand," Nahla says eagerly. "Is it alright, Sitt Marriam?"

"Of course, as long as she lets you. She has a mind of her own."

"Amal has a mind of her own, see?" I say.

Nahla feeds me the delicious dessert, and it feels like long ago, when she fed me kenapheh after each beating. Still, her coming here is not such a good idea. I feel I'm being forced to return to those days of red-hot Gehannem. *It's good to have you back, but you're taking me where I don't ever want to go. Your kena-pheh feels like a bribe to drag me back.*

I panic and tell her, "Go home to your children, Nahla. But come back tomorrow and we'll have coffee together, you and I. Just you and I. And we'll read each other's cup, and I'll have a chance to read the paper. Just the two of us. Promise?"

"I promise," Nahla replies. She bends over and kisses me on both cheeks. "Is there anything you'd like me to bring you tomorrow?"

"Roasted almonds and pistachio! And English chocolate! And rolled grape leaves."

"Anything you wish, habeebty! Now I have to go and begin my duty at the desk. Tomorrow I'll tell you how I got the job. Rest well."

Both appear to have left the room. I wonder what they're talking about. What else, but about me? I'm on everybody's mind and tongue. Ah, how the wheel of life turns! Here Nahla, with little education, a nonchalant attitude toward life, married to an older man, a kinder sort than most, loses him and somehow manages to raise her children to become successful. And she finds herself a good job. And me, look where I ended up! Justice is no more than a blind bastard!

Although I envy Nahla, I'm pleased for her. She was a true friend, kind, generous and, above all, courageous. She would never have stood for the abuses I put up with. I wish I had her . . . Oh, Nahla is deserving of her good fortune. If I had listened to her, I might be in a better place now.

CHAPTER 35

IN THE WINTER of 1947, the British, unable to quell Zionist attacks and Arab retaliations, decided to end their mandate and began their gradual withdrawal. That signalled the clashing forces to unleash their fires throughout West Jerusalem and many suburbs, towns, and villages, leaving death and destruction in their trail.

When Amal read the newspaper, she feared for her little nephews and niece. She wondered about Kareem's fortunes—heavy investments in the collapsed Samiramis hotel, and in real estate in the prestigious Katamon area that he planned to develop as a huge recreational and entertainment complex. Although she resented the role he'd played in her miserable marriage, she did not wish him harm.

The terrified residents of Katamon banded together to protect their neighborhoods. They armed themselves and fortified their homes with barricades, which they manned nightly. Their wives and children lived in terror of the whistling shells and the shuddering of the earth from explosions.

Many wealthy Arabs left everything behind and went to Egypt, Syria, Lebanon, or Jordan. Kareem was in a dilemma. He struggled against the thought of leaving his investments and fleeing to another Arab country, but when he found a bullet on his veranda, he was quick to abandon everything and decided to take his family to a safer place, until the dust finally settled.

The next day, a Saturday, Kareem left his wife and mother packing their valuables and clothes, and went to Jerusalem beg his brother and Amal to come with them.

When he saw that Boulos was not home, he explained the plan to Amal. She felt safe in the Old City, especially as Nahla and everyone else were staying. Everyone within the Old City believed Zionists would never shoot one bullet inside the walls, for fear of destroying their own holy places.

"Thank you for thinking of me, but I'm not afraid as long as I stay in the Old City. My family is staying in Bethlehem, and if need be, I'd stay with them until things calm down." She now had her little freedom and her precarious dignity, which she did not want to abandon for any promise of security. "I've put my trust in Allah!" *And I'm not such a fool to allow myself to become a maid again for Shamiran and your mother.*

"Won't you reconsider? Shamiran and the children want you to come along."

"I do appreciate the thought, Kareem, but I'm staying." As he turned around to leave, she said, her voice breaking, "Kiss the children for me. Allah be with you along your journey, and bring you safely back!"

Kareem rushed to his office to finalize last minute details. There was Boulos, standing around, looking anxious.

"There you are. I've just come back from your house. It's getting far too dangerous here. No one knows what the outcome of this war will be. I would like you and Amal to come with us to Damascus, until things settle down."

"What would I do in Damascus?"

"I might have to leave the family there and come back here to look after my affairs. The family would need a man there to take care of them while I'm away."

"I'm staying here."

"You have nothing to keep you here, except . . . " he stopped in mid-sentence. The more he argued, the more intransigent Boulos became.

Frustrated, Kareem took a small stack of bills and stuck it in Boulos' coat pocket. He kissed his brother on both cheeks, told him to stay out of trouble, and to take very good care of Amal. "Your wife deserves a lot more than she gets."

Boulos pursed his lips, clenched and unclenched his fists, but said nothing.

On May 17, 1948, the British mandate ended, most of the British forces left and, in their wake, came waves of horror, destruction, and bloodshed. Soon the Arab diaspora was complete.

Refugees poured into every city or town for shelter. Amal was glad she had decided to remain in the safety of her home, within the walls of the Old City, comforted by Nahla's friendship and the knowledge that Old Jerusalem remained in Arab hands. She had no idea where Boulos was, and hoped he would remain away. However, she was not entirely at ease. With Boulos, she had learned that she should never let down her guard. She had to talk to Nahla.

Nahla told Amal that Aida and Ed did not leave with the British forces. Ed wanted to leave on the *Frigonia*, along with the British soldiers and citizens, but he wouldn't go without Aida. "Those two have a marriage blessed by heaven," Nahla said.

Nahla also recounted other news she had heard from Aida. Friendships and alliances forged between Arabs and Jews, men and women, who had fallen in love, married or lived together, in many cases had come to a sad end. Arab husbands had to let their Jewish wives go back to their families for their safety.

Then Amal told Nahla of her own fears.

"Amal, don't worry. You know I'm here. If he comes back and lays a hand on you, I'll call the police."

"What police, Nahla? In this time of chaos, there's no police or government. These are lawless times."

"Ed will take care of him for you. He's taller and wider than Boulos, and trained as a soldier. One punch to his stomach, and Boulos will be finished."

Amal was silent for a few seconds, deep in thought, then said, "Nahla, you're the only one I can trust. I'm afraid of him, and afraid of what he could do to me now that his mother and brother are going away. I want to bring you things for safekeeping, just in case . . . in case something happens to me."

"What are you talking about? Nothing's going to happen to you. Haven't you heard what I've been telling you?"

"I've heard, Nahla, but . . . "

"Stop it, Amal. It's the war that has everyone on edge. Even my kids scream during the night."

Two days later, Amal was in the kitchen slicing eggplants while one batch was sizzling in the pot. The noise of frying prevented her from hearing the soft padding of the rubber-soled shoes on the stairs.

As she turned toward the pot, she spotted him from the corner of her eye. She froze. He stood just outside the kitchen doorway, his shoulders slumped, his arms hanging loose, a smirk on his face, his bloodshot eyes staring at her fiercely. "I see your hands are busy as your tongue has been," he said mockingly, his speech slurred.

He almost tripped down the two steps into the kitchen and grabbed a handful of her hair at the back of her neck. Immediately she retreated two steps.

He jerked her head forward, his arrack breath spewing in her face, and deliberately and slowly said, "You've never learned how to keep your ugly tongue shut up where it belongs. But I'm going to help you with that." He dealt a hard blow to her face.

Now, for the first time, unafraid, Amal shouted in his face, "You let me go right now, or . . . "

"You have the boldness to threaten me! I will have to break your teeth and cut out your tongue so you'll never again speak ill of me to my family. I'll take 'better care of you,' alright, since you 'deserve better care.'"

He yanked her hair and with all his strength pressed her cheeks together to force her mouth open. She remembered the knife on the table behind her. In one frantic movement, she reached for it and drove the blade deep into his stomach.

He stared, his eyes large and incredulous. She stood, quivering but ready to lunge again if he dared attack her. Blood bubbled from his mouth and he dropped to the floor of the small kitchen.

The sight of the blood at first froze her to the spot, rendering her utterly unable to think. Then, it registered. And she began to wail.

In horror, Nahla, who had been in the courtyard, was listening. Something unspeakable had just happened. From the stoop, she could see Amal standing in the middle of the kitchen wailing, the knife still in her hand. At her feet, lay the crumpled, motionless body of Boulos.

Paralyzed, Nahla stood and watched the hysterical behavior of Amal as she dipped her hands in a small pool of blood and rubbed her hands and arms with it. Words froze in Nahla's mouth and her legs shook. Amal appeared oblivious to Nahla standing in the doorway.

Nahla stepped inside. "Amal, listen to me!" Still hysterical, Amal kept moaning and whimpering. "Listen," Nahla commanded, shaking her shoulders. "He drove you to this. Stop behaving like a madwoman."

Amal heard Nahla's voice and stared at her friend as though she was seeing her for the first time. Then she began to wail again.

"Yes, weep and wail, you poor woman." She held Amal's shoulder and walked her out of the kitchen. "Sit in this chair and don't move until I get help. Do you understand what I just said?" She repeated herself to make sure that Amal understood. Then she closed the door behind her and turned to go down, but suddenly remembering that Boulos was visible, she shut the kitchen door that opened to the stoop.

Panting, she told her eldest daughter, fourteen-year-old Therese, to run to the nearest shop and call Aunt Aida and Uncle Ed and tell them to come immediately. "Tell them something terrible has happened to Amal."

Nahla ran back up. Amal panicked as she saw her coming toward her with two dripping towels in her arms. As Nahla cleaned up the bloodied face and arms, Amal continued to weep and wail.

In less than half an hour, Aida and Ed arrived with an English friend, one of those who had remained with their Palestinian wives. Both were disguised in Palestinian police uniforms. Nahla quickly told Aida what had happened. Then she took them upstairs.

Amal saw Ed, but did not recognize him, nor understand what he said. She continued to whimper and wail, now and then slapping her face and pulling her hair. Nahla wrapped a black shawl around her head and, with Aida's help, got Amal into her coat. The two men held her arms and lifted her off the chair. Nahla whispered to Ed to take her to her parents' place, opposite Rachel's Tomb, on the outskirts of Bethlehem. Amal heard that and struggled to free herself from their grip.

Ed and his friend hurried her out of her house and rushed her down the winding alley and all the way up and out of Jaffa Gate. Ed signalled for a taxi and put her in the back, next to him, and they sped to Bethlehem.

Amal, continued to mumble unintelligibly. In minutes, the taxi driver located the Dannos' home. She would have run away had not the Englishman overpowered her. Soon her mother came out with Gabby, and both followed Ed into the car.

In a few minutes the taxi left the asphalt and turned onto the dirt road. Sudden clouds of dust obstructed their view, and soon the taxi slowed down and stopped at a formidable metal gate.

Quickly Ed got out and rang the bell. Soon, a tall, middle-aged man, wearing a red fez, appeared. Ed disappeared inside and minutes later returned to the car and whispered to Gabby. Amal caught one word . . . "shock."

Two orderlies approached the car and dragged the screaming Amal out. Gabby and a weeping Marta followed behind and disappeared behind the gate of the daunting fortress.

CHAPTER 36

IT'S MORNING AGAIN, and Doctore Boone is back to examine my eyes. He's talking too fast for me to follow all of what he says. But I manage to catch his final pronouncement: "Tomorrow you can go back to Bethlehem."

That gives me time to see Nahla again. She'd promised to come this afternoon with coffee. On the one hand, I feel good that she even wants to see me. On the other hand, I dread having her near me. Her presence brings everything back, and I writhe in anger, fear, and guilt. But I must admit, I owe her much. If it hadn't been for her, I don't know what hell I'd be in now.

I have a dilemma, though. How do I talk to her while Sitt Marriam is listening? I want to have a serious discussion, like we used to do. If only Sitt Marriam would leave us alone!

I feel better now that I can open my eyes, even just a little. I can't wait to have these eggshells taken off.

Sitt Marriam is back, and I'm tired. I can't understand how I can be tired when all I do is lie in bed and jabber away. Sitt Marriam must be tired as well. She's not saying much today. "Go to sleep, Sitt Marriam. You're tired."

"I'm reading this magazine. Would you like me to read to you?"

"No, habeebty! There's nothing good in magazines or newspapers."

"There are some useful bits of news," she says in a matter-of-fact tone.

"Nothing but tar. Go to sleep! I want to sleep."

Slowly I drift away and then, suddenly, I hear Sitt Marriam. Is that Nahla with her?

"She has her good days and bad. But she's a character."

"You should've known her in her younger days. She was so good, so kind. But one thing she didn't have was luck."

"The poor woman went into shock when she saw a man kill her husband right before her eyes," Sitt Marriam says.

"A terrible sight. Her husband always hung around with a bad sort of people. One of them must've taken his revenge."

"Poor soul! She's very intelligent and funny, but when she's riled up—Allah help us—you don't want to be around."

"She can't help herself. I don't know of anyone who had a life worse than hers." Nahla paused then asked, "Sitt Marriam, would you let me have a little time with her alone?"

"I'm not allowed to leave her alone for more than a few minutes. If anything happens, I'll lose my job."

"I assure you nothing will happen to you. Doctore Boone is in charge here. I need a few private moments with her, like in the good old days. Please!"

"All right. It may do her some good. I'll go for a cup of tea in the lunchroom and return in, say, half an hour."

"Shookrun, Sitt Marriam."

"Amal, I've brought some fresh coffee just like in the old days. Wake up. I have only half an hour, and I want to talk the way we used to do."

I pretend I'm suddenly awake from a dream. "No *naddaraat*! Never."

"Amal, it's Nahla, habeebty. I hear you're much better today."

"Better . . . worse . . . all the same!"

"Things have to get better. Here, let me raise your bed a little so you can drink your coffee."

"You don't give coffee to a *majnooneh*."

"We both know you're not a majnooneh."

"Everyone knows I am. That's how it is."

I wish I could see the expression on her face as I tell her, "Nahla, I had a dream in which a voice said I went mad after seeing a man kill my husband."

For few seconds she was silent and then said, "Well, that's what happened. Everyone knows that."

"Everyone?"

"Everyone except a handful of us."

I take the first sip, and the rich aroma of Arabic coffee suddenly fills me with all the wonderful, warm memories of those afternoons when we poured our hearts out to each other. A sudden rush of pain tightens my throat, and I find it difficult to swallow. The tears flow, and Nahla panics.

"Amal, habeebty, what's wrong? Is my coffee so bad?"

I force myself to stop the tears and tell her jokingly, "Your coffee is now so-so, watery and too sweet. You've lost the touch, Nahla, and so have I."

I take a few sips. "Nahla, I was joking. It's the best coffee I've had . . . in a very long time, anyway . . . since that day . . . how long ago was that, Nahla?" I meant to ask that question, because I want her to tell me all that has passed since that ill-fated day.

"Nine years, I believe."

"Just nine years? That's impossible! I'm sure it's been at least forty years."

"It might feel like forty to you, but this is 1957, and you went . . . away in '48. Anyway, do you see your mother regularly?"

"I don't have a mother."

"What do you mean? Has anything happened?"

"She never came. No one came. Not family, not a friend, nor an enemy, except for Soeur Micheline."

"Who's she?"

"A nun who loved me and didn't forget me." I mean to make Nahla feel guilty.

"I'm sorry, Amal, I couldn't visit you. The first few years after the war, my life was hell. My husband was killed by a stray bullet, a week after you . . . went to . . . to Bethlehem. My days then were from Gehannem. I had to clean houses to put bread on the table. Thank Allah, the girls excelled in school. A distant cousin of my husband was the administrator of this hospital. I went to see him about a job.

"He offered to marry me. I didn't want to marry again, but I thought what do I do with four children and no money to send them to school? So I used my head and married him. He wasn't much to look at, and even older than Saleem—Allah's mercy on his soul—but he was good to me and to the children. He built a house in this area and supported all five of us. He's the one who found scholarships for the girls. Last year, he died suddenly from a heart attack. He left me everything—the house, his money, and his pension."

"You were always lucky with men, Nahla."

"Not as lucky as my daughter!"

"What do you mean?"

"Oh, I'm very grateful, but I'd be more grateful if I could marry again, this time someone young and handsome, someone with more . . . "

"Did you say things have changed, Nahla?" I ask with a smile. I can't help but love her, even though she sometimes talks like indecent women.

There's a pause, a long pause, and neither one of us knows how to go on. Suddenly, I ask, "Nahla, what happened . . . at my house?" I ask, almost in a whisper.

"That . . . well, I sent word to the Catholic priest to come right away. When he came, Ed told him someone broke in and killed Boulos with the kitchen knife, and you lost your mind from shock. The priest took care of the mass and burial that same day. It was wartime and the priest notified the police headquarters, but they didn't even come. They had bigger problems on their hands. An old widow now lives in the house."

"What about Shamiran and Kareem?"

"I heard they came back from Damascus one year after the war ended. Kareem lost all of the businesses in West Jerusalem. He lost his house in Katamon. Several chauffeurs disappeared with the taxis, and no one could find a trace of them or their families. He has two or three taxis left, I hear, and only one other business. People say he's sick—diabetic—mostly from grief over his losses. Those who ran the bakery for the year Kareem was away claimed part-ownership of it. He's spent a lot on lawsuits with no good results, people say. He lives in a rented house now, and apparently, he's aged a lot.

"You should see your sister. She looks careworn and so much older. But you will never believe the rumors about Hilaneh. The day she was supposed to leave with Kareem for Damascus, she disappeared with her suitcases. The way people tell it, she was in another part of the house, while Shamiran was packing. Shamiran went to Hilaneh's room, but she and her suitcases were gone. According to gossip, she left with her man-friend. Aida thinks she went to Yaffa. Can you believe it?"

"I can believe anything. But what she did isn't more than a smudge compared to the dark stain on my hands."

"Amal, someone should've done it to him long before—that offspring of the Shaytaan. What he did to you shocked everyone. All the neighbors and everyone who knew him said he deserved what he got! They wondered how you took it for so long. One woman told me, 'If he were my husband, I'd have poisoned him ages ago.'"

"Still, I've got his blood on my hands and my soul."

"Amal, you can't harp on it. Now, before the nurse comes back, I want you to know that the money and jewelry you left with me are safe. Anytime you want them back, just ask. I have to admit that I borrowed the money when times were difficult, but I put it back as soon as my financial situation improved. If you want me to give it to your fam . . . "

"I have no family. If ever I have a need for it, I know how to reach you. It won't do me any good now or in the hereafter. So take it all, Nahla, or give it to the poor—to some unfortunate woman."

"As you wish, but I still hope you'll be able to make use of it yourself, while you live. Isn't there something you need now in that place?"

"What I need no one can give—except Allah. But . . . " I find myself choking with tears.

"Amal, don't. It's not good for your eyes. For years you suffered so much but kept going, and now you're giving up. This is not the Amal I knew."

"I'm not the woman you knew. I'm someone other—lost, damned, full of fear."

"Amal, Allah must have understood how that man drove you to that point. He must have forgiven you."

"If He has, why is my mind on fire and my heart in agony?"

"Because you won't let go. You're hanging onto that one hideous moment and you won't let go. Any other person would have cracked long before."

A knock, and the door opens. The nurse asks sweetly, "Have you two had a nice visit?"

"Yes, very nice, Sitt Marriam," Nahla replies.

"It looks like Amal will be going back tomorrow. She's doing very well."

"Do you think I could come tomorrow to say good-bye and bring something special? I wanted to bring a nice meal for her today, but last night I couldn't manage. Today I'll leave work early."

"That would be good. Right, Amal?"

"Right, wrong, sweet, sour. I don't know."

Then Nahla puts her arms around me and kisses me on the cheeks and on my head. My throat is constricted again, but I drive the tears back—tears of being denied the love of a mother. Nahla says she'll see me tomorrow, her voice scratchy. She's trying to control herself, too.

Suddenly she says, "I almost forgot the almonds and chocolatta in my purse. There they are. Enjoy them when you feel like it."

The door closes, and I let the tears run. Sitt Marriam strokes my hair and shoulders, all the while telling me how happy I should be about having such a good friend. "I wish I had a friend like Nahla. You're so lucky, Amal. Not everyone has such a loving friend. You're blessed."

Slowly I begin to think of Sitt Marriam's wish for a friend like Nahla. I never thought of her having or not having friends. She sounded sad when she said that. She envies me? What a joke! But maybe she *is* friendless. She has a mother, though, and I don't. I did have a loving nun, an angel, a surrogate mother. But it's been six years since she last came. I'm so ashamed of the way I behaved then. Blinded by my own pain and anger, I didn't see how Soeur Micheline might have been suffering.

She visited me regularly in the first three years I was in the Oasis. On the last few visits a novice had accompanied her. I never thought to ask why she was there. During those visits I was usually in a quandry, uncertain whether to act like a mildly deranged woman, or to be true to my real self. I wanted to reveal the truth to her, in hopes of receiving some direction toward peace, but I always succumbed to my fear of confessing and exposing my crime.

I could not bring myself to utter the horror I had committed, so I resorted to my usual pretense of madness. "Where's Jesus? He hasn't come to visit in a long time. He doesn't love me anymore."

Soeur Micheline put her arm around me. "He loves you more than you know, Amal. Pray and ask Him to help you, chère."

I whimpered, then broke into a giggle. "What did you bring me? Roasted almonds and pumpkin seeds?"

The good nun handed me some chocolate and watched as I snatched the Cadbury bar and began gobbling it. "Slowly, slowly, Amal. No one is going to take it from you."

Suddenly, my eyes filled with tears. Soeur Micheline patted my back and asked, "What is it, ma fille? Tell me."

"I want to die. Why haven't they come? Where is my family? Why have they deserted me? Even my mother has never come to see me, not once!"

"She did come, Amal. She came twice, but you refused to see her."

"That was a long time ago when I was like a raging beast. I was angry at everyone."

"You are still angry, chère." The old nun looked doleful. "Pray for Jesus to come into your heart and cleanse it of all the anger. Ask for forgiveness and the wisdom to forgive those who have hurt you."

"Jesus is deaf, like His Father. They're busy with good people. They have no time for a bad madwoman! And why should I ask for forgiveness? Allah's the one who should ask me to forgive Him for what He's done to me! And the others? My family? I hate them all!" My voice reached the rafters.

Soeur Micheline's faced turned ashen at my blasphemy.

"Turn toward love, Amal. Begin by forgiving your mother. She loves you very much. She weeps for you. The sweets and almonds I bring each time are from her, a token of her love for you."

I turned to stare at her, then jumped to my feet and hurled the rest of the chocolate and nuts at the wall. "That's what I do with her token of love. You tell her that! I don't need her token, I don't want her love. I don't want her to come and see me, that spineless coward. I curse her and the day she conceived me!"

The nun sat motionless and silent. Then she grimaced and put her hand near her heart. Seconds later, she held out her arms, beckoning me. When I knelt before her, she put her hand on my head and said, "Chère fille, my prayers will always follow you and my love will always find you. May God soothe your cankered soul."

I saw how pale and tired she looked as she struggled to her feet and moved toward the doorway where the novice waited for her. But as usual, I was wrapped in my own misery.

And where is my Soeur Micheline now?

CHAPTER 37

"HEY, AMAL, wake up. What a night you've had—talking away!"

"You know, as soon as Doctore Boone comes, we're going to get ready to go back to Bethlehem."

"I want to see Nahla before we leave."

"She said she would come, and she will. Don't worry."

A sudden knock, then the door opens. I hear Doctore Boone's voice, "Good morning!"

"Good morning, Doctore!" I say it in a slow, singsong fashion, just as we used to chant in class every morning.

He removes the taped eggshells over my eyes and examines them—pulling at the eyelids, shining the light into my eyes. He asks how many fingers I see. I see his five fingers, though not clearly, but he says, "Very good."

I don't know how good that is when I can't see details. He gabbles something to the nurse. I wish he would speak more slowly. With his hand on my shoulder he says something, and the nurse translates. "Amal, il doctore says your eyesight is quite good. You just have to be careful to protect your eyes from infection. You have to keep them covered a little longer while you sleep, or when you're outdoors. Then, in a few weeks, you can be fitted with eyeglasses. After that, you'll be able to see well again."

Il doctore pats my shoulder and says, "Good luck. Good-bye, now!"

"Good-bye, Doctore." And since he is Nahla's son-in-law, I add, "Thank you for taking care of this blind woman."

I'm nervous and fidgety; I don't know why. Maybe it's because I don't want to leave Nahla again. At first I didn't want to see her, but how quickly my feelings have changed. I yearn for those days we chatted over coffee. That's what I miss—a connection with someone who truly loves me. Nahla's visit has awakened in me the longing for love, a longing I had suppressed all these years. I hope she will visit me now and then, but I'm not going to ask or beg.

Someone knocks on the door, but it's a strange knock, like someone is hitting the door with something other than a knuckle. The nurse welcomes Nahla in.

"Sorry, Sitt Marriam. Both hands are full, and I had to knock with this pot."

Nahla comes over to hug and kiss me. "How are you today, Amal?"

"Flying above the wind!"

"You'll feel like flying above the wind when you see what I brought you."

I've got to get rid of the nurse. "Nahla, we should give this good nurse a break. I give her little rest, day or night."

"Yes, she is a great nurse, and well deserves a good rest."

Sitt Marriam takes the hint. "Why don't you two enjoy each other's company. I'll come back in a little while."

Sitt Marriam raises my bed and leaves.

Nahla puts a warm plate on the table and I eat. "Oh, Nahla, this is enough to heal the heart and soul!"

"So, I'm good?"

"You're the best."

"I had the best teacher!"

"Nonsense!"

Then she puts a cup of Arabic coffee in my hands. It tastes heavenly.

Nahla says, "I'm sending the rest of the food with you. Sitt Marriam will give it to you tonight for supper, and tomorrow for lunch. I've been here a few years and I can tell you, nurses like her are rare."

Nahla clears her throat and I know she wants to say something serious. "Amal, I have to start my duty in a few minutes, but I'll see you in the front before you leave. Please, take care of yourself, and keep your spirits up, because things will be better. I'm going to say a special prayer for you every night and light a candle for you at the church of Sittna Marriam. I promise to see you soon."

Nahla leaves, and I begin to feel the same kind of abandonment I felt when Immie left me at beit il-majaneen nine years ago. Is this another of those times that fill me with hope, only to disappoint?

I begin to sink again into my dark world. But Sitt Marriam's cheerful voice soon rouses me. "We must get ready to leave, Amal. Let's get ready before Ghassan comes."

Without a word, I do what she says. Inside me are many colliding emotions, which cause me to be irritable, but I remain silent.

A while later, I hear Ghassan's voice at the door, "Sitt Marriam. Are you ready?"

She holds my arm and guides me out the door, through dark corridors, and finally outside the hospital.

Suddenly, I hear Nahla, "Amal, I brought you these dark glasses to wear when you don't need the cotton patch. They'll give you protection from dust or sunlight. Use them until you get the real eyeglasses."

"At your command!" I say, and everyone laughs.

Nahla kisses me again and promises to come visit me soon.

"Tomorrow!" I say.

"At your service, your Highness!" Nahla says. That draws chuckles.

As the taxi speeds back toward Bethlehem, my mind goes over and over the last four-and-half days—especially Nahla's visits. I never thought I'd see her again.

Then the chauffeur says, "Here we are at Rahail's Tomb, where the wind blows ten times harder than anywhere else."

I'm so near and so far away.

Sitt Marriam asks, "What do you mean?"

What do I mean? I must've spoken aloud. I must be more careful. "I mean beit il-majaneen."

In a short while, the taxi slows down. We must be getting closer. The taxi stops, and Ghassan opens the door and helps me out. Then Sitt Marriam takes my arm and guides me to the gate and bangs on it.

I hear Abu Salem's congenial voice. "Ahlan, ahlan, Sitt Marriam! Ahlan Amal!"

"Sitt Amal," I correct him.

Sitt Marriam laughs, and the old man apologizes. "I'm so sorry. It's my fault! You're right. Sitt Amal!"

Sitt Marriam guides my steps inside the gate. "Where am I going now?"

"To the same room in the Sick Ward. We have to make sure nothing disturbs your progress. When you get the new glasses and you can see very well, you'll go back to your ward. Doctor's orders."

I'd like to be with Khadeejeh and the rest of my friends. The few days at the eye hospital made me realize I need to be with others. On the other hand, I like the peace and quiet of the Sick Ward, having my own room, and my own nurse. Such a wonderful nurse! I can't wait to see what she really looks like.

Once I'm back in the Sick Ward, an idea strikes me. "How about bringing Khadeejeh to have supper with us?"

"Perhaps. Just stay nice and quiet until I come back."

"At your command, Colonel Marriam!"

CHAPTER 38

SITT MARRIAM brings Khadeejeh in for ten minutes. My poor friend! She's so excited she never stops hugging and kissing me, spraying me with her spit. I keep wiping my face and thinking it a blessing. It's Saturday—bath day. It's very cold outside and not so warm inside the wards. But here, I can't complain. In a few weeks I'll be back with my friends.

Khadeejeh says, "Amal, habeebty, we have to start our lessons. Immie came and brought me paper, but the bastards took it away. You have to talk to Sitt Marriam about that."

"Khadeejeh, we have to wait until I can see."

"When's that?"

"I don't know—soon, when I can see better with the glasses."

"Tell them you need them very soon."

"It's not up to me, Khadeejeh."

"You have to tell them. All the time you've been away, the

voices have been screaming in my head. We have to start soon, habeebty."

"Of course! I'll tell Sitt Marriam."

Sitt Marriam is in the room all the time when Khadeejeh visits. She tells Khadeejeh it's time to leave. "But I just came. I haven't even eaten my food."

"You have, Khadeejeh. You've been eating and talking at the same time. I'll take you back, and bring you again tomorrow for a little visit. I have work to do now."

"Liar! They're all liars. Don't believe a word she says," Khadeejeh spouts off angrily.

"It's all right, Khadeejeh. You'll come again, and soon I'm going to be back with you."

"And never leave me again?"

"Never!" I say, aware I can't be sure of anything. She kisses me again and again. As the nurse leads her toward the door, she promises, "I'm coming again tomorrow."

I must admit, going to the Hospital for Ocular Diseases has done me a lot of good, especially seeing Nahla again, and hearing the most incredible tale of how the bastard was murdered. "Someone killed him," Nahla said. I wish someone had, and saved me the trouble of bloodying my hands and staining my soul.

Nahla's version also helped me remember the interview with the elderly doctore, who questioned me the day they took me in. In the state I was in, my disconnected answers flitted from east to west, as did my emotions.

Whenever he asked about Boulos' death, I stood and danced, belting out a zaghrootah. Then I wailed and beat my head hard with both hands. He asked why I was doing that. I didn't know what to say and blurted out that someone in my head told me to do it. Then he asked who that "someone" was, and I told him it was a woman. And he wanted to know more about the "woman," and I told him I swore on the Koran not to tell or the Shaytaan would get me. I don't know how I thought of the Koran when, as a Christian, I should've said the Gospel, and from my name he knew I was Christian. Then, thinking mad people are hysterical, I started to laugh and cry in an alternating pattern.

When he asked if I knew who killed my husband, I was shocked. I stopped and stared at him and had no idea how to answer.

Sometime in the midst of my raving, a nurse admitted my mother and brother. I saw them out of the corner of my eye. I didn't let on, though, and never once looked at them directly.

Il doctore started telling my brother that he thought I'd had a shock, and I might also have some "sophrenia." Gabby didn't know what it was, but il doctore explained to him about a type of hysteria, when voices talk to the afflicted and tell them all sorts of things. Gabby denied that the family was ever aware of that.

Before the visit ended, my mother turned to me and wanted to embrace me, but I clutched the nurse who stood beside me all that time and tried to hide as from some attacker. I remember saying, "Don't let her touch me! She's going to hurt me! Don't let her hurt me!"

When I peeked at her, I saw the agony in her face as she sobbed, and I thought, *Good! Suffer, you whimpering coward! Look what you've driven me to!* That was the last time I saw her or any one of my family. I suppose they stayed away to avoid the shame of having a madwoman in the family. Or maybe they never really loved me. Not even my mother or Gabby.

I spend my time counting the hours and the days to the next Sunday when Nahla might come. She promised, but will she? Time has now become important to me. Before that hideous Soraiya clobbered me, days melted into nights and I didn't care what day or month it was.

I ask Sitt Marriam what day it is, and she says, "You've asked three times now, and three times I've told you it's Friday; tomorrow is Saturday, bath day, and the day after is Sunday."

I didn't forget. This is part of my plan—just in case she got a whiff of my conversations with Nahla. That worries me. I repeat what she says, slowly, and then ask if Nahla's coming on Sunday. She says, "We'll see. I hope so."

"Maybe she'll bring me kenapheh and roasted almonds and Syrianni melon seeds."

"She always does. Everyone spoils you. You are one lucky woman."

"You have no idea how!"

She wishes me good night and leaves.

"It's Sunday!" Sitt Marriam brings me breakfast. "And you're lucky again!"

"Your brain is twirling in your head again. I knew something was going to happen to you sooner or later, poor girl!"

Laughing, she says, "Look! Can you see what I'm holding?"

I see two small, oval-shaped whitish objects, one in each hand. "Looks like eggs, but it can't be!"

"Bravo! You guessed it," she says cheerfully.

"Where do you get eggs in winter? They can't be chicken eggs!"

"Yes, they are. Now we have modern chicken farms in Amman. We can get eggs all year round."

"From Amman? Where's that?"

"Our new capital. My mother boiled them this morning."

I feel overwhelmed with such generosity, and guilty because her mother's an old widow with only a daughter to support her. I feel like I'm stealing from her but can't refuse her kindness. "Your mother is an angel from heaven."

"My mother has a heart of gold. And . . . she has fallen in love with you and the stories I tell her about you."

I can't believe what's happening to me these days. Strangers are acting like my family, sending me food, showing concern for me. Nahla might come today, and I know she won't come empty-handed. I'm feeling so good that I'm afraid of slipping and giving myself away.

"Am I going back to the ward to sleep in the same room with all my friends?"

"Yes. Do you like that?"

"Yes. No!"

"You can't decide? Tell me why you like being here."

"It's quiet. I can th . . . " I stop abruptly. I can't be rational with her. "Will you give me chocolatta, when I go back to the ward? I can't live on Im Issa's horrible food."

There's a knock at the door. "Nahla!" I shout, excited. And I feel her breath around my neck and hear her friendly voice. "Marhaba, Amal! How are you, habeebty?"

"As good as I look. What do you think?"

"Much better than the last time I saw you, when your eyes were bandaged."

"You talk like Sitt Marriam, diplomatic like." And they laugh.

"I brought you a surprise."

"What's going on? One surprise after another! I'm starving. They starve me here, Nahla."

Sitt Marriam says, "You're such a poor, spoiled woman." They laugh, and Nahla says, "She deserves all the spoiling we can give her."

I eat from the food Nahla brought. The nurse says, "I'll save the rest for tomorrow."

"Nahla, she always takes away my food."

When the nurse leaves, I whisper to Nahla to play along with me when Sitt Marriam is in the room.

"You give her a hard time, Amal. Why?"

I signal to her with my index finger to come closer. She leans her head against mine, and I whisper in her ear, "That's the way to keep them believing I'm mad. Otherwise, if they think I'm sane, they'll ask me to leave, and where would I go, Nahla?"

Sitt Marriam returns and says to Nahla, "I'll be in the next room, in Doctore Jamayelle's office. I'll keep the door between us unlocked, but the door to the outside is locked."

"Shookrun, Sitt Marriam. Amal is so lucky to have you as her nurse."

As soon as the nurse leaves, Nahla whispers to me, "Amal, you can't spend the rest of your days in this place. Why, it's a prison."

"That's right. It's not a nice place, but it's right for the likes of me. How long were we neighbors, Nahla?"

"Nine years."

"And how long has it been since that day?"

"Nine years."

"Figure it out. I was almost twenty-four when I married. So, how old am I now, Nahla?"

"Forty-two, forty-three?"

"Now how could an old woman like me survive, Nahla?"

"You have me. I'll help you find a job at the hospital where I work, and maybe they'll train you to be a nurse, or you can be a cook. Forget the past and look ahead."

"And have fingers point at me at every turn. Not as easy as it sounds, Nahla!"

"Even ants do more for themselves than you're doing, Amal. They never stop searching for food. Small as they are, they have such a will to survive."

"I wish I were an ant!"

"I'm not smart enough to make you see, unfortunately. But try to look at life differently, Amal. Next Sunday, I'm coming with my daughter Therese and her husband Doctore Boone. He wants to check your eyes. Another friend of his, an optometrist, will come with him. Doctore Rajani will decide what kind of eyeglasses you need. And there's something else. Something you and I need to do."

I panic every time she comes up with a new idea. "What's that, Nahla?"

"I've asked permission to take you to mass Christmas Eve at the Church of the Nativity."

"Have you lost your mind, Nahla. Never!"

"But why? I can't understand you."

How can I make her understand! I feel like an outcast, like a leper in Biblical times. I don't belong anywhere anymore, except here. "What if someone recognizes me? All faces will turn toward me, their lips whispering, 'Isn't that the Dannos' daughter, the one who went mad and hacked her husband to death!'"

"Well, then, we'll go on Monday, mid-morning, when very few people will be there, mostly tourists."

"And I'm a tourist from Gehannem! Forget it!"

Sitt Marriam knocks and walks in. Nahla thanks her. "We've had a good visit. Right, Amal?"

"Right," I say in a flat voice.

Nahla kisses me and leaves. I lie there, confused and worried. All I want is sleep. Maybe when I wake up, today will have been a bad dream.

CHAPTER 39

THIS IS THE SUNDAY Nahla promised to come with il doctore to examine my eyes and test them for glasses. I'm dreading today. All those people all at once! Nine years of isolation, and now, it seems, the whole world wants to see me. It's difficult to handle.

I also worry about persuading Nahla against taking me to the Church of the Nativity. I can't go. But now I have to deal with my immediate worry—how to handle these visitors. Curse Soraiya who started it all, and the imbecile Pharha!

I've had my breakfast, and I wait for the nurse. I feel the bone-chilling cold, in spite of the woollen socks I wear, socks that Sitt Marriam's mother had knit for me. How I wish I had a mother like hers!

No matter how I try to focus on pleasant things, I end up turning to anxious, somber thoughts. I'll try to sleep until Nahla comes.

I see the vast courtyard in front of the Church of the Nativity, the colorful scouts and playing bands from every denomination, all lined up on both sides of the court, and the main street leading to it. Motley throngs gathered to see the Patriarch, surrounded by dignitaries, walk up to and through the small entrance to the huge church.

Suddenly, I spy a girl of eight who, with her small gang of friends, sneaks away to join in the excitement of the day. The scene is as vivid as if it were happening right now.

My two friends and I are elbowing our way through the crowds. We get pushed out a few times, being told how rude we are, how our parents didn't raise us well. We don't care—we're determined to see the procession.

Finally, we manage to crouch behind some women and peek out between their long skirts. We make sure our fingers don't touch their legs, or we'd get a good kick from their heels. We hear the people behind us. "These imps under our feet!" We remain quiet, and they ignore us.

What a thrill it is to watch the parade of scouts from every Christian sect—Room Orthodox, Armenian Orthodox, Copts, and Syriann Orthodox. Our Orthodox feast comes two weeks after the Catholic feast. Every Orthodox believer thinks our feast is better—our scouts look more colorful, our drums beat louder, and the archbishops that follow the scouts look more impressive. But the Catholics around our enclave—all natives of Bethlehem—believe their feast is the best. We don't argue with them. There are more of them, and they have more money, and own most of the homes and property in Bethlehem.

Now each of the Orthodox churches has its own Patriarch,

bishops, and elders inside the Church of the Nativity, and policemen stand at the small entrance to guard against intruders—children without parents, like us, trying to get into the crowded church. We have to leave now and hope we can sneak in to our homes unnoticed. We pray our mothers didn't miss us during that enchanting hour, but we brace ourselves for possible punishment. On our way down the steep hill from the square to Wadi M'ali, we plan our strategy.

We're at the gate of our enclave, and Nadia sneaks in first, to test the waters. Nadia's mother is lenient, compared to Siham's mother and the red-fire Sitty. We don't see Nadia come out for few minutes and wonder what to do next. Then we see her walking slowly toward the gate and stopping just outside it. "They suspect we went to the parade, but I told Immie we were playing in the fields below. She doesn't believe me. I have to stay inside for three days."

I persuade Siham to go next. Then, after a few minutes, I walk in, and guess who's waiting for me? Who else? I insist I was with Nadia and Siham in the fields below. Sitty looks at me with narrowed eyes and says, "You think I was born yesterday, offspring of the imps?" Immie, however, believes me, or pretends to believe me. Sitty rushes toward me, and I run and hide behind my mother. Sitty tries to catch me, but I'm too quick for her, and Immie tells her to end this game before she falls and breaks her neck. Sitty stops, but not before condemning me to house arrest for a week. I'm happy I didn't get a thrashing with the broom in her hand. Immie should use that trick every time Sitty goes after me. I feel like laughing but don't dare. Instead, I put on a sad face, like I've been punished unfairly.

I wake up to Sitt Marriam's voice calling me. I hear hushed

voices. I want to return to my dream. But Nahla comes near my bed, kisses me and inquires about my health.

"You look good! Say marhaba to everyone here—Doctore Boone, Doctore Rajani, and Therese. They're staying only as long as it takes to test your eyes. Then we'll have lunch."

"Marhaba, Tante!" says Therese. "You look better than you did three weeks ago."

"Bless your sweet tongue!"

"My husband will check your eyes first, and then Doctore Rajani will give you the test. In another week or two, you'll see as well as anyone here. Here is Doctore Boone!"

"Marhaba," he says in his funny accent, and I'd laugh if it weren't rude. He examines me as usual, very gently. "Very good. Everything looks very good. I think we're ready for specs."

Sitt Marriam doesn't need to explain. I understood him.

"Amal," he says my name in the funniest way, "Doctore Rajani will give you the eye test, and he will make you the best specs—naddaraat."

I giggle at the way he spoke.

"If you're laughing at the way I speak Arabic, blame Therese. She's my teacher." Then everyone laughs.

Now Therese comes near me and says they have to leave.

"Allah fill your home with many children, habeebty!"

She translates what I said for her husband, and he laughs. "Not so many. We Inglizi have one or two. That's enough."

I tell Therese, "Foreigners are strange. Imagine having one or two! You should have at least six or seven."

She translates again, and they all laugh.

"If I have a girl, I'm going to give her your name. I've always loved your name, Tante."

"Allah bless you." I whisper in her ear, "Don't use my name."

"Why, Tante?"

"It's cursed!"

"No, Tante, there's no such thing, and your name means hope. What's more beautiful?"

I feel relieved now that they're gone and Nahla says, "That wasn't bad. You worried about it, and everything went so well. Now you must be hungry."

"Famished!"

The thought of Sitt Marriam listening to me talk to Nahla worries me. I can't let her doubt my condition.

"Nahla," I shout, "I'm dying from hunger. They haven't fed me for days." And just as I say that, I hear the door open and shut.

"Sitt Marriam has gone to get plates and forks."

"She's a rare gem! The trouble I gave her at first would have tried the patience of Ayyoub! What an angel!"

"That she is."

The door suddenly opens. Sitt Marriam comes in. "Hope you had a good visit."

"We did. Thank you," Nahla says.

Finally, Nahla gets up and asks if I'm ready to put on the clothes she made for me, and to go with her to the Church of the Nativity.

I feel my insides shudder. "Nahla, I love you and am deeply grateful, but it's impossible. I can't do that."

"Amal, just try. You can't say no without trying. Give it a chance. And I do so want to see you in the lovely dress and coat I made. Do it for me."

I feel powerless. All my previous resolve is now smothered. The nurse helps her to dress me, and both of them keep flattering me, telling me how good I look with the new outfit, coat and shoes. Then, the nurse fits on the sunglasses Nahla gave me to protect my eyes. Nahla and the nurse take me, each holding an arm, and the nurse says, "Let's go!"

I'm trembling as they walk me out to the waiting taxi. "We won't be long, no more than half an hour and we'll be back," Nahla tells the nurse.

Nahla holds my hand and tries to comfort me. My trembling and anxiety increase as the taxi leaves the dirt road and goes faster on the asphalt. "In just a few minutes we'll be at the church," Nahla says.

Now my tears come and I shake like a leaf. "Nahla, we have to turn back. Take me back, I beg you!"

"Amal, try to calm down. There won't be too many people there. We'll go in, say a couple of prayers and leave."

I begin to lose control and become hysterical. Nahla has no choice but to tell the chauffeur to turn back. I feel terrible doing that to sweet Nahla. Perhaps she will never come back to see me. I have disappointed her.

The nurse is surprised that we have returned so soon. "She refused to go and became hysterical," Nahla explains.

"I'm sorry. Perhaps you can try at some other time."

Nahla sounds sad, "Amal, it's alright. Maybe it wasn't the right time for you. I'm sorry. I didn't realize how strongly you felt." She kisses me, promises to come again, and leaves.

CHAPTER 40

IT'S THREE WEEKS NOW since Nahla's last visit. Alone in bed, I listen to the wind. I've never liked winters, not only because of the cold, but mostly because of the wild winds that unleash their fury, whistling, keening, and roaring menacingly. Unable to sleep, I keep tossing in bed thinking—the worst thing to do.

I'm certain Nahla's upset and she should be. I'm so ungrateful. Perhaps, I should've just closed my eyes, kept my fears bottled inside, and gone with her to church. This *should've* is like a permanent, dull toothache that eventually wears you down. Sometimes I wish Nahla hadn't re-entered my world. Would've been easier to continue to rot until the end of my days. And that is no way to think. I want to change the way I feel, think, and live. But bringing about change is more difficult than the dreadful present.

Eventually, I surrender to sleep.

I'm sitting on a rock, surrounded by untended fields and groves, no one around except birds chirping while looking for food. The sun is red-hot. I'm full of anxiety because I only have a vague sense of the reason I'm here. It's a strange feeling of waiting for something but not knowing what that something is.

The thought nags at me that I must be going before darkness falls, though I have no idea where I must go. Suddenly it is dusk, and I feel the urgency of leaving before it's dark and the evil spirits of the night are on the prowl. I've heard of such things. It's cooler now and the day is drifting into night. Get up, I tell myself. Now!

Just as I try to get up, I make out the dark shape of a woman moving in my direction. Perhaps she knows where she's going, or where I'm going. As she comes closer, I see an old woman, all in black, like someone in mourning. She is dabbing her face, a web of deep wrinkles mars what might have once been handsome. A black scarf covers her head.

"Where are you going, ya Khalty?"

"To the Haj, my sacred pilgrimage," she says weakly.

"But the Haj is in Mecca, not here."

"No, it's this way, child. It's late, but I must be going."

I decide to go with her. Perhaps, I'll remember where I'm supposed to go. After a while I say, "It's too dark now, and I'm afraid."

"It is, but I've waited too long to do this, and now there's no turning back."

A short while later, she points at a large rock some distance away, and says, "There it is. We will pray there."

I'm angry. I've been following a mad woman who has dragged me to a rock. "Kneel and pray by yourself, I'm leaving."

As I walk away, she begins to wail. "Stop your wailing! You'll bring the wolves down on us." I continue to walk faster and faster under an inky sky, on rocky road, without a sense of place or time.

Suddenly, I hear wolves howling in the distance. I panic and run as fast as I can, afraid of stumbling. I glance behind me and see two pairs of small fireballs bobbing in the dark, approaching. Very soon after, I hear the heavy breathing of the beasts padding behind me. I let out a scream. I'm at a ledge and face a drop to a terrace far below. The wolves are a few feet away and I jump.

My feet don't find the ground, and I'm so afraid I'm falling into a bottomless dark hole. Then, out of nowhere, arms catch me, and I see the old woman in black. "Don't be afraid, child," she says. "I'm taking you to safe grounds."

I scream and struggle in her arms. I don't want the safer grounds of a mad woman!

Suddenly, I hear Sitt Marriam. "Amal, wake up! It's all right."

My arms are still thrashing as Sitt Marriam holds me. I'm shaking and terrified, and begin to sob. "It's just a bad dream,' she says gently.

"A nightmare from Gehannem." She gets me up and walks me to the washroom and splashes cold water on my face.

"I'll get you something to drink. Stay in the chair and don't move until I return."

I am still in the wake of the nightmare, hard as I try to shake it off. The nurse comes back with a glass of lemonade. I drink it fast and I feel the nightmare losing its grip. "Soon, I'll get your lunch and you'll feel much better. Stay in the chair. Sleeping during the day is not a good thing any longer."

Yes, so many philosophers and advisers these days! Everyone wants me to do this and that.

"Do you want to tell me about your dream?"

"Not now. Let me rest." I know there's no rest. I'm still lost in that dark wilderness, alone and frightened out of my mind, believing the jaws of the beasts are tearing away at my flesh, or that old woman is planning to carry me away to some terrible place.

After lunch, Sitt Marriam tells me my wardmates have been asking for me. "How would you like to see them. It might do you some good."

"Let me think about it. Maybe a change is what I need."

She leaves. The nightmare still hovers over me. Maybe Khadeejeh and her jabber will help dispel my anxiety.

After lunch, Sitt Marriam puts the gray hospital coat on me, covers my head with a scarf, and leads me to the room where the patients stay during the day in winter. Before we enter, she puts the sunglasses on me. She opens the door, and Hala's voice rises in a zaghrootah:

Ayee, ya alf ahlan bi-Amal;
Ayee, biss-ssinna wil-hana, widd-dalal;
Ayee, mish msad'een in-shoofek'
Ayee, lanhoutt itt taj ala rassek!
Lulululululululu!
Ayee, a thousand welcomes to Amal;
Ayee, in joy, good health, and wealth;
Ayee, we can't wait to have you back
Ayee to place the crown on your head!
Lulululululululu!

I can't believe how good I feel at the way they're welcoming me back. They let Khadeejeh embrace and cover me with kisses first. One of them yells, "Enough Khadeejeh! Leave a little of her cheeks for us!" They all laugh, and I find I can't stop smiling. So many questions all at once that I have to plead for help. "Settle down! I only have two ears and one mouth!"

They laugh, and then begin to argue over who should sit beside me. They push and shove, competing for first place next to Khadeejeh. They don't want to push her around. She's not only my best friend, but the tallest and strongest.

Now Sitt Marriam tells them we only have half an hour, and each is allowed one question. After I've answered all their questions, Sitt Marriam tells them she will take me back, but will allow me to come for an hour everyday.

I feel better than I've felt in a while. They treated me like a celebrity and that warmed my heart. But that night I have the same nightmare, and the night nurse comes running. She holds my thrashing arms and tries to wake me up. She keeps asking me what is frightening me so, and I tell her, "the wolves . . . woman in black . . . "

CHAPTER 41

FOR A WEEK NOW, I've been having the same nightmare, waking up the night nurse with my screaming. During the day, I try to convince myself it's nothing. Other times I search for the meaning, but I quickly abandon that. I'm afraid and don't want to know what it means. I've convinced myself that dreams are nothing but a figment of the imagination. Oh, I do have some imagination! I become more anxious as we get closer to night time.

It must be the weather. All week long the raging wind bellows night and day.

Now they sedate me at night to stop the nightmares. I've become quiet again, uninterested in talking or eating. I'm tired. All I do is sit or sleep.

One afternoon, a nurse walks in and tells me I have a visitor. I tell her I don't want to see anyone. "It's your friend Nahla."

My first reaction is to send her away. Seconds later I

remember that she's my only link to the outside world. I sit up. This must be Sunday. She has finally come. I've been thinking she's abandoned me.

In the Visitors Room, Nahla hugs me and kisses me. Then, we sit down. "You're so quiet. Are you upset because I haven't come sooner?"

"I was beginning to think you'd never come back."

"How could you think that! I've had a very bad cold and have been quite busy with a few matters. So now I'm here. How have you been?"

"So-so."

"I spoke with Sitt Marriam. She told me you've been having nightmares."

I look at her, not knowing what to say. "Is it true, Amal?"

"True. I'd rather not talk about them."

"Amal, talking about them might help. I'd like to know. You know, a friend of mine has a book on dreams and often talks about their meanings. Maybe we can figure out what your dreams mean."

"Maybe it's better not to know, Nahla."

"That's not like you, Amal. We're sisters. Please, tell me."

So I tell her.

"The beginning is terrifying, Amal, but the ending is good. Somebody is saving you from the wolves. Don't you think so?"

"I don't know what to think anymore."

"I'll speak with my friend about it. She might have an interesting interpretation. Now, I have a few things for you. Some sweets, and your new glasses. Doctore Rajani wants to know how they fit and how well you see with them. Shall we try them on? Do you like the brown frames? I thought they would suit you."

"Do I have to try them on now?"

"Of course! I have to tell him how you see with them. Let me help you put them on. And look at you. I do like them on you."

I take a quick look at Nahla, and I'm shocked, and try to take them off.

"No, keep them on, Amal. You have to get used to them."

I look at the floor, the walls and ceiling, avoiding Nahla's face. The Turkish rug is the usual strong reds and blacks. On the wall facing me is a landscape—lush green meadow and giant trees, all vivid colors. I never noticed it before. It must be new. Nahla takes my face in her hands and turns me around to face her. "Now tell me what you see."

I don't want to describe her. She is not the Nahla I knew. She's so changed.

"I'm waiting, Amal."

"Well, you've changed some."

"I've changed a lot. And who hasn't! Everyone has. So, how do you like my graying hair, and my wrinkles?"

"I don't see wrinkles."

"If you don't, I'll have to take the glasses back to have them made stronger."

"There's no need for that. I see very well with them."

"I see. You didn't want to hurt my feelings, then."

We laugh and I begin to feel better. "Thank you, Nahla. I could never repay you for what you've done for me."

"I'm not sure about that. You've done so much for me in the past. We're for each other anyway. Sisters forever." She hugs me and it feels good.

"Are you going to have something to eat now?"

"Thank you, Nahla. Maybe later. I had a big lunch."

She chats on about her family and some friends for a few minutes, just to keep the conversation going. Then, suddenly, Sitt Marriam comes and takes a few steps inside the room. Behind her white-stockinged legs is a pair of legs in black. I freeze. What's this? My heart is pounding, and fearfully, I look at Nahla, then at the nurse, and back at Nahla. I'm speechless. Sitt Marriam speaks, "Amal, you have a visitor." She moves sideways and I see an old woman in black. I am seized with the terror of my nightmares.

I feel Nahla's arms around me. "Amal, it's alright. This is not a ghost. Take a look and see who it is." The nurse moves out of the woman's way, and I see her. Now, the anger of a lifetime floods my heart and I scream at her, "No, go back! Go back!" She's weeping. "Now you weep. I don't need you or your tears." I turn to the nurse, "Take her away. I will not see her."

The nurse leads her out of the room. I'm so angry that I'm shaking in Nahla's arms. "Nahla, whose idea was this?"

In a sober voice she says, "Mine, Sitt Marriam's, and your mother's. Last month she came to see me first, then Sitt Marriam, pleading with us to bring her to you. She's wearing black mourning, first her mother, and six months later for her husband. Amal, there comes a time to leave the past behind and face the present."

"Let me go, Nahla. I don't feel good." I get up to go, and my legs buckle under me. Nahla and the nurse lift me and lay me on the divan. I'm half conscious of Nahla's anxious voice calling me. Someone puts a cold damp towel on my forehead. My head slowly clears.

The nurse keeps talking to me, and then asks if I could stand up. They help me get to my feet and walk me to my room. There they put me to bed, and I hear weeping. "Amal, I'm sorry if I did the wrong thing. I thought it a good idea to bring peace to both of you. She's suffering, too, Amal. Forgive me if I made things worse."

I gather enough strength to speak. "Nahla, whatever you've done it was with a good heart, I know. But I was not prepared. I've known this would happen sooner or later, that the woman of my nightmares would come! But I tried hard not to admit it openly. I need time to think. It must be getting late. You can leave, Nahla, before it gets dark."

For days I remain in a somber mood, pensive, reflecting on the past, the present, and the future, nothing easy or simple. I still can't figure out what to do. They think I'm in depression, and perhaps I am.

Unexpectedly, Sitt Marriam brings in Khadeejeh. She throws herself on me, hugging and kissing. "Amal, habeebty, it's so lonely without you. You promised to get pencils and paper. How are we going to make it to the mountain, if you don't teach me to read?"

"Khadeejeh," I say quietly, "I'll teach you to read. I just need a little more time."

"You always say that, but when, Amal? When?"

"Soon." Then I ask Sitt Marriam, "Can you give Khadeejeh some chocolatta?"

"Yes, Amal, but, Khadeejeh, you can't tell anyone. If you do, you won't get any more. These are Amal's that she's sharing with you. You understand, Khadeejeh?"

"Of course. If I tell, then they'll want some too, and there won't be any more for me. I won't tell."

"Good," the nurse says. She leaves for a couple of minutes and returns with chocolate and gives it to Khadeejeh who jumps with joy, "Allah reward you, Sitt Marriam!"

"It's from Amal."

"And reward Amal and make her happy again, the way she used to be."

"That's a good one, Khadeejeh. Did you hear that Amal?"

"I heard. Inshallah, Khadeejeh. Don't forget to drink some water to wash the taste from your mouth before you go back."

"I'll stay here until the taste goes away."

"No," Sitt Marriam tells her. Amal is tired, and you have to go back before they miss you. Here is some water."

"Good-bye, Amal. Don't forget—paper and pencil! And chocolatta!"

"Good-bye, Khadeejeh."

During Nahla's last visit, I asked her for paper, pencils, and some primers to start teaching Khadeejeh. She needs to get permission to bring them in. I'll ask Sitt Marriam to move me back to the ward. I need to be with my wardmates. Perhaps I'll feel better there.

CHAPTER 42

I'VE BEEN BACK in my old ward a month now. Sometimes I wish I were back in the Sick Ward where it's quiet. Being with my friends, though, has chased away the terrifying nightmare. Perhaps, it's because now I'm constantly thinking of ways to resolve my problem—that is when the women quiet down.

At times, it is good to have distractions from those who babble about anything that pops into their heads. Some are forever wagging their tongues about things only they understand. Others silently sit in their corners, away from the rest.

But when night comes, I struggle with my demons. At times I blame myself for not having done things differently. I should've had more courage early on and changed the course of my life, difficult as that might've been. Now, I'm bent on finding a way out of the present.

I find comfort in meeting with Sitt Marriam on Tuesdays, supposedly for an eye checkup, or so the wardmates believe.

They'd rebel if they knew she brings me treats. Lately though, I've refused her generosity, but asked her to save the sweets. I feel guilty for this privilege when the rest are deprived of so much. I'll think of a way to share the treats with my mates someday.

Another Sunday and, perhaps, another visit from Nahla. I sit on a bench next to Khadeejeh inside the Day Room of our ward, listening to her unintelligible one-sided dialogue. She's worse on visitation days, wondering if her mother will come. I have concerns of my own today. I'm wondering if Nahla will bring the things I asked for.

Soon, Sitt Muna comes to the Day Room and announces, "A visitor for Amal. Let's go."

I turn to Khadeejeh. "I'll bring you something good when I come back."

"Hurry," she says.

As soon as I am in the doorway of the Visitors' Salon, Nahla rushes toward me. She embraces and kisses me.

"Nahla, I don't deserve such loyalty."

"Enough nonsense! You deserve a lot more than most people. And my heart tells me Allah will reward you in the end. I've brought you the things you like."

The heavenly smell banishes my promise not to accept the gifts of food. After all, I have had such slop all week, and my resolve blows away with the wind. I only have one pastry and keep the chocolate in my pocket for Khadeejeh.

She asks how I like the eyeglasses. "I can see well, though they feel strange. But I will get used to them." Then, with hesitation, I ask, "Nahla, were you able to get the supplies I've asked for?"

"Of course! In fact, Doctore Jamayelle has agreed to allow a small room to be used as a reading room. He'll supply the books and magazines for those who care to read."

I can't believe my ears. I spring to my feet and hug her. She laughs and says, "I'm happy too, Amal. I told you good things will come your way."

"You mean you will make things happen. Good things don't come on their own. You're the miracle worker!"

I tell her about Khadeejeh and her fixation about learning to read the Koran so she could go to Mount Markel to meet her prince.

Nahla wants to laugh but only smiles. "You're not afraid that she might hurt you?"

"Khadeejeh? She's my protector. I would never have been beaten had she been with me. She was on kitchen duty that day. You wouldn't give a red penny for her looks, but she has the pure heart of a child."

"Amal, there's something I must tell you. Stop pretending to be insane with Sitt Marriam. She knows you're not. She's figured it out on her own, from things you've said at times. I think it will make it easier if you don't pretend with her."

I'm struck dumb. For a moment I stare at Nahla in panic. "I don't want her to tell what she knows before I've figured out the course I must follow."

"Never worry! She's interested only in helping you, just like so many people are."

"So many people?"

"Soeur Micheline!"

"Where is she? It's been years since I've seen her. Sometimes I think she must be with the angels."

"No, she's still with the living, but she hasn't been well. A stroke. Now she walks with crutches, and none too well. She has kept in touch with Sitt Marriam to know how you're doing."

"She doesn't deserve such trouble," I say through tears.

"No, but she's strong. I've met her Amal, and she wants to see you."

"How is she coming when she has to use crutches?"

"She's determined."

"I'd love to see her. I had lost hope, but now . . . I . . . I don't know what to say about life's surprises."

"Or miracles! Amal, I have one favor to ask of you."

"You know I wouldn't refuse, even if you asked for my eyes!"

"What I'm asking, Amal, is big. But I ask it with a wish and a prayer."

"Go ahead, Nahla. Just ask!"

"I want to bring your mother here next Sunday. I would like you to sit down with her and have a talk, clear the air."

"Nahla, I wish you had asked for my eyes instead."

"Will you, Amal? For me?"

All sorts of emotions are roiling in my head and I can't think. "Nahla, I don't think I could face her."

"Please, Amal. For me?"

"I can't say yes, Nahla, I can't."

Nahla's gaze leaves mine. She leaves, and I find myself more worried than ever.

It's been a week since Nahla's visit, and I wonder if she's coming today. Maybe she'll use her head and stay home in this howling wind and whipping rain. I know we need rainwater to store in our wells for the long, hot summers, but a winter like this makes me wish for a scorching summer.

We are in the Day Room, trying to beat the cold by rubbing our hands and jumping around to warm our feet.

Out of nowhere words of a song I learned as a little girl, suddenly appear, their lovely tune humming in my head. How strange memories are! I loved that song about gathering basil leaves and smelling the exhilarating fragrance. I used to dance and sing it to my friends' clapping. Sitty used to scold me for such foolishness.

I have no idea how Lila is going to react to the competition, but it turns out better than I expected. She joins the rest clapping to the beat of my song.

Gather and smell the basil leaves,
The heavenly fragrance, and lovely blooms
Gather and smell the basil leaves.

I planted each with these small hands,
And watered them with both my eyes,
In Allah's name I beg you, friends,
To pour some water on the basil plants.

A few get up to dance, and the rest clap and sing the refrain. After a while, they stop and sing other songs.

I can't wait to have the promised books and magazines and other supplies. That would help Khadeejeh and a few others, but mostly, it would help me. I need to do something, now that I can see.

Suddenly, we hear the door unlock and open, and Sitt Muna walks in and announces, "Someone for Amal!"

I'm surprised that Nahla has come. I must give her a lecture about going out on such miserable days.

Nahla is standing in the doorway of the Salon. She hugs me tight and says "You have a special visitor. Look!"

I am afraid to look, but when I see it's Soeur Micheline, I run up to her shouting out her name. "Easy, easy, Amal!" Nahla warns. I had forgotten about the poor nun's weak condition.

She beams as I hold both her hands in mine. "I've missed you, too, chère! We have much to talk about. Sit beside me."

"I thought I would never see you again."

"As you can see, time has taken its dues. But I'm still alive by the grace of le Bon Dieu. And how are you faring, chère?"

"Like February winds! I swing here, there, and everywhere. But now that you've come back, everything will be better."

"Amal, I'm going for half an hour's walk to give you two a chance to catch up. I'll be back before you know it," Nahla says cheerfully, and leaves.

The good nun says, "Amal, I know of all that you've been through the last few months. Little birds tell me."

"I know you have two birds that speak like angels."

"So you know my birds! And they're your angels, Amal, and a blessing in disguise. They are like agents sent to pave the way for your entry into a state of grace."

"Oh, I've tried for years to get there, but failed terribly."

"You haven't failed. You haven't found the way yet."

"Such a long and difficult journey to face the charred pieces of my life! I don't see why Allah has carved my fate in black granite."

"Allah carves no fate. It is we who carve our present and future." Soeur Micheline looks intently into my eyes. I don't believe what she has said, but decide to go along. She may be my last hope.

She continues to speak gently for a long time about love and hate, kindness and cruelty, goodness and depravity. These contradictions are the essence of our humanness, she tells me.

A knock at the door, and Nahla enters. "Soeur Micheline, it's getting dark and I have to take you back before I go to Jerusalem."

"We will take a minute to pray together. Will you join us, dear Nahla?"

Nahla and I kneel, while the nun remains seated. She asks the Lord to help me understand, forgive, and be forgiven. We help her to her feet. I take her hands and kiss them, and she plants a kiss on my head. "Dieu's blessings on you, my dear Amal."

CHAPTER 43

DURING THE THREE WEEKS after Soeur Micheline's visit, I felt detached from everyone and everything around me. My wardmates kept their distance, some out of consideration for whatever is troubling me; others out of fear of Khadeejeh, who always stands by me like my personal guard. They'd never seen me so silent and remote.

Sitt Marriam has offered to take me to the Sick Ward to have the quiet I need, but I refused. My days and nights are haunted by remembering, trying to understand. There's so much to dig up, and to mull over that soon anger rises again, and I have to stop.

I keep going over Soeur Micheline's words—understanding, love, forgiveness. But how do I find those things? No one has the recipe for that. I must lay out my part in this sorry tale. Could I have left my terrible marriage? Was I a coward? Surely Allah would rather have forgiven a renunciation of marriage vows than the deadly sin that has blackened my soul. How can He forgive me for that? How do I forgive myself for that! Can I?

And as for those who refused to raise a finger to help me, or those who tortured me, I can't find a way to forgive them. I won't!

It's Sunday, and Nahla never misses more than three Sundays. I'm sure she's coming and hope Soeur Micheline will come with her. But what I need now is some rest.

Suddenly I'm awakened by Sitt Muna, who helps me up and toward the Visitors Salon, except she leads me to a special salon that I had never seen before. There Nahla and Soeur Micheline are waiting.

First, Nahla hugs me and walks me toward the nun. She opens her arms to embrace me and a wave of warmth fills my heart. "And how's my favorite student doing?"

"Better now that both of you are here. I hope you're feeling well."

"As well as could be. Have a seat, chère. Sit right here and tell me how you really are."

Nahla gets up to excuse herself, but I insist she stay. "There is nothing you shouldn't hear, Nahla. It's too cold outside. Please, stay."

I swallow my fear and open my heart to the nun, telling her all my thoughts, the confused jumble of emotions that trouble me; how I've begun to see my own part in the troubles that have hounded me, but have not accepted the failure of those who should have been my fortress; how rage and anger toward my family still wash over me like an incoming tide. I confess my anger against an Allah who would permit a lifetime of suffering to fall on one so powerless. I tell her of the fears and hypocrisy of hiding beneath the veil of madness, of living in horror of Judgment Day, of how I am steeped in the painful memories of the past and terrified of facing the present. Exhausted, I stop.

Both Nahla and Soeur Micheline are silent. Then the nun starts to speak quietly. "Troubled souls commit troubling acts. To diminish their own suffering, they commit crimes against the vulnerable. The tormented become the tormentors—a vicious cycle. Do you understand what I am saying?"

"I think so, but . . . how can I forgive my parents for binding me to a man who didn't love me and, even worse, for refusing to raise a finger to answer my cries for help?"

"In their ignorance, Amal, they thought they were doing something good, giving you a husband who would provide for you. They did not mean any harm to you."

"Alright. That, maybe I can understand, but I will never accept their excuses for not coming to my rescue."

"Your father was bent on saving his name. He had been dislodged from his homeland and had lost his identity. He was struggling to redeem his dignity, even at the cost of your misery."

"And I'm supposed to understand that and forgive?"

"That is your choice, chère—to understand their motives and forgive their ignorance, or to remain condemned to misery. Now come here, into my arms."

I embrace her with tears in my eyes and a premonition in my heart that I may never see her again.

CHAPTER 44

THE MORE I THINK about it, the more I am not certain I will ever be able to forgive my father. My sister and brothers seem like strangers to me. In the end, whatever is left for me to do is between me and my mother and my own sins.

But for now, this is my place in the world. I turn my thoughts to the project with Sitt Marriam. All the nuts, biscotti, and chocolatta I've been saving with the good nurse I would like to share with my wardmates. And I have begun to teach Khadeejeh to read. I can tell this is a challenge of a lifetime. But if it makes her happy and keeps her hopeful, it is a good challenge.

Khadeejeh is not my only student now. She was so excited that she told everyone about learning to read and a few others asked to join. I've had to get permission from Doctore Jamayelle, and now I have a schedule for four people. I want to start art lessons, too, even though I have no formal training. I'll show them what I know. I think it might be of help.

Today is Sunday, and I know Nahla is bringing my mother. I'm apprehensive, but I think I am ready. Soon, Sitt Muna comes to the Day Room. "Amal you have guests."

Slowly I walk toward the salon and stand outside the doorway a few seconds to quiet my mind and heart. All my plans of what to say and how to conduct myself have disappeared and I am lost.

Suddenly, Nahla steps to the doorway. "Amal, you look good. Come, come in." She knows I'm nervous and says, "She's not here. Sitt Marriam is talking with her."

"Thank Allah! I'm a bundle of nerves, Nahla, and my stomach is in knots. A few minutes ago I was calm and ready to see her, and now . . . I don't know what's happened to me."

"She feels the same way. Sitt Marriam had to take her away to calm her down."

"Nahla, I don't feel up to it anymore. I don't know what I should do or say to her."

Sitt Marriam walks in alone, smiles and asks how I'm doing. "You look uncomfortable."

"Nervous, is more like it."

She comes close to me and wraps herself around me—a friend, not my nurse any longer. I look toward the door and see my mother, in black, her hands covering her face. Nahla's hand taps my back to hint at what I should be doing. Slowly, I stand up on shaky legs and find myself walking toward her. I have no idea what to do next. Then words come from somewhere within. "Come and sit down."

As soon as the words are out, she brings her hands down and I see her wrinkled face and quivering lips. She looks so much older. She wants to put her arms around me but I'm not ready.

The nurse leads her to a chair. "How I've prayed for this moment, to see you again," she speaks through tears.

"And how, for so many years, I longed for you to become my mother."

She flinches, as if I had struck her. Without tears now, she speaks quickly. "I wish I could erase the past and rewrite it. You'd see a mother who would challenge not only the will of mother and husband, but the red-hot fires of Gehannem to rescue you. Forgive my cowardice, daughter, forgive my sin. I beg you."

I struggle to gather my thoughts, and the words tumble out. "You have no idea how long I have waited to call you 'Immie.'"

"You've always been in my heart. I, too, lived like a prisoner to the will of others. I was a coward, but give me a chance to be your mother again. That's all I want from this world now." She pauses, then takes a breath and begins again. "Amal, I have plans for us. I want to rent a small house where we can live together. You need to get away to a better place, ya binty."

I'm stunned at the audacity of her plan. This is too much for me. And not enough. I shake my head.

I look at my mother and wait to be angry. But I'm not. I'm struck by an overwhelming sadness that this woman who—Allah knows—loves me, was never the mother I needed her to be. That same Allah knows I am now stronger. And my mother sees it too. The not-mad madwoman who bought herself liberation through sin.

"I'm not going anywhere," I tell her. I don't say that I don't need her anymore. Perhaps one day.

I tell my mother I will see her whenever she likes, but our visits will be here, in the asylum. This is my home, at least for now. My friends and protectors are around me. And I am their friend, protector—and now, perhaps, their sometime teacher. With Nahla, Soeur Micheline, and the others, I have as much of the outside world as I want. There are still too many demons beyond the madhouse for me.

I move closer to my mother, not really wanting to hurt her more than I must. "There is no better place for me, Immie. I will always be the outsider, the majnooneh, marked for life. Gossip will follow me wherever I go. It's better that I stay here."

I know she wants to say more, but doesn't. She remains the loving coward, whom I no longer need to rescue me. Less mother and daughter now, perhaps we can build something new. We hold each other.

Here in this house of the insane I will rescue myself.

Acknowledgments

In the five years it took me to write this novel, I have been fortunate in the kind of support I received from my family and friends.

I owe much gratitude to many people who have helped in various ways. I must thank my husband for his patience while I spent many hours a day at the computer and for eating leftovers a few days a week; also to my son Nabil, who encouraged me and offered critiques and advice; to my younger son Farrid, who spent many hours teaching me to use the computer effectively. I am thankful for the steady support of my six siblings, especially Elias and Ruth Nimeh, Samira Norma-Alexander, and Yvonne Nimeh.

I would like to thank Patricia Anderson, a literary consultant, for her lessons in writing and editing, and encouragement. To my friend Tina I owe much, not only for her support, but also for her willingness to help me in preparing the manuscript. I must thank my friend Mary Khoury for recalling the traditional wedding Zaghrootahs. And last but not least, I owe thanks to Mrs. Badee'a Williams, a nonagenarian with an extraordinary memory of life in Palestine from the dawn of the nineteenth century until the end of the British Mandate.

However, I must recognize and thank three very important people who are responsible for making this novel possible—Carolyn Jackson, the managing editor of Second Story Press; Margie Wolfe, the publisher; and Anne Millyard, my editor. I owe much gratitude to Carolyn and Margie for believing in my novel, and to Anne for her lessons and insights. Thank you!